ANITA MILLS
FALLING STARS

A TOPAZ BOOK

TOPAZ
Published by the Penguin Group
Penguin Books USA Inc., 375 Hudson Street,
New York, New York 10014, U.S.A.
Penguin Books Ltd, 27 Wrights Lane,
London W8 5TZ, England
Penguin Books Australia Ltd, Ringwood,
Victoria, Australia
Penguin Books Canada Ltd, 10 Alcorn Avenue,
Toronto, Ontario, Canada M4V 3B2
Penguin Books (N.Z.) Ltd, 182-190 Wairau Road,
Auckland 10, New Zealand

Penguin Books Ltd, Registered Offices:
Harmondsworth, Middlesex, England

First published by Topaz, an imprint of New American Library,
a division of Penguin Books USA Inc.

First Printing, September, 1993
10 9 8 7 6 5 4 3 2 1

A LESSON IN LICENTIOUSNESS

"You do think that I am fortunate to have snared Count Volsky, don't you," Kate demanded, wishing to see the smug superiority banished at least for a moment from Lord Bellamy Townsend's heartbreakingly handsome face.

"Actually, I haven't thought about it at all." he replied. "But to tell the truth, I cannot think you are a match for Volsky."

"What an awful thing to say just because I do not want two gentlemen fawning all over me," Kate said.

"Ah-ha! There is more life in you than I thought," Bell murmured.

But Kate was trembling with the discovery that there was more power in passion than she had ever imagined. . . .

FALLING STARS

"An astonishing achievement . . . superlative. Anita Mills is a brilliant shooting star of the genre."
—Kathe Robin, *Romantic Times*

*This book is dedicated to everyone
who reads the last page first.*

Monk's End: *July,* 1802

It was hot in the tiny attic schoolroom, and Katherine Winstead fidgeted over her lesson, her mind clearly elsewhere. She glanced sideways at her sister, wishing Clarissa would complain of the heat. Mama would not fault Miss Beckwood for yielding to Claire.

At seven, the younger girl was already possessed of the beauty that gained her everyone's favor. With her fair skin and gold hair, she was the fairy princess, while Katherine despaired of being anything other than a small, dark elf. And there did not seem to be a day that passed that Mama did not make the unfavorable comparison, always sighing that "Poor Kate favors the Winsteads, I'm afraid."

But Harry, the eldest of the Winstead brood at seventeen, was quite handsome, prompting Papa to predict that one day Katherine would be just as pretty "in her own way" to his skeptical wife. Some days Kate herself suspected it was a hum, but nonetheless she clung to the notion that it *could* happen.

The sound of a carriage barreling down the long lane brought Katherine to her feet, and despite the governess's frown, she ran to the attic window.

"He's here! Claire, he's here!"

The younger girl looked up. "Mama will say you are not being a lady, Kate."

"But he is here! And there is someone with him!"

As Katherine watched, Harry turned to say something to another boy. Ignoring the latter, she studied her brother eagerly. "How tall he has grown! Look, Claire—I think he is as big as Papa!"

But Beckwood and Claire stared at his companion. Harry said something to him, causing him to look up, and Miss Beckwood gasped, "Why, just look at him!" Even Katherine could see it: Boy or not, he was beyond handsome. He was strikingly beautiful.

"Oh, just look at him!" the governess said again.

"Harry?" Katherine asked loyally.

"I think she means the other one, Stoopid," Claire hissed.

Forcing herself away from the window, Miss Beckwood recalled her duty. "Back to work, both of you, else you'll not get to go down at all."

Reluctantly, Katherine sat and took the quill. Glancing to where Clarissa's head was once again bent so low that her hair obscured her paper, the woman sighed. "Katherine, you must try to be more like your sister."

Kate knew Claire was shamming it. She stared at her own page, thinking resentfully that the lesson would take far too long. And she did not care how much imaginary bolts of sateen and ribbon cost. She'd much rather go fishing with Harry.

But as she worked, she could not help being disappointed that her brother had brought someone home with him. Before he'd gone away to school, he'd treated her more like a younger brother than a sister. He was like Papa, only not quite so busy.

"Here now—what a pulled face for your favorite brother!"

Katherine nearly knocked the ink pot from its holder as she jumped up. "Harry!" she squealed. "You're my *only* brother!"

"Hello, poppet." Grinning, he opened his arms, hugging her.

"Oh, Harry!—I am so very glad you are home! I have even had Old Joe show me how to bait my fishing hook, so you will not have to do it for me. And I can fire Papa's hunting piece, even if I do not hit anything."

"Actually, we won't be here long—Bell and I are going fishing up in Scotland." As her face fell, he felt instantly sorry. "But I've brought gifts from London."

Guiding her away from the door, he half turned to the other boy. "Told you Kate was a hoyden, didn't I? Kate, make your curtsy to Bellamy, Viscount Townsend."

"Miss Katherine," the youth murmured. "I hear you are forever getting into scrapes." He possessed her hand, then released it, smiling. "So am I, I am afraid."

"Yes," she said simply. Turning to her brother, her quivering chin betrayed her. "How long do you mean to stay?"

"Not above a week. But I shall return for a few days before term begins."

Amelia Beckwood hesitated, then with uncharacteristic forwardness, she thrust her hand out to the young viscount. "And I am Miss Beckwood, the girls' governess—and you must forgive Katherine's sad lack of manners."

"My dear Miss Beckwood, I should think you scarce out of the schoolroom yourself," he declared gallantly.

To Katherine's utter disgust, the woman blushed. "How improper you must think me, sir. I—"

"On the contrary." He flashed a smile that lit his extraordinary gray eyes. "And I like improper females."

"Pay him no heed," Harry advised her. "Bell's a shocking flirt."

"What did you bring me?" Claire wanted to know. "Will I like it?"

"I certainly hope so." He drew two small velvet pouches from his pockets. Handing one to her, he opened the other himself. In his palm lay a lovely oval locket and chain. With his thumbnail, he flicked the enameled gold open to reveal a small compartment.

"When you are older, it is big enough to hold a lover's lock, Kate," he teased her.

Clarissa held up a smaller heart-shaped locket, then pouted when she saw Katherine's. "Ooooh—I want that one. Please. She won't care." Tossing her curls for effect, she looked up coquettishly at her brother. "She'd rather have a fishing pole—or a grubby dog."

He shook his head.

"I'll ask Mama," she threatened.

"Mama didn't buy it—I did. For Kate."

Claire's lower lip thrust out farther as she appealed to the governess. "Beckwood, tell him I must have it."

"No."

Tears welled in her eyes. "Mama'll make her give it to me—I know she will!" she declared angrily.

"If she does, I'll never buy you anything again," Harry threatened.

The young viscount intervened, asking, "May I see it?"

Claire eyed him suspiciously for a moment, then held the gift out. "I don't want it—I want the other one."

He pulled a single strand of pale blond hair, rolled it around his little finger, then slipped it inside the small heart. Snapping the locket closed, he polished it on his coat sleeve, then handed it back.

"There," he announced, smiling. "You have your very own lover's lock, Miss Clarissa."

The tears stopped on the instant, and a slow smile of triumph curved Claire's small mouth. "Put it on for me, will you, Beckwood?"

"If you must bicker, his lordship will not think you are ladies," Amelia Beckwood reminded them. Her eyes met Bellamy Townsend's, and her cheeks pinked becomingly. "It was terribly kind of you."

Harry's gaze took in the paper on Katherine's desk. "Finish your lessons, Kate, and I promise I shall ask if you can dine downstairs tonight."

"Downstairs!"

"What about me?" Claire demanded plaintively. "She's only ten, and I—"

"And you are only seven," he finished for her.

"Mama won't—"

"I'll ask Papa," he countered.

"It's not fair!"

He ignored her. "For now, Kate, I've got to go on down—haven't bathed since London. And I expect Bell will want to sleep an hour or two—he played deep at the Black Boar last night."

"Harry!" Claire shrieked.

Attempting to mollify her spoiled charge, the governess bent to study the heart-shaped locket. "How pretty it is, Claire," she murmured soothingly. "Do you not agree, Katherine?"

Kate wasn't attending that. She was listening as her brother and Bell Townsend spoke from below.

" 'A lover's lock,' " Harry mimicked. "It's a wonder you aren't bald."

"Always keep the females happy, old fellow, and they'll give you anything you want."

"Someday," Harry predicted, "you're going to have hell to pay for keeping too damned many of 'em happy."

Within two days, Harry's friend had charmed nearly everyone in the house, exerting himself to be agreeable, joining in every amusement, whether it meant fishing or playing bowls with Harry and Katherine, riding the pony cart with Claire and Miss Beckwood, or target shooting before all of them. Even Katherine found herself liking him.

But Beckwood acted as though she were the schoolgirl, making a silly, giddy fool of herself for Bell Townsend. Where lessons had once been of paramount importance, she now said, "It would be a shame if the girls did not get the fullest possible visit with Master Henry." Then the woman accompanied them everywhere, always smiling dreamily at the viscount.

And Claire declared baldly, "When I am grown, I shall be Viscountess Townsend!"

"Fiddle. He will be far too old for you by then," Kate shot back.

"He is but seventeen like Harry," Claire retorted. "And Papa is nine years older than Mama."

Mama. At dinner, she directed most of her conversation to Townsend, laughing at his every attempt at wit. At one point, she voiced the hope that his influence could "rein in Henry's vices."

Keeping a straight face, the young viscount reassured her, "Oh, he don't get into scrapes around me."

"What a dear boy you are," she murmured approvingly. "You remind me of your mama—such a lovely creature, you know."

"Yes."

"She always called you her angel, as I remember."

Katherine looked up at that and caught his wince. "Mama always had hopes of me, I suppose," he said.

"No—no, she was quite right. One has but to look into your countenance to see you are everything she could have wished."

Harry choked. Coughing until tears streamed down his cheeks, he finally had to turn away from the table.

"Really, Henry, you forget your manners," Lady Winstead complained. "Drink slowly, I beg you."

"I don't think it was anything he drank, Mama," Kate spoke up. She waited until her mother's attention was claimed by her father, then she mouthed the word "angel" at Townsend. His gray eyes met hers as his lips formed "brat" in response.

After dessert, Lady Winstead rose. "I find myself rather tired," she said, addressing her husband. "Do you go up also?"

He nodded. "I thought to partake of one brandy in my book room, my dear, then I shall join you while the young people play cards."

"Cards?" Her mouth flattened in disapproval, as though the word itself were sinful.

"I told Henry I didn't mind it if they played a few games of whist," he answered mildly.

"There are more than enough gamesters in this house, I think," she responded stiffly. "And I do not want Katherine—"

"Oh, Mama—it is but a harmless game," Harry insisted. "And it requires four to play it."

"Humph! There are no harmless cards, Henry." She eyed her husband reproachfully for a moment, then sighed. "Miss Beckwood, I hope you understand there is to be no money wagered."

"Yes, Lady Winstead."

"Ten o'clock at the latest, then."

With that pronouncement, she left them. Katherine's

father sighed, then shrugged his shoulders. "I guess woman is meant to be man's conscience—eh?" With that, he started for the door, stopping only to ruffle Katherine's hair. "For luck, Kate," he murmured. "Play 'em close, you hear? And play 'em to win."

As Katherine crept into the bed she shared with Claire, her sister rolled over and sat up. "Don't think I won't tell Mama," the girl said crossly. "The clock's struck midnight."

"I know. But we were winning, and Miss Beckwood did not want to come up."

"You *gamed*? Mama would never approve!"

"Mama knows." Katherine rolled onto her side. "Good night."

Reluctantly, Claire lay back down. "Well, I will still tell her that you did not come to bed until past midnight," she decided. She turned away and hugged her pillow. Just when Katherine supposed she slept, the younger girl muttered, "Why does it always have to be you and Harry? Why doesn't he favor me?"

"Probably because of Mama," Kate answered.

Claire's breathing evened out quickly. Turning her head against her own pillow, Katherine savored her win—Harry had teased that if she'd been at White's, she'd have been rich. It was a hum, and she knew it—what defeated Bell Townsend and Beckwood had been Papa's "medicinal" rum, which Harry had discovered in a cabinet.

He and Bell had persuaded Miss Beckwood to have "a drop." Eventually, she'd had a great deal more than that. By the end of the evening, all the woman could do was giggle, she remembered with disgust. And Townsend was not much better.

The clock struck the half hour, dividing the darkness, and as the sound receded, Katherine thought she heard a door squeak slowly open. She lay silent, listening as someone quickly passed in the hall. For a moment, she wondered if she merely imagined what she heard, but then the servants' stairs creaked.

Katherine crept to her window and peered into the

moonlit garden below as a woman emerged from the house and darted down the garden path toward the maze. At the last instant, she looked back as though she feared to be followed, and Katherine stared. It was Miss Beckwood.

But what on earth would she be doing out in the middle of the night? Then the answer came—she'd had far too much rum, and it did not take much to guess that she was sick. After all, when Harry'd gotten into Papa's Madeira, he was up half the night retching, and everyone knew it. And poor Beckwood could not afford such a thing, for if it ever came to Mama's ears, she would be turned off.

Katherine ran down the back stairs and outside. The cobblestone path was wet with dew, the grass slippery beneath her bare feet. Her heart pounding, she stopped at the edge of Papa's prized maze and hesitated. There was no sign of Beckwood. But what if she herself got lost? What if she could not find her way back before morning? She shuddered to even think of the peal Mama would read over her. For a long time, she listened, wavering, thinking perhaps she should go back and let Beckwood take care of herself.

Then she heard the woman's cries, followed by strange, animal-like grunts. Poor Beckwood. Swallowing her fear of the dark, she ran toward the sounds, not daring to call out that she came. She stopped when she saw them.

The governess was lying on the ground, her bared, thrashing legs pale in the moonlight. Above her, a man rocked on his knees, his pantaloons pulled down around his ankles. The woman's cries became louder, more frantic, but he did not stop. To Kate, it looked as though Beckwood fought him.

She found her voice and screamed, "You are killing her! Stop it—oh, stop it! Papa! *Papa*! *Help*!"

Beckwood's attacker cursed loudly as he separated awkwardly from her and staggered to his feet. He lunged toward Katherine, nearly tripping over his clothes. Behind him, Beckwood sat up and covered her face with her hands, crying, "We are discovered! What have I done—oh, what have I done?"

"Kate! What the *hell* are you doing here?"

Katherine froze at the sound of Bellamy Townsend's voice. He was still pulling up his pantaloons when he reached her. He caught her shoulder, shaking her. She stared, wide-eyed, when he released her.

"Oh, lud." He ran his fingers through his hair. "Look, it isn't—I mean—she—" His gray eyes reflected the moon. "Look, I didn't hurt her, I swear."

It came to her then—*Whatever he'd done, Beckwood had wanted him to do it.* Mortified, she broke away and ran. At the edge of the maze, she stopped, her heart pounding, just long enough to catch her breath, then she hurried back toward the house.

Still in his nightshirt, her Papa appeared at the door. "Kate! What in the devil are you doing out there?" he demanded.

The awful look on Beckwood's face floated before her as she clung to her father. "I thought I saw a ghost, Papa," she lied.

"Where?"

"In—in the old monastery."

His arms tightened around her for a moment, then he sat her back from him. "Why are you outside, Kate?"

She couldn't tell him the truth. She couldn't tell him what she'd seen. Looking at the ground, she mumbled, "I had a dream, Papa—and there was something chasing me—it wore a long robe," she added, inventing. "And I couldn't see its face. But the chains made a noise, and then I awoke in the monastery."

The footman behind him nodded. " 'Twas the murdered monk."

"That will be enough," her father said, interrupting the fellow. "She has quite a sufficient imagination as it is." He took her hand and headed toward his study. "Dinkins, before you retire again, two glasses of hot milk, please." He waited until the footman disappeared before he sank into a chair. Looking up at her, he pursed his lips.

"A ghost, Kate?" he asked softly. "I have never known you to be afraid of anything." When she didn't answer, he sighed. "I know a whisker when I see one, my dear."

She didn't want to lie, but neither did she wish to hurt her foolish governess. So she remained silent.

Her father did not speak again until Dinkins brought the milk, apologizing, "It ain't real hot, my lord, 'cuz the fire's nearly dead in the stove."

"Thank you. That will be all. You need your sleep— go on back to bed." As the man left, John Winstead sipped his milk, then looked over the rim of his glass. "Do you know what trust is, Kate?" he asked slowly.

"I think so, sir."

"Trust is loving someone enough to believe what he says." His eyes met hers. "Trust is believing someone has a good reason to withhold something. Do you understand me, child?"

"Yes, sir." She stared into her milk for a moment, then answered slowly. "You think I might be untruthful, but you are willing to believe I have a reason for it."

He nodded. "Precisely."

She dared to look up. "I have hopes you will not tell Mama."

"I won't." He finished his milk. For a time, he seemed to grope for words. "You and Harry favor me, Kate," he began, "and I'm afraid I have been somewhat of a disappointment to your mother." He stopped to stare at the shaft of moonlight that sliced across the dim room. "My father was a gamester, I am a gamester, and no doubt Harry will be one also. It is in the blood, I'm afraid."

"You don't have to explain Mama to me, sir."

"I know." He stood and reached for her hand. "Come on, you've got to get to bed."

As she walked up the steps beside him, she was nearly overwhelmed by the gratitude she felt for him. At her door, he bent to kiss her cheek.

"Always remember you are my darling child, Kate," he said softly. Straightening, he spoke more lightly.

"And always remember gamesters make miserable husbands."

"Yes, sir."

As she turned toward her room, she saw that Miss Beckwood's door was ajar. As soon as the baron disappeared into the darkness, the governess whispered, "Kate?" The candle in her hand betrayed her wet face. When Katherine did not come to her, she stepped cautiously into the hall. "Please—I'd like to speak to you."

"I've got to go to bed."

"Please," the woman repeated. "I know I do not deserve to be heard, but—"

Reluctantly, Katherine followed her into the tiny chamber. Beckwood's eyes were red, and her hands shook. Suddenly, her face crumpled, and she began sobbing. "He's going to turn me off—I know it! He's going to turn me off! I didn't mean to do it—it was the rum, Katherine—it was the rum!"

"I didn't tell him anything."

It was as though the woman did not hear her. "Do you know what I am? A spinster—an ape-leader," she blubbered. "I have no fortune and no hopes of one—none at all!"

"Beckwood, I didn't tell Papa anything!"

The woman blew her nose in a soggy handkerchief, then went on. "It isn't as though anyone would ever wish to marry me! I just wanted to be held. I—"

"Miss Beckwood, I said I saw a ghost!" Katherine all but shouted at her.

The governess stared for a moment. "You said you saw a ghost?" she repeated blankly. "Why?"

"I had to say something."

"Then he does not—I mean—you did not tell him?" she asked incredulously.

"No."

"Oh—you dear, dear child!"

"I did it for Harry. I didn't want him to know about it."

Beckwood wiped her wet cheek with the back of her hand. "Well, I think he knows now." Sniffling, she added, "They are going in the morning, because Lord Townsend says he cannot stay after this." Then, as though to comfort herself, she said, "But he promises he will come back."

"Good night, Miss Beckwood."

"Good night, Kate."

Later, as she lay beside an oblivious Claire, Katherine stared at the ceiling, feeling somehow betrayed by Bell Townsend. Everyone had liked him, everyone had welcomed him, and he'd misused their trust to make a fool of a lonely, silly woman. But even worse, he'd caused her to lie to her father.

London: *Summer,* 1814

Despite the warmth of the air, despite the beauty of hundreds of lanterns that vied with a clear, star-studded sky to illuminate the limestone mansion's lawn, Katherine shivered as her brother handed her down from their town carriage. Behind her, Clarissa observed excitedly, "It is the very best of nights, Kate! Only fancy—we shall see Czar Alexander!"

"I would that we did not," Katherine muttered as she pulled her silk shawl more tightly about her shoulders. "One has but to read the papers to know he is mobbed wherever he appears."

"Be still, you foolish girl," her mother snapped. "A crowd is to your advantage, if you will but use it."

They were nearly to the pilastered porch. As late as they were, the lanterns flickered above the heads of some of the highest of the *ton* still waiting entrance. A knot formed in Katherine's stomach.

Lady Winstead turned to survey both daughters critically, and her lips tightened as her eyes moved over Kate. "Straighten your shoulders and remove your wrap. You look as though you are a short Egyptian," she decided irritably. "And you ought to have let Marsh apply the rouge, for you seem more than half-dead ere the evening has begun." Reaching out, she pinched Katherine's cheeks hard.

As she turned her attention to Claire, Harry moved closer. "Buck up, Kate—you look fine."

It was a lie, but she was grateful for it. Since their father's death, Harry was the only one who cared a button for her. If it were not for his bad rep with the ladies,

she would have wished to live with him. But she knew
her mother would not hear of it.

If Harry didn't watch himself, he was going to be as
dangerous to know as Bellamy Townsend. Well, perhaps
not quite that dangerous, she conceded. At least no one
had divorced his wife over him like the Earl of Longford
had done over Townsend.

"Are you coming, Katherine—or are you wool-gathering?"
Lady Winstead demanded, cutting into Kate's thoughts. "Tonight I pray you will make at least some attempt at conversation, lest Sally Jersey believes you are an imbecile."

Harry sighed. His mother refused to understand that
Kate could not help her shyness in company—no more
than she could help her short stature, her ordinary face,
or her unfashionably dark hair and skin. And she certainly could not help the lingering scandal that hung over
all their heads.

Clarissa was already creating a mild stir as several
bucks turned around to admire her. Kate's hands were
clammy. Loosening her grip on her fringed shawl, she
wiped the damp palms on her slim muslin skirt. Her
mother looked back to her and demanded sourly, "What
are you doing *now*?"

"Nothing, Mama," she answered.

Lady Winstead observed plaintively to Harry, "In
company, there is not a bit of life to the girl, is there? I
daresay John was right three years ago when he wanted
to take her to Bath for the Little Season. We'd have been
saved a great deal of worthless expense."

"Leave off," he muttered. "Kate is an Original."

"An oddity, you mean," his mother snapped back.

"Two years ago we were in mourning," Clarissa spoke
up. "And last year Harry feared the scandal had not yet
been forgotten—"

"Hold your tongue, missy! We are agreed we shall not
rake that up again!" Lady Winstead said sharply.

"Well, I for one do not mean to forget Papa," Kate
declared loyally. "It was not his fault."

"Well, I am sure *I* did not put a period to his existence," her mother said acidly. Pasting a smile on her

face, she managed to push her way inside and catch the Countess of Jersey's attention. "La, Sally, but what a crush!"

For a moment, Lady Jersey looked at her as though she were an encroaching fool, then her gaze moved to Harry. "Ah—what a pleasure, dear boy!" She smiled and tapped him coquettishly with her fan. "You must share the latest crim-cons with me over tea soon."

"You have but to ask me," he assured her. "You know my mother and sisters, I believe."

Lady Jersey's bright eyes swept over them, making Kate want to cringe. "Miss Winstead," she acknowledged to Katherine, then she discovered a smile for Clarissa. "You *are* in looks tonight, my dear. Is Cranston here? Or Hargrove?" She let her voice drop speculatively. "I wonder."

Claire would have been in looks had she been in sackcloth, Kate thought privately, while her own gown did not become her at all, no matter how much her mother insisted that white made "even an ape-leader appear more virginal." It was a hideous lie, for it made her appear utterly sallow. The only thing worse was yellow or the palest pastels, her mother's other favorite colors for her.

"So, does Alexander come?" she heard her brother ask the countess.

"My dear Harry, he is here! You do not think everyone should wait like this for anyone else, do you?" Sally Jersey replied. "They are all come—even that Cossack Platov! Linking her arm in Harry's, she pulled him toward the Russians.

For a moment, even Katherine was carried by the excitement of those around her as she glimpsed the tall, blond autocrat of all the Russias standing beside the punch bowl. The rich gold braid of his military uniform caught the light from the chandeliers. Beside him, the Grand Duchess Catherine of Oldenburg, spoke to an over-decorated gentleman that Katherine guessed must be the King of Prussia.

"Look, Kate—there's the Cossack savage!" Claire whispered.

Katherine followed her sister's rather indiscreet point to a group of military officers gathered at one end of the table. There was no mistaking Platov—unlike the others, he'd eschewed formal dress and wore instead a military jacket over loose-fitting trousers that were tucked into high black boots. A wicked-looking sword hung from a belt at his waist. He was tall, dark, exceedingly ugly, and rather unkempt by civilized standards. As hetman of the ferocious Don Cossacks, he was attended by two menacing armed men.

One of the Cossacks' guards tried to gain Claire's attention by mouthing words at her, then pointing to his wrist, grinning. Embarrassed for her sister, Kate announced urgently, "I'm not feeling quite the thing, Mama—really. It is the heat," she lied. "Could we not sit down?"

"Oh—look, Kate," Claire whispered excitedly, "there is Lord Townsend, and he is watching me."

"I would doubt that," Katherine answered dryly. "You are not someone else's wife."

"Oh, Kate! We have known him for an age—and—and he used to run tame at Monk's End! How could you say such a thing?" Claire demanded.

"Everywhere he goes, there is a scandal. And Mama would not wish you to encourage him."

"No, of course not," Lady Winstead agreed hastily. "Too much nasty gossip there. Oh, look—there is Mr. Thurgood, Katherine. If you were to give him any hope—"

"Mr. Thurgood is ancient. Please, Mama, I am unwell," Kate insisted desperately.

Seeing that the old man was already peering nearsightedly elsewhere, her mother responded waspishly, "Sometimes I do not know why I bother at all. Go on, Claire—help her."

As Kate headed gratefully for the chairs that lined one wall of the huge room, her sister grumbled spitefully, "Why must you always ruin my evening? Bell Townsend was going to single me out!"

"I expect he'll be old and raddled before his salad days are over," Katherine muttered with asperity.

"Kate! How dare you say such a thing?"

"Without difficulty. Rakes make damnable husbands."

"Kate!" Claire squeaked again. "Who said that?"

"Harry—and I expect he should know."

"Miss Clarissa?"

Claire spun around to face a young officer in the uniform of the Horse Guards, and immediately she smiled radiantly. "Captain Rigby. How very nice to see you again."

"I hope I am not too late to secure a waltz?"

"Well, I—" Claire's eyes sought Bell Townsend, discovering he was conversing with Harry, then she looked down demurely. "I should have to ask Mama, for she still thinks the waltz quite fast, sir."

"Then let us ask her," he suggested. Nodding to Kate, he said, "I trust you will pardon us."

"Yes"

"Damn," Harry muttered. "Poor Kate."

Bell turned to look at her. Despite the fact that Katherine Winstead was an odd little creature, he pitied her for Harry's sake. There was no question about it—she wasn't going to take, no matter how many parties she attended. "The girl ought never to wear white if she can help it," he decided.

"I know."

Bell nodded. "Makes the girl look like an Antidote. Sorry to say it to you, but she's got no color and no style."

"Mama won't pay for anything she does not choose. Not that her clothes matter all that much—Kate still would not play the game right. She gets damned near tongue-tied in company."

"She used to talk to me." Bell looked at her again. "The only things she's possessed of to make a man look twice are her tart wit and her smile," he observed wryly, "and if she will not use them . . ."

"She spoke because she knew you. And she knew Mama wasn't going to throw her at your head. But whenever someone drags an eligible *parti* to meet her, she turns into wood, I swear it."

As Bell watched, several other girls sought seats near
Katherine Winstead, and he felt even sorrier for her. Not
very many gentlemen could be expected to brave a whole
line of plain girls. The idle thought crossed his mind that
while nothing short of a miracle could bring her into
fashion, he could certainly see she was noticed—if she
would let him. He half turned back to Harry, only to
discover that Lady Childredge and her daughter had the
poor fellow cornered. When he looked again to Katherine Winstead, kindhearted Maria Sefton was taking an
obviously reluctant youth to meet her.

Turning on his heel, Bell walked not toward Katherine
Winstead, but rather toward the punch bowl. He was as
yet too sober to approach her.

The evening was passing slowly. Katherine sat, her
feet tucked beneath her chair to hide that she'd slipped
out of her shoes. As she watched, Claire managed to
have a partner for every dance. It didn't matter, Katherine insisted to herself. She'd rather sit like a statue than
be led out again by another old man—or by some green
boy pushed at her.

The Season would soon be over, and she would again
be home at Monk's End. But not without a price. Her
mother would be sure to vent her vexation a hundred
times over, reminding Katherine that she had failed to
achieve every girl's expectation of a husband. And if
Claire succeeded, it would be worse, for then there would
only be Mama. And somehow not even Kate's horses and
dogs could entirely compensate for that.

"Miss Winstead—Kate—may I join you?"

Startled, she looked into a perfectly tailored gray evening coat, then raised her gaze to meet Bellamy Townsend's arresting eyes, and for a moment, she was
surprised. "What a signal honor," she murmured faintly.

The girl was still short and a trifle too thin for his taste,
and the only color about her was the rose pinned to her
shoulder. The thought crossed his mind that he must be
more drunk than he'd felt, else he'd not be standing there.
Nonetheless, he proceeded gamely.

"Actually, I thought to speak with you." Dropping to sit beside her, he reached for her dance card. One blond eyebrow rose quizzically as he read it. "Well, you certainly stay with the safe ones, don't you? I thought Thurgood died last year."

She snatched the card back. But she could not quite control the twitch at the corners of her mouth. "He would be wounded to hear you say that—if he could hear it at all. One has to shout at him, you know."

"Poor old soul," he murmured sympathetically. "I suppose he regaled you with a dozen ailments."

"No." She smiled ruefully. "He went to a great deal of trouble to assure me he *wasn't* on his last legs."

"You ought to let yourself smile more often, Kate—it becomes you."

"Stuff." She eyed him suspiciously. "To whom do I owe this—Harry?"

"You wound me."

"Impossible." Frowning, she scanned the crowded ballroom. "Claire ought to be returning, I expect."

"I'm not looking for her. Truth to tell, I have come to beg a waltz with you."

Her dark eyes widened briefly, then were guarded. "Oh? But why would you wish to do that?"

"Come now, Kate Winstead. I've known you since you were a little chit in the schoolroom," he said, betraying a trace of impatience. "Look, I saw you here, and—"

"And you thought I would wish to dance with you?" she asked incredulously. "Lord Townsend, I assure you—"

"Cut line, Kate," he interrupted abruptly. "Listen, do you want me to bring you into fashion?"

"If coming to more of these affairs is fashion, I'd rather not. Besides, you could not possibly manage it," she added candidly. "I am even beyond Brummell's powers."

"You ought to watch your sister—the chit knows how to engage a man's attention," he told her. "Smile, tilt your head just so, ply your fan as though it were meant for something besides a breeze. As it is, you appear flat and green."

"And you think that is what I wish to do? Bellamy Townsend, I should rather be forever on the shelf than pretend to be an empty-headed wigeon!" she declared with feeling. "And you have described me as though I am a—a lawn!"

The last strains of a minuet played. On impulse, he caught her hand, pulling her up. "One waltz, Kate."

Stark terror assailed her. "I cannot! Please—my shoes—"

"Go barefoot and start a new fashion," he replied cheerfully. "Scandalize 'em."

"No!" But he was already tugging her toward the floor. "Wait!" He stopped but did not release her hand. She struggled to wriggle her toes into her slippers. "Townsend, you are no gentleman," she muttered. "And I cannot think why—"

"Told you—bringing you into fashion."

She tried to pull away, then became aware of the curious stares. "Oh, lud—I cannot! I'll disgrace you," she threatened him.

"Now you are showing a bit of spirit, my dear."

"I'm not your dear—and no one would believe I was."

"Come on, they are playing our waltz," he murmured wickedly. As Kate ceased struggling, he favored a disapproving matron with a dazzling smile. "You may give it out that I am once again storming the bastions of maidenly reserve."

"You, sir, are outrageous!" Kate choked out. "There is no telling what she will say!"

"Does it matter? You'll be on every tongue," he assured her, grinning.

Aware that more people watched, she felt blood rise to her face. "It matters a great deal," she managed through gritted teeth. "I should rather have it thought that I would not go to the nearest corner with you. Your shocking rep, you know."

"How uncharitable of you." At the edge of the cleared dance floor, he put his other hand on her waist. "Smile, Kate, for they look at you."

She felt like a wooden stick, but he pretended not to

note it. Finally, as the music wafted across the ballroom, seemingly carried by the soft summer breeze from open windows, she began to count out the steps to herself.

"Pretend we are alone, that the candles above are but the stars of a summer night," he murmured at her ear.

She closed her eyes and nearly lost her balance. "I—I cannot."

"Think of summer stars, summer falling stars Kate," he whispered. "There is nothing prettier—or more magical."

His hand was warm, his body far too close, and he was, after all, Bell Townsend. It would be so easy to dream of a man like him. And a lot of females did. Resolutely, she recalled how foolish he'd made Amelia Beckwood.

"You do not dance badly, you know."

"If you meant it, you would say I danced well," she countered. "And I have practiced with Harry."

"You'll never take, Kate, unless you learn to turn that tongue to wit."

"Everyone else claims I do not have one."

"You are not being fair to Harry."

She nearly stumbled. "He—he didn't say that, did he?"

"Not in words, but you worry him. Try not to tread on my feet, will you?"

"Where is your vaunted address?" she asked through clenched teeth.

"I try not to waste it."

"And I shall consider that a compliment."

As the music ended, he turned her around, then led her from the floor. "Did you think of falling stars?" he quizzed her.

"No," she said simply. "I thought of Miss Beckwood."

"That was an age ago."

Before she knew what he meant to do, he leaned into her for the briefest moment, and his lips brushed her cheek. As the color flooded her face, she could hear the gasps of those around her.

"How—how *could* you?" she choked furiously. "Now Mama will be saying I am fast!"

"Dare to be lively, Kate—let those dark eyes flash a bit of fire," he whispered, bowing over her hand. "You don't have to be a drab."

As he left her, she could not help noting the curious stares. And for a moment, she wondered if Claire had seen her waltz with him.

"Ah, *cherie,* such a handsome chevalier, *n'est-ce pas?* May I sit with you, mademoiselle?"

Katherine half turned to look as an elegant auburn-haired beauty took the chair next to hers. "You have the advantage of me, I'm afraid," she admitted.

"I am Madame Malenkov, *ma petite.* And you?"

"Miss Winstead—Miss Katherine Winstead."

The woman fanned herself for a moment before smiling at Kate. "It is—how you English say it?—a shocking thing?"

"Squeeze—a shocking squeeze."

"I do not blame you for sitting—my feet are tired also." Madame Malenkov lifted her slim skirt above her ankle to reveal small green satin slippers that matched her gown. "They are too tight." When Katherine said nothing, she shrugged creamy bare shoulders and went on, "I shall long for the quiet of Russia before I am there."

"I collect you have been to all the parties," Kate murmured politely.

"*Cherie,* I have been everywhere! My mind is like a top, whirling constantly, and still it cannot catch up to my body! It is exhausting!" Madame Malenkov sank back in her chair and fanned herself more. "And that terrible affair at Carlton House!"

It was difficult to remain aloof to the woman. Kate unbent enough to ask, "You were at the Regent's dinner?"

"Yes. Yes—a disaster, *ma petite*—a disaster. It was so hot I thought to faint, and Lexy had to remove me back to the Pulteney. I know not how your Regent stood it himself, for I have always thought fat people do not tolerate heat. But it was a boring event, so I did not mind leaving at all," the Russian woman confided. "And the Old Queen—so dull. But I should not be—how you say it?—critical of your government, for I do not live here."

"Your English is quite good," Kate observed, warming to her.

"Well, I speak French more, but Lexy and I had the English tutor for years. Your people do not seem to speak anything else, do they?"

"Some of us speak French also."

"Well, none speaks Russian that I have met. But then many of the *boyars* in my country do not also."

"There you are, you naughty girl!"

Katherine cringed at the censure in her mother's voice. "I am but resting, Mama." Then, hoping to forestall a scene, she gestured to the woman beside her. "This is Madame Malenkov, Mama. Madame, my mother, Lady Winstead."

"Charmed, to be sure." There was nothing in Lady Winstead's tone to indicate anything of the sort.

"Madame Winstead." Madame Malenkov smiled, revealing perfect teeth. "You must be mother to Baron Winstead, then. Such a man—so very—" She groped for a word and finally settled on, "accomplished."

"You mean he is a shocking flirt," Kate guessed. "And he is that."

"Katherine! Henry is no such thing! Really, madame, but—"

"No, no—she is quite right." Madame Malenkov rose, looking down at the card that hung from her wrist. "But I am promised. And I am not found here, I think. Until later, *cherie*."

"Katherine, it does you no credit to sit with a woman like that. You cannot show to advantage, for every man will be looking at her," her mother declared. "And what on earth were you thinking of, missy?" she demanded, her voice rising as she recalled her purpose. "Townsend! I vow I thought that Drummond-Burrell woman would choke!"

"It was but one waltz, Mama."

"She said she thought he had kissed you in front of everyone! I vow I thought I should have the vapors!" Lady Winstead reached for Katherine's dance card and studied it. "Well, at least Thurgood would appear interested. He has five thousand pounds, you know."

"And three dead wives," Katherine remembered.

"Yes, well, George Maxwell is here, and—"

"It would not signify, Mama."

"If you would but smile at him—"

"Lord Leighton is pleasant to everyone," Kate answered tiredly.

"Then Barstowe. He is—"

"Old. Mama, he must be forty!"

"Not too old to want to fill a nursery," Lady Winstead insisted. "And not so old as Mr. Thurgood."

"Mama, I should rather die," Katherine declared flatly.

"You are not getting any younger, and I fail to see how you can dismiss—"

For a moment, Kate's temper flared. "Why don't you just throw me at our vicar's head and be done? He may be a widower in his dotage, but surely he must meet your requirements by being alive!"

Across the room, Madame Malenkov pinched her brother's sleeve, then discreetly directed his attention toward Katherine. He frowned for a moment.

"*Voteta?*"

"*Da.* That one." She whispered, "She is perfect to our purpose, Lexy. She is a mouse."

"*Ya nye znayu,*" he murmured doubtfully.

"Of course you do not know. But I can make her presentable enough." Pulling him after her, she made her way back to Katherine, where she murmured apologetically, "*Pardon,* Madame Winstead."

Kate's mother whirled around, ready to snap, then her mouth gaped. There with Madame Malenkov stood a dark-haired officer. Even before he was introduced, he bowed slightly, and the medals on his chest caught the light from the candles above.

"Lexy, this is Madame Winstead—and her daughter,

Katherine.'' The woman smiled encouragingly at Kate.
''Miss Winstead, this is my brother, Count Volsky. He
admired you very much when you were on the dance
floor.'' Patting her brother on his arm, she looked up at
him. ''There. You are introduced, Lexy. The rest is up
to you.''

He was taller than Townsend, possibly as tall as Harry,
and his shoulders filled his uniform coat perfectly. As he
bowed over her hand, his straight black hair gleamed. He
looked straight into her eyes.

''Mademoiselle, I have begged for the introduction,''
he murmured, smiling at her.

She wasn't sure she could speak. ''Count Volsky,'' she
managed. Then, unable to think of anything else, she blurted
out, ''Are you enjoying England, sir?'' As she said it, she
felt utterly foolish.

''But of course,'' he answered, smiling. ''It is all so
charming.''

''Were you in the war, Count Volsky?'' she heard her
mother ask him.

''Yes, yes. One cannot be Russian without having
served against Napoleon, madame. We fought the mad-
man for our very existence.''

Obviously impressed by the array of medals on his
chest, Lady Winstead observed, ''You must be quite the
hero, sir.''

His smile faded, and for a moment he was sober before
he answered. ''In my country, there are no living heroes
but Alexander—there are only the survivors.''

''But you were wounded in the war, surely,'' her
mother insisted. ''Your cheek—''

His hand touched a red, triangular-shaped scar that
marred one jaw. ''*Mais non,* madame. He smiled ruefully and shook his head. ''This I had in Paris, I'm afraid.
The French are quarrelsome, far too ready to fight over
everything.''

He glanced down at Katherine's bare wrist, then again
to her face. ''You have not a dance card, mademoiselle?''

"I—uh—I must have lost it," she lied, not wanting him to see how seldom she'd actually been asked.

"How very fortunate. Now you cannot be expected to remember everyone on it, do you think?"

"Uh—no."

To her astonishment, he lifted her wrist to his lips, murmuring, "Then I must surely be next."

As she hastily retrieved her hand again, she could feel the hateful color rise to her cheeks once more. To her relief, he addressed her mama.

"Madame, do you trust me to waltz with your daughter? I promise you I shall not be the savage."

For the second time in a matter of minutes, Lady Winstead was stunned. She looked at him as though he must surely be mistaken. "You—you have not met my other daughter, have you, Count Volsky?" she stammered.

"Miss Clarissa Winstead?" His next words were the most endearing Katherine had ever heard. "We were introduced, I believe."

Letting out her breath, she dared to speak. "Please, Mama—I—I should like it."

"Well—yes, of course, my love—of *course*! I would not for the world have Count Volsky think the English rude or inhospitable." Her mother tittered slightly. "You will find my Katherine a trifle shy, Count Volsky."

"I shall find her pleasant, I am sure, Madame Winstead."

The musicians had finished a round and were just beginning the first strains of a waltz. It was not until she preceded the handsome Russian toward the cleared dance floor that Katherine realized what she had done. Her palms went damp, her throat dry, and her heart pounded. At least she'd known Bell Townsend. Briefly, she considered covering her mouth and running.

"I—uh—well, I am not particularly good at this," she admitted helplessly. "I don't know why I said I—"

"Ah, but with the waltz, you have but to follow, *cherie*. Besides, I have seen you do it. This Townsend—he is your particular acquaintance?"

She nearly choked. "No," she assured him. "He is

but a friend of my brother. Unfortunately, I have known him more than half of my life.''

''And you do not waltz on short acquaintance? Come—I shall make it all right,'' he promised.

As Count Volsky's hand rested at her waist, Katherine closed her eyes. Falling stars—Townsend had said to think of falling stars, she told herself, trying to calm the terror she felt. If she did not think about the man holding her, if she pretended he was but Harry . . .

''You can look at my shoulder. All you have to do is follow where you are taken.''

His shoulder was all she could see. She fixed her gaze on his medals. Silently, she began to count the steps.

''No, no—follow.''

Once again, her terror subsided as the music crowded it out. ''You were untruthful, Ekaterina,'' Volsky said low. ''You are doing very well.''

''Thank you.''

''You wear perfume,'' he observed softly.

''No—it is lemon in my hair. Mama would have it a lighter shade, but it is still dark.''

''Your mother is wrong.''

''I beg your pardon?''

''There are too many blondes.''

She nearly misstepped at that. ''They are all the rage here, sir.''

''The rage?''

''The preferred fashion.'' She tried to turn the subject slightly. ''Madame Malenkov is very beautiful.''

''Lena?'' He appeared to consider, then nodded. ''Yes. Before Cyril, we had many offers for her. But now she is widowed, for he died during the war.''

''Oh. I'm sorry for it.''

''They were ill suited. Galena Petrovna despised him.''

''Galena Petrovna? She was married twice? I'm sorry, I should not have asked such a thing.''

''It is most confusing, I suppose,'' he conceded, ''but in my country, one is called by one's father. Ours was Peter Mikhailovich Volsky, so I am Alexei Petrovich Volsky, and Lena is Galena Petrovna Volskaya Malenkova.

But you cannot rely on that always," he added, his blue
eyes twinkling, "for some daughters are skayas, some
ovas or ovnas, and some evnas, depending on the name
of the father."

"Oh." Not wanting to ask where the "a" came from
in Malenkova, she fell silent. As her body responded to
the music, she felt she must surely be dreaming, and she
was afraid that when she waked, she would discover there
was no Count Volsky. But for now, she felt as though
she were the envy of every girl in the ballroom.

"Your father—what is his name?" he asked suddenly.

"His name was John. He—uh—he died some time
ago."

"I'm sorry. Who is the head of your family?"

"My brother Harry. Actually, his name is Henry, but
he dislikes it."

"Well, in Russia, you would be Ekaterina Ivanova
Winstead, and you would be addressed directly as Ekaterina Ivanova, and you would be spoken of as Ekaterina
Winstead—or actually as Ekaterina Winsteada. We have
the habit of adding the feminine sound to your name."

"And Harry?"

"He would be Henry Ivanovich to his face. Your John
is our Ivan, you see."

"He is Baron Winstead here."

"We have not the title. We are counts, princes, and
grand dukes, among other things—but not barons."
Smiling, he added, "In Russia, your Prince Regent would
be a grand duke and his title would be czarevitch, showing he was the czar's son. But perhaps I bore you—no?"

"Not at all. I find the differences fascinating," she
answered sincerely. "We know so little about your country, I'm afraid."

"Tell me," he asked suddenly, "if you had seen the
Tower of London, the Mint, Almack's, and Hyde Park,
where would you go after that?"

"Well, I—" She hesitated for a moment, wondering
what he meant. "Do you ask what I would do were I new
to the city—or do you ask what I most like to do?"

"What you like to do."

"Well, quite my favorite thing is to walk among the flowers in St. James Park. It is lovely and quiet there in the mornings." She looked up at him, then dropped her eyes shyly. "But I should not think a visitor would count it worth seeing—not after all the other places one usually goes."

"I have always enjoyed flowers, Ekaterina."

All too soon the music ended. Suddenly self-conscious, she stepped back. "My thanks, sir."

Returning her to her seat, he bowed over her hand. "Perhaps I will see you again while I am in your country, Ekaterina Winstead." He seemed to hesitate for a moment, then he murmured, "*Au revoir*, mademoiselle."

Her gaze followed him as he disappeared among the crowd. Telling herself she had to have dreamed everything, she bent to secretly slip her shoes from her feet.

"Never say the Russian trampled them?"

She looked up into Bellamy Townsend's faintly sardonic smile. The blood rose hotly in her cheeks. "No, of course not," she said shortly. "He mastered the steps better than I did."

Townsend studied her for a moment, then smiled. "Apparently you are more in fashion than you thought."

To her utter surprise, he took the chair beside her. "Are you quite certain this is not a wager?" she asked. "I mean, I cannot think you—"

"Actually, I am merely waiting for someone."

"Oh."

He leaned back, resting his head against the French paper on the wall. "However, if I were you, I should not waste my time throwing my cap over the windmill for the dashing Count Volsky. He won't be here very long."

Her back stiffened. "I am not so green as to set my cap for the first gentleman to waltz with me, my lord," she retorted coldly.

"That would be me, Kate—and, no, it wouldn't do you any good if you did. My salad days," he declared definitely, "are far from over."

His manner infuriated her. "Bell Townsend, if I lived in medieval times and discovered I was promised to you,

I should rather have shaved my head and taken religious orders," she told him with feeling.

"Ah, there you are, *mon ami*!" For a moment, Katherine thought Madame Malenkov addressed her, but it was Bellamy Townsend's hand the woman took. He rose as she held out her dance card. "I am promised to you this time, *n'est ce pas*?"

Just then, Kate caught sight of Alexei Volsky standing by her sister, and her spirits plummeted. Why did he have to notice Claire also? Just once, she would like to be the one with the triumphs to tell. But it would not happen—once Claire exerted herself to flirt with a gentleman, he never looked at Kate again. And tonight, she could not bear it.

She found her brother lounging along the opposite wall, a glass of wine punch in his hand. His face was flushed, either from dancing or drink. He raised his glass to her.

"To the Russians, Katie!"

It was drink. "Harry, I should like to go home."

He blinked. "Waltzed twice—saw you with my own eyes—the Jersey remarked it. Dash it, but now's not—"

"My head aches abominably."

"Wouldn't know it by—" He stopped and peered more closely at her. "Do look peaked."

"Please, Harry."

He downed the wine and set the empty glass on a passing tray. "Well, not much left but supper, anyway," he conceded. "Party's a crashing bore. Tell you what—get Mama and Claire, and I'll set you down on my way to White's."

She shook her head. "Claire won't want to go. Perhaps Lord Hargrove could be persuaded to take her."

"Can't send her off alone with him."

"Mama can go with them, can't she?"

He digested that for a moment, then nodded. "Wait here, and I'll tell them. Ten to one, Mama will be like a cat over cream at the thought. Anything to nudge Hargrove along, you know."

"Yes, I know."

In the carriage, she pulled her shawl tightly about her

shoulders and leaned back, closing her eyes, hoping her brother did not mean to tease her. A silence, broken only by the rattle of the iron-clad wheels on the cobbled street, descended. It was not until they were nearly home that Harry spoke up.

"Volsky asked me about you."

"And I suppose you hinted he should dance with me," she muttered.

"No. Why would you say a thing like that?"

"I don't need pity, Harry. And I know you must have asked Bell Townsend."

He blinked. "No—got that all wrong, Kate. It wasn't me, I swear it. Just as surprised as you, if you want the truth. Can't say I wasn't glad, though, 'cause it ain't your fault you don't take. If Mama would leave you be—"

"She cannot make me taller—and she cannot make me pretty."

"He inquired as to how old you are, by the by."

"Don't be absurd. He knows precisely how old I am."

"Not Bell. Volsky."

Somehow that was a lowering thought. "So now he knows I am but one step from being an ape-leader."

"It wasn't like that at all."

"Harry, don't you fun with me, for you are not the least bit amusing!"

"You must have a devil of a headache," he murmured sympathetically.

"It is getting worse." She leaned her head against the coolness of the door pane. "Much worse."

"You ought to go to bed as soon as you get home. Maybe Peg can do something for it."

She sat up abruptly. "Oh, lud—don't tell her, I pray you, for the last time she burned feathers. It was weeks before the smell left my pillows."

He was silent again, and this time she could scarce stand it. Finally, her own resolve not to discuss the dashing Russian crumbled.

"How old is he?"

"Thirty."

"I knew it for a hum! I should scarce call that *old*."

"I should hope not. I'll be there next year, and so will Bell." He leaned forward slightly. "You know, what with Bell and Volsky dancing with you, things might be better now."

"Harry, you are disguised."

"Remarked—I swear it." He looked out the window briefly, then back to her. "In any event, we are home."

Opening his own door, he jumped down, then went around the front of the coach to wrench hers. "Catching her by her waist, he lifted her out easily. "There. You know, tomorrow I'm going to tell Mama to buy you something with a little color."

"She won't agree." Standing on tiptoe, she brushed a quick kiss against his cheek. "Good night, Harry—you are quite the best of brothers."

Once inside the house, she hurried to her chamber, undressed quickly, and slipped into bed. Lying there, she clasped her arms over her breasts and tried to relive every minute of her waltz with Alexei Volsky. For this one night, for a few brief moments, she had felt almost pretty. But as her mind began to wander in that hazy world before sleep, it was Bellamy Townsend's handsome face that floated before her, Bellamy Townsend's gray eyes that teased her, telling her she was green.

K atherine pulled her pillow over her head and tried to ignore the persistent pounding on her door. She'd spent an utterly miserable night, tossing and turning, plagued by wild, utterly impossible dreams. When it became obvious that the knocking was not going to stop, she rolled over and called out crossly, "I pray you will go away, for I am still abed!"

The door opened, and her sister slipped inside. "Kate, you cannot mean to sleep all day."

"I have the headache," Katherine muttered.

"Still? Then perhaps you ought to have Peg burn some feathers for you. The last time—"

"The last time the smell made it worse."

Clarissa moved closer to peer into Katherine's face. "You did not partake of the wine last night, did you? Mama would not—"

"Of course not!"

"Well, I daresay when you are up and about, it will go away." Having afforded all the sympathy she had, Clarissa plopped down on the end of the bed and began regaling Kate with her triumphs. "You left far too early, you know. I vow it was the most exciting party of the Season! Only fancy—I danced with all the Russians— except that hatman—and the czar, of course."

"Hetman," Katherine corrected her. "Platov's title is hetman."

"Except the Cossack then. Really, Kate, but what does it matter how he is called? Now—where was I?"

"Dancing."

"One would think you do not wish to hear the best of

all,'' the younger girl declared peevishly, throwing up her hands. "It would serve you right if I didn't tell you!" When Katherine did not respond, Clarissa leaned forward. "I danced with Count Volsky—and—oh Kate!—I vow he is nearly as handsome as Bellamy Townsend!"

"If you danced with all of them, I expect you did," Katherine responded dryly. "Really, Claire, but I do have the headache.''

Ignoring that, the younger girl continued to chatter eagerly. "Anyway, he is quite taken with me—I could tell it!"

"I expect he was." Not wishing to hear more of Alexei Volsky, Katherine tried to turn the conversation away from him. "What of Hargrove? Did he bring you and Mama home?''

"Actually, he was quite pleased to do it.''

"And I trust Mama was in alt over that?''

"She toad-ate him all the way home." Not to be denied, Clarissa returned to the exciting part of her story. "But we were speaking of Count Volsky, Kate.''

"And the rest of the Russians who stood up with you, no doubt.''

"Oh, *everyone* danced with me! I vow I was the toast of the evening! There was Ponsonby—and Palmerston— even Brummell himself!"

"And Lord Hargrove—Mama would not have you forget him, for I think she has quite fixed her hopes there.''

Clarissa tossed her head, practicing the effect, then made a face at Kate. "Now *he* tried to get me to waltz thrice with him!" Giggling like a schoolgirl, she confided, "He was ever so jealous of Count Volsky, I swear it.''

"Well, he cannot be blamed, for you have certainly led him on full half the Season.''

"Kate! I did no such thing!"

"Well, if you didn't, you are a shameless flirt."

The younger girl stared for a moment, then recovered. "I shall consider that envy merely," she declared haughtily. "Just because you came home with some megrim—''

"Caused by boredom.''

"Well, if you had not sat there like some sort of Antidote, I daresay somebody might have taken pity on you."

"I don't want anybody's pity."

Not wanting to lose the opportunity to crow over her greatest triumph, Clarissa leaned to pat Kate's hand. "Of course you do not," she murmured soothingly. "Believe me, I should like nothing better than to see you suitably settled."

"As Mama will not require that I be fired off first, I fail to see why," Katherine murmured mildly.

"Goose! You are my only sister, after all."

"Claire—"

"Well, I daresay it does not signify. I expect you will get some sort of offer this year. There is Mr. Thurgood—"

"I am not going to be anyone's fourth wife, Claire."

"Well, I daresay that does not signify just now, anyway." Clarissa's lovely face took on the look of a cat after cream. "Only fancy—he took me in to sup!"

The knot in Kate's stomach tightened. "Who?"

"Why Count Volsky, of course! And he has such address!"

"How nice for you," Kate said without enthusiasm.

"We were but six seats from His Imperial Highness— six seats from the czar, Kate! He must be quite rich, don't you think?"

"If he is autocrat of all the Russias, I expect he is."

"I wasn't speaking of the czar!" Clarissa snapped, irritated. "I meant Volsky! Usually you are not such a slow-top."

"I expect it is the headache."

"Yes, well, I sat between him and Count Platov. Kate, I think he has a particularity for me!"

"Somehow I cannot quite envision you in a Cossack hut, Claire."

"Not the hetman, ninny! Volsky! You *are* a slow-top!"

Katherine sat up and swung her legs over the side of the bed. "I should not refine too much on a dance with Count Volsky." She managed a slightly lopsided smile.

"After all, I expect he danced with everyone. Indeed, but even I waltzed with him."

The younger girl gave a squeal of triumph. "I knew it! You are as jealous as Hargrove! And a dance is not of the same particularity as supper!"

Kate rose and reached for her wrapper. "No, I am not so foolish as to think a waltz meant anything." Tying it around her, she moved to ring for her maid. "Do you stay to drink your morning chocolate with me?" she asked mildly.

"Lud. no! I had mine ages ago. I vow I could not sleep for thinking of him!"

Her back to her sister, Kate murmured, "Hargrove?"

"You know very well whom I meant!" Claire retorted. "Lord Hargrove is a crashing bore!" She flounced toward the door. Stopping there, she turned back. "I can fix his interest, you know," she declared smugly. And there was no doubt whom she meant. With that, she left.

While Katherine waited for Peg to come up, she took a chair to the window and sat down. It did no good to tell herself that her sister's flighty barbs did not hurt. She had but to look at a fellow for Claire to get him. It was not fair in the least. Her one consolation was that Volsky would leave—and soon, and she would not have to see an ignominious repetition of the pattern. Then she recalled Bell Townsend and wondered why she'd forgotten to mention him also. Now that would have taken the wind from her sister's sails.

"I brung yer chocolate—and I took leave ter put yer breakfast with it, miss."

"Just leave it on the table."

"Ye ain't blue-deviled, are ye?"

"No—I have the headache."

The maid set the tray down and came closer. "Well, ye do look a bit hagged," she decided. "Maybe ye ought ter get back ter bed. I can tell yer mama—"

"I daresay it will go away after I have eaten." Katherine stood up and glanced down from the window. What she saw made her heart nearly stop. "Just go on, Peg—I'll call you when I am done."

"But I ain't set it out fer ye, and—"

"Go on. I can tend to it for myself."

Muttering that "Miss Kate is out o' reason cross ter-day, and 'tis a shame, it is, for the sun's shining," Peg left.

But Katherine wasn't attending her. Below, Madame Malenkov and Count Volsky stepped from an exceedingly smart landau. The Russian nobleman's head was bare, and his black hair shone in the morning sun. He was in full uniform, with his hussar hat tucked beneath one arm. His black boots had a shine that would have shamed Beau Brummell. As he mounted the steps, Kate forced her gaze to his sister. The curled brim of the lovely widow's green hat showed her auburn hair to advantage. As Kate stared, they disappeared inside.

She could hear Clarissa running up the back stairs, ordering Peg to find their mother's dresser quickly. She could not face Count Volsky "looking like the veriest wreck!" Kate's already low spirits plummeted, and she considered going back to bed. They had not come to call on her, anyway.

Galena Malenkova's warm voice carried upward, followed by the deeper, yet softer sound of Alexei Volsky's. Kate listened as her mama directed them into the front saloon. Apparently, the Russians did not know that they were supposed to merely leave cards in the tray in the hall, that it was too early to be actually received. And equally apparent, her mother did not care, for her voice betrayed her excitement. Everyone was enamored of all Russians, Kate reflected almost sourly. By nightfall, every female Lady Winstead knew would be apprised of this signal honor. The only thing better would be if Czar Alexander himself had come with them.

Reluctantly, Kate turned to her chocolate. This morning it was too thick and too sweet. Setting it back on her tray, she covered it with a napkin to hide from Peg that she had not drunk it. Well, let Mama and Claire toad-eat them—she herself did not intend to go down. It would be quite enough to listen to her sister boast of this newest conquest when they were gone.

Peg slipped through the door, scarce able to hide her excitement, then blurted out, "They are asking fer ye, miss! And her ladyship said I was ter fetch ye directly down," she added. She stopped. "Ye ain't dressed."

"Of course not!" Kate retorted crossly. Almost as soon as she spoke, she was contrite. "Oh, Peg, I'm sorry—it is not your fault that I am not quite the thing today."

"Ye ain't going ter let her steal the march on ye, are ye?" the woman demanded.

"Look at me—I cannot go down," Kate protested. "I cannot show to advantage beside her."

"Humph! Seems ter me ye ain't going to have ter— they asked for you, not her."

"There must be a mistake—they have the names confused, I expect." For a moment, she was torn, then Claire's words echoed in her mind. *I can fix his interest, you know.* "Tell Mama to advise them I have the head-ache," she said dully. "Perhaps another day."

"Here now, missy—what's this?" Lady Winstead stepped into the room and surveyed Kate. She winced visibly, then declared, "You'll do no such thing, Katherine! I myself can scarce credit it, but Madame Malen-kov insists they are come to take you up—something about a promised trip to St. James Park."

"St. James Park?" Kate repeated blankly. "Oh—I col-lect they wish to see the flowers."

"There are flowers everywhere," her mother replied sourly. "You will make yourself presentable immediately and come down."

"Mama, I have the headache!"

"I don't care if both limbs are broken," Lady Win-stead snapped. "This is your chance to be seen with them, and you'll not let it pass, missy!"

"They cannot bring me into fashion, Mama!" Kate wailed. "They are leaving!"

"I'll have none of this missish behavior—not now, Katherine." With that, her mother turned and walked away.

Kate stared after her. Volsky had come to see her?

There *had* to be a mistake. Or else she'd misled him last night into thinking that St. James Park had to be seen. That must be the case.

"Ain't no time fer woolgathering, miss," Peg said, cutting into Kate's thoughts. "Miss Clarissa ain't going ter be ready ere she can make 'em wait, don't ye know?"

Kate turned around and untied her wrapper. Slowly,. it sank into her consciousness—Volsky had come to see her, not her sister. And Claire was not yet down. *Claire was not yet down.* "Fetch a walking dress, Peg," she ordered, tearing at the buttons on her night rail, feeling a certain urgency.

"Which one?"

"It does not matter—none of them becomes me in the least."

Pulling the nightgown over her head and letting it fall to the floor, Kate reached for her zona. Her fingers worked frantically at the laces, tightening and tying them. She had to hurry. Quickly, she put on her stockings and rolled them at her knees, knotting them there. Peg presented her with her best slip, and she fairly dived into it, then turned to take the dress. It was pale blue lustring, plainly cut, and no doubt it made her look even plainer than she was, but there was no time to waste choosing another. As she fastened the small buttons at the neck, she glimpsed herself in the mirror, and her resolve deserted her.

"Oh, Peg—I cannot! I look like the veriest frump!"

"Here now—none of that, miss. A bit of the rouge pot'll fix that."

"And my hair—'tis naught but tangles!"

"I'll comb it fer ye—all ye got ter do is sit a minute," the maid promised.

"I'm hopeless!"

"Not if his lordship was ter want decent conversation," Peg murmured, dragging the brush through Kate's dark hair. "We can pin it a bit here and there. Besides, you'll be wearing a hat."

The woman's hands worked dexterously, hiding the smashed curls beneath a high-crowned hat. When she moved away, Kate made a face at herself in the mirror. There was no hiding it—she *was* an Antidote.

Peg studied her for a moment, then reached for the rouge pot. "Just a dab," she promised. "Too much and you'll look like one of them fancy pieces."

Despite everything, Kate told herself that she did not look as bad as she thought—she could not. Rising, she settled her shoulders and took a deep breath.

"Go on with ye—all ye got ter do is talk to 'em," Peg said firmly.

On the stairs, Kate stopped to wipe wet palms against her dress. Behind her, Claire called out, "Wait for me— I am quite ready also."

Kate half turned, and what she saw made her heart sink to her stomach. Claire wore a blue-figured muslin that set off her pink blondeness to perfection. In one hand, she carried a matching parasol, and in the other, a broad-brimmed, flat-crowned hat, its blue ribbons trailing. She looked like a painting.

Kate wanted to flee, to run back upstairs and hide, but her mother's voice stopped her. "There you are, my love—you dear, naughty child," she chided. For a moment, Kate thought she spoke to Claire, but when she turned to face her, her mother was smiling up at her.

"Mama—" she began desperately.

"Dearest Kate, Count Volsky and Lady Malenkov have waited an age for you."

There was an unmistakable edge of warning. Swallowing, Katherine nodded and moved slowly down the stairs. Count Volsky had come out into the hall and was looking upward. Claire, ever conscious of the effect she had on men, waited until Kate was nearly down before she hailed him.

"So kind of you to call, my lord," she said, smiling, drawing his attention.

"Miss Winstead," he acknowledged before turning his attention to Kate. "And you, *ma petite,* the headache is gone?" he inquired solicitously. "They said you left before we went to sup."

"Yes."

"I should hate to think the fault mine, for you seemed to be in health when we danced."

"No—no, of course not."

Her hand felt like ice as he possessed it and bowed low over it. "You should have apprised me, and we could have sat instead."

"I scarce thought it your concern, sir." Aware that she sounded stiff and wooden, she tried to make amends. "That is, I did not expect you to concern yourself." That sounded worse. "I mean, we are scarce acquainted, and—"

"I am sure Count Volsky quite understands, Katherine," her mother said frostily. Smiling almost rigidly, she added, "I have ordered cakes in the front saloon."

But Volsky shook his head. "The morning escapes, Madame Winstead. Tell me, Ekaterina," he murmured, addressing Kate, "do you take pity on this visitor to your city? Can you find the time to show Galena and myself this St. James Park?"

"Of course she can!" Lady Winstead insisted. "Though I am not sure St. James—well, I mean there was that unfortunate business about the Pagoda—"

"The fire? Yes, yes—Platov told me of it," he said dismissively. "But we do not go to see the building, I think." Once again, his clear blue eyes sought Katherine's. "We go for the flowers, *n'est ce pas*?"

"Uh—yes, yes, of course. I—uh—I should be delighted, sir," she stammered. "But—"

"Good. And I am called Lexy by nearly everyone, Ekaterina."

"I am afraid we are a trifle more formal here, Count Volsky," Claire said, moving to stand beside him. "As she is the *elder* daughter, she is Miss Winstead."

"Ah, but there should not be such formality among friends, I think," he responded smoothly. "I shall address her as Ekaterina—unless she should object, of course."

He'd set-down Claire. As the younger girl's face flushed, Kate hastened to ask him, "And your sister, sir—she is well?"

"Ah, *cherie,* so kind of you to inquire," Galena Malenkova answered softly from the saloon door. "But of course I am always in health, little one." She hurried forward to plant a quick kiss on Kate's cheek. "It is you who have worried Lexy. When he heard you were unwell, nothing would persuade him we must wait until after the noon to see for ourselves."

"It was nothing, madame."

"I am glad to hear of it. Lexy has rented a troika— well, it is not a *troika* exactly, for there are but two horses," she corrected herself.

Clarissa made one last effort. "Poor Kate—she will not tell you when she is feeling not at all the thing, Count Volsky, but as you can see—" She paused, giving him time to look at her plain sister. "Well, I should be happy to show you and madame the park, sir."

"The offer is appreciated, Miss Winstead, but I am promised to Ekaterina—*n'est-ce pas,* little one?"

Before Kate could answer, Madame Malenkov spoke up. "Alas, but the conveyance is crowded, else we should take you also, Miss Winstead. Perhaps another day."

Clarissa's face fell, then her lower lip protruded in a pout. Her mother touched her arm in warning, insisting to the count, "I am sure Claire would not wish to intrude, my lord."

"Exactly," Galena Malenkova murmured. "Such a lovely child."

"Well, then—shall we proceed, Ekaterina?"

"I should be delighted, sir."

Alexei Volsky offered Kate his arm, promising her mother, "I shall take care not to overset the conveyance, madame."

"We shall have her back before the sun sets," Madame Malenkov added.

"So long?" Lady Winstead frowned. "I am not at all sure—that is, I would not have it bandied about that she is fast, madame. You understand, of course."

"Of course. And no one who should see your daughter could think her anything but proper," the Russian woman reassured her. "But there is so little time in your wonderful country. Lexy had thought perhaps a visit to the park, with a nuncheon in a basket provided by your Gunther's—and later we should like to partake of ices in his establishment. And if it is convenient, perhaps we shall make her known to the grand duchess. I shall need to stop at the hotel again, I think.''

Lady Winstead's mouth gaped. ''The czar's sister?'' she asked weakly.

''Perhaps. And who knows—? If Alexander is there, perhaps him also.''

''Mama!'' Claire wailed.

''Be still, you foolish girl!'' her mother snapped. Seeing the tears that threatened to spill over, she added more kindly, ''While Katherine is out, I daresay we might go to Hookham's.''

''I don't want to read a book!''

''Clarissa!'' Turning to Count Volsky, Lady Winstead apologized, ''You must forgive my daughter, for she is overtired from so many parties.''

''He did not note it,'' Madame Malenkov assured her.

As Dawes, her mother's butler, held the door for them, Kate could hear Claire. ''Well, I never! Are they blind?''

To which Lady Winstead replied, ''I can scarce credit it myself. Even Townsend waltzed with her last night— while you were conversing with Lord Hargrove and his mother.''

''Bellamy Townsend!'' Claire cried. ''I don't believe it!''

''Most improperly, I might add,'' her mother recalled. ''Indeed, if Mrs. Drummond-Burrell can be believed, it looked as though he kissed her.''

''Kissed her! Mama! And—and you did nothing?''

''Well, I did not see it, of course—and it was but a peck on the cheek, I am told. Besides, I did not wish to create an unpleasant scene there, and she was already asleep when we came home.''

''If Bellamy Townsend has kissed Kate, the whole world has gone mad!'' the girl declared forcefully. ''Mad!''

At the curb, Alexei Volsky handed his sister up, then

reached for Kate's elbow. Leaning closer, he murmured, "I shall hope to enjoy the flowers." As her eyes widened, he favored her with an almost conspiratorial smile. "You did promise me flowers, did you not?"

Despite the quickening of her heart, she tried to keep her voice light. "I hope you will not be disappointed," she answered sincerely.

His other hand possessed hers. *"Nyet."* Still smiling, he added, "Someday, my little *Angleechahnka*, you must learn to speak Russian."

The sun was bright, the sky unclouded, and the scent of the flowers seemed to permeate the clear, warm air. Moreover, the company was light. Madame Malenkov walked ahead toward the ruined pagoda, where the Prince Regent's earlier fireworks display had gotten quite out of hand, burning the five-story building.

Katherine walked more slowly, keeping pace with Alexei Volsky, who seemed inclined to linger. Ahead of them, three bucks of the *ton* strolled, and to her chagrin, one of them was Bellamy Townsend. Galena Malenkova stopped to exchange pleasantries, prompting Kate to frown.

"I am not at all certain I should recommend Lord Townsend to your sister, sir."

Beside her, Alexei Volsky stopped. Looking down into her eyes, he smiled. "He is a rake? It does not matter, I think. I would not expect Lena to encourage him before my eyes."

"No, of course not."

He reached to take her hands. "My apologies, Ekaterina. It is kind of you to wish to warn Galena. You do not mind that I call you Ekaterina, do you?"

"No." She dared to look up at him. "Indeed, I rather like the sound of it."

"And forget what your sister tells you—I am Lexy—or Alexei, however you prefer to say it."

There was such warmth in the blue eyes that Kate wished he could stay in England forever. Afraid that the Russian could somehow see into her thoughts, she looked down.

"I should not have spoken, I know. It was that I have known Viscount Townsend much of my life." As his eyebrow went up, she hastened to explain, "He is my brother's dearest friend, you see. But even Harry would agree Bell has the most inconstant heart."

"I think he is more inclined to note Sofia Verenskaya, little one."

"I don't know her."

"Marshal Sherkov's wife. She was at the ball last night."

"Oh."

"And before you worry for her, Sofia will probably seduce this Townsend before he seduces her. She is, I am afraid, the pretty young wife of an ill-tempered old man."

"Oh. Well, if she is lovely, she will have no difficulty getting his attention. She has his paramount requirement," she observed. "He has an affinity for married ladies."

"There you are—Galena is a widow."

"But she is so beautiful. I cannot think Madame Sherkov could compare with her."

He looked to where Townsend, accompanied by lords Leighton and Carew, stood pointing out the charred ruins to his sister. "Galena," he said slowly, "is different. Since Cyril's death, she devotes herself to me." Turning back to her, he tucked her hand into the crook of his arm, then patted her fingers. "But why must we speak of others on such a fine day, I ask you? No, Ekaterina, but we must enjoy ourselves."

She was acutely aware of the nearness of him, so much so that she could scarce think. He was so tall, so straight, and so solid. And when the sun caught the gold braid on his uniform, he was as handsome as any.

"I must rely on you to name the flowers, little one."

"What?" She flushed, feeling caught at thinking of him. "Oh, I do not know all of them, I'm afraid. I merely like to admire their beauty."

"Then let us admire whatever they are together."

They walked amid the brightly blooming plant beds

saying little. From time to time, she noted the admiring glances cast Count Volsky's way, and she could not help the surge of gratitude she felt. On this day at least, she knew she was envied.

At one end of the walk, there was a small booth for selling flowers. He stopped before it and turned to her. "Which are your favorites? Must I guess, or do you tell me?" he asked, smiling. "Roses?"

"Actually, I have scarce met a flower I did not like," she admitted.

He studied the assortment, then selected a small bouquet of mixed blooms. "For you, Ekaterina," he said softly as he presented them. "You like the country blossoms, eh?"

Embarrassed by his kindness, she bent her head to sniff the heady fragrances. "Yes," she answered simply.

"So do I," he admitted as he started to walk again. "At my home, there are many, many flowers, but alas, the season for growing them is much shorter than here." Finally, he gestured to a bench. "You must be tired, Ekaterina." Stopping to sweep it off with his hand, he murmured, "I hope you are enjoying this as much as I."

"Oh—I am—I am," she said sincerely.

"Good. Then you shall not mind it if I ask you to ride in Hyde Park tomorrow?" His blue eyes twinkled as he added, "I show to much greater advantage when I am on a horse, I promise you." His hand covered hers where she gripped the bench. "When I was young, my tutor told me all Englishwomen ride well."

"I love to ride, but I cannot vouch for how well. I can sit a horse, but we do not keep one in London—other than the carriage pair, that is."

"Then I shall obtain one."

"I am not at all certain that Mama—" she began doubtfully.

"Galena will come for your English propriety, little one."

"I would that you did not call me that," she blurted out. As he looked down at her, she colored uncomfortably. "Mama hates it that I am short, and she is forever remarking on it, you see. As though that will make me grow—which it does not, of course.''

"Poor Ekaterina," he said soothingly. "What is it that you would be called?''

"Kate—or Ekaterina.''

"Kate.'' He appeared to consider it for a moment, then shook his head. "It sounds strange to me, but perhaps I will get used to it.'' He reached to lift her chin with his fingers, making her look at him. "There is nothing wrong with being small, Ekaterina.''

"Perhaps not, but when you are small and plain, I suspect life is different. Everyone seems to favor beautiful people, you see.''

"How tall are you?''

"With or without my slippers?'' she countered, smiling. "I like to say I am five feet and one inch, you know, but truth to tell, I am merely five feet in my stockings.''

"And I am six English feet in my boots,'' he admitted. Cocking his head to look at her, he decided, "You have a lovely smile, Ekaterina—you must employ it more often. And the dark eyes, I like them also. There is a mystery to dark eyes, I think.''

"My nose is too long.''

"It is defined, that is all,'' he assured her. "Who would wish for a short one?''

"I must admit I have never thought about it in quite that way,'' she murmured.

He was silent for a moment, then he said quietly, "Galena could make you pretty.'' His finger moved from her chin to trace her jaw, then to her nose. "I can see it.''

She wanted to believe him, but her good sense told her differently. Still, she managed to hold her tongue.

"Ah—you think I am offering you this Spanish gold—no?''

"Yes.''

"You think perhaps I would seduce you?''

"Of course not.'' Embarrassed, she tried to draw away from him. "Hopefully, you would wish to be friends.''

"Lexy! My poor feet must rest, and we have wandered everywhere looking for you. Ah, you have bought her the flowers—how very gallant you are.'' Galena approached, smiling at the men with her. "Not that the escort is not charming, of course. You are acquainted with Ekaterina Winstead, *n'est-ce pas*?'' she asked them.

"Don't know her precisely,'' Lord Carew murmured, "but I am acquainted with Baron Winstead.''

"Miss Winstead,'' Lord Leighton greeted her.

"And of course you know her,'' Galena reminded Bell Townsend.

His gray eyes rested on Katherine, and he nodded. "I ran tame at Monk's End long before she was out of the schoolroom. Hallo, Kate.''

His carefully brushed Brutus was now tousled by the soft breeze that wafted over the canal. It gave him that boyish look that endeared him to all the ladies—the dangerous combination of angel and devil in one.

He turned to Volsky. "Harry tells me she is a veritable bluestocking—but I've never persuaded her to share much beyond a sharp tongue with me.''

"Bluestocking?''

Knowing full well that any pretense to intellect was offensive to fashionable men, she sought to turn the charge aside. "Well, I would not say that precisely. I like to read, that's all.''

"Ah—the English romantic novels,'' the count murmured, nodding.

"Doing it too brown, Miss Winstead,'' Townsend insisted. "I have it on excellent authority that you are as well-read as an Oxford don.'' Once again, he grinned at her companion. "Likes politics, too—though a trifle radical, I am told. The Whigs, isn't it?''

"Townsend—'' Her voice was little more than a growl.

He grinned. "You are overmodest, Miss Winstead.''

"Well, now that you are found, Lexy,'' Galena spoke up, "I think we should discover a place to eat. Lord Townsend tells me there are bugs in the grass.''

"Fiddle.'' Kate shot the viscount a defiant look. "As a dandy, he is afraid to get his clothes dirty.''

"Then we will eat here, after all,'' Galena decided.

"Alexei, order the boy to bring everything." But as she spoke, she waved toward the rented conveyance.

As Alexei and Galena tried to gain their tiger's attention, Kate hissed at Townsend, "You wretch—why did you say that?"

"That you are a bluestocking?"

"Yes."

"I had hopes of helping you with your Russian swain, my dear."

"They don't even know what a bluestocking is. You make it sound as though I am a complete oddity. And he is not my swain," she added crossly. "I hope you do not mean to eat with us, else I shall be put off my food."

"Not at all. We are promised elsewhere, my prickly radical."

"Bell Townsend, I am not your anything," she retorted acidly. "And you had no right to make them think me odd."

But later, as she and Galena and Alexei Volsky sat down to eat, the count poured wine into glasses, then held his up to Kate's. "To the lady with the blue stockings," he murmured. His blue eyes betrayed a faint amusement. "However, I must beg of you not to discuss politics with Alexander."

"As if I should presume to speak to him."

"Ah, but you will, Ekaterina, I promise you. However, while he professes to admire the Whigs here, you must not forget he is the autocrat in Russia."

It had been an extraordinary day, one that Kate would never forget if she lived to be a hundred. She looked down at her hand, thinking her mama would never believe Alexander of Russia had touched it, or that she had taken tea with the grand duchess. Still, she was quite nervous, for despite his promise to her mother, Alexei Volsky was not returning her home until it was already quite dark.

Leaving Galena in the vehicle, Alexei escorted Katherine to her door. The night sounds surrounded them, and above, the stars were brilliant in the clear sky. He stopped just short of the portico and turned her to face him. The moonlight seemed to reflect off his eyes.

"I have seldom spent such an agreeable time, Ekaterina," he told her, smiling. "You must enlighten me more on the morrow." His hand brushed her cheek lightly. "Until then, Kate."

Not knowing if he were serious, or if she'd bored him with her assessment of the recent war and British policy differences between the Tories and the Whigs, she felt quite self-conscious. Apparently, he guessed her thoughts, for his next words were a relief.

"It does not displease me that you have a mind. Beauty without intellect is tedious. As you surely must have noted, Galena wears the blue stockings also."

Embarrassed, she said quickly, "You are kind to say it, sir—Alexei, that is. And again I must thank you for the lovely flowers."

"It was nothing. Until tomorrow, then?" He stepped closer. "Any who thinks you plain is wrong," he murmured. "It is the hat that is plain."

He bent his head to hers, and his breath caressed her cheek as his lips brushed it. Then he straightened.

"Good night, Ekaterina," he said softly.

The door opened, and Dawes cleared his throat. "That you, miss? Her ladyship has been asking if you was at home."

Katherine jumped guiltily. "Good night, sir—er—good night, Alexei." Grasping her hat and the wilting flowers before her like a shield, she went inside to face her mother.

He returned to the carriage, where he sank back against the squabs. Looking across at his sister, he sighed.

Galena reached for his hands, clasping them in hers. "*Fychom dyela?*"

"*Neechevo.*"

"Lexy, I swear I can see that you will not be disgusted with her." When he did not answer, she massaged his fingers, saying earnestly, "You do this for us, Lexy—for *us*. It will be all right—you'll see. Trust Lena," she coaxed.

Inside the house, Lady Winstead, instead of reading a peal over Katherine, was unusually pleasant. It was Claire who was mad as fire. Her color heightened, the younger girl met her in the hall.

"Of all the scandalous behavior! You kissed him—I saw it! And it is now common gossip about Bell Townsend! I vow I have never been so shocked by anything!"

Still shaken from her parting from Count Volsky, Kate answered dreamily, "You are mistaken, Claire—it was *they* who kissed *me*."

"Brazen hussy!"

"Really, Claire, but it was no such thing. I—"

"Clarissa!" Lady Winstead moved to intervene, saying firmly, "That is quite enough. I will not stand for a brangle."

Unused to the censure in her mother's voice, Claire's lower lip trembled, and her eyes filled with tears. "But Mama—she—she stole him from me!" With that, she fled up the stairs. Her door banged loudly as she slammed it.

"A fit of vapors—nothing more," Lady Winstead said mildly before turning her attention again to Katherine. A small smile lifted the corners of her mouth. "I have ordered ratafia for us, my love. Shall we repair to the saloon for a comfortable coze ere you ready yourself for Lady Hargrove's musicale?"

"Uh—I don't feel like going, Mama," Kate protested. "I am rather tired."

"Nonsense," her mother declared briskly. "It will be all over town that Count Volsky has singled you out."

"Mama, you have gossiped all day, and it is no such thing!" Kate swallowed as Lady Winstead's smile flattened. "That is, he will be leaving shortly, so I should not refine too much on a basket nuncheon in the park," she managed in a more reasonable tone. "But," she added to mollify her mother, "the Volskys did take me to the Pulteney, where I spoke the merest commonplace with the czar and his sister."

That stopped her mother for a moment. "He actually did take you to meet them? Kate, it is a signal honor!"

"The grand duchess poured tea," Katherine remembered. "And Czar Alexander said he much admired the English people."

"No! Oh, wait until—" Lady Winstead caught herself, and returned to her earlier intent. "I have heard that the Volskys are *unbelievably* rich, Katherine," her mother went on. "And there is no saying but what their tastes are a trifle different from ours. And if you were presented to the czar—"

"Mama, you must not refine too much on a courtesy!" Kate insisted, alarmed. "Besides, they are leaving!"

"Lady Sefton told Mrs. Barclay that he means to go to Vienna for the peace conference, my love."

"You discussed him with everyone, didn't you? Mama, if you have spread the gossip that he has any particularity for me, I daresay he will cut me when he hears of it. And I do not want any ratafia."

Lady Winstead glanced at Dawes, who continued to linger in the foyer, listening. "You are merely overset, for you are unused to such attention, Katherine," she said smoothly. "And one small glass of ratafia will do you good." Standing back, she waited for Kate to pass her into the saloon. Then she followed, carefully shutting the door.

"Servants gossip, I'm afraid."

"No more than ladies, apparently," Katherine muttered under her breath as she sat down.

"What?"

"Nothing, Mama."

"Do not mistake me, my dear Kate—I have not the least hope that Volsky himself will come up to scratch. That would certainly be too much to ask," she conceded. "But it does not mean we cannot use his attention to show you to advantage, after all. We should be fools to ignore the opportunity."

Kate sat very still. Her mother's manner meant that rather than going back to Monk's End, she would be forced to try harder to catch a husband. And she knew she could not do it. She didn't want any of the rakes and dandies—and certainly none of the aging widowers likely to favor her.

"Kate, you are woolgathering!"

"Yes, Mama."

"We shall go to the Hargrove affair while people are still speaking of the Russian's singular attention, my love." Lady Winstead surveyed Kate critically for a moment and winced. Recovering, she added, "When you are dressed, I shall send Marsh up to do something with your hair. And you may wear my diamond pendant."

"Mama, I cannot be out half the night."

"Why not?"

Sucking in her breath and letting it out slowly, Kate announced simply, "Because Count Volsky and Madame Malenkov have invited me to ride in Hyde Park with them in the morning." As soon as she said it, she wished the words back. At Lady Hargrove's, her mother would be certain to spread that about also.

"Really?" Lady Winstead peered into Kate's face again. "Well, the Russians are a different people," she decided, "so perhaps they do not note that you are a trifle dark. And after seeing Count Platov for myself, I am inclined to think that beauty does not matter to them." Recalling a bit of gossip she had gleaned in her calls, she added, "And I am told he means to dance for us after the Italian woman sings. Count Platov, I mean."

"That should be diverting," Kate murmured without enthusiasm.

"Yes—well, do run up and ready yourself. I shan't mind being fashionably late, but I should dislike missing the Cossack dance."

Claire had been sullenly silent all the way, and her mood had not lightened until they were set down at the Hargrove mansion, a stately brick Georgian home in Piccadilly. Being late, they were spared the receiving line, but Lord Hargrove was waiting for Claire. He was a solidly built young man, handsome in a ponderous way. Every time Kate saw him, she thought he looked as German as old King George. He held out his hands to her sister.

"My dear Miss Winstead, you have never looked lovelier," he declared. Then, "You are wearing the flowers I sent you."

Claire smiled and manipulated her fan. "You are too kind, sir."

"An Incomparable," he assured her, kissing her fingers. Looking to her mother, he asked, "Do you not agree, Lady Winstead?"

"We are all quite proud of her." Quickly pinching Kate's arm, she pushed her forward. "I have hopes of both my daughters now, my lord. "Only fancy, Kate has been to the Pulteney to meet the czar—Count Volsky and his sister took her there."

"Mama—"

Hargrove glanced at Katherine, then appeared to dismiss her. "I am told the Russians will be leaving within the fortnight—and a very good thing, too, I might add."

"Yes, a very good thing," Claire agreed readily.

"A dark, strange people," he said, ignoring the fact that Czar Alexander was fairer than half the Englishmen. There was no mistaking whom he disparaged. "So very uncivilized."

"Madame Malenkov says the count speaks five languages," Kate said, feeling it incumbent to defend the Russian.

"I did not mean his scholarship, Miss Winstead," he responded coldly. "I was rather referring to his temper."

"Indeed, he appears the gentleman to me," she insisted loyally.

Clearly, Hargrove did not like to have his views disputed. "I am not at all sure the French would agree with you, Miss Winstead," he replied stiffly. "I understand he fought a duel there over his sister."

Fearing that Kate would set his back up further, Claire intervened hastily. Forcing a brittle laugh, she tapped his sleeve with her fan. "My sister has hopes of him, I'm afraid, so you must not refine too much on her opinion. Come," she wheedled, smiling up at him, "you must procure some punch for me else I shall die of thirst."

Kate's cheeks were hot. Humiliated, she whispered to her mother, "I knew it—I should have stayed at home."

"Do not be a fool!" Lady Winstead snapped. "The right gossip often does what appearances cannot, Katherine."

"Mama, if he hears what you have done, Volsky will give me the cut direct!"

"Nonsense. If he is a gentleman, he will know you had nothing to do with it. Leave the matter to me, my dear."

"Mama!"

"Hush." Smiling, Lady Winstead waved at Lady Jersey.

Out of the corner of her eye, Kate caught sight of Bellamy Townsend returning from the punch table, and for a rare moment, he was alone. In the ordinary way of things, she might have crossed the room to avoid him, but this was different. Slipping past her mother, she intercepted him.

"Is Volsky here?" she demanded.

One blond eyebrow shot up. "My dear Miss Winstead, were I a vain man, I should be wounded," he murmured. "You might have greeted me first. In fact, I *am* wounded."

"Your pardon." She dared to meet his gray eyes. "Please—if he is, I must find him."

He relented. "You are saved, Miss Winstead. Alexei has gone to White's."

Aware that he must have heard the gossip also, she looked away. She ought to be relieved that Count Volsky was not in attendance, but instead she was disappointed. "Oh," she managed, forming the word silently. "Yes, of course. I expect he is tired of parties."

"No doubt."

Her face was like a mirror, and once again Bell felt sorry for the plain girl before him. "Buck up, Kate— what do you care if a handful of biddies talk? Within the week, they'll be diverted to something else."

"I daresay you are used to gossip, my lord, but I am not. I just wish that Harry were here."

"Alas, but he has gone to White's also."

"I would that Mama had not done it," she said miserably, "for I know not how I shall hold my head up when he hears I have set my cap for him."

"Have you?"

"No, of course not! I am not a complete fool."

"Ah, Lord Townsend—how fortunate," a woman murmured with an heavy accent.

She was ravishing, prettier than Galena Malenkova even, and the spangled gown she wore made Kate want to escape. It clung to her body, revealing every curve, leaving little to the imagination. It was obvious that she did not wear a petticoat beneath.

Bell turned around, caught her hand, and lifted it to his lips. "Ah, the charming Sofia." Releasing her fingers, he turned back to Kate. "Miss Winstead, have you met Madame Sherkov?"

The Russian woman's gaze swept over her, then dismissed her as unimportant. "We are not acquainted, I am sure." She slipped her arm through his possessively and looked up at him with eyes bluer than Alexei's. "I have need of you, *mon cher ami,* for I have no escort. Poor Gregori is abed with a complaint and did not come," she added, pouting seductively. "Such a shame, do you not think?"

"A shame," he agreed readily. To Kate, he said, "I would not worry, my dear."

As they moved away, his words were no comfort at all. The Russian woman's throaty laughter floated back. "So that is Lexy's English conquest. How clever Galena is."

Kate could not hear the viscount's murmured reply. At her elbow, her mother demanded, "What was that about, missy? Volsky is one thing—Bellamy Townsend quite another. And after last night—well, need I say more?"

"It was nothing, Mama. I merely asked him if he had seen Harry."

"Though he was used to visit us in his youth, I cannot entirely forget the unsavory Longford affair," Lady Winstead went on. "Indeed, it surprises me he is received."

"Men are usually forgiven anything," Kate reminded her, "and I am about as likely as Count Platov to raise his interest."

Somehow, she managed to pass the evening, mostly by trading inanities with the Misses Rockwell, two equally unpromising females, one of whom had the misfortune to be utterly freckled, the other merely tall and thin. Finally, as everyone watched Count Platov and his two bodyguards whirl about the floor, their loose coats flying, Bell Townsend sat beside her.

"You have nothing to worry over, Kate—everyone who has heard the tale dismisses it," he whispered. "And I have set it about that the friendship is between you and Madame Malenkov."

"Thank you," she answered low.

"It was the least I could do for Harry." Rising abruptly, he bowed. "Good night, Kate."

"Miss Winstead, that was Townsend!" the elder Rockwell girl squeaked. "He spoke to you."

"He is a friend of my brother's," Kate replied listlessly.

"Then Mama was right! She said it was all a hum—that last night was an aberration," the younger one confided. "Oh—I daresay I should not have said that, Miss Winstead. I pray you will forgive me."

"Yes, of course."

But as she said the words, Kate felt rather dispirited. She almost wished she'd led them to believe Bell Townsend was flirting with her. Just once, she wished somebody could think someone other than Mr. Thurgood could develop a *tendre* for her.

In his carriage, Bellamy Townsend considered stopping by one of his clubs for a game or two. But he really didn't know what he wanted to do with the rest of the night. Reaching beneath his seat, he drew out his silver flask and opened it. He look a long satisfying pull, savoring the taste of France's best. The yellow balls of gaslight glowed, illuminating St. James Street. He could see the bow window of White's, and for a moment, he hesitated. Harry Winstead would be there, but lately Harry's luck made him dashed near unbeatable. No, he didn't want to play at White's.

He leaned back, passing the establishment. For a moment, his driver slowed the carriage to a snail's pace, then lacking the signal to stop, the fellow flicked the reins and urged the horses on. Taking another deep swig, Bell pondered whether to go to Brooks's—or whether to call it a night and take himself off to bed. But it was deuced early for that.

The trouble was, he reflected ruefully, that he was bored with nearly everything. He had been ever since Elinor Kingsley had refused him. Momentarily, she came to mind, her copper hair and eyes drawing him once more. She was the epitome of a man's dreams, the only woman he'd ever offered his name. And she wanted Longford.

Longford. He supposed there must be some sort of justice, but he could not appreciate it, whatever it was. They'd been friends then, before Diana, and were now, after her. But not without scandal and near ruin for all of them. He still didn't know why he'd done it—drink perhaps—but she had seduced him with disastrous consequences. Longford had not proven a complacent husband, and he'd divorced Diana for it, naming Bell.

And now Elinor loved Longford. It was as though some sort of circle had been completed. As though divine retribution had descended. It was rich, Bell thought; full half the women of his acquaintance—wives, widows, and even chits just out of the schoolroom—threw themselves at his head. Then he fell head over heels for Elinor, and she wouldn't have him. Whenever he thought of her, he still felt the pain beneath his breastbone. Indigestion, Harry had told him, insisting he had no heart to bruise.

He was getting maudlin. Forcing his thoughts away from Elinor, he reached into his pocket for his watch, and as he drew it out, a small bit of paper came with it. He frowned, then remembered—Hopewell's wife had slipped the note to him while he danced with her. Unfolding it, he held it up to the inside carriage lamp and squinted to read it.

H. has gone back to Yorkshire and I shall be lonely tonight. There was no mistaking her meaning. He balled up the note and threw it onto the carriage floor. She was like so many others—faithless, rich, and as bored as he was. And it seemed that every errant wife thought he wished to tumble her.

What he needed was sleep, and he knew it. He leaned back and drained his flask, seeking a dreamless oblivion. His carriage rolled to a halt before his yellow stone town house. It was dark, unwelcoming, and suddenly he didn't want to go inside. He needed someone to chase Elinor Kingsley from his mind. He hesitated, then reached to tap the roof of the passenger compartment with his walking stick. His coachman jumped down and peered in the door.

"Ye ain't stayin', my lord?"

"Hopewell House in Harley Street, Tom."

Clearly, the man was disappointed, for he could be heard muttering something under his breath about sleep. Well, if Bell stayed the night, he'd send them home without him. And if not, it would be a short visit. Sometimes

he could not bear the way a woman clung to him afterward. Sometimes he had to escape.

The Hopewell mansion was dimly lit, owing to the
hour, but he could see the curtain over a window above
lift as his carriage halted at the curb. Then it fell discreetly down, silhouetting the woman behind. The front
door opened, throwing a faint slice of light onto the portico as he mounted the steps. A girl, probably Fanny's
maid, stood there expectantly, a candle in one hand.
Placing a finger over her lip, she stepped backward, then
whispered, "Her ladyship is upstairs. I'll light your
way."

The house was silent, so much so that the heels of his
patent dress shoes clicked loudly as he crossed the foyer.
At the bottom of the stairs, he removed his silk-lined
evening cloak and tossed it casually over his arm. Then
he followed the girl up. The flickering candlelight cast
tall, eerie shadows up the papered walls.

She stopped, nodding to indicate the door, then hurried away, as though she did not want to be an accomplice. He inhaled deeply, let out his breath, then reached
for the knob, turning it. The door swung inward, revealing a richly appointed bedchamber. Several braces of
carefully placed candles blazed, bathing the room in a
soft, intimate glow.

Her body outlined beneath a shimmering gossamer
cloud of sheer silk, the blond woman turned around,
smiling. "You came, after all. I'd begun to fear you'd
not read my note."

"I almost didn't," he admitted. "I very nearly went
home to bed."

"But are you not glad you did not?" she asked softly,
moving fluidly toward him. As her body brushed his, she
reached to twine her arms about his neck, pulling his
face to hers. The intoxicating scent of jasmine floated up
from the warmth of her skin. "Well?"

"I think you are a damned fool, Fanny," he answered.
"A damned fool."

Her smile faded to a mock pout, then she pulled his
head down, whispering, "I'm tired of Hopewell—I want

a young man inside me. I want you, Bell. Her lips parted, inviting him to taste, as her breasts pressed into his chest. "Don't make me plead, Bell."

His arms closed around her and he bent his head to hers, teasing her lips with his tongue, then as his own desire rose, his mouth possessed hers. Her fevered body moved seductively against him, heating his blood. Her hands slid to his shoulders, holding him, clinging tightly.

He let himself savor the familiar feeling as his hands moved from her back down over her hips, cupping them, pressing them against the rise of his body. The thin gown fell open, slipping from one white shoulder, and he left her mouth to trace hot, demanding kisses there. Finally, she broke away, panting.

Her eyes large and luminous in the candlelight, she shed the silk nightgown, letting it slide downward to reveal her body. Barefoot, she stepped out of it. He could see the rise and fall of her rose-tipped breasts, the flat plane of her stomach, the pale, almost downy thatch below. His pulse raced, pounding in his temples, and his mouth was dry with desire.

"Please, Bell—I'd not wait."

He slipped off his shoes and shrugged out of his coat. Turning around to seek a chair, he began unbuttoning his waistcoat. He undressed slowly, prolonging the moment, and when he swung back to face her, she was already lying upon the bed, her pale body made pink by the soft reflection of rose satin sheets. She raised her arms as he went to her, then settled beneath him, pulling him down.

He kissed her thoroughly, deeply, then moved his head to her breasts. Her fingers dug into the waving hair that clung to the back of his head, pulling him back to her mouth, and all the while, her body writhed hotly beneath him. She moaned gutterally and spread her legs for him.

"Now, Bell—*now*!"

He slid inside her and lost all conscious thought. Driving, pounding, he pursued his pleasure relentlessly, not knowing, not caring about anything beyond the heat that consumed him. Dimly he was aware he cried out, then he felt the ecstasy of release, and he collapsed over her, his body wet with sweat. He rolled off, then lay there, catching his breath. When he opened his eyes, she was watching him. He sat up and swung his feet over the side.

"You are not leaving?" she cried. "But I wanted you to stay the night!"

This was the thing he always hated. "We both got what we wanted, Fanny," he said, starting to rise.

"Not quite." She twined her arms about his neck from behind and knelt there, holding him, and then she began pressing kisses along the nape of his neck. A shiver coursed down his spine. "Fan—"

"Charles is seldom gone from home, Bell," she whispered, moving one hand downward to touch his shrunken self. "I'll make it good for you." Her fingers played with him, and as he grew, he felt renewed desire. Groaning, he rolled back into the bed and gave himself over to the exquisite sensation. It was, he decided, going to be a long night.

He came awake slowly and wished he'd not, for his head ached like the very devil. And last night's wine was sour in his mouth. His hand groped for the decanter he always kept by his bed, but as his arm slid over the satin sheets, he remembered. He sat up carefully, holding his temples with both hands. Then he saw her. She sat in a chair watching him.

"I thought you meant to sleep the day," she murmured.

"Got to go—the servants—" he croaked.

"They already know."

He blinked at that, and it dimly occurred to him that she wasn't concerned. "Discretion—got to have discretion—" The room spun around him. "Too weasel-bit to think. Need a hair of the dog—"

She rose and poured him a glass of Madeira, then brought it to him. He tossed it off gratefully, then lay back down until the pounding stopped. It occurred to him that he drank far too much, but now was not the time to stop. Not while he had such a head.

"Feeling more the thing?" she asked solicitously.

"No. What time is it?"

"Past noon."

He sat at that. "Got to get home. Don't want Hopewell—"

"I want him to know it, Bell—I want him to know."

"Oh, God," he groaned. "No. You cannot—you don't know—"

"He's old!" she retorted. "And I am too young to wither, all the while listening to his complaints! He even wheezes when he sleeps! I want a young man, Bell!"

He had to get out of there. As woolly as his mind was, he knew that. The last thing he needed was another scandal. And old men tended to be less understanding about errant young wives than the rest of them.

"Look, Fanny, I don't—"

"I want you, Bell. For a long time, I've wanted you."

"Dash it, but you cannot!" With an effort, he flung himself toward his discarded clothes. "You don't know what you are saying. It was a tumble, that's all."

She stared, then said spitefully. "No, you are mistaken. It was much more than that, Bellamy Townsend. It was my freedom."

"You cannot want a scandal, Fanny." He pulled on his stockings and pantaloons, quickly slipping the straps under his feet, then looked for his shoes. "Don't be a goose. Count Hopewell's money, amuse yourself discreetly, and wait for him to die."

"I am tired of waiting for him to die! I cannot stand him, Bell—I cannot! I hate him!" She brushed at hot tears that spilled onto her cheeks. "You cannot know what it is like to have a—a *limp* old man on top of you!"

He turned back. "That, my dear, is none of my affair."

She sniffled, then dabbed at her eyes and nose with a fine lawn handkerchief. Looking at him through wet lashes, she could see her tears were having no effect. He stood, as unmoved as if he were stone, until she could stand it no longer.

"I could make you love me."

He shook his head. "No. I don't love anybody, Fan—

not even myself. And I had enough hell living down Longford's wife." As he spoke, he pulled on his shirt, muffling his words. His tousled blond head emerged, and he set to tucking the tail into his pants. "My affections, I fear, don't last."

"I wrote Charles, and—and I told him we were lovers."

He started, then stared. "What the deuce—?" His gray eyes narrowed. "You jest surely." He could see she was quite serious, and a knot formed in his stomach. "Why, Fanny—*why*?"

"But I had to! Don't you see?"

"No, I do not!" he snapped. "It isn't the way the game is played!"

"I need your help, Bell! I—I want to be rid of Hopewell!" Her chin came up defiantly. "I wrote him that I am carrying your child."

He was thunderstruck for a moment. Then he found his voice. "*What?* The devil you did, Fan!" Recovering, he shook his head, reassuring himself. "No, it won't fadge. I have spent full half the year in Cornwall with Leighton."

"You don't understand—"

"Now there you are right!" he said angrily. "What were you going to do? Wait a month or so, then try to pass it off as mine?

"No, of course not."

"Then whose brat is it?"

She looked at the floor. "There isn't one. But there could be. I was not careful, and neither were you."

He ran his fingers through his hair, trying to understand her. "It makes no sense—none at all. Why tell him you have slept with me? And why tell him you are with child when you are not?"

"Because Charles would believe it! Everyone knows what you are!"

"No. Acquit me, Fanny. I don't need this—not now. You'll have to get yourself out of this alone."

"I told you—I have already written him!"

"When?"

"I posted it just past noon yesterday. I expect he will have it tomorrow—or the next day at the latest."

He poured himself another glass, then gulped it down. "Do you know what you have done?" he asked finally.

"Yes."

"He'll call me out."

"But you are a crack shot—everyone says so."

It came to him then—she expected him to kill Charles Hopewell for her. "No," he said abruptly. "You've mistaken me, Fanny. I won't do it."

"You'll have to! Don't you see?—he'll divorce me. And—and you'll be named. And there'll be none to believe you innocent. Bell—"

"I don't think you have thought this out, my dear," he said with more calm than he felt. "I kill your husband after being named as your lover. No two ways about it—you are ruined, and I'm afraid I'm not a marrying man. Besides, you wouldn't want me if I were, I assure you. Now—where does that leave you? In the basket—alone," he answered for her. "Good day, Fanny." He reached for his coat and cloak, then left her.

"You'll have to marry me!" she shouted after him.

As he descended the stairs, he heard glass breaking, then the door slammed with such force that it rattled the chandelier in the foyer. The maid who'd let him in the night before peered around a corner, while the butler inquired politely, "Shall I call up your carriage, sir?"

"No."

Outside, he found the coach still waiting. His coachman and driver favored him with reproachful looks, but as he climbed inside, he knew they'd slept. A carriage rug was still rolled up on the seat where it had been used for a pillow. Well, he'd see each of them got a pocket of silver when they got home, he decided. Leaning back to ease his aching head, he eyed the flask regretfully. It was like everything else this day—as empty as his luck.

Once home, he did not even pause to examine the pile of scented missives in the basket in the foyer, choosing instead to head straight for his own bedchamber. If anything, Fanny Hopewell's Madeira had made the pain worse. At least he had a bit of brandy on his dressing table. As he reached for the decanter, his reflection stared back at him from the mirror.

He leaned closer, drawn to the almost perfect symmetry of the finely chiseled features. Adonis, Brummell called him, as though these looks were Aphrodite's gift. He laughed mirthlessly. A gift? In truth, they were more a curse disguised. As far back as he could remember, beginning with his mother, females had petted, cosseted, and courted him. "My pretty child," his mother had called him. "Me handsome, beautiful lad," the Irish maid who had seduced him was wont to say. And it had never stopped, not since that first tumble more than fifteen years ago. He frowned, thinking that one day he would be naught but an aging roué. A caricature of himself.

He studied the mirror again, seeking some consolation in his face. It had always seemed to get him what he thought he wanted, and he had to admit that it kept women from looking at the shallow cad beneath. But someday it was going to get him killed.

He drew back and picked up the decanter. Removing the stopper, he drank directly from the bottle, letting the fruity fire warm his throat. Taking it to the table beside his bed, he sat to undress, all the while trying to figure a way out of this unexpected coil.

He did not doubt the *ton* would be titillated by this new scandal in a matter of days. An old fool, a young wife, and Bell Townsend—the perfect broth, they'd say. The Hopewell affair. No matter how much he denied it, there would be knowing looks, whispered rumors—until Hopewell would have to call him out. Fanny's words echoed in his ears. *Everyone knows what you are.* No, he was not ready for that. The Longford thing had nearly finished him.

Then they'd all had to leave the country. Longford had taken himself off to war, Diana had fled across the Atlantic, and he'd gone to India. He could still remember the exotic palaces. And he could still recall the awful

heat, the terrible misery he'd seen. No, he was never
going there again.

He drank from the decanter again, then lay down, his
arms behind his neck, to stare at the ceiling.

Longford would be coming back soon, and he was not
at all certain he could bear hearing that the earl and Elinor Kingsley had wed. For the briefest moment, he allowed himself to remember her, then resolutely pushed
her from his mind, replacing her with Sofia Sherkova.
The woman had invited him to St. Petersburg, saying that
"Poor Gregori is too blind to know what I do." And
although the last thing he needed was another irate husband, there was a certain appeal to a repairing lease in
Russia.

The soft, pale hues of dawn fell across her bed from the window, and still Katherine had not slept. All night, her thoughts had tumbled incessantly within her mind, plaguing her until she could not stand it. Finally, when the clock in the hall had struck the hour of three, she had crept downstairs for milk. It had not helped in the least.

And now she dared not sleep, for Count Volsky was coming to ride with her. Part of her wanted to believe he would come—but there was that nagging voice inside that told her to expect a note begging off. Perhaps it would be kinder, she told herself, perhaps it would save her from making a fool of herself.

Yet whenever she closed her eyes, he was there, haunting whatever dreams she had. As her mind had whirled in that fanciful world just short of sleep, she'd heard him again and again. She could hear him tell her she was *"small yes, plain no . . . Galena could make you pretty, Ekaterina."* Ekaterina. In the Russian's soft accent, it sounded almost beautiful.

Downstairs, someone was banging on the knocker. She rolled over and squinted at her mantel clock. It was but six. Nobody came then, not even the tradesmen. But the noise did not stop. Finally, there were hurried steps on the stairs, the unlocking of the door, then her brother's voice demanded that someone wake his mother. He sounded more than a little disguised with drink. Dawes tried to placate him, but he was insistent.

More steps, a furtive tapping at her mother's chamber door, muffled voices. Curious, Katherine threw on her wrapper and crept to listen. Opening her own door a crack, she peered out as her mother passed, her night rail hastily covered with a Norwich shawl.

"Henry, if this is your notion of a jest, I shall not forgive you," Lady Winstead told him sourly.

"Mama, I bring you news of the first import," he assured her.

Hearing the soft slur in his voice, Kate decided he was too foxed to realize what time it was, that he'd merely stopped on the way home from his club. Sighing, she padded back to bed, where she removed the robe and lay down again.

Mentally, she reviewed what she could wear in case Count Volsky did come. Both of her habits were drab and sadly out of style, but until now she'd scarce considered their lack. Now she was embarrassed to be seen in them. Perhaps if Peg could add a bit of bright braid . . .

No, that was silly . . . there was no time.

The stairs creaked, and she guessed that her mother came up again, but the steps stopped at her door. Three sharp raps sounded, then there was a clearing of throat before Dawes said apologetically, "Sorry to be waking you, Miss Winstead, but you are wanted below." He waited a moment, then knocked again. "Did you hear me, Miss Winstead?"

"Yes."

"His lordship said there wasn't any need to dress."

"All right."

Mystified, she rolled to sit, then reached for the wrapper again. Standing, she thrust her arms through the sleeves, pulled it close over her night rail, and knotted the tie at her waist. If he was but drunk, she was inclined to read a peal over him herself.

Her heart thudded as she descended the stairs and walked to knock on the book room door. It opened beneath her hand. Harry was half-sprawled in a chair, a wineglass in his hand. Behind him, her mother stood, her expression quite odd. Perplexed, Kate glanced from one to the other, then back again.

"Well," she asked finally, "is anyone going to tell me why I am summoned."

"Oh, my dear!" Words seemed to fail her mother.

"Look like you've not been to bed, Kate," Harry observed, reaching to pour more wine. "Here, you'd best have one also. He filled a glass, sloshing some of the red liquid onto the carpet. Any other time, her mother would have taken him to task for that alone, not to mention that he'd offered her wine, but this time she did not seem to notice. She merely stood there, apparently dazed. He rose unsteadily and handed the drink to Katherine. He held up his own.

"I wish you happy."

"You are disguised," Kate decided, disgusted.

"Not disguised," he corrected her thickly. "Surprised. Dashed surprised." Taking a long sip, he met her widened eyes. "If you'd have him, Kate, Volsky would wed with you."

The room spun around her as her glass slipped from nerveless fingers. For a moment, she could only stare at him. Then she managed to find her tongue. *"What?"*

"Word of a Winstead," he declared solemnly, raising his right hand as though he took an oath. "Fellow's damned generous, I might add." A slow grin curved his mouth. "Well? Cat got your tongue, Kate?"

She turned to her mother. "He's funning with me, isn't he?"

Lady Winstead's lip trembled and her eyes were wet. "Oh, my dear—my dear child!" Overcome, she burst into tears, then dabbed at her cheeks with the ties of her wrapper. "It is more than I have ever dared wish for you!"

"You don't have to take him if you don't want," Harry said behind her.

Stunned, Katherine could not think. As though she were in a trance, she dropped into the nearest chair. "But—but we are scarce acquainted," she mused faintly. "He cannot wish—"

Moving to stand beside her, her brother touched her shoulder. "Apparently, he does, for he has offered not only to forgo the customary Russian dowry, but also to frank everything—your wedding, your bride clothes— everything. And if you accept, he has agreed to settle five thousand English pounds on you.''

''There must be some mistake—he must have been foxed—''

''Do you not see?'' Her mother's voice rose, betraying her excitement. ''Katherine, Count Volsky has offered for you!''

''If you wish time to consider, I'll fob him off,'' Harry offered.

''Harry!'' Lady Winstead shrieked, ''There is nothing to consider—she is not like to receive any comparable proposal!''

Alexei Volsky had offered for her. *Alexei Volsky had offered for her.* It could not be. ''Are you quite certain, Harry?''

'' 'I'd marry Ekaterina,' he said as plainly as I am speaking to you now.''

She was still afraid to believe him. ''Did he say *why*?''

''Katherine, if you refuse Count Volsky, I shall quite wash my hands of you!''

But Kate waited for Harry to answer. ''He must have said something,'' she prompted him.

''He said he admired your excellent mind and character.''

''Oh.'' Disappointed, she chided herself that she could scarce expect Alexei to declare himself head over heels for her after one waltz and a picnic in the park.

''I daresay marriages are merely arranged in Russia,'' Lady Winstead said. ''No doubt the Eastern influence. The point is, Count Volsky wishes to marry you, and I for one am ecstatic!''

The way her mother said it indicated that she considered Alexei's taste beyond understanding. And for once, Kate agreed with her. ''That was all?—my mind? He said nothing else?''

''Well, we discussed the terms, of course.'' He cleared his throat and glanced nervously at Lady Winstead. ''He will be leaving for Vienna to attend to some of the pre-

liminaries there, then he expects to return to Russia. But
Madame Malenkov is to remain with you to oversee your
wardrobe and make preparations for your journey there.''

"*I* shall tend to her wardrobe, Henry," their mother
declared stiffly. "I do not need—"

"He was most specific on that head, Mama." Turning
his attention back to Kate, he said, "If you accept, you
will be married quietly at Monk's End. There will not
be time for much of a wedding trip, but I have offered
the use of my hunting box in Leicestershire, should you
both wish it.''

Aware that her daughter was still looking rather blankly
at Harry, Lady Winstead shouted at her, "Katherine, you
will be pleased to accept!"

Settlements. Wardrobe. Wedding. It was all nearly in-
comprehensible to Kate. All that she could think of for
the moment was that Alexei had offered for her. That,
for whatever reason, he wanted her.

"Mama?" Clarissa peered sleepily in the door. "Is
aught amiss? I heard Harry, and then you were speaking
so very loudly.''

"Naught's amiss, my love," Lady Winstead assured
her. "Only fancy—Count Volsky has asked Henry for
Katherine's hand!''

It was Claire's turn to stare. "*What?* I don't believe
it!''

Her mother nodded. "And most generously so, I might
add.''

The younger girl turned to Kate. "How could you?
You did this to spite me—how *could* you?" Her lower lip
trembled and her eyes filled with tears. "You—you
hussy!''

"That is quite enough, missy! You must wish your
sister happy, dearest. Besides, I have hopes of Hargrove
for you.''

"I don't want him!" Claire cried. "He is naught but
a stuffy stick!" Ignoring Lady Winstead's thinning lips,
she declared defiantly, "Very well then, I shall have Lord
Townsend!''

"You'll do no such thing!" her mother snapped. "I

have spent far too much for you to fling yourself at a profligate's head!''

''Bell's not a marrying man,'' Harry said. ''You wouldn't want him.''

''Much you would know about it!'' the younger girl retorted tearfully. Covering her face, she ran from the room.

''Clarissa! You will come back this instant!'' When there was no response, Lady Winstead hesitated. Looking to her son, she sighed. ''Should I go after her, do you think? I'd not have her looks spoiled by crying.''

''If anything is spoiled, it is Claire rather than her looks,'' he observed dryly.

Irritated by his criticism, she snapped, ''It is no such thing, Henry Winstead! She is a trifle high-strung, that is all.''

''Mama, you have petted and hovered her from the first time any thought her pretty, and well you know it,'' he countered, unmoved. ''I think it quite just that it is Kate who took, if you would have my opinion.''

''Yes, yes, of course, and you must know I am pleased to fire her off at all.'' To Kate, she said, ''It *is* a brilliant marriage, my dear.'' With that, she hastened to comfort Clarissa.

Harry waited until their mother was out of hearing. ''You don't have to make up your mind just now, you know.'' He squeezed her shoulder reassuringly. ''In fact, you do not have to accept Volsky at all. And if Mama makes life too miserable for you, you can come to live with me.'' Releasing her, he stepped back, then walked to the window. The sun was barely up. ''The choice is yours, Kate.''

''Harry, I—''

''Russia is far away, the language foreign, the customs sometimes unfathomable, I should expect. You will not have Mama, or Claire, or me there.'' Abruptly, he swung around to face her again, his expression sober. ''Only you can decide whether you would spend the rest of your life with Volsky, my dear.''

"You make it sound so—so very grim." Lifting her eyes to his, she asked, "And if I accept?"

"You will be Countess Volsky, a very rich woman, Kate. And you will have Galena Malenkova for support, I think. She seems to have developed a liking for you."

She swallowed. "When—when does he have to know?"

"I expect he would give you a couple of days."

"And if I accept?"

"He will send the announcement off to the papers, you will make an appearance together here, Madame Malenkov will see you are properly fitted, then we shall retire to Monk's End for the wedding before Volsky leaves."

The thought of leaving all she knew was painful, but so was life at Monk's End. This way she would not be a failure, this way she would not have to envy Claire when Hargrove or some other handsome and wealthy lord came up to scratch. And she would have Alexei.

"Well?" he prompted gently. "Should I say you are wishful of more time?"

"It is so sudden—I scarce know him, but—" She sucked in her breath and let it out slowly. "But I think I could love him—no, I *know* it."

He nodded. "I'll tell him this morning, then." A heavy sigh escaped him. "I told him I would stop by the Pulteney on my way home. Oh—supposed to tell you, he won't be able to ride today, but he will bring his sister to consult with you and Mama."

She walked up the stairs in a daze, and it was not until she reached her bedchamber and sank into a chair that she realized she was shaking. Volsky wanted her. It did not seem possible. Volsky wanted *her*. She sat staring, seeing Alexei in his full dress uniform, his medals gleaming, his dark hair bared, his hat under his arm. If Bellamy Townsend was the epitome of English style and looks, then Alexei Volsky must surely be his equal in Russia.

Then she realized what she had done. And for an awful moment, she panicked. Why had she accepted him? Just so she would not be on the shelf? So everyone would envy her? She hoped not. She hoped it was because she thought she could make him love her. He was, after all, incredibly kind—and incredibly handsome. And usually those two things did not come together.

It would be all right, she told herself resolutely. She would be in no worse case than half the females on the Marriage Mart, for they were often betrothed blindly, with far more attention given to their looks and the gentlemen's money than to any pretense to affection. At least Alexei Volsky wanted her enough to ask Harry for her, which was more than she could say for any English buck of the *ton*. And, as Harry said, she would have Galena Malenkova.

With that comforting thought came the realization that Mama would no longer choose her clothes, that she could have what she liked. And with Galena's help, she would have things that flattered her. No more frilled white gowns to make her look small and sallow.

Rising, she moved to the mirror to stare at her reflection, wondering what had gained her Alexei Volsky's attention. Her hands crept to her dark, sleep-flattened curls, pulling them down at the sides of her face. No, she was still plain. She sighed regretfully, grateful that he had seen something she could not.

thought she couldn't make him love her. He was, after all, dreadfully kind and incredibly handsome. And usually those too handsome to be come fondness... As she'd thought earlier... she told Kate. "Really," she murmured, "it was mine to do... he... keep those with one... before... were... as used to that... with... of one... they dared to do...

With the possibility any problem... Alexei... knew that got enough... see Harry for any... thought... that she could... to word... brown... well...

K ate came down the stairs more than half-afraid he'd changed his mind, but Alexei Volsky smiled up at her. When she reached the foyer, he bowed over her hand.

"You behold an honored man, Ekaterina," he said, smiling. "And Galena is pleased."

Behind him, Madame Malenkov smiled also. "Ah, *ma petite*, I shall welcome you to the family." As Alexei released Kate's hand and stepped back, Galena moved forward to clasp the girl's shoulders. Pressing a kiss against each of Kate's cheeks, she said, "We shall make you happy, I promise you." Still holding Kate, she scrutinized the pale lemon yellow muslin, frowning. "But first we go shopping, I think." She shook her head as though the garment offended her. "I hope this is not your favorite color, *cherie*."

"No, of course not," Kate said quickly.

Abruptly, Galena Malenkova turned to her brother. "We must visit the modiste today. She cannot go to Russia in rags, I tell you. How much should we spend, do you think?"

"Madame Malenkov," Lady Winstead began stiffly, "naught's wrong with what she has, and—"

"Nonsense. It is not befitting for Alexei's countess to be a drab," Galena declared. Her gaze returned to Katherine, and she winced visibly. "*Ma pauvre petite*, you shall have Galena now," she murmured soothingly. "We will have no more of these over-washed things. You need more color to show to advantage, and we shall find what suits you."

"Madame Malenkov, I am quite capable—" Lady Winstead began stiffly.

"But of course you are! I have seen how the other one is dressed, but they are not at all alike, I think," the Russian woman said flatly. "She must be to Alexei's taste, however." Turning to Kate, she asked, "You are wishful of new things, are you not?"

"Yes, but—"

"*Mais non*—it is of no consequence to Lexy, I assure you. He can afford anything you should wish. Lexy?"

He drew a thick leather folder from beneath his uniform coat. Counting out a wad of bank notes, he handed them to his sister. "If it is not enough, you may draw on the embassy's credit."

Lady Winstead was speechless. " 'Tis a fortune," she managed weakly when she finally found her voice.

"My dear Madame Winstead, she will be a countess," Galena reminded her shortly. "And she has nothing."

Taken aback, Katherine's mother tried to recover in front of Dawes. "Well, I should not say that, but I am sure dearest Kate is most pleased, in any event. Now, I expect there are other things to be discussed, and I'd as lief not decide them before the servants."

Galena Malenkova lifted her fine brows. "You did not settle everything with Baron Winstead, Lexy?"

"We discussed the arrangements."

"There. You see, madame, he has already done it."

Katherine's mother motioned for Dawes to go on. "Yes, but there are preparations. The wedding—"

"There is not time," Galena countered dismissively. "The wedding will occur late next week at this monk's place, then Alexei will leave the week after. I shall stay with Ekaterina, of course, until we can return home."

"We will have a ceremony in Russia also," Count Volsky said, looking to Katherine. "In late October."

"Monk's End," Lady Winstead said, correcting Galena.

"A strange name, I think."

"It is an old and much-admired estate, madame—held

by the Winsteads since Elizabeth's reign,'' the older woman responded stiffly.

Before either could provoke the other further, Kate hastened to intervene, explaining, ''During the reign of Henry VIII, a monk was murdered there, giving the place its name. Our house sits where an old chapter house was burned by rather zealous supporters of the king. The abbot, we are told, was reluctant to embrace the new religion.''

''How very interesting, *cherie*. Now, Madame Winstead, I cannot think what else is to be settled between Lexy and Baron Winstead. Oh, except—is it your wish that Ekaterina stays with me at the Pulteney Hotel, or would you have me come here after Lexy is gone?''

''Well, I am sure I don't—''

''Then we shall let Ekaterina decide, for then she is a married lady, *n'est-ce pas*? Now, *ma petite*, you must get your shawl.'' She winced as she looked again at the pale muslin. ''We shall buy the best of London today.'' Her eyes rested of Lady Winstead briefly. ''You are most welcome to come, of course—and the other one also, if she wishes.''

''As if any of the premier modistes should be available now. You are better advised to employ a seamstress,'' Clarissa said, moving into the foyer from the saloon where she'd been listening. ''Good dress lengths and trimmings are to be found in linen drapers' shops—I should suggest Leicester Square, I think. Or perhaps Clark and Debenham's in Wigmore Street.'' Stopping in front of Alexei, she glanced up at him just so, then dropped her gaze demurely. ''Count Volsky,'' she murmured.

''Mademoiselle,'' he acknowledged, bowing slightly.

Disappointed, she turned to his sister. ''Madame Malenkov, you must forgive me for intruding, but I should be more than delighted to assist you in discovering bargains here. I mean, there are several bazaars and emporiums where ribbons, lace, gloves, and all manner of things are to be had quite cheaply.''

It was Galena's turn to be affronted. "Mademoiselle Winstead, I assure you Alexei does nothing cheaply."

The younger girl's color heightened perceptibly. "Madame, I only wished to be helpful."

"Yes, of course. So it is settled, *mais non*?" she addressed Kate's mother. "I have asked of Lady Jersey, and she has referred me to a modiste—a Madame Cecile, I believe."

"Madame Cecile!" Clarissa gasped. "Oh, but she won't—"

"That we shall see," Galena said firmly. "Now, Madame Winstead, do you wish to accompany us?"

"Well, I had not expected—but, yes, of course, I shall go."

"Go on, Ekaterina, get your shawl," Galena urged Kate. "We waste time."

Clarissa, who had never once been privileged to glimpse inside Madame Cecile's rather exclusive establishment, pleaded with her eyes. "Mama—?"

"Very well. Madame Malenkov has said you may come, my love."

"I shan't be long," the girl promised. "I have but to get my parasol and shawl."

It was not until Claire caught Katherine in the upstairs hall that she dared betray her excitement. "Madame Cecile's! Did you *ever* think to see it, Kate?" Then, recalling herself, she sniffed. "Well, I daresay we shall be turned away."

"I expect."

"One would think you were not the least excited," Claire retorted. "As though you are not surprised that Count Volsky came up to scratch."

"Perhaps I am still stunned. And I have no very great expectation that a few dresses from even the best modiste can make me what I am not, Claire." Having reached her chamber door, Katherine stopped. "Besides, it is so new that I am afraid I shall waken and discover I have but dreamed everything."

"I vow I can scarce stand nor walk anymore," Clarissa complained, sinking against the padded carriage seat.

Beside her, her mother appeared dazed. "I cannot credit it," she murmured more to herself than anyone. "My Kate. I never thought—" Collecting herself, she straightened in her seat. "Well, Count Volsky is *most* generous."

"Pah, it is nothing, I assure you."

Kate stared out the window as the coach rolled away from the curb. Nothing? Despite the sinking feeling that Alexei must surely complain of the extravagance, she felt like a fairy princess. Nothing? When all the things they'd ordered came, she would have everything. She was not even sure she could remember it all.

The day had become a dizzy whirl of Madame Cecile's, other assorted mantua makers, milliners, a hosier's, and a corset maker. Kate had been measured and remeasured more times than she could count while her mama and Claire had eagerly perused the fashion plates in the *Lady's Magazine* and *La Belle Assemblee* with Alexei's sister. The only brangle had come when Lady Winstead had suggested that the gowns should be of light muslin or lawn, to which the Russian woman had haughtily replied that silks and satins would serve Katherine better in her role as Countess Volsky.

And silks there were, ranging from tissues to the heavy twilled bombazines. Carriage dresses, walking dresses, evening dresses, ball gowns, riding habits. It made one's mind dizzy to think of all of them. And the colors— Madame Malenkov had been adamant about that—there had to be colors. Pomona greens, willows, warm, deep peaches, and nearly everything else imaginable—except white or yellow. The lone concession had been a pearl-colored silk to be cut into a short-sleeved, square-necked gown trimmed with tiny glass beads and pearls. That would be Katherine's wedding dress. And to offset the lack of warmth in the hue, madame had chosen a ring of peach-colored silk roses to hold the nearly floor-length silk scarf on the bride's head.

Leaning back, Kate closed her eyes and tried to assimilate what was happening to her. She had to be dreaming. Plain girls did not get offers from wealthy and dashingly handsome gentlemen. Plain girls with merely respectable fortunes did not go to Cecile's. She was going to wake up in Monk's End and find none of this had happened, she was quite certain.

"I am disappointed that nothing can be delivered before the weekend—and not all of it until we are returned to London," she heard Galena say. Then, "Does she perhaps have a colored underchemise—something elegant?" To which, Lady Winstead replied she'd not expended greatly for that which was not to be seen. The Russian woman sighed expressively before saying, "Then I shall have to have one of mine cut down when I return to the hotel. I have an excellent maid who can do it."

"Madame—"

"*Mais non.* It does not matter, for I have many. But alas, we are not of the same complexion, Ekaterina and myself." There was a brief silence, followed by decision. "I shall send a rose one, I think. And my silver net *jacquette* to wear over it. Yes, I think so, for we are provided tickets to the opera for tonight. The Catalani sings in *Idomeneo*, I believe."

"Madame, I scarce think an unmarried female like Katherine—" Her mother's protest died, possibly of a look from the Russian.

"She must now show to Lexy's advantage, Madame Winstead," Galena answered her. "You may put your white muslins on the other one, if you wish, but I shall dress Ekaterina to suit my brother."

"But it is not proper," Clarissa demurred, finding her voice.

Somehow the thought of appearing in underwear with naught but something of net over it was rather daunting, and for once she was inclined to agree with Claire. "Madame—Galena, that is," Katherine amended hastily, "I don't think I should be comfortable in your undershift."

"Nonsense," the other woman said dismissively. "You would have the world see that you are flesh and blood."

Her hands possessed Kate's in Kate's lap. "While yet you are here, Galena will make you the fashion."

"I do not want to appear fast. Alexei might think—"

"Alexei is a man, Ekaterina. And your bosom is good, so we must show a bit of it, I think. Yes, most definitely."

Unconvinced, Kate held her tongue, not daring to dispute with Alexei's sister. Then she heard again his words. *Galena could make you pretty, Ekaterina.* And she wanted desperately to believe them. Desperately. For how else could she expect to hold him once he'd wed her?

Alexei's sister squeezed her fingers. "Trust me, *ma petite*, for I know what I am about." Sitting back, she addressed the others. "And you are invited also, of course. That Maria, she is so very kind, *n'est-ce pas?* We shall sit with the Seftons in their box."

Lady Winstead, who could scarce consider herself in the fashionable Sefton circle, nearly choked. "It is a signal honor," she managed finally.

But Clarissa was not so certain. Somehow the thought of fading into the background, even in the Sefton's box at King's Theatre, did not appeal to her at all. "But, Mama—the Fevershams—we are promised to the Fevershams," she recalled plaintively.

"Hush. We shall send a card 'round. I daresay they will quite understand."

Galena nodded. "Exactly. There is to be a party of us—Marshal Sherkov and his so charming wife, and Alexei's aide, Maxim Boganin. And one of the Prussian princes—I forget which—and *cher* Bellamy, of course. You are perhaps acquainted with him, no?"

"Lord Townsend?"

"Is there another Bellamy, do you think?"

"No, of course not."

"I did not think there could be," the Russian woman murmured. "So very engaging, would you not say?"

"When he wishes to be," Katherine responded before Clarissa could be cast into transports. "But if you are promised to the Fevershams, perhaps you ought to go there, Claire."

The younger girl favored her with a look that bordered on dislike. "Well, I should not for the world refuse to appear with you and your betrothed, Kate," she declared. "Besides, I am sure we can go to the Fevershams' anytime, don't you think, Mama?"

"Precisely." Looking very much like the cat who'd just swallowed cream, Lady Winstead assured Katherine, "Madame Malenkov's chemise will be just fine, I am sure. But if you wish, you may borrow my Canton crepe shawl, dearest." To Galena, she asked, "And will Lord and Lady Sefton be in attendance also?"

"But of course! It is their box, after all."

"Well, I did not know—"

"You must not worry. Lady Sefton said she believes she knows you, and that is all that matters, *n'est-ce pas*?" Glancing out the carriage window, Galena caught sight of a clock above a shop. "But we must hurry if I am to get the chemise altered and to you." Rapping on the ceiling, she called to the driver above, "*Vite! Vite!* We are out of the time!"

It was not until they were set down at home and Galena had gone on that Lady Winstead dared to admit her awe. "The Seftons' box! I vow I am in alt, my dears!" Then, following Kate up the stairs, she added, "I know not how or why it has happened, my love, but we are to move in the first circles!"

Left behind, Claire felt hot tears of envy scald her eyes. As they threatened to spill over, she ripped up at Dawes. "Well, why are you watching me?" she demanded angrily. "Am I the only sane person in this place?" Tearing at the ribbons that anchored her fetching gypsy hat, she pulled it loose, then flung it to the floor. Kicking it with a dainty kid slipper, she muttered, "I shall be well rid of her, anyway. I hope she goes to Russia and disappears."

For the first time in her life, Katherine basked in the glow of being envied. As she sat in the Seftons' box, she was acutely aware of the admiring glances cast at Alexei Volsky, and she could scarce wait for the *Gazette* to announce he was hers. As her borrowed opera glass took in a number of gentlemen whose glasses were trained on her, she was also uncomfortably aware that, fashionable or not, she was nearly naked in Galena's rose satin shift and the silver tissue *jacquette*.

Then she saw her brother. He sat in a box across the pit and one level below the Seftons', and beside him was an exceedingly lovely female Katherine did not know. She was unquestionably his latest Fashionable Impure. But at least he was a bachelor, unlike many who flaunted mistresses. Then another, utterly awful thought occurred to her; one that did not bear thinking. She scarce knew Alexei—what if he should be the sort to have bits of fluff? She glanced sideways at him, and noticed he wasn't paying any attention to the beautiful women who openly admired him. He was turned around, talking to Galena.

Halfway around the horseshoe, Lady Oxford sat with her complaisant husband. If all the rumors attending that lady were true, he must surely be a saint, for he could scarce help knowing that few of his children were actually his own.

"We have much opera in Russia," Alexei said suddenly.

"I should like to hear of it—Russia, I mean."

A slow smile warmed his blue eyes. "You will see for

yourself, Ekaterina. And I will take you to the opera in
St. Petersburg.''

She fell silent at that, thinking how far away she was
going, wondering if she would ever feel at home there.
It did not matter, she told herself fiercely. She would
have Alexei and Galena.

Apparently, her thoughts were rather transparent, for
he leaned closer. ''You will learn—you will learn.''

''Yes, of course.''

Nonetheless, she found herself looking away. And out
of the corner of her eye, she saw Madame Sherkov pass
Bell Townsend a note. For all the differences, some things
were the same. Apparently, everywhere there were
women ready to stray for him.

From behind, Galena leaned forward to pat Katherine's shoulder. ''Everything is fine, *cherie*,'' she murmured.

''I don't know—''

''Of course it is. You leave everything to Galena, and
you will have St. Petersburg at your feet—before we go
to Domnya.''

''Domnya?''

''Our estate near Voronez on the Don. It is our prin-
cipal residence, and there are seven thousand serfs on
the land there,'' Galena said proudly. ''You will like it.
The house is big and built on the Western design by an
Italian favorite of Catherine the Great, so it is not old.''

''I am afraid I shall not know how to go on,'' Katherine admitted.

The Russian woman smoothed the silver tissue over
her shoulders, then patted her soothingly again. ''I know
everything seems difficult now, Ekaterina, but you must
not worry. Galena will take care of you.''

''You are cold, *daragaya*?'' Alexei asked her.

Daragaya. She did not even know what it meant. She
would have to ask Galena later. ''No—not at all.''

''So solemn,'' he chided, teasing her. ''I give you the
long face?''

''I was merely thinking how strange it will be to me.''

The curtains were going up, and a hush fell over the

crowd as the candles were doused quickly. Katherine strained for a glimpse of the Catalani, but the first singers were men. The music was beautiful, romantic. As Katherine closed her eyes, she felt Alexei's fingers brush her arm, then rest there. It was going to be all right.

When the Catalani came onstage, she sang with the voice of an angel. Katherine listened, so raptly attentive that she was disappointed when the curtains rang down for intermission. But Alexei rose, stretching, saying that he saw one of the Prussian princes there also, and he believed he would pay a call to the box.

"You may come with me, if you wish," he told Katherine.

"You go on, Lexy," Galena told him. "Ekaterina will wish to hold court for the gossips, I think."

The Russian woman proved right, for no sooner than he had left, several girls, all properly chaperoned by their mothers, came to the Seftons' box. It was obvious they came from curiosity, for there were numerous politely phrased but nonetheless probing questions directed her way. Galena fended them off for her, hinting that perhaps they would learn more by reading the papers.

Oddly, Lord Townsend had not left the Seftons' box, but had instead chosen to linger half-hidden by the hangings. On this night, the premier buck of the *ton* seemed strangely withdrawn and disinclined to much society. Finally, as the music began to play softly again and Alexei reclaimed his chair, the viscount rose and touched Galena's arm.

"Madame, a word when you are available."

"Ah, *cher* Bellamy, you have but to ask. But of course."

The curtains were ascending once more, and the great house was darkening as Townsend and Galena stepped out into the corridor. Their low voices were drowned in the music. It was not until the Catalani had sung for several minutes that they returned. As his sister slipped back into her seat, Alexei turned around.

"Fychom dyela?"

"Nothing is the matter. If you do not mind it, he means

to accompany Ekaterina and me to Russia. I told him you would be grateful.''

He appeared displeased, then said something undistinguishable in Russian. Galena laughed lightly. ''Ah, Lexy, you are worried too much. I know enough to be careful of him. Besides, Ekaterina and I will welcome the escort. Is that not so?'' she asked Kate.

Bell Townsend going to Russia? For a moment, Katherine was too surprised to answer.

Galena smiled smugly. ''You see, Lexy? You have not the need for jealousy, I think.''

''You meddle too much, Lena,'' Alexei muttered, turning his attention again to the stage.

Finally, the last encore was given, and the curtain rang down. As the pits emptied, someone outside took up the chant, ''Alexander! Alexander! Alexander!''

''He is not even here,'' Alexei muttered, ''and now we shall be set upon.'' He turned to grasp Galena's arm, pulling her back. ''Do not go that way—they are coming!''

But he was already too late, for those in the pits turned back, driven by the crowd that waited outside. Panicked, people fled, pushing and shoving for other doors. Kate tried to hold onto her betrothed's other arm, but she could not.

''Lexy! Lexy! Where are you?'' she shouted, unable to see any of her party. Panicked, she tried to turn back, but it was impossible. She was suffocating in a mass of bodies.

''Kate! Kate Winstead!'' She could not see who called her, but she felt someone pull her, dragging her through the pushing crowd.

''Air!'' she gasped. ''Please—someone—''

It was no use. She held on tightly, clinging to the hand as though it were salvation, stumbling, reeling, twisting. Buckles and buttons raked her as she struggled between the mass of bodies. She thought her arm must surely separate from its shoulder. She felt Galena's tissue *jacquette* tear just before she finally emerged into air.

Apparently, they were in back of the theater. As her

rescuer released her hand, she grasped at a lamppost and caught her breath. When she looked up, she realized it was Bellamy Townsend.

"My-my thanks," she stammered out. "What happened?"

"Someone mistook a prince for the czar. Are you all right?"

"Yes, but Alexei—"

"I couldn't reach him."

His hat was missing, his coat pulled off one shoulder, and he looked more like a boy just come from a mill than like a buck of the *ton*. "If Brummell could see you now—" she began. Then she looked down, and her words died on her lips. "Oh, my!"

He started to take off his coat, then cursed loudly. It looked as though the footpads had discovered them, for three men circled expectantly, much like crows over carrion.

"Ooo—'e's a swell! Well, me fine buck—yer purse or yer gizzard," a dirty fellow demanded.

"Oooh, Billy—lookee!" A drunken accomplice lunged, tearing the rest of the tissue *jacquette* from Katherine. On the other side, someone caught at the shoulder of her chemise. Terrified, she struck at him.

He chortled gleefully. "We got us a gentry mort!"

Hoping to distract at least one of them, Bell threw his purse into the street, then barreled into a man who held her, butting him down. "Run, Kate—for God's sake, run!" he shouted at her.

"*Oww*, guv'nor!" the fellow howled. "Get 'im, Jack!"

One of the others swung, and Katherine saw Bell Townsend fall. She knew she could not leave him. Grabbing her slipper, she turned back to beat on the man. "Please—someone help!" she screamed. The big fellow turned on her, advancing. "Billy don't like fer no mort ter—"

Townsend jumped on him from behind, riding him, clawing at his face, trying to get his eyes. When the other one caught his arm, Bell yelled again at Kate, "Don't be

a fool—run!'' Instead, she kicked hard, catching the man
between his legs, and he rolled to the ground, his knees
drawn up to his body. At almost the same time, Bell
found his own mark.

"*Owwww!* Ye've blinded me, ye bloody arse!'' The
thief shook Townsend off as his hands went to his face.
"Me eyes! Ye've put out me lights!''

"Come on, Kate!'' Bell shouted urgently. "Now!''

Once again, he caught her hand and ran, dragging her
after him. It wasn't until they had covered several blocks
and turned the corner onto a dark street that he stopped.
Out of breath, he leaned against a wall. Finally, he managed to gasp out, "Why didn't you run the first time?
You could have escaped.''

Shaking, she closed her eyes and held onto the same
wall. "He would have robbed you.''

They stood there for several minutes before either
spoke again. Finally, he said, "I've had my pockets slit
before.''

"I was afraid they'd slit your throat,'' she admitted
breathlessly. "Besides, I didn't know where to go.''

He grinned. "That was a prime kick, Kate.'' The grin
faded as his gaze dropped. "Damn.''

She could barely see him in the moonlight, and she
was grateful. Her hand found the torn chemise and pulled
it up over her breast.

"Damned fortunate it's not cold out,'' he observed,
struggling out of his coat. "Here—you are more in need
than I.''

Blood rushed to her face. Alexei would never understand, she knew it. And Mama—well, that did not bear
thinking either. "I—I cannot go home like this—I cannot.''

"Put it on backwards, and it will cover more. Come
on—then I'll get you home.''

"With *your* reputation?'' she asked incredulously.
"Thank you, but I should rather make the attempt myself.''

"Look, you do not have anything I have not seen, but

I rather doubt your mother will understand it if you arrive half-unclothed.''

"I have always known you were not a gentleman," she muttered, struggling into his evening coat. "Where are we?"

He didn't answer.

"We've got to get to Alexei's carriage—we've got to find him, lest he think the worst," she insisted.

"I'm not going back into that mob—if you were Prinny himself, I wouldn't do it for you."

"But he will not know where I am! And what if something has happened to him—or to Madame Malenkov?"

"If they have any sense, they'll manage. By now, they are probably halfway to the Pulteney."

"I should rather think he looked for me," she told him shortly. "Please, Bell—"

"I'm not going back." He moved closer and tried to button his jacket over her back. "There—more than half-crooked, my dear, but it will suffice."

He started walking, leaving her no choice but to follow. Struggling to keep up, she nearly tripped. "*Will* you wait for me?" When he slowed down, she added, "And *do* you know where we are?"

"I think so. And it's a devil of a long walk."

"Can we not hail someone?"

"And risk a scandal?" he countered. "I'd think you'd rather go on foot."

"Perhaps a hackney?"

"I left my purse in the street. Unless you are an exceptional female and carry money in your reticule, I'd say we are without luck."

"I lost my reticule in the crowd."

"Then we are even, aren't we, Kate?"

"Not quite." She fell in beside him, trying to match his stride in her narrow-skirted chemise. "I suppose you are going to Russia to dangle after Sofia Sherkova, aren't you?" she asked sourly.

"No."

"Alexei will not like your attentions to his sister."

"As much as it may surprise you, Kate Winstead, it is not my intention to dangle after anyone."

"And everyone knows that for a hum!" she scoffed.

"Let us just say I am in need of a bit of distance between myself and England."

"A repairing lease?"

"Something like that," he admitted grimly.

"You've lost your fortune," she hazarded.

"No." For a moment, he was silent, then he sighed. "I don't want to kill anybody."

She started to tell him he ought to expect such things if he insisted on seducing other men's wives, but she managed to hold her tongue. Finally, she suggested practically, "Well, I expect you could delope, couldn't you?"

He stopped abruptly, and as he turned to her, the smoky light from a street lamp reflected in his eyes. "You really despise me, don't you? If I fire into the air, you know damned well he'll put a ball into me."

"I don't suppose you could blame him."

"I ought to have left you back there," he muttered.

"Why didn't you?"

"I don't know. Because you are Harry Winstead's sister, I suppose." He began walking again. "Watch where you step, will you? If you sprain your ankle, I won't carry you," he warned her when she caught up to him. "I'm not quite as big as Harry—or Volsky. I only show to advantage in my own milieu, I'm afraid."

"Reclining?" she asked sweetly.

"Now that, Kate, was unworthy of you." But even as he said it, the corners of his mouth twitched. "You haven't spared me since you were a little chit, have you?"

"No—not since Beckwood," she reminded him. Yet there was something within her that wanted reassurance from a premier buck of the *ton*. "Townsend," she asked suddenly, "why do you think he offered for me?"

"Thurgood? Or Volsky?"

"Thankfully, Mr. Thurgood never came up to scratch."

"Well, it wasn't your manner or your clothes. You had no color and no style, Kate."

She wished she hadn't asked.

He could see he'd hurt her, and he stopped again. "Look, I'm not Volsky, so what does it matter? You are not plain, but you've got no town bronze. I don't know how you can be Harry Winstead's sister and be as green as they come, but you are. Utterly green," he declared flatly."

"You think I am fortunate to have snared him, don't you?"

"Actually, I haven't thought about it at all."

"No, I suppose not."

"But if you want the truth, I cannot think you are a match for Volsky."

"What an awful thing to say! And I am not green!"

"Green," he repeated definitely.

"Just because I don't want a gentleman fawning all over me, and—"

He stopped at that, and his gray eyes gleamed wickedly. Without warning, he caught her shoulders, and before she knew what he meant to do, his arms slid around her, and he kissed her thoroughly. For a moment, she caught at his waist to steady herself, savoring the first real kiss of her life. It was a heady, powerful feeling to be in a man's arms. Finally, he released her.

"There is more life in you than I thought," he murmured, releasing her.

Mortified by her response to him, she spat out, "You are disgusting! I did not give you leave to kiss me!"

"Am I? My dear Kate, that is precisely what you ought to want from a man. Otherwise, you will have a passionless marriage, and Volsky will be looking elsewhere for his amusements."

Shaking, she wiped her mouth with the back of her hand as though she could clean it. "If Harry even thought you had touched me, he—"

"He'd understand the lesson, Kate—and you do need lessons, I can tell you. But you liked it, and that's a beginning," he added, smiling broadly at her.

"Bell Townsend, you are no gentleman!" she choked. "And I did not like it!"

He shrugged. "I don't need to be—and believe me, no matter what a female says, the last thing she wants is a namby-pamby gentleman." As he spoke, one of his eyebrows lifted skeptically. "And if you did not like it, you are one hell of an actress, Kate Winstead."

"Oh, of all the conceit! Thankfully, Alexei's not like you, not at all. He's kind and—and I think he loves me," she finished definitely.

"How do you know?"

"Because he offered for me—and because he has never attempted to maul me!"

"Remember the lesson, Kate," he advised softly. "No man wants a piece of wood in his bed."

"I don't know how you would know what a decent man wishes," she retorted. "All you have ever done is chase cyprians and immoral women." She started walking quickly, leaving him behind.

"Proper wives ought to ask themselves why there are cyprians and immoral women," he said, catching up to her. "If there are no buyers, there are no wares."

"I am sure Alexei does not share your utterly disgusting views," she muttered, walking even faster.

But truth to tell, she wasn't sure what Volsky thought. And the closer she got to her home, the more she worried about what he would say when he saw her. Hopefully, he would not be there, and he would never have to know.

C ount Volsky's rented carriage was at the curb, and the portico was lit by lanterns. Kate stopped beneath a smoking street lamp and took stock of herself, and what she saw did nothing to bolster her waning courage. Bell Townsend eyed her critically.

"I'd better go in with you."

"As if that should help," she muttered. "But I daresay you will wish me to return your coat."

"It *is* Weston's finest, you know."

"I hate a dandy," she muttered.

She looked like the veriest street urchin. Her hair straggled, her nose was smudged, the rose satin chemise dirty and torn, her stockings rent. She reminded him of the grubby hoyden who'd fished with him and Harry years ago at Monk's End. Her dark eyes met his for a moment, then she squared her small shoulders, and started toward the house. He'd give her one thing—plain and shy or not, she was pluck to the bone.

Bell reached for her hand, then dropped it. The last thing either of them needed was for Volsky or Lady Winstead to see that. It was his turn to settle his own shoulders manfully and prepare for the worst. Under the circumstances, if Volsky cried off, he knew he'd be expected to marry her. And he wouldn't do it.

The Winstead butler opened the door and stared, his mouth agape. " 'Pon my word" was all he could manage to say.

"It is all right, Dawes," Katherine said, her voice low.

"Kate!" Her mother nearly swooned when she saw her. For an awful moment, her eyes raked the backward coat, the torn chemise, and her lips flattened into a straight line. Then she saw Bellamy Townsend. "Claire, my salts!" she wailed. "Oh, you foolish girl—whatever is Count Volsky to think?"

"I don't know, Mama," Kate answered tiredly, "but Lord Townsend and I have walked all the way from King's Theatre."

"Walked!"

"Lady Winstead, I can explain," Bell assured her. "We were set upon by footpads after we were separated from you. Indeed, but I possibly owe my life to Kate." He grinned boyishly, but to no effect. Katherine's mother continued to regard him balefully.

"Mama, I cannot find—" Claire stopped to stare at her sister. "What have you got on? Well, of all the indecent—Mama, just look at her!"

Two red spots rose in Katherine's cheeks, but she managed to keep her voice even. "I should be very much more indecent without it, I'm afraid. Please—if you would excuse me, I am going up to bathe and go to bed." Turning to Bell, she extended her hand. "Thank you, my lord, for seeing me safely home. If you wish to wait, I shall have Peg bring your coat down to you shortly."

Volsky had come into the foyer and was standing behind her. For an awful moment, Bell half expected to be called out. But it was Madame Malenkov who spoke.

"Ah, *cherie,* but we have been so very worried!" the Russian woman said, hurrying to embrace Katherine. "You poor child—Lexy, do you see? What she must have been through!"

"You are all right, Ekaterina?" he said solicitously.

"Yes."

"When the people charged the princes, we could not see you, and when we reached the carriage, we waited, hoping you would find us." Alexei turned to Lady Winstead. "Someone must find the baron, I think."

Kate frowned. "Harry? Whatever for?"

"He saw everything, but he could not reach us," her mother explained. "And now he is gone searching for you."

"Mama, are you going to let her stand there like a shameless hussy?" Claire demanded.

"I am more covered than you are," Kate retorted. "Please, I should like to retire." She looked down at her bare feet. "I do not think I can stand any longer."

"Ma pauvre petite," Galena crooned. "Lexy, you must help her up the stairs." As she spoke, she slipped a small box into his hand. "He has a surprise for you, I think."

"Yes, yes, of course." Alexei viewed her awkwardly for a moment, then he put his hand under Katherine's elbow. "It must have been terrible for you, Ekaterina," he told her as he guided her up the stairs. "When you are in Russia, you will not have to worry for your safety. We do not let such things happen in my country."

Bell exhaled his relief. "Well, no harm done, really, is there? Lady Winstead, tell Kate to direct my coat home, will you? Madame Malenkov, your servant."

"But how do you get there, *cher* Bellamy?"

"It isn't terribly far."

"Oh, Lord Townsend—your hand!" Rushing to his side, Claire pointed to a scrape on his wrist. "You must have gotten that defending our Kate! Mama, look!"

Embarrassed, he shook his head. "It is nothing—I daresay I scraped it when I fell." Before she could touch him, he added ruefully, "But you are mistaken, Miss Clarissa—it was Miss Winstead who defended me."

"You were used to call me Claire," she reminded him. "And," she added slyly, "she was always the hoyden."

"Clarissa!"

"Well, she was, Mama."

"Ah," he said lightly, "but that was when you were a little chit in the schoolroom, wasn't it? Now that you are grown, I should not presume."

He was in his shirtsleeves, his cravat askew, his pantaloons soiled with street dirt, and his blond hair rumpled from losing his hat. But he was still almost too beautiful for his sex; he was still Adonis. It was not fair that Kate should have been the one to have spent more than an hour alone with him.

For a moment, Claire considered making more mis-

chief, then decided against it. It was bad enough that
Kate was marrying Alexei Volsky, but at least she would
be going to Russia with him. The worst thing possible
would be for the count to discard her, forcing Viscount
Townsend to make an offer. Claire bit back words she
knew she would regret bitterly.

"Well, I expect that Kate must seem younger to you,
for she never knows how to comport herself," she said
instead. "And she is such a brown little thing."

He didn't answer her. Alexei Volsky was coming back
down the stairs, and once again the hackles rose on Bell's
neck. The Russian smiled. "The maid tends her, so everything is well, *n'est-ce pas*? She will have a bath and
sleep, and in the morning, it will not seem so bad." He
looked to his sister. "It is done," he said low to her.

"We owe Lord Townsend our gratitude, Lexy," Galena reminded her brother. "Poor Bellamy, he is forced
to walk home. You should take him, I think."

"Yes, yes, of course." Volsky passed a hand over his
eyes. "It has been a very tiring day for me also, but it is
nothing to set him down at his house."

"I should be grateful," Bell murmured.

"Yes, well, then naught's more to be done, is there?"
Lady Winstead asked, trying not to betray her own relief.
She held out her hand for Volsky to kiss, then turned to
Bell. "This has been a terrible blow to my nerves."

"I understand."

"Yes, well, I expect we shall sleep late after this.
Claire, you'd best get on up to bed. Good night, Madame
Malenkov."

"Oh, but I shall stay with Ekaterina," Galena announced. "For Lexy's sake, I must see that she has the
best of care."

Affronted by the implication, Lady Winstead started to
protest, then held her tongue also. "As you wish, madame," she replied frostily. "I am sure a bedchamber
can be found for you."

"It is not necessary. I shall sleep on the chaise in Ekaterina's room. I do not think she will mind." Galena's
gaze found her brother, and she frowned. "I expect she

is terribly overset now that Lexy has told her the czar demands his attendance most of the time. I would be there for her.''

''Really, madame—''

''I am unused to it, but I will manage, I am sure. I must tend to Alexei's interests, you know.''

Once outside in the cool summer night air, Bell drew a deep breath and let it out slowly. ''I hope you do not think that Miss Winstead and I—''

''Of course not,'' Volsky cut him off abruptly. ''One has but to look upon Ekaterina to know she is an innocent.''

''Very.''

Volsky said nothing to that. Silence descended as they mounted the carriage and continued for several blocks. Finally, Bell spoke up. ''If you do not mind it, I should rather return to King's Theatre. Hopefully, my own conveyance is still there.''

''Not at all.''

''I'll look for her brother.''

''He was most distraught, but what could I say? She was torn from us by that mob.'' Another long silence, then Alexei Volsky leaned forward to look out his window. ''We are there. Is that your carriage?''

''I cannot tell for certain in the dark, but I expect so. And if it is, my driver will be asleep in it.''

They drew close enough to see the Townsend coat of arms blazoned on the door, one of the last self-aggrandizing acts of his late mother. Bell opened his door and started to jump down, but Alexei Volsky touched his arm.

''If you are coming to Russia for Galena, I should not advise it, my friend.''

''No.''

''And if it is Sofia, I warn you—Gregori Sherkov can be a cruel man.''

''Kind of you to tell me,'' Bell murmured.

''Good night, Townsend.''

Bell walked the several steps to his coach. Wrenching

his own carriage door open, he was surprised. As the driver hastily got out of his way, he could see that Winstead waited for him. Harry stared at Bell's shirtsleeves for a moment, then demanded, "Where's Kate?"

"At home. I walked her there." Bell slid into the vacated seat. "She's quite safe, and Volsky is not in a taking over it."

Obviously relieved, Harry sank back. "We were all in a taking, I can tell you. When I saw that crowd, and then she wasn't with Volsky, I half expected the worst. By the time I could get across the street, everything was nigh over, and she was nowhere to be seen. I've been up and down these blocks a dozen times and more, looking for her." He looked at the darkened theater, then sighed. "Sometimes I forget how small, how frail she is."

"I wouldn't call her frail, old fellow." Leaning forward, Bell reached under the seat for his flask. "Kicked a fellow where it hurts."

"She wouldn't even know that."

"Deuced lucky, then." Bell took a gulp from the container, then passed it. "I pulled her to what I thought was safety, and damme if we weren't set upon by cutpurses. Kate kicked one of 'em, and I blinded another, then we ran."

"You're certain she wasn't hurt?"

"I told you—she's all right. Her feet may be sore and her dignity wounded, but I got her home. Not that your mother was particularly pleased by the sight of me," Bell admitted cheerfully.

"How'd they get your coat?"

"I'm afraid circumstances demanded I loan it to your sister. Someone nearly pulled her dress off her."

"Egad." Harry drank deeply, then wiped his mouth with the back of his hand. "Where's Volsky?"

"He just set me down."

For a moment, Winstead was pensive, then he sighed again. "It'd kill Kate if he cried off. Only offer she's had, you know. I'm dashed glad he didn't make an issue of this."

"It didn't seem to bother him—deuced calm, in fact.

Thing is, I wondered why he wasn't looking for her himself.''

"He's not familiar with London."

"No, I suppose not." Bell retrieved the flask and drank again. "What do you think of him?"

"I think Kate's damned fortunate. Why?"

Bell shrugged. "I don't know. Russia's a long way from England," he murmured noncommitally.

"I know." The carriage lamps betrayed Harry Winstead's twisted smile. "Is that why you are going, my friend?"

"I'm going because I didn't like India," Bell answered simply.

"Petticoat trouble?"

"Got to play least in sight for a while." He met Harry's gaze, then looked away. "Fanny's told Hopewell I got her with child. She wants me to kill him for her."

A low whistle escaped Winstead, then he sobered. "You cannot afford this. You'll be cut everywhere if Hopewell makes a dust over it."

"Devil of it is, it's not true."

"Nobody will ever believe that."

Bell held up his nearly empty flask and smiled grimly. "To Russia, Harry. When I am come back, he'll know she lied."

A watchman passed them, calling out, "Two of the clock! Two of the clock!"

"You going home?" Harry murmured.

"Without a coat, I can scarce go anywhere else. You?"

"Got a prime article waiting for me, if she's not gone to bed. Want to set me down in York Place?"

"Might as well. Do I know her?"

"No, and you're not coming in with me—there are some things I don't share."

The carriage traversed the mostly deserted London streets, its wheels rattling on the paving stones. Inside, there was relative silence. Finally, when they were nearly there, Harry exhaled heavily. "Look, I know you and Kate do not deal well together, but—"

"But you want me to look in on her," Bell finished

for him. "I don't think so. For one thing, how's it to look to Volsky? And for another, she wouldn't welcome me."

"You don't know that."

"Actually, she's quite plain on that head."

"I'm not asking you to play nursemaid to her—just write once in awhile to let me know how she goes on." Before Bell could argue with him, Harry explained, "Oh, she'll write home, but she's not one to complain much."

"I doubt I shall even see her, once we are there."

"But if you do."

It was a small favor for a good friend. "All right, if I see her, I'll let you hear of it."

On his way back from York Place, Bell felt almost out of charity with Kate Winstead. The night was still young, and he had no wish to go home. He ought to have kept the damned coat and gone to White's. He passed Amy Wilson's house and thought of her sister Harriette, wondering how she fared with her sugar merchant. It didn't matter. When she came on the market again, he would be in Russia.

Idly, he recalled the admiring looks cast his way by another Fashionable Impure, the one everyone called Venus Reclining. He drained the flask, then tossed it onto the opposite seat. Knocking on the ceiling to gain his driver's attention, he called out, "Somers Town!" As the carriage swung into the turn, he leaned back. If no one else was there, he was inclined to do a bit of reclining with the fair Venus. Hell, he was already half-undressed. Besides, he was certain of a welcome.

K ate could not sleep. She lay abed, trying not to cry, telling herself she was but foolish. Still, she could not help feeling terribly hurt and disappointed. Finally, she rose and went to the window. Below, a damp fog from the river lay like a blanket, mingling with the smoke from the lamps, obscuring much of the street.

At least he'd not repudiated her. She shivered and rubbed her bare arms, not from the cold, but rather from an excess of nerves. Lexy loved her. *Lexy loved her,* she reassured herself. He must, for why else would he have offered for her? Why else would he have given her his mother's magnificent diamond and ruby betrothal ring?

"Is everything all right, Ekaterina?" Galena asked from the darkness.

"Yes, of course." But even as she said it, Katherine could not quite keep the tremor out of her voice. "I am all right."

"Oh, *ma pauvre petite,*" the woman murmured soothingly, coming up behind her. "It is Lexy, is it not?"

"Why—why would you think it, madame?"

"Because he told me earlier, but I did not wish to ruin your triumph for you. If he waited until you were at home, the fault is mine, Ekaterina. I told him to tell you in private when he gave you the ring."

"But surely he could discover time for me!" The words burst out before she could control them. "The notice will be in the *Gazette*! How is it to look if I am to go about unescorted?"

"Shhhh—you are overset merely. You have but to hold

out your hand for everyone to know how much you mean to him,'' Galena reminded her.

Katherine swallowed hard. ''But I wanted—''

''You wanted everyone to know, and they will. I understand. They will say there is no one in all of England with such a ruby, I promise you.''

''And now he says that the czar demands his attendance until the wedding. Madame, I shall be marrying a stranger!''

''Hush. You will be returning to London a married lady, Ekaterina. And we will be going to Russia to join him in the autumn.''

''Is it because of tonight?'' Katherine cried. ''If so, I can assure him that I don't even like Bellamy Townsend!''

''He knows that Viscount Townsend saved your life, Ekaterina, and he is grateful for that. You must not think such things—I tell you Lexy is besotted! Look at your hand, Ekaterina—look at your hand! If he did not love you, he would have given you a mere bauble rather than that.''

''And Claire—how she will go on about it,'' Kate continued tearfully. ''She will say he does not care for me at all!''

''Pah. That one—she is a viper in the nest, little one. Tell her she will be fortunate if this Cosgrove gives her something even one-third the value of what you have.''

''Hargrove—it is Hargrove.''

''Does it matter who he is?'' Galena put her arms about Katherine's shoulders. ''Come, let us sit down and decide what is to be done. Here—let me see your ring,'' she coaxed. ''Ah—how I remember it. Every woman in Moscow envied my mother for this, Ekaterina—every woman.''

But Katherine was not easily appeased. ''There is nothing to be done. Alexei has made it quite clear to me that he does not have the time to dance attendance on me before the wedding.''

''He has his duty, Ekaterina.''

"Everyone will say 'there is Miss Winstead, but where is her betrothed?' "

"And later they will say 'there is Countess Volsky,' " Galena said softly. "The ruby her husband gives her can be seen across the room."

"Followed by 'where is her husband?' no doubt. Madame, I shall be marrying a stranger!" Katherine cried again.

"But a very kind one who wishes to love you," Galena countered. "And how many English girls know their husbands? They have a few dances, the man offers the settlements, and it is done, *n'est-ce pas*? Already you have possibly spent as much time with Alexei as many of your females have with their betrotheds." Taking Katherine's arm, she directed her to a chair. "Come, you are disappointed, and with every reason, *daragaya*. But you must not let this spoil your triumph. Only you will wed Alexei Volsky, Ekaterina—only you will be his countess. Only your children will carry his name."

Katherine sat reluctantly. Folding her hands in her lap, she did not look at Alexei's sister. "You think me quite foolish, don't you?" she said finally.

"Of course I do not! Ekaterina, you are all Lexy and I could have hoped for!" Dropping to a seat nearby, Galena persisted, saying, "We shall be so very busy ourselves, little one. Even if Lexy should have time for us, we will have no time for him."

"I am not at all certain I can marry anyone on a week's acquaintance, madame."

"Lena. What is this 'madame,' Ekaterina? We shall be sisters at Domnya." The older woman sighed. "Will it help if I speak to the grand duchess? Alexander listens to his sister, and perhaps something can be arranged." When Katherine did not answer, she sighed again. "Very well. I shall see that Lexy is made available for at least one event. A reception at the embassy for you, perhaps. Yes, for then Alexander must be there also." Satisfied with the notion, she leaned to pat Katherine's hand. "You must not be sad, little one, for you have Galena. And I will call on Alexander's sister for you."

"I would not wish to cause Alexei any difficulty, madame—Lena, that is."

"Pah. It is nothing. I know not why Lexy did not think of it." Galena squeezed Katherine's hand, then released it. "Believe me, you have answered my prayers for my brother. Together we make him very happy, no?"

"I hope so."

"Good. Now if you cannot sleep, we shall call your maid and require heated milk for you."

"Peg is asleep, I'm afraid."

"In Russia, it does not matter. We own everyone who lives at Domnya, and they will do whatever is asked." Galena smiled encouragingly. "Did I tell you there will be seven thousand serfs there to do your bidding? You will be a powerful woman at Domnya."

"As if I cared for that," Katherine responded low. "It is enough if Lexy loves me."

"Ekaterina, we shall both love you, and you will wish for nothing. Every jewel, every fur, every gown you covet, you shall have," the Russian woman promised. "And when you come back to visit, the viper will envy you. Galena will stay home at Domnya with the children."

Somehow the thought of children had seemed but a distant possibility. And for all that she'd fallen head over heels for him, Alexei Volsky was still too much the stranger for such intimacy. Perhaps that was what worried her the most—she had only one week to become better acquainted with him. When she dared to look at Galena, Alexei's sister shook her head.

"That woman, she tells you nothing, does she?"

"I don't understand."

"About what is expected. It is just as well, after all. The day you are married, you come to Lena—do you understand? I can tell you how to make Lexy happy."

"Mama—"

"Pah—that woman! I think she does not know how to live, Ekaterina. That is why she watches your sister. The men, I think, they never came to her."

"Papa wed her."

"But were they happy?"

"I don't know—no, I don't think so."

But even as she said it, Katherine could still remember that night she'd found Bell Townsend in the maze with Miss Beckwood. The night when her father admitted he was a disappointment to her mother. It was the only time he ever spoke of the unhappiness between them.

"That woman, she could not make a man content. There is too much bitterness in her."

"You are very observant, Lena."

"I do not observe, Ekaterina—I know. Just like I know you are the right wife for Lexy." Galena stood. "And if we do not get back into bed and go to sleep, everyone will wonder what he admires in you. Come, for today we shop, and then I go to the grand duchess."

Katherine crawled between her covers and pulled them up over her shoulder. Turning over, she said, "Thank you, Lena—I know not what I should ever do without you."

"Ah, Ekaterina, you must not worry—I will never leave Domnya. Never."

She felt a rush of gratitude wash over her. Galena would see she had a betrothal reception or a party at the embassy. Galena would see she had a little time with Alexei. Galena understood.

Monk's End: *July* 3, 1814

Galena had been right. The time had passed far too quickly, marching Katherine through a seemingly endless round of fittings and the embassy party, and now the wait was over, and the interim had been sustained by a daily posy and love note from Alexei. Now she would wed in the same small chapel where she'd been christened and confirmed.

Even Claire, who had been so spiteful in the beginning, was caught up in the bittersweet excitement. She'd cried the night before, saying she could not bear to part with "the sweetest of sisters," then she'd dabbed at her tears, adding that Kate was so very fortunate.

Walking alone through the fine mist that shrouded the ancient graveyard, Katherine sought the courage to carry through with this giant step in her life. One part of her said that she barely knew him, the other argued that her mama was right—she *was* fortunate to have gained a man like Alexei's notice. And while she could not have done better, she certainly could have done worse. She had only to think of Bell Townsend to know it.

Off to the side, just beyond the old stone wall, she found her father's grave and stopped. Leaning down to brush wet leaves that clung to the limestone marker, she stared at the deeply chiseled letters. *John, 11th Baron Winstead, b.1753, d.1812.* It still did not seem possible that at fifty-nine, he'd taken his own life.

The pain cut through her breastbone, leaving a hollow ache within. That was why she so seldom came here—she could never help asking why. But now she looked down at the glistening grass, thinking of him, remembering his easy laugh, his twinkling eyes, the smoky smell of his coats. She'd been the daughter that trailed him to the stables, that rode with him about the manor. She had to hold back tears and fight the lump in her throat to speak.

"I am getting married today, Papa. I-I wish you could have been here, you know. I'd know if you liked him. And I-I'm afraid, Papa—I mean, what if—"

"Kate, whatever—? This is not the time for a pulled face," Clarissa chided, coming up behind her. "And you are getting wet."

Kate turned around, then blurted out, "Oh, Claire, what if I cannot hold him? What if I cannot make him love me?"

"In any event, you are a very rich woman," her sister answered practically. "Besides, you cannot cry off now, else Mama will be mad as fire."

"But I am not beautiful like you!"

"No, you are not, but there is no accounting for the Russian taste, I suppose, though Madame Malenkov— well, it does not signify, anyway. You are fortunate he is marrying you." She looked down at Kate's hand and sighed. "I should take the hetman himself for a ruby like that, you know."

"Yes, yes, I know I am fortunate, but—"

"And at least you will have that woman to dress you instead of Mama. Even I have to admit you look much better."

"Better," Kate repeated. "Better than what? An Antidote?"

"What does Count Volsky say?"

"That I look well! As though I have been ill!"

"Kate, I have never known you to be such a goose!"

"But I don't really know him!" Kate wailed. "And I am afraid! There—I have said it, Claire. I am afraid!"

"Of what? Of being a married lady?"

"I don't know! Maybe he won't love me!"

"What difference does that make? You will be Countess Volsky. Really, Kate, but sometimes I just don't understand you."

"Nobody does! Not you—not Mama—not Harry even!"

Clarissa sighed. "Kate, you do not have time for this. Alexei has already gone to the chapel, and you are not even dressed. Come on—before the sky pours, and my hair is quite ruined."

With an effort, Katherine sniffed back tears, then managed to smile sheepishly at her sister. "I guess I am a bit of a goose, aren't I?"

"Yes, and I shall be a shocking fright also, if you do not stop this." Catching Kate's hand, Claire started to pull her back toward the old manor house. "I wasn't going to tell you, but Sally Jersey thinks you have done exceedingly well for yourself."

"I know—everywhere I go, someone whispers the same thing. 'It is the Winstead girl as is betrothed to the Russian,' " she mimicked. "'With her looks, she is so very fortunate.' Do they all think me deaf, Claire?"

"Kate, where have you been?" Lady Winstead demanded anxiously from the porch. "We have been looking for you for an age! It is nigh to half past nine—and the vicar will be there at ten!"

"I went walking. I wanted to tell Papa."

"In this?" Her mother's voice rose incredulously. "And look at you! I vow I shall swoon!"

"Nonsense," Galena Malenkov cut in briskly. "She does not need to be overset on her wedding day." To Kate, she said much more kindly, "Come, *ma petite,* and Galena will help you ready yourself. And if Lexy must wait, so be it." She reached out to take Katherine's cold hand. "You have a bit of fright, *mais non*?"

"Yes."

"A natural thing for a young girl," the Russian woman reassured her. "Now, I have that Peg heating the tongs again, so you are not to worry. And the gown is readied. You have but to get dressed, and we will fix the hair a bit here and there, put on the veil, then voilà!"

"You are very kind, Lena."

"Pah. We are to be sisters, after all."

"And I cherish you already," Kate said sincerely.

"We will do very well together, I think. And when the children come, you will have Galena to rock them. We shall be happy, Ekaterina."

But after Peg had done her best, after the exquisite gown was on, and the long tissue silk scarf flowed from the crown of flowers on her head, Katherine stared hard at her reflection. What she saw did not comfort her—she was still naught but a plain girl dressed finely.

Despite the warm, musty dampness of the old stone chapel, Katherine felt as though her whole body had turned to ice. For a moment, she wanted to tell Harry that she could not do it, but then she saw Alexei Volsky waiting for her at the altar. And the parish vicar looked expectantly toward her brother. There was no more time. She smoothed the skirt of her gown and straightened the circlet of roses on her head, hoping that the long scarf fell straight. She was as ready as she was ever going to be. She nodded to Harry, and he took his place beside her.

The old vicar cleared his throat, then began, "Dearly Beloved, we are gathered here . . ." She held her breath, scarce hearing him until he asked, "Who giveth this woman?"

"I do," Harry said clearly, placing her cold hand in Alexei's. He turned and walked to sit beside their mother. Behind the count, his groomsman stood woodenly, as though he were a palace guard. Beside Katherine, Clarissa waited also, ready to witness. As the vicar cleared his throat again, the younger girl leaned close to whisper, "Buck up, Kate—'tis a wedding, not a funeral."

Katherine was so aware of the man holding her hand that she could think of little else until she was asked if she would take Alexei Petrovich Volsky for her husband. He asked twice, prompting Alexei to squeeze her fingers, and she managed to nod, saying almost too low for any to hear, "I will."

There was an air of unreality to all of it. And all too soon it was over. She looked down at the diamond and ruby ring on her finger, thinking she'd tied herself to him forever. She was irrevocably Katherine Elizabeth Mary Winstead Volsky—or was it Volskaya? She was not even sure of that.

The parish book was signed, witnessed, and dated, and there was nothing more to do but leave the chapel. She looked briefly at the crucifix that hung behind the altar, thinking a quick, silent prayer. *Please, God, let him love me.*

He settled his shoulders as though a burden had been lifted. "Well, it is done."

"Yes."

The rain had intensified, and when they emerged from the stale air of the chapel, it was truly pouring as though the sky emptied buckets. Alexei caught her hand and ran for the carriage. "Let us hope this is not an unfavorable omen!" he shouted. He pushed her up, then heaved his body in after. Sinking back against the leather squabs of Harry's traveling coach, he brushed at the rain spots on his coat. Looking up, he forced a smile.

"The gown becomes you, Ekaterina. Galena has transformed you."

"Thank you." She dropped her gaze to her clasped hands in her lap. "I am most grateful to her."

"We can leave immediately after the wedding breakfast, or if you prefer, we can stay here tonight and hope the rain ends."

Somehow the thought of going off with a stranger was suddenly quite daunting. She colored uncomfortably, then blurted out, "I should rather stay here."

"As you wish. Galena thought perhaps you would rather be away from your mother and sister."

She fought rising panic, telling herself everything was going to be all right, that she already loved him. He was handsome, kind, and considerate—what else could she wish for? If only he would say something to let her know he could love her . . .

"You are quiet, Ekaterina."

"It is all so new to me. And I have scarce seen you. I—"

"Do you not think I regret that?" he asked, sliding

across to her seat. Reaching to lift the ring of roses from her hair, he carefully folded the soggy silk scarf attached to it, then set them on the other side. "Galena has kept her promise to me, and you do not shame me, *dara-gaya*," he said.

Snuggling against his wet coat, she felt the cold metal medals, but she did not care. Everything was going to be all right. *Everything was going to be all right*.

His hand lifted her chin, and his blue eyes blurred before hers. The softness of his breath against her cheek sent a shiver through her. She sat very still as his mouth pressed against her lips. Then she felt his other hand brush her breast lightly. Her face flamed as she caught his fingers.

"Alexei—no!"

He released her and leaned back, watching her, frowning. "Do they teach you English girls nothing?"

"I'm sorry—it is just so terribly new to me." But as she said it, she remembered Bell Townsend's ruthless kiss, and could not help comparing it to Alexei's blood-less one. It was, she told herself fiercely, that Alexei Volsky respected her.

Her husband stared silently out his window for a moment, then observed abruptly, "We are arrived."

Harry threw open the door, grinning. "I thought you'd stolen my coach and made off for Leicester without eating."

"Actually, we have decided to stay the night here," Alexei announced. He jumped down and reached for Katherine, lifting her by her waist, then letting her slide the length of him. His hand closed over hers. "Come, Ekaterina, for the guests await."

Like the ceremony itself, the wedding breakfast was a private family affair. There had not been time, Lady Winstead had complained repeatedly, to do justice to "dear Kate's marriage," but that could not be helped. It was a miracle that anything had gone right.

The irritated cook had outdone himself despite griping, "I shall have to serve naught but pastries and a joint on this notice.'' What he had actually managed was a full five-course meal that would have done the chef at the Pulteney Hotel in London proud. But Kate scarce noted it.

While Alexei and Harry manfully carried the conversation by discussing everything from the weather to the late war, Kate sat silently, pushing her food from one side of her plate to the other. When Lady Winstead noticed, she urged her to ''eat rather than play'' with her food. But Harry insisted she be left alone. And Madame Malenkov nodded, saying that poor Kate was but tired, and who could blame her?

''Ekaterina has lived in the whirlwind these last days, *n'est-ce pas*? I for one think that she must rest after the bride cake is eaten,'' she declared firmly. ''Do you not agree, Lexy?''

He nodded. ''It cannot have been easy for her.''

''But what will you do?'' Kate blurted out. A new flood of color rushed to her face, and she felt utterly foolish. ''That is—''

''If the rain stops, Harry will show me the ruined monastery, I think. And if not, perhaps he and your sister can be persuaded to play the cards.'' He smiled, then patted her hand. ''You are our responsibility now, Ekaterina.''

Finally, the dishes were cleared and the cake eaten. For all that it had been called a breakfast, the clock in the front saloon chimed two. Harry lifted his glass one last time.

''To Kate and Lexy—may they have a long life together!''

Galena sipped, then held hers up again. ''And may they make me an aunt many times over.'' Her eyes met Kate's. ''Ah, *ma cherie*, but you cannot know how I have longed for a child to hold. Now these arms will carry an infant of yours one day.''

Alexei clinked his glass against his sister's. ''God grant your wish, Lena,'' he murmured.

Harry cleared his throat. ''Well, do you join me for a bit of brandy in the front saloon ere we tempt the rain again, Lexy?''

"Most gladly."

Lady Winstead rose. "Then all is settled for the afternoon, is it not? If Madame Malenkov does not mind it, I think I should like to lie down myself."

"But of course I do not mind it," Galena murmured, rising also. "Come, *ma petite*—I will go up with you, and we will leave the men and Claire to their amusements." She cast a warning look at Alexei. "I trust you will *not* speak of the politics, for we all know you would be a Tory if you were English."

"I do not need you to tell me what I can say, Lena." In front of them all, he leaned to brush his lips against Kate's cheek. "Until later, Ekaterina."

With Peg's help, Kate removed the circlet of roses and the scarf, then stepped out of her wedding dress. She'd hoped Galena had wanted to speak with her, but Alexei's sister had gone to her own chamber. And Kate had not been able to bring herself to ask her anything with Peg hovering nearby.

Far too unsettled to sleep, she lay down and stared at the ceiling. It was, she reflected apprehensively, quite one thing to wish to be married, and quite another to contemplate sleeping in the same bed with him. She touched her zona, remembering how his hand had brushed her breast, and shame flooded through her.

He would do more than that, she did not doubt it. But what? And would he be pleased with her? Or would he be as disappointed as he was in her brother's carriage?

K atherine sat before her dressing table, pulling her hair this way and that, wondering which way Alexei might like it. It didn't matter—after a rainy day, it was hopelessly flat. She made a face at herself, then saw Galena in the mirror.

"I am caught," she confessed, sighing. "It is impossible, I fear."

"Nonsense." The older woman moved closer and picked up the hairbrush. "We pull it back like this," she said, "and then we put a turban over it."

"To sleep?" Kate asked doubtfully.

"Not to sleep. But by the time it comes off, Lexy will not care what your hair looks like, Ekaterina."

For a moment, Katherine went cold. All day long she had hoped either her mother or Galena would say something to her, and now she longed to ask, but she could not. Now she had only perhaps a few minutes before the stranger she had wed would come up to her.

"There."

It seemed as though someone else looked back at her. "I don't know."

"Believe me, it is all right." Galena moved to the front and adjusted the embroidered lawn nightgown. "Not that this will stay on very long," she murmured.

"Lena—"

"Yes, yes—I know you are worried, Ekaterina, but there is no need. Lexy will be all that is kind to you."

"I cannot think I must take my night rail off."

"I expect he will take it off for you. Some men will only lift up the hem, but it is such a mess that way."

Katherine swallowed hard. "I don't know, Lena," she whispered miserably. "What if I do not please him?"

"Humph! Men are such selfish creatures, that they please themselves." Seeing that the color had left Katherine's face, the Russian woman put her arms around the girl's shoulders. "I will tell you what to expect, Ekaterina, but it sounds worse than it is. You forget what is happening in the passion of the moment, I promise you."

"I will try not to give him a disgust of me."

Galena dropped down onto the padded bench beside her. "You are a good girl, Ekaterina Ivanova, but a man wants much more than that. Now, when he comes up to you, you should be in the bed, and you should smile at him. And when he undresses, you must not appear afraid of what you see." She reached to pat Katherine's hand. "When the clothes are off, he will lie down beside you."

"All of them? The clothes, I mean?"

"I expect he will not wear his nightshirt until later. It gets in the way. Then he will touch you."

"Where?"

"Everywhere—even where you scarce touch yourself. But you will like it, I promise you. It is only the act itself that might hurt a little, and then it is only the one time. But he must be inside you, or else a babe cannot be made."

"Inside me?" Katherine echoed faintly. "Oh, Lena, surely—"

"You will like it," Galena repeated. "It is quite pleasant when you get used to it. And if Lexy is not too selfish, you will find you wish him to come to you often."

"Lena, I don't think I can do this," Katherine whispered desperately.

"Pah. Tomorrow you will think yourself a silly goose for being afraid of him." Rising, Galena leaned to kiss Katherine's cheek. "But for now, Ekaterina, I must go. It would not be at all proper for me to be here when he arrives."

In the distance, a clock struck over and over again, telling her it was quite late. "I expect he still is having brandy with Harry," Kate decided.

"Just remember to wait in the bed." Galena surveyed her critically one last time, then reached for the rouge pot and the hare's foot. "Just a little," she murmured, "lest he think you a ghost. And perhaps a tiny bit of perfume—not too much, for he will wish to breathe. There. You are ready, Ekaterina."

The girl was going to be a cold piece of wood and Galena knew it, but it couldn't be helped. The longer Lexy waited, the worse it would be for both of them. Galena went downstairs to the book room and rapped lightly on the door before opening it.

Harry Winstead sat sprawled, his coat open, his vest hanging, his cravat loose, and it took no great powers of perception to realize he was utterly foxed. And her brother was opposite him, a large brandy glass in his hand.

"Shame on the both of you! You are disgusting," she chided them.

"Not disgusting," Harry insisted. "Disguised."

"It is Ekaterina's wedding!"

With an effort, Katherine's brother rose, weaving unsteadily on his feet. "Ought to go to bed," he mumbled thickly. "Cannot make it."

"*Garçon! Garçon!* What is it you say—footman? *Footman!* Come aid your master!"

"Don't need—"

But as one of the lower footmen appeared, Galena snapped her fingers imperiously. "You—take him to bed," she ordered. She waited only until she could hear Harry Winstead trying to sing as he was helped up the stairs, then she rounded on Alexei.

"And you! Alexei Petrovich, you are *pyanee*!"

"*Nyet,* Lena. I have not had nearly enough."

"You belong up there beside your wife!" she hissed at him. "She awaits you!"

"Lena, I don't want—"

"I don't care what you want!"

He ran his fingers through his disordered hair. "Lena—"

"Lexy, we were agreed!"

"I don't want to play games anymore," he muttered

defensively. "I do enough for you. You have given me a plain woman, Lena."

"What difference does it make? She will serve very well."

"She is like kissing a stone. I should have taken a Russian woman."

"But this one will not understand the gossip—nor will she run home to her family, Lexy." She moved closer again and reached to brush his cheek with the back of her hand. "Lexy, it will work—had I not thought it, I should never have suggested Ekaterina to you." Her hand moved across his lips. "She is more than half in love with you already."

"You did not see her in the carriage, Lena."

"Lexy . . . Lexy . . . Are you so used to harlots that you do not know how to treat a virgin?"

"Strange words coming from you," he muttered, turning his head away.

"Seduce her," Galena advised him. "Everything depends on you—everything. You need a wife, Lexy—you need an heir for Domnya."

"Do I do this for Domnya, Lena—or for you?"

"Both. It means everything to me." Once again, she touched him. "You can make her love you, Lexy."

"Lena, it is not right."

"Lexy . . . Lexy . . . what is wrong? We give her a title and wealth, and you cannot say she will ever have that here. There will be children at Domnya, Lexy," she argued passionately. "She will have her sons and daughters around her."

"What of me, Lena? What of me?" he asked bitterly.

"Ah, Lexy," she said softly, "for you it will be as always."

"I do not like it that Townsend comes to Russia," he muttered.

"Are you jealous?"

"Of course not! But if I am married to the *Angleechahnka*, I can complain, can't I?"

"Yes. But you worry too much. *Cher* Bellamy has other reasons for coming to Russia, Lexy."

"I do not want Sherkov for an enemy." He reached to pour himself more of the brandy.

She knocked the glass from his hand. "No more, lest you cannot do the deed."

. He raised his hand to protest, then dropped it. "The things I do for you, Lena—the things I do for you." He caught her arm and rubbed his face against the flesh. "Why can you not come to Vienna?"

She pulled away and stared at him for a moment. "I have to take care of Ekaterina. Now, you will delay no longer—you will go to your wife, Alexei Petrovich!"

He looked away, saying nothing.

"Seduce her, Lexy—seduce her," she urged him.

The ormolu clock seemed to tick more loudly, keeping time with her heart, as she waited. Once again, Katherine sat before her mirror, brushing at her hair. The turban lay on the dressing table, discarded because she didn't want to wear it. Somehow it had seemed foolish to put something on her head if she were going to be naked everywhere else.

Galena had told her to wait in bed, but somehow Katherine could not bring herself to do it. She was still nervous and more than a little frightened, for the Russian woman's description of the marital act had been revolting, no matter how many times she'd insisted Katherine would like it. Every time Katherine thought about it, her blood ran cold in her veins, turning her body to ice.

Part of her wanted him to come, to get it over with, and part hoped he drank so much with Harry below that he would not come at all. But it did not matter, she told herself resolutely—no matter what he did to her, she was not going to resist. Her whole life depended now on making him love her.

The ancient floorboards creaked beneath the carpet in the hall, and for a moment, her heart paused. Footsteps drew nearer, stopping outside the bedchamber. The door swung inward. She could see him in her mirror, but she still could not force herself to turn around, not knowing what Galena had told her. As she watched, her breath held in abeyance, he discarded his coat, hanging it over the back of a chair. His waistcoat and cravat followed. Her heart pounded in her ears as he loosened his frilled white shirt at the neck.

He moved behind her, and stood there for a long moment. The mirror reflected the snowy whiteness of his shirt against his darker skin. Black, curling hairs were visible beneath his open shirt. He chest rose and fell evenly. The sweet, clove scent of Imperial water floated downward. He'd probably used it to wash the brandy from his breath. With an effort, she found her voice.

"Galena said to smile, but I cannot."

His mouth twisted wryly. "Galena. What a little mother she is to us, eh?"

"Yes—and I am most grateful for her."

There was an awkward silence, then he reached for her brush and laid it aside. "The dress you wore at dinner becomes you, *daragaya.* I liked it nearly as much as the wedding gown."

"Thank you. Galena chose it."

"She will manage everything for you, if you let her."

"She is the kindest woman I have ever met," she said sincerely.

His eyebrow rose at that. "Ah, but then you are most acquainted with your mother and sister, are you not? Perhaps that explains your opinion," he murmured. "But I did not come to discuss any of them, I think."

The way he said it sent a shiver down her back. "What does it mean when you call me *daragaya?*" she dared to ask.

He smiled, revealing fine, white teeth. "In the English? An Englishman would say 'sweetheart' or 'darling,' I suppose." His hand dropped to her shoulder, and he leaned over her. His black hair gleamed in the soft light. "Ah, Ekaterina, it would be easier to kiss you if you stood," he whispered, his voice soft and enticing. She felt his lips touch her bared skin at her neck, and his breath was warm, alive. She closed her eyes briefly and tried not to shiver again. When he drew back, she rose to face him, her heart pounding so loudly that she could scarce think.

"Are you still afraid, little one?"

She nodded, then raised her eyes to his. "But there is nothing you could do to me that would make me hate you, Lexy," she answered bravely.

He smiled again and moved closer. Lifting her chin, he bent his head to hers. "Put your arms around my neck, *daragaya,*" he whispered against her lips. "I need the feel of you against me, if I am to do this."

As her arms came up to twine about his neck, his mouth sought hers, tentatively, gently, until her embrace tightened, then his kiss deepened, sending a flood of heat through her. She clung to him, letting him probe and taste, scarce noticing when his hands slid down over her back and hips. He was taking her very breath, and she did not care. This time, she would show him that he'd not made a mistake by marrying her.

When he raised his head, there was desire in his eyes. His fingers found the tasseled ties of her wrapper, tugging at them until they loosened, and the robe fell open as his hands slipped inside. A low sob escaped when he found her breasts, and she began to tremble.

"I'd take you to bed now, Ekaterina," he said.

She nodded, not trusting herself to speak.

He swung her up easily and carried her to the already turned-down bed. As he straightened to unbutton his pantaloons, she rolled onto her side and looked away. She felt the mattress give with his weight and his warm, bare leg brushed against hers. Momentary panic rose within her as he reached for her, turning her over.

For a long moment, he stared into her face. "You are my wife, Ekaterina."

"Yes."

He waited no longer. Lowering his body over hers, he began kissing her again. Her arms came up to clasp his shoulders as she felt the heat of her own desire. When he eased the hem of her night rail upward, she remembered faintly that Galena had said he would take it off.

His mouth found her breast beneath the thin silk, and

he shocked her by sucking at her nipple. Her hands clasped and unclasped in his hair as her nipple hardened, tautening something deep within her. And then she felt his fingers between her legs. She stiffened with fear and would have pushed him away, but he shifted his weight over her and lowered his body, separating her legs with his knee. There was the feel of wet flesh against wet flesh, then he grasped her hips and thrust inside. She cried out as she tore, then her body closed around his as he filled her.

She lay there, not knowing what to do while he rode, his body straining against hers, and then his frenzied moans rose into a loud cry. She felt the warmth inside when he collapsed over her and lay there, his weight supported by his arms. It was done.

With an effort, he disentangled his limbs from hers and rolled away. As they separated, she felt the warm flood between her legs. Embarrassed, she could not meet his gaze.

Still panting, he gasped, "Now you are Countess Volsky."

Beneath her embarrassment, she felt vaguely dissatisfied, as though there must be more to it than that. She wanted him to hold her, but he didn't. Instead, he turned to her, murmuring, "You had better clean yourself."

Gathering what dignity she could, she managed to get up and pull her wadded gown down. A sticky liquid ran down her leg as she hobbled to the basin. As she poured water into the basin and dipped a cloth, she was painfully aware that he watched her. Her back to him, she lifted the night rail and washed, and when she withdrew the cloth to wring it out, she saw the blood Galena had mentioned. She was now his wife—in fact as well as name.

"You are all right?" he asked finally.

"Yes."

She finished washing, then went to her chest to draw out a clean nightgown. Stepping into the deepest shadows, she pulled off the other one and slipped into a demure lawn, which she carefully buttoned at the neck.

Acutely aware of the awkwardness between them now, she hesitated.

"Is there something wrong, Ekaterina?"

"Uh—no. No, of course not."

To her horror, he rose from the bed, seemingly unconscious of his nakedness, and walked to the tray Peg had set out earlier. He poured wine into the two goblets. Turning to face her, he lifted one. "A toast, Ekaterina." When she did not move, he held out the other. "Come, let us drink to these children we will give Domnya."

Not daring to look at him, not knowing what to say, she reached for the glass. It shook in her hand.

He smiled over the rim of his goblet. "Go on."

She managed a shy smile as she lifted her wine to her lips. "To my husband, then."

Wife. Husband. It sounded so strange, but she would get used to it. And she would get used to him. She drank deeply, draining her glass.

She awoke slowly and stretched languorously, only dimly aware that she was not alone. Then her toes touched his leg, and the memories of the night brought a blush to her cheeks. "Good morning, Ekaterina."

Everything was all right. She turned to snuggle close to him, burying her head against his bare shoulder.

"Lexy," she murmured.

He held her for a moment, then rolled away to sit. Slapping her backside lightly, he told her, "If you do not get up, we will not get to this hunting box tonight, I think."

Disappointed, she turned over and reached for her wrapper, retrieving it. When he rose, she struggled to pull it on and cover herself. He padded barefooted across the carpet to find the clothes his manservant had laid out for him.

"It does not bother you to dress before me?" she dared to ask him.

He shrugged. "Why should it?"

"You act as though you have been naked in front of a woman before."

"I am thirty, Ekaterina." He pulled on his inexpressibles and turned around. "Aren't you getting up?"

"Have there been many?" As soon as the words escaped, she had to look away.

"Many what? Women?"

"Yes."

"Only one."

"I'm sorry—I should not have asked."

"But only you are my wife—only you are Countess Volsky, Ekaterina Ivanova—only you are Volskaya." He smiled wryly. "And it is late to ask such a thing now."

"I could not bear it if there should be others, Alexei. Not after—"

"Ah, Ekaterina," he murmured, coming to her. Leaning over, he brushed her cheek with his lips. "I shall never look for a woman beyond my own home. There, I have said it."

Her arms reached for his neck, pulling him down. "And I promise I shall not be like other wives also, Lexy. I will never want anyone but you."

"Then we must surely be happy. Now, let us eat breakfast. As Harry tells it, we have far to go today."

As he finished dressing, she slipped from the bed to get her own clothes. Peg had hung her new traveling dress, a pomona green twilled silk trimmed in dark green braid, on the back of her wardrobe door. And in the hatbox, there was a matching bonnet, an exquisite creation with a curled brim and two dyed pheasant feathers perched jauntily beneath a grosgrain ribbon. Galena had insisted that Lexy would like it. Katherine turned away and tried to dress without being seen.

"I will get your maid."

"No!" As his eyebrow lifted, she blurted out, "I don't want her to know what I have done!"

"Ekaterina, it was expected. And I do not travel with a wreck."

"No, of course not. I can—"

"I will send Galena up to you, and she will summon the maid," he decided firmly. "They can get you ready while I am shaved."

He left her then, and she could hear him calling for his sister. It was different for a man, she supposed, but everything was still too new to her. She glanced to the bed, saw the tangled covers, and blushed anew. Hurrying to them, she tried to smooth everything over, as though she could somehow conceal what she and Alexei had done. Then she saw her bloodstained silk night rail. Stooping to pick it up, she whisked it behind her as she heard voices in the hall.

"Ah, Lexy—and how is the bridegroom this morning?" Galena asked teasingly.

"Leave me alone, Lena," he responded shortly.

There was a rapping on the bedchamber door. After stuffing the telltale nightgown into the bottom of the wardrobe, Katherine went to open it.

"Ah, *ma cherie*, but you are lovely this morning!" Galena announced. "You see—everything was all right." She walked across the room to throw open the curtains. "And what a beautiful day you will have for your trip!" She turned back to Katherine. "You are most fortunate, Ekaterina. I was wed to an older man, so I can say it."

It was all too new for her to discuss Alexei now. Seizing on a chance to turn his sister away from that, Katherine asked, "But did you not love him?"

The woman shrugged. "He was pleasant enough, but it was an arranged marriage. My mother and father decided it was time I left Domnya, and it was done."

"How awful for you."

"Well, they are both dead, and now I am returned to Domnya," Galena observed philosophically.

"Don't you think you could remarry someday? I should not like to think that we—that Alexei and I—kept you from your own happiness," Kate murmured.

"Never. Alexei—no—*you* and Lexy have need of me, *ma petite*. And it is so good to be needed," she added smoothly.

"But you are not old, Lena," Kate protested. "And you are quite beautiful!"

"I am two and thirty, Ekaterina, but that is not the problem." She smiled. "It is so kind of you to say I am beautiful, but a man would have more than that in a wife.''

''And you are so kind!''

Galena sobered abruptly. ''Ah, Ekaterina, I would that I could find a good husband, but he would want children, and that I could not give him.'' Seeing that Katherine stared, she nodded. ''I lost one babe, little one, and the doctors despaired of my life. They did everything—the leeches on my stomach to draw out the poison, purges—everything. And now they tell me there are too many scars inside. I cannot have another,'' she said sadly. She forced a weak smile and took Katherine's hand. ''But you, Ekaterina—you will not mind that Aunt Galena loves your children, will you?''

''No, of course not. I will always need you at Domnya,'' Kate answered sincerely. ''Indeed, but I should not know what to do without you. I mean, the language—the customs—everything! Galena, I shall know nothing!''

''Ah, Ekaterina.'' The Russian woman embraced her warmly, then held her away to look into her face. ''Together we will make Alexei very happy. And in turn, he and I will make you very happy. It is a good arrangement—no?''

''Yes.''

''I will teach you everything, *ma petite*,'' Galena promised. ''And Lexy will see that you want for nothing. You are happy—no?''

''Yes—yes, I am.''

''Good. And now we must make you presentable for your wedding trip, *n'est-ce pas*?'' Releasing Katherine, she walked around her. ''Ah, yes—very good. You look very well today. Some powder, a little rouge—and a few curls at the side of the bonnet—yes, it is good.''

''As Mama cannot spare Peg, I know not what I shall do when we are in Leicestershire,'' Katherine said, sitting down before her mirror. ''He will be displeased—I know it. He said he cannot abide a wreck, and that a countess must do nothing for herself.''

"In Russia. Here he cannot expect everything, I think. But if you wish, I will speak to him."

"I shall always be plain, you know."

"But it is what Lexy thinks of you that matters, *ma petite*—not the lies of a mirror. Pah! What is that? Silvered glass, that is all."

As Galena leaned over her to reach for the powder box, Katherine could smell the warm scent of sandalwood mingled with something else. There was something so very comforting about Alexei's sister—something that told her not to be afraid of everything. It was as though God had sent her a guardian angel.

It had been a pleasant, quiet week, and she did not want it to end. She told herself she would remember forever the morning mists, the days spent in walking or riding about the countryside, the trips to visit the castle where Mary Queen of Scots had been held, and the tour of Bosworth Field, where the Wars of the Roses had finally ended. Now she would be going back to London a married lady.

On this, their last morning in Leicestershire, she lay beside Alexei, savoring the sound of his even breathing. She did not want to move for fear of waking him. They would be leaving, returning first to Monk's End for Galena, then to London, where he would depart for Vienna without her. And despite the promise of more new gowns and some jewels, the fact that he would be going on still disappointed her.

As though thoughts could waken, he stirred slightly, then opened his eyes. Despite her welcoming smile, he yawned widely, then frowned.

"What time is it?"

"Does it matter?" she asked softly, hoping he meant to take her into his arms.

But instead, he rolled away to sit on the edge of the bed, his back to her. Reaching for his discarded watch on the table, he opened it.

"*Dyevyat*," he muttered.

"What?"

"Nine."

Reluctantly, she sat up. Leaning her head against his

back, she murmured, "Do we have to leave? Could we not stay one last day?"

"No. I will be overlate in returning to Alexander's side already, Ekaterina, and he will not be pleased." He pulled away, disappointing her again, and stood up. Turning back to her, he smiled wryly. "For all that he is the liberator here, you must remember he is the autocrat at home."

She lay back, watching dreamily as he dressed, thinking he must surely be the handsomest man on earth. And she the most fortunate female.

"You had best get up, if we are to reach Monk's End by nightfall," he said, his voice muffled in his shirt. When she did not move, he became impatient. "Come on—we have not all the day."

"No, I suppose not."

She sighed and rose to find her clothes. The hunting box was staffed only by a couple Harry employed to watch the place, and it was obvious the woman had never been a lady's maid. Katherine's dress was merely draped over a chair, her undergarments laid on top.

Seeing that he was already nearly ready, she dressed quickly, then moved to the small dressing table to make herself presentable. As she sat down, Alexei left the room, saying he hoped Mrs. Crowe meant to fix a decent breakfast.

Taking a cloth from the washstand beside her, Katherine wet it and began to wash her face. She stopped to study her reflection in the mirror. It was the same face she'd always seen, but now it did not matter so much that she was plain. She could accept it, for she had Alexei.

"His lordship's a-wanting his tea with his eggs, Lady Volsky," Mrs. Crowe announced from the open door. "Would ye be having the same—or would ye prefer a cup o' chocolate?"

"Tea will be fine, thank you. I don't think they drink coffee in Russia."

"Humph!" The woman sniffed her usual morning disapproval. "I'll warrant there's a great deal they don't do there. If I was to have it, he'd be eating caviar on his toast, he says. Well, when yer ready, my lady, I'll have breakfast awaiting ye.''

My lady. *Lady Volsky.* Even the sound of it made Katherine's heart leap. A month ago—three weeks even—if any had said she would be wed to a handsome Russian count, if any had said she would even be betrothed to anyone, she would have been the first to laugh. But it had happened. She was Katherine, Countess Volsky, and soon she would be on her way to a new life in Russia.

For a moment, that gave her pause. There was so much she did not know about her future home. There was so much she did not know of her new family. So much that Alexei had not yet told her. So much that she'd forgotten to ask. What was Domnya like? All he'd ever told her was that it was a grand estate beside the Moskva River; "within a day's ride of Moskva itself.''

Moskva. The Russian word for Moscow. There was so much to learn that the task seemed nearly insurmountable. New language. New customs. New people. New places. But she would do it. She would learn whatever was necessary to please Alexei.

"You are not ready, *daragaya*?''

"Uh—yes.'' She half turned to look up at him and smiled ruefully. "I was merely woolgathering.''

"Woolgathering? In here?''

"An expression, Lexy. Daydreaming.'' As his brow furrowed, she explained further. "Thinking of you, I'm afraid—and of all I will need to know before I am truly mistress of Domnya.''

He came to stand behind her, putting his hands on her shoulders. "Ekaterina, it pleases me that you would learn, but you must not think you have to know everything. You will always have Galena to help you.''

"Always? Always is a very long time—what if someday she should find someone and wish to marry?''

His hands tightened perceptibly. "You need not worry—Lena does not leave Domnya.''

"But if—''

"She does not leave Domnya,'' he repeated definitely.

"It is her home." Abruptly, he released her shoulders and stepped back. "Come—the food is getting cold."

The carriage wheels bounced over the rough road, jostling Katherine, but Alexei did not seem to notice. Instead, he stared out the window at the countryside, saying nothing, as though he were lost in his own thoughts. Then he spoke suddenly, startling her.

"I do not like it that Townsend goes with you to St. Petersburg, Ekaterina."

"Because of Galena?"

"Yes. And because of Gregori Sherkov."

She started to remind him that she'd tried to warn him, but didn't. "She will not be alone—I will be there. Besides, he says he does not intend to dangle after anyone," she recalled.

"Do you believe him?"

"No," she admitted truthfully. "It seems as though scandal follows him everywhere."

He leaned across the seat to possess her hands as his eyes met hers. "In Russia, Galena will take care of you, Ekaterina. I would have you do the same for her on the voyage. Promise me you will watch him for me."

"All right."

"And you must not tell Lena." He let go and sat back.

"Why do you not speak of this to Galena?"

"Galena is—" He paused, seeking his words carefully, then went on, "Galena believes she can meddle in the affairs of others, and that there will be no price to pay. Sometimes she believes herself more clever than those around her."

He fell silent, and his face was distant for a time, making her feel as though she were already alone. In two days he would be on the way to Vienna, and she did not know how she could stand it. Finally, she turned her thoughts forward to Domnya. "What are they like? The rest of your family, I mean."

He shrugged. "They are a family—what is there to say? Galena will—"

"But I want you to tell me. I want you to tell me about

everything—about the Volskys—Domnya—Russia." She looked down at her lap. "I would see it all from your eyes, Lexy."

"Everything?" A black eyebrow rose. "Ekaterina, we have not the time to tell everything."

"Alexei, I will know nothing."

Sighing, he relented. "We can begin, I suppose. There are not that many Volskys, Ekaterina. There is Galena, who is the eldest, then myself, followed by two brothers and two sisters. You will meet them, but you do not need to concern yourself with whether they like you or not. Viktor is still in school in Moscow, and therefore he is still dependent on my goodwill, so he will not trouble you. Anya is married to Prince Golachev and lives a great distance from Domnya, and Tatiana lives most of the year at a boarding school in Novgorod noted for its discipline."

"And the other brother? You have left out one, I think," she murmured.

"And Paul." He sighed again, this time heavily, then looked away. "Nothing will please Paul, I am afraid."

"Why?"

"Where do I begin? In my country, a firstborn son can be set aside. We *boyars* have long resisted your way of inheritance, you see. And Paul—Paul believes he was— and is—the more deserving son. It is a bitter disappointment to him that our father gave him Omborosloe rather than Domnya. And it was I who wished him to have that even. Papa would have seen him in the army."

She nodded. "And he is jealous of you."

"Yes. And it does not help that Olga Vladimovna prefers Domnya also."

"Olga?"

"His wife. She is Prince Narransky's younger daughter, and the Narranskys have always intrigued—for centuries they have plotted to advance themselves. She is too much like her family, I am afraid." Settling his shoulders as though he had unloaded an oppressive thought, he forced a smile that did not warm his eyes. "What else would you know, Ekaterina?"

"Domnya must be quite beautiful."

"It is the greatest of the Volsky estates," he declared proudly. "Not the prettiest, I suppose, but the greatest. Most of my serfs belong there. And the palace itself was given my grandfather by the Empress Ekaterina." He paused, and his smile broadened. "For his services. She was always generous to her lovers, and there were many of them. In this case, the estate was near Moscow rather than St. Petersburg—quite obviously a parting gift, for it took him away from her. But he did not complain. She was getting old and was not nearly so attractive to him as his own wife."

"The palace," she echoed hollowly, scarce having heard the rest.

He nodded. "Not nearly so large as the Sheremetievs', of course, but quite respectable. There are one hundred and seventeen or twenty-nine rooms, depending on how they are counted—not including the guest houses."

"Alexei! You jest, of course!"

"You think you wed a poor count, Ekaterina?" he asked softly. "Your sons, *daragaya,* will be heir to much. And your daughters can marry into the best families in all of Russia."

"Well, I did not think you poor, of course, for Harry said the settlements were generous, but—"

"I am a generous man."

She fell silent at that. Trying to assimilate what he'd told her, she could only think of the enormity of his house. He'd not only made her a countess, but she would be a rich woman in Russia, she would be mistress to more than she could begin to comprehend. And he'd chosen her.

"Something is the matter?"

"No, of course not," she answered slowly. "But if your family can marry princesses, it is a wonder that you chose a mere English baron's sister."

"The mind does not always rule the heart," he murmured.

His words sent her spirits soaring. As improbable, as

impossible as it seemed, he'd truly wanted *her.* Indeed, he'd all but said he loved her.

"You are disappointed, Ekaterina?"

"Oh, Lexy—no!" Her mouth twisted as she fought the urge to cry from her happiness. "I think I must surely be the most fortunate of females!"

"I hope you will always believe that," he responded soberly. "I hope we will make you happy at Domnya."

October 22, 1814

The salt air was bitterly cold as Katherine walked the *Marskoy Zvyizda*'s deck. The Sea Star, as Galena had explained the name, was old, dating back to the early years of Catherine the Great's reign, and the sails were heavily patched, showing splotches of white and gray against the dingy, yellowed canvas. But when Townsend had preferred to wait at Helsinki for another, somewhat better ship, Galena would not hear of it. Alexei was already in St. Petersburg, she said, and he would expect them.

Crossing her arms against her fur-trimmed pelisse, Katherine stared into the churning gray water below. "It is going to storm," the captain had warned them, "and this time of year, the Baltic can be treacherous because it is so shallow." It looked as though he was right—already heavy, whitecapped waves rolled in the distance, and the sky was a mass of thick, ominous clouds. A lone tern swooped in the distance, then was gone, leaving the ship in seeming isolation, one exceedingly small island of wood and canvas bobbing on an increasingly turbulent sea.

It was all of a piece, Katherine reflected wearily, for she'd been abed, unable to eat, for most of the journey. Galena had said that it would not be long ere the awful sickness passed, that it did not usually last much beyond the fourth month. That gave her perhaps another three or four weeks, and Katherine did not know if she could stand it. She breathed deeply of the raw air, hoping it could somehow stay the queasiness that threatened again. She knew if she went below, it would only be a matter of minutes before she had her head over the basin. Only air and a lack of food seemed to help.

"I'd begun to think you had died."

Still holding the rail, she half turned to face Bellamy Townsend. "What an awful thing to say," she muttered hostilely.

The wind ruffled his blond hair, making him look younger, and his gray eyes reflected the sky. "Well," he murmured, "it was either that or the conclusion that you had taken me in such dislike, you had given up eating to avoid me."

"I was ill—surely Galena told you that."

Even as she said it, she felt a pang of guilt, for she knew she'd failed to keep her promise to Alexei. Whenever Galena had come down, she'd tried to bolster Katherine's sagging spirits with everything Bell said or did.

He leaned on the rail beside her. "Actually, she did, but I've missed your tart tongue. Sea travel is deuced boring, you know."

"Yes, it is," she agreed readily enough.

He squinted at her, then nodded. "You do look as though you have lost weight rather than gained it. And you had none to spare in the first place."

She was tired and out of sorts. "Since she has told you nearly everything else, it surprises me she has not explained I am increasing," she muttered.

"Actually, she did. She seems quite pleased for you."

"Inordinately so."

"And you are not?"

"I am getting used to the notion."

"Blue-deviled?"

"No," she lied. "Why would you think that?"

"It shows."

For a moment, she looked at him, then returned her attention to the sea below. "Galena is very kind, but I have missed Alexei," she admitted, sighing. "Despite the fact I am increasing, it is still difficult to think of myself as a married lady when I have scarce seen my husband. She bit her lower lip, then shook her head.

"Very soon, I shall be all ugly and misshapen, you know, and he will scarce be able to remember me as I was."

"Well, I have never had a wife," he answered, "but if I cared enough to get myself leg-shackled, I don't think it would bother me."

"You don't think, but you do not know." She pushed away from the rail. "And you probably have already sired a dozen."

"None that anyone's laid at my doorstep."

"How fortunate for you that so many of your conquests have complaisant husbands. Except Longford—and Hopewell, of course."

"Diana's brat wasn't mine, and Fanny is lying."

"And yet you are running—you ran then, and you run now, Bell. Papa was always used to say that fewer people doubt when you stay to face the consequences of what you have done."

"Is this a lecture? If so, I don't need one."

"Papa would have said it was cowardice to run."

She was a queer little creature, usually shy in company, but in the years he'd known her, always ready to rip up at him. Ever since that encounter with her governess, he'd been in and out of her black books, usually out.

"Do you ever really care about anyone?" she asked him finally.

"Occasionally—but not often," he admitted.

"People say you are like Byron. I think they are possibly right."

That brought a lift to his brow. "Perhaps with females, but I have never consorted with men. Harry and I are friends only, I assure you."

"I did not mean any such thing, and well you know it," she retorted. "I was merely likening Fanny Hopewell to Caro Lamb."

"Well, you are wrong, in any event."

"You use foolish females, Bell—you use them."

"And they use me."

"Well, it is disgusting. How can a man wish to seduce so many women? It is as though the intimacy he seeks is about as meaningful as a handshake."

His expression remained blandly amiable, but his jaw tightened. "Is this tirade because I kissed you, Kate? If so, you are wide of the mark. I have never—I repeat, never—had the least interest in you."

"Of course not! But I would that you left Galena alone! There—I have said it! Now, if you will pardon me—"

"I told you—"

"Despite what you said that night after the opera, I think you are seeking to entertain yourself until you are reunited with Sofia Sherkova," she said tartly. "Marshal Sherkov's *wife*, to be precise."

"Now that, my dear Lady Volsky, is none of your affair."

"Alexei will not like the attention you are giving Galena, my lord."

"We are friends merely."

"Friendship between a man like yourself and any female is remarked. Neither Alexei nor I would see Galena's reputation harmed."

"Acquit me. I have done nothing to you or to Madame Malenkov to warrant this." He bit off each word precisely. "If I have been pleasant to you, Kate, let me assure you the notion was Harry's. I promised him I would see you safely to St. Petersburg." With that, he pushed off from the rail. "Good day, Lady Volsky."

She felt chastened. No matter what he did, for her own sake, she ought to learn to be civil. And for all that Alexei would protect her, Galena was a widow who ought to know a seasoned rake when she saw one.

"Wait!"

He half swung around. "I don't think so."

"Please—I ought to beg your pardon."

"Ought to?" His eyebrow lifted. "Can this be half an apology, Kate?"

"Yes." She wet her wind-dried lips with her tongue, then looked at the deck. "I have no right to censure you, my lord—none at all. Aside from Galena, nothing you have ever done is any of my concern."

"Not even your Miss Beckwood?"

"I don't know. She was very foolish, wasn't she? And so very lonely—I expect she threw herself at your head."

She raised her eyes to his. "But you trespassed on my father's welcome, you know. You were a guest in his house, and that seems almost as wrong as the other."

"I sense your apology disappearing," he chided.

"At least I tried to say it. I cannot help it that I do not approve of the way you live your life. It is possible to like a person, and yet despise what he does, isn't it?"

His anger gone, he returned to the rail. "I suppose the truth is painful sometimes. And I owe you an apology also—I should not have kissed you in London. It was boorish of me, I'm afraid."

"I had quite forgotten that," she lied.

"Now I truly am wounded," he murmured, smiling. "You know, you are an odd sort of female—a sparrow with lion's teeth, so to speak."

"I am sorry. I usually am only like this to Harry."

"No wonder he left home."

"Harry left because of Mama, if you would have the truth. She got a maggot in her brain that he ought to offer for Miss Pinkston, and they quarreled half a year over it."

His brow creased for a moment. "Miss Pinkston. I don't—"

"It was an age ago—years, in fact."

"Oh—*that* Miss Pinkston."

"I collect you recall her."

"Horse-faced with bags full of money."

She bristled. "Why is it that supposed gentlemen always must describe a female by her looks? You could have said 'the wealthy Miss Pinkston,' you know."

"Why is it supposed ladies always describe a man by his money?" he countered. "Because," he answered himself, "a man is a fortune hunter for mentioning it, while a woman is forgiven the same greed, thank you."

"Well, anyway, Harry has repaired his fortune another way."

"And he's been deuced lucky at it."

"You would think after Papa—" She stopped, unable to finish her thought. "That is, you would think he would know luck to be rather fickle, wouldn't you?"

"It has been to me."

"You?" she scoffed. "You have everything, and you did not have to make the least push to gain any of it."

"But it couldn't buy me what I wanted," he said bitterly. Once again, he left the rail. "I think I shall go down—and I'd advise the same for you. According to Captain Ryshuskin, it is going to storm—and by the feel of that wind, it may even sleet."

Sighing, she turned her thoughts to Alexei. His last letter had said he would be at St. Petersburg waiting for her, that once she had been presented formally, they would go to Moscow, where the metropolitan there would recognize his marriage to her. But she would have to nominally embrace the Orthodox faith. Like the czarinas, Empress Elisaveta Alekseevna, who had been Princess Louisa of Baden—or the Dowager Empress Maria Feodorovna, who had been Princess Sophia Dorothea of Wurttemburg—she would have to take a Russian name.

It was silly of her, she supposed, but she did not wish to deny everything from her childhood. Indeed, but the whole matter seemed rather silly, particularly since she had been born not a royal princess, but merely plain Miss Winstead of Monk's End.

In this case, Galena had supported her brother. There must be no impediment to the legitimacy of the child Katherine carried, she insisted. It was as though both of them had centered all their dynastic ambitions in her, and to be worthy, she must become as Russian as they were. No, that was not entirely true, Katherine conceded—what counted was that she must *appear* to become Russian before the church and state. At home, they said, she could be anything she wished. In fact, Galena said she did not have to learn the language if she did not want to.

"Russian," Galena had declared, "is much more difficult than the English to understand. And so many of us speak French, anyway."

"Lady Volsky!" someone shouted. When she turned around, a man pointed downward, calling out, *"Vneess! Vneess! Bistryeye!"* As she did not move, he caught her arm, looking up. *"Boorya!"*

The thick clouds had blackened, giving the sky the look of evening rather than midday. And as if by the man's direction, the wind blew harder, carrying with it a hail of frozen rain. As the first hard drops hit her face, Katherine needed no further urging. Above her, the aged sails flapped wildly, nearly drowning out the shouts of those who tried to lash them against the weathered spars. The masts, buffeted by a strong blast, groaned beneath the weight of the rigging.

The Russian sailor caught her arm, pulling her toward the shelter of the stairs. As they reached them, the door banged shut under the force of the now howling wind. The sleet came down in sheets, blinding her, stinging her face, as the gale forced her against the door. The sailor struggled to pull it open, then pushed her inside.

The door hit her, sending her reeling down the darkened steps into the narrow passage. The wooden floor beneath her feet creaked and yawed, rolling her first against one wall, then the other. She reeled like a sot and tried to hold on, while the ship rose and fell as it strained to ride the rising waves of the storm. She slipped, falling against a cabin door, and it gave, sending her sprawling inside. A lantern swung crazily from the wall, then went out, leaving the room in utter blackness, and Katherine heard Bellamy Townsend curse.

Struggling to regain her footing, she clung to the wall as the floor rocked beneath her. Then she felt arms about her, pulling her away, and, as the ship listed suddenly, Townsend sprawled over her. He caught the door hinge and held on, his weight pinning her beneath him. She flailed wildly, trying to right herself.

"Lie still—or you will hurt yourself! You cannot walk!"

Her stomach dropped with a wave, then rose, seemingly toward her mouth. "I'm going to be sick!" she shouted.

"Not now! For God's sake, not now!" Nonetheless, he stumbled to his feet and lurched for the basin, which had slid beneath a table.

He was too late. She barely had time to sit before the

wave of nausea hit her. She tried to swallow as her whole body went wet from the sickness, but it was no use. The pitifully few bits of bread and cheese she'd managed to eat earlier spilled onto the floor.

"Oh, God," he muttered, thrusting the bowl beneath her face. He sank to sit beside her and braced her heaving shoulders. "Come on, Kate, you are all right—you are all right."

Finally, there was nothing more, and she stopped. She sat there, gulping for air, feeling utterly mortified. Suddenly, the ship pitched wildly again, then there was a loud noise, and it felt as though the whole vessel meant to roll onto its side. Terrified, Katherine threw all modesty to the wind and clung to him.

"We're going to die!" she cried. "We're going to sink!"

"Don't be silly!" he yelled, his voice scarcely recognizable. Even in the darkness, she could see her terror reflected in his eyes. One of his hands held the door frame, and his other arm was wrapped tightly around her.

She began to pray, unable to hear her own words as she repeated them over and over. Above, a cabinet door flew open, spilling clothes and books onto the floor. He buried his head in her shoulder and held on, wincing as a sconce chimney shattered over him.

"Are we aground? Are we taking water?" she cried.

"How the hell would I know?" he shouted at her. "I don't think so," he added, without much conviction. But the ship rose again to ride a wave, and he exhaled his relief. "We're all right, Kate. It's just a devilish bad storm."

She could hear the rigging creak and groan in the wind, but she shared a sense of survival. Looking down, she saw the mess on the floor and basin. "I'm sorry," she mumbled, embarrassed.

"It is all right—I've been weasel-bit a few times. Once I even woke up lying in the stuff." He dropped his arm from her shoulder. "Are you all right?"

"I think so."

They sat, listening to the howling wind, feeling the rise and fall of each heavy swell. Loose papers spread across the cabin floor, then collected before sliding again. Two small benches and the table were overturned, and everything not secured was scattered.

Katherine shuddered. "I am never sailing anywhere again," she declared with conviction.

"Ekaterina! Ekaterina! *Gdye tebya?*" Galena's frantic voice carried over the wind. *Ekaterina!*"

"Oh, lud," Katherine groaned. "What will she think?"

"If she sees the basin, she'll acquit me," Bell answered.

There was a loud thumping in the narrow passage outside, then the Russian woman staggered in, lantern held high. "Oh, Ekaterina, merciful God, but you are safe! When you did not come down—and that Maria!" She spat out the maid's name with disgust. "Well, she was useless! She would not look for you."

"I am all right."

"The storm—it is terrible!" Galena nearly lost her balance and had to grab for a wall. "And the ice—it is everywhere! I was afraid when you did not come down that you had gone overboard."

"You went up? Galena!"

"For you and the babe, I do anything. But I am assured the damage is not significant. Someone said we scraped something," she added breathlessly. "*Cher* Bellamy, help me, will you?"

Townsend managed to get the lantern and hang it on a hook as the Russian woman staggered. Sinking to the floor, she held onto Katherine. The hem of her skirt narrowly missed the basin. "Oh, *ma pauvre enfant*," she murmured. "You have the sickness again?"

"This time, I think I was seasick."

"I do not doubt it, but the worst, it is over. Still, I am told the sea will not calm for hours. I think, Ekaterina, we should have you lie down in our cabin."

"Yes, of course." With an effort, Katherine stood on shaking limbs and held onto her sister-in-law for balance.

Turning back to Bell, she managed low, "I thank you for your prompt assistance."

Murmuring soothing words in Russian, Galena propelled Katherine to the cabin they shared. In one corner of the room, the maid still huddled.

"Get up."

The Russian girl shook uncontrollably. *"Pazhaloosta—ya—"*

"Glupeya dyevooshka!" Galena snapped impatiently. "It is over, I tell you! You will help me get Ekaterina Ivanova to bed—now!"

"I can manage," Katherine protested. "Besides, I don't—"

"Nyet. We do not care for ourselves in Russia." Gesturing toward the maid again, Galena ordered imperiously, *"Tyepyer!"*

"Da, gaspazha." The girl rose slowly, her eyes round in her colorless face.

"Leave her be. She is still frightened."

"Nyet. Maria—"

"Da."

Satisfied, Galena turned her attention to Katherine. "We must take care of our little mother, *ma petite.* The future of Domnya is in you."

Without removing her gown or her shoes, Kate dropped to her bed, where she clung to the mattress as the floor beneath them went up and down, up and down. Closing her eyes, she tried not to think of the movement. Never again, not under any circumstances, was she going to sea.

Galena sat at her feet. "I hope you are not still frightened, Ekaterina. It would not be good for the babe."

"No."

"That Captain Ryshuskin said he would inform us," the woman recalled irritably, "and we do not hear from him. Maria! I will send her up to ask that he attend me."

"I should rather have him on the bridge."

"Pah. He does not ignore Galena Petrovna, I tell you. Lexy will have his head for it."

"Lena, I think I am going to be sick again."

"Ah, Ekaterina." Galena rose and leaned over to smooth Kate's hair. "What are we going to do? If you cannot keep your food down, the babe will be poor—and Lexy will say I have brought him home a little twig. Try to keep it down—for Lena, you must try."

"I am," Kate whispered. Then, "I cannot."

"Maria!" Galena barked. *"Syaychass!"*

"Da, dahma." The girl came back to fetch the bowl, sitting it on the floor beside the bed.

Leaning over the side, Katherine retched, bringing up naught but bile as Alexei's sister watched. Finally, she lay back, utterly exhausted.

"Everything will be better when we are at Domnya, Ekaterina," Galena promised her.

Kate closed her eyes again. No, everything would be better when she saw Alexei. Everything would be better when she had him to hold her. To tell her he was glad about the child.

Not even the ground at Helsinki had looked as welcoming as the docks of St. Petersburg. Katherine saw them in the distance, and for the first time since she'd left England, her heart actually leapt. Her hands tightly clinging to the ship's rail, she stared at the tiny figures that dotted the piers, trying to see Alexei.

Beside her, Galena said, "It is beautiful—*n'est-ce pas*?" Drawing in a deep breath, she savored it. "It is Russia," she announced proudly.

Russia. Until now it had been but a place in Katherine's imagination. Now it would be her home. But it looked so different from what she had expected. Onion-shaped domes and gold-tipped spires dotted the skyline, giving it a decidedly foreign appearance. And as the ship closed with the land, she could see that the city encompassed several islands.

Galena followed her gaze and nodded as though she knew the younger woman's thoughts. "*Da*. You can see the Cathedral of St. Peter and Paul—the one with the straight golden spire—on Zayachy Island. It is the tallest building in all of St. Petersburg, and Peter the Great is buried there. Beneath it, although you cannot yet see it, lies the Peter and Paul Fortress. It was to have been used to defend us against the Swedes, but now it is a very bad prison."

"Like Newgate," Katherine murmured.

"Not like Newgate at all," Galena insisted firmly. "It is the worst place the czar's enemies can go—worse even than Siberia. If they come out at all, they are usually made insane by the experience." She shrugged. "But

none of the Volskys have ever gone there, I thank God.''
She caught Katherine's arm, directing her attention else-
where. ''You think you see the sea, but now it is the Neva
River, and we will debark there—on the south island.''

The younger woman nodded. ''It is much like the Sev-
ern—so wide where it comes into the sea.''

It seemed as though the ship slowed to a snail's crawl,
making minutes feel like hours as Katherine scanned a
group of waving men eagerly. And she thought she saw
Alexei.

''Look—there he is!''

''Who?''

''Lexy!'' Katherine began waving her handkerchief at
him.

But Galena caught her hand, pulling it down. ''It is
unseemly, Ekaterina,'' she said sternly. ''And that is most
definitely not Lexy. He does not come to the docks like a
common person.'' Releasing Katherine, she added more
kindly, ''He will await us at the Winter Palace, where we
shall be guests of the czar until we leave for Domnya.''

''But—''

''A state carriage will be sent for us, Ekaterina, and
soon you will see him. It is an honor to be at the Winter
Palace.''

''Oh.'' It was difficult to hide her disappointment in
the face of Galena's pride. ''I thought—that is, I expected
he would wish to meet us,'' Katherine managed lamely.

''And he does. Come—not a long face, *ma petite*. You
are the Countess Volsky, and there will be much curiosity. You must not betray his confidence in you.'' When
Katherine said nothing, Galena patted her hand. ''But do
not despair, for I will guide you. There are many in-
trigues in Russia, Ekaterina.''

Bellamy Townsend joined them. ''St. Petersburg,'' he
said softly as he leaned on the rail. ''Impressive.''

''But of course.''

''Are you coming to the Winter Palace also?'' Katherine asked him.

''Alas, no.'' His mouth quirked downward, twisting
his smile wryly. ''I'm afraid I am unworthy of such ex-

alted company, Lady Volsky. But I have been invited to view the city's defenses with Marshal Sherkov, as he has been kind enough to offer me his hospitality.

Galena frowned. "You will be most careful, Bellamy. Gregori Mikhailovich is—" She hesitated for emphasis, then declared, "—a most *dangerous* enemy. If he should even suspect that you—well, you would not leave Russia alive, my friend."

"Madame Malenkov, you regard a newly prudent man," he assured her. "You are better advised to address your warning to Madame Sherkov."

"And so I shall. But you must come to Domnya also, I think, and perhaps he will not wonder quite so much."

"I should be honored."

Knowing full well that Alexei would not be pleased, Katherine demurred, "Galena, I don't think—"

"Nonsense. But of course he must come to visit us. Listen, *ma petite*—there will come a time when you will long for an English voice at Domnya."

"Alexei—"

"Alexei Petrovich will not mind if I invite your countryman, Ekaterina."

Katherine knew better, but she held her tongue. Alexei could guard his sister himself now.

Never in all of her life had she seen such a carriage. The dark red lacquer glistened as though it were wet, and the gold trim shone in the afternoon sun. On the doors, ornate crests had been carved and gilded in relief. And in front, a team of four white horses, their tails braided with gold, stamped restlessly beneath ornate harnesses. Two coachmen, both in dark red trimmed with gold braid, stood at attention on either side, while a third offered Galena a white-gloved hand.

Alexei's sister mounted the carriage step without so much as a glance or word to the man who helped her. Katherine forced a smile and mumbled her thanks to him as she was thrust into the coach. Galena looked displeased.

"*Dastachna*—enough. You are Countess Volsky, and therefore you must not be free with your kindnesses."

"He was good enough to give me his hand," Katherine retorted, stung by the cold, clipped tone in her sister-in-law's voice. She turned to the window. "Where is Maria?"

"She will ride in the cart."

Silence descended between them as the carriage began to roll, then picked up speed, weaving through crowded streets. Katherine leaned forward to look at the strange, majestic palaces and public buildings. Peter the Great's city. Forgetting her pique with Galena, she took it all in, marveling at the visual feast of it.

"That is the Winter Palace."

Katherine stared at a seeming wall of windows that did not appear to end. "Where?"

"We are passing it—it goes on nearly forever, you will think, for there are more than a thousand rooms. It is said to be an English mile in length."

"This?"

"Yes. The Empress Elisaveta built it for herself more than one hundred and fifty years ago, *cherie*. But the inside was redone by the Empress Ekaterina in the fabulous style. I do not think there is anything to compare in England."

"If there is, I have not seen it," the younger woman admitted.

"It shames Versailles," Galena declared.

Finally, the carriage slowed, then halted before the immense building. As Katherine watched, the coachmen approached an Imperial guardsman, apparently explaining that she and Galena were to be guests. Most of the words she could not understand, but she heard "Malenkova" and "Volskaya" quite clearly. Papers were presented, examined, and returned. Then the carriage door was opened, and the coachman mumbled something apologetically.

"*Doorak!*" Galena told him furiously. "*Ideeot!* What is the delay?"

"*Neechevo, dahma.*"

Galena threw up her hands in disgust. "I am served by imbeciles, Ekaterina—imbeciles!" She turned to look at the palace, discovering his error. "We are at the wrong entrance!"

The fellow paled and stammered something, but Alexei's sister was not mollified.

"We will enter here, and a chair will be sent for us," she said sourly. "And Alexei Petrovich will punish this fool."

After another discussion with the guards, two pole chairs were brought out, and Katherine and Galena handed into them. It almost reminded Kate of Bath, but the surroundings were far more sumptuous. As the chairs bobbed on the shoulders of the bearers, they were carried through splendors beyond Katherine's imagination—long, arched marble corridors, ornately vaulted and gilded rooms, exquisite portrait galleries—all of it overwhelming, sating to the eyes.

Beside them, the hard heels of the guards clicked loudly, resonating, echoing through seemingly cavernous halls. Finally, they stopped, and a liveried servant hastened to open heavy, carved doors. A group of military officers turned at the sound, and Kate saw Alexei. He excused himself from his companions and made his way across the exquisitely tiled floor to her, stopping first to say something to Galena, followed by sharp words that sent the servant scurrying from the room. Swallowing her disappointment, Katherine waited as Galena was helped from her chair. Alexei kissed his sister's cheeks.

Then he turned to Katherine and barked something to her bearers. She was set down hurriedly, and the side door opened. As she leaned out, her husband's strong hands caught her elbows, and for a moment, she thought he meant to embrace her. But he merely steadied her as she stepped from the chair, then he stepped back.

"Galena tells me you have been ill" were his first words to her. "You must take care of yourself now."

"It will pass," she promised him.

"I hope so. How can you bear a babe when you are so thin?"

It seemed as though she faced a stranger. She wiped suddenly damp palms against the wrinkled skirt of her traveling dress and waited, ill at ease, as his gaze moved over her. Finally, he offered her his arm, and when she took it, he started back to the group he'd left.

"*Maya zhena,*" he announced. "Ekaterina Ivanova."

There were a few curious stares, followed by nods, then he presented each of them to her. As he named them, each one clicked his heels together and bowed over her hand.

"Petr Andreivich, Count Steremsky. Feodor Gregorivich, Prince Danshekin. Stephan Zacharavich, Count Bashtir. Yuri Aseikov. Igor Dmetreievich, Prince Pahlin."

To each, she smiled and did as Galena had schooled her, saying, "*Raht pazna-komitsa*" politely. They exchanged amused glances, then Prince Pahlin told her, "We are pleased to meet Ekaterina Ivanova also," in English. His gaze moved to Alexei's sister, who stood behind her. "You enjoyed a pleasant voyage, Galena Petrovna?"

"*Nyet.* It was terrible."

"A pity."

"We were nearly shipwrecked. And Ekaterina Ivanova is not a sailor."

As she stood there, the conversation became a mix of English and Russian, but it did not seem to matter. To Katherine, it was obvious that there was little difference between polite inanities in England and Russia. Finally, to her relief, Alexei took her arm again, and they moved on.

"You will need to make yourself presentable, Ekaterina," he murmured. "You will go with Galena." He nodded to one of the servants who hovered nearby. "He will show you the way."

It was scarcely a lovers' reunion. She managed to swallow her disappointment again. "When will I see you?" she asked.

"I will be up to dress for dinner." He patted her arm as though she were a child. "Go on with Lena, *ma petite.*"

As they walked behind the uniformed footman, Galena caught Katherine's hand and held it, saying soothingly, "I know, *daragaya,* but when we are at Domnya, he will not be so formal, I promise you. He will make you a good husband." When Katherine said nothing, the Russian woman squeezed her fingers. "Here he is too busy to attend us, so while he conducts his business, you and I will shop. There is so much to buy, Ekaterina."

"I have trunks of clothes."

"The clothes, yes, but you have not the furs, and those you will need. *Bab'e leto* is over, and now we face the winter. Winter at Domnya is cold, very cold," she said definitely. You will need fur hats, fur cloaks, fur muffs— everything—or you will not go outside." She stopped walking for a moment. "Ah, *daragaya,* I know you are lonely for Lexy, but when he is not with us, we shall spend his money—all right?"

"I do not feel like shopping, Lena."

"Ekaterina . . . Ekaterina . . . When you are at Domnya, we will have him all to ourselves," Galena promised. "Come—you must smile," she coaxed. "A man does not like the long face." With her free hand, she reached to pinch Katherine's cheeks together to force the smile. "This is what a man would have, Ekaterina—always. And if he does not get it, he will look elsewhere."

"You think me foolish, don't you?"

"*Mais non, ma petite.* I think you love Lexy—and I will help you keep him. We are allies, Ekaterina—allies. I will tell you how to go on, I promise you."

"If he should turn from me, I could not bear it!" Tears welled in Katherine's eyes. "And—and he does not even seem pleased to see me!"

"Hush, little one." Galena's arms closed around Katherine, holding her. "He is most pleased—I know it. You are merely too tired, that is all. Come—you will lie down before we dress for dinner. And tomorrow we shop."

She awakened to the sound of angry voices, Galena's accusing, Alexei's defensive. And then they faded to a low murmur. Katherine lay there, trying to hear, but everything was said in Russian. Finally, she sat up and reached for her wrapper.

The door opened suddenly, startling her, and he stepped inside. "I did not want to waken you," he said apologetically, approaching the bed. Dropping to his knees beside her, he reached for her hands. "Ah, Ekaterina," he said softly, "what a boor you must think me." His head bent to press his lips in first one of her palms, then the other. "You behold a contrite husband, *daragaya*."

As she looked down on his thick black hair, she could not resist touching it. Her fingers ruffled it as his head rested on her lap, and longing washed over her. "She should not have told you," she managed, her throat nearly too constricted for speech. "I would have gotten over it."

"No. You do not deserve the stranger, Ekaterina," he whispered, his breath warm through the silk that covered her legs. "How do you feel? Does the babe overset you?"

"I am fine now that you are here."

"Good." He rose and began undressing.

In the dim light of an oil lamp, she watched him, trying not to betray her eagerness to be held by him. To her it seemed he moved slowly, deliberately drawing out the exquisite hunger. Then before he removed his pantaloons, he shrugged into his nightshirt, pulling it down over his body, disappointing her. Then she realized he was trying to avoid any awkwardness between them. She laid her wrapper aside and waited.

He blew out the lamp, and as the wick smoked, he came to bed. Lying down beside her, he smoothed her hair. "The babe pleases me, you know."

"I know." She snuggled against him. "Oh, how I have missed you, Lexy," she whispered.

"And I you."

When he still made no move to hold her, she reached to touch his cheek, to trace the fine profile of his jaw. With a boldness she did not feel, she dared to press her lips against his throat. He was very still.

"You do not have to worry that you will hurt our child, Lexy." Even as she said the words, she felt like the veriest hussy. "I love you so much."

He rolled onto his back. "It would not be good tonight."

Humiliated, she felt the blood heat her face. "But why—?"

"Galena—she is in the next room."

"She will hear nothing."

She knew then he did not mean to take her, that he did not want her—after three and one-half months of separation, he did not want to hold her like that. And she wanted to cry. She rolled onto her side, drawing her knees against her, acutely aware of the dampness between her thighs and the ache inside her.

Finally, she could stand it no longer. "Do you love me, Lexy?" she choked out.

"Ekaterina, you are my wife, the mother of my child. How could you doubt such a thing?"

"You have not held me! You have not kissed me!"

"I did when I came in."

"My hands!"

"Shhhhh. Galena will hear you," he cautioned her.

"I don't care! Everything is Galena, isn't it? What about me, Lexy? I have come all the way from England to live with you!"

"Ekaterina, please." He reached to turn her back to him. "What is it you want from me?"

She stared hard at him, trying to read his eyes in the dark. She wanted to cry out that all she wanted was for him to love her, to act as though he were glad to see her, as though he cared. But she could not say it.

"I want," she whispered finally, "the man who married me."

"Ekaterina, I am tired."

Tears trickled down her cheeks and her throat ached too much for speech. He thought her childish, demanding, she supposed.

His hand touched her face lightly, then drew back. "You are crying *daragaya*."

She couldn't answer.

He sighed. "Little one, Lena will kill me if anything should happen to this babe—or to you." When she still said nothing, his hand slid over her hip to her thigh.

She felt her nightgown easing upward, and she sucked in her breath, holding it, waiting, until his fingers touched her there. An almost anguished sob escaped, then was stifled with his mouth. "What Galena does not know will hurt nothing, Ekaterina," he murmured against her lips. "But you must be quiet."

As though he feared discovery, he was quick to roll over her, and then he entered her, thrusting rapidly, and it was as though he held his breath until he was done. When he left her, she felt somehow unclean, as though they'd done something wrong and furtive.

And with that came the shame. There must be something wrong with her, she must be some sort of hussy to want more of him than that. But after three months' absence, she'd wanted him to hold her, to love her.

"Is something the matter, Ekaterina?" he asked finally.

"I don't know."

"You are tired. Perhaps you should go to sleep."

The Russian court had proven to be a den of licentiousness, with Galena forever pointing out who was committing adultery with whom. More than once Katherine had caught admiring, flirtatious glances cast at Lexy, and she had to admit to herself that she was jealous. But always Galena insisted that he would have nothing to do with any of them. Still, Katherine was glad enough to leave St. Petersburg for Moscow.

To pass the long days within the confines of the carriage, Galena began schooling her for her interview with the metropolitan. She must be certain to dispute the ascendancy of the pope in Rome while not dwelling on the Archbishop of Canterbury or the king's position at the head of the Church of England. Doctrinal similarities rather than differences must be stressed. And above all, she must indicate her willingness to attend the Orthodox church.

"It does not matter at all what you are to us, Ekaterina," Galena insisted over and over, "but for your children's legitimacy, you must say you accept our czar's religion. Though," she added, "it is not always certain that Alexander himself is as Orthodox as the church would have him. He has discovered spiritualism and Bible study, you see."

"The Church will ask you to take a Russian name, that is all, Ekaterina," Alexei reassured her. "He will not examine you too closely. Now if you were wed to the czar—"

"Bah. I suspect the Empress Elisaveta cares not a fig for Orthodoxy, Lexy," Galena retorted.

"But she was confirmed, and he was crowned at the Uspenskii Cathedral," he reminded his sister.

"*Da*. But that was *paleetika*. Besides, where is she now? Where is she while Alexander gets bastards of Maria Czetwertskyna?"

"Galena—"

"It is common knowledge," she declared, unchastened by his tone. "Now—where was I? The icons, I think."

At that moment, there were shouts from the roadside, and when Katherine looked out the window, she saw the street of a small village lined with ragged people. One woman held a half-naked child against her breast, using her arms to shield it from the cold. The man beside her stretched out his hands in supplication.

"Beggars!" Galena fairly spat out the word. "If they get in front of the carriage, Lexy, you must tell Nemsky he is not to stop."

"Lena, they look as though they are starving!" Katherine protested. "Surely we—"

"Pah. The serfs, they are always starving," Alexei's sister retorted. "Besides, it is not our responsibility. I think they must belong to Beschertnik."

But Katherine already had dug into her reticule and withdrawn her small purse. Galena covered her hand to stop her. "Ekaterina, you must not."

Turning to Alexei in disbelief, Katherine appealed to him. "But we have so much—and they have not enough clothing for a child. Please, Lexy—I'd give something."

"And they will beg again and again," Galena insisted. "Besides, it would be an insult to Beschertnik. Tell her, Lexy—you must tell her."

He appeared to be studying his hands for a moment, then he turned his palms up helplessly. "I am sorry, Ekaterina, but we cannot interfere."

"Interfere! Lexy, it does not look as though they have food!"

"I am sorry," he repeated.

"You can say I did not know it was an insult," she

argued. "You can blame it on my English blood, Lexy, but I'd still give them something."

Instead, he thumped the roof of the passenger compartment and shouted, *"Pashlee!"* The carriage, which had slowed, picked up speed.

"Lexy!"

"Oospakoytiss!" Galena snapped. "You must calm yourself," she repeated in English. "It does not matter."

"Does not matter!"

Without looking at her, Alexei muttered, "They are serfs."

"They are your countrymen!"

"Ekaterina!" Galena said sharply. "It is done."

"But—"

"Done. There is nothing we could do if Alexei wished it. They are someone else's problem, and I for one do not mean to anger their master."

Finally, Alexei sighed. "Please, Ekaterina, you must not worry over a few hungry serfs."

"In England—"

Alexei straightened in his seat. "You are not in England," he told her coldly. "You must not concern yourself with what you do not understand."

She was helpless, and she knew it. Even if she tried, she could not make herself understood to Alexei's driver. And clearly both her husband and his sister were vexed with her. But she had to try one last time. This time, when she touched his sleeve, she did so gently.

"Please, Lexy—I cannot let anyone—not even a dog—go hungry in this weather. Those people are cold and hungry."

His jaw worked visibly, then hardened. "It is not your place to do anything for them. We are late enough as it is."

"If you must concern yourself, Ekaterina, perhaps you will wish to pray for them," Galena suggested smoothly. "Or when we reach Moscow, you may leave a donation in one of the churches."

"What good will that do?" Katherine asked bitterly.

"It is all we can do. If we stop, there will be a mob, and you would not wish that," the older woman offered reasonably. "It is not safe to stop on a road when we are not escorted by guards. We could be robbed."

Katherine stared out the other window, utterly unconvinced. Finally, as his anger with her ebbed, Alexei exhaled heavily. "Ekaterina," he said more gently, "you will have to realize that we are not like the English. When you are here longer, you will understand."

"Never."

An uncomfortable silence descended, leaving each to his own thoughts. It was a long time before anyone spoke, and then it was Galena.

"We cannot reach Babino by nightfall, Lexy. It will have to be L'uban, don't you think?"

"We will stop at the river, Lena. At least I know of a place that has clean beds."

"*Ya galadna.*" She sighed. "You wish to eat also, no?" she said to Katherine.

"I'm not hungry."

"Well, perhaps when we are arrived."

"Anger fills her stomach," Alexei muttered. "Leave her alone." His eyes moved from Katherine's stiff back to Galena's face. "You cannot stand silence, can you?"

"No. And I dislike unpleasantness. Come, Ekaterina—we shall speak of the clothes to be had in Moscow, and poor Lexy will be punished by the loss of his money to the shopkeepers."

"Lena, you beggar me to spoil her."

"Lexy, her condition makes her have the sensibilities," Galena protested. "You forget what she is to Domnya."

"I do not forget she is my wife."

"I could not possibly wear anything more," Katherine said tiredly. "If you cannot find it in your heart to feed the poor, you may keep your money."

"Well, it has always been a long journey to Moscow—and I expect this one will seem even longer," Galena said philosophically. "Let us hope we shall arrive in charity with each other."

Once again a determined silence descended, and this time it did not break until the carriage halted before a village inn. The sun was low in the sky, and the air was getting colder when one of the coachmen opened the door. Galena shivered and pulled her fur-lined cloak about her.

"We are arrived, Ekaterina."

Even before they could step from the carriage, the innkeeper and his staff stood bowing obsequiously at the door, welcoming them in Russian. Galena brushed past them regally, then beckoned for Katherine to follow. Alexei said something to his driver, who then communicated it to the innkeeper.

Inside, they were shown clean but starkly furnished rooms. Katherine watched, embarrassed, as her husband lifted the coverlets to see the linens. The innkeeper hovered him, eager to please. As soon as Alexei nodded, he breathed a sigh of relief, then turned to shout orders down the hall.

"We shall eat as peasants," Galena muttered. "Mutton dumplings, sour milk soup, boiled carp, beets, and black bread."

"If you had ever traveled with an army, you'd be grateful for this," Alexei told her.

Katherine's stomach revolted. "I am too tired to eat," she decided.

"The babe makes you too thin as it is," he said. "You will eat."

In truth, if she had not known what was served, Katherine would have enjoyed everything but the carp. As it was, she picked at her food, eating the dumplings and the bread. And when a bottle of vodka was produced, she excused herself to go up to bed.

But after she'd undressed and washed in the basin, she did not think she could sleep. Every time she closed her eyes, she saw the rag-covered woman, her half-naked babe in her arms. How could he and Galena care so much for the child within Katherine and not give a pin for the suffering of their own people?

She heard Galena's steps on the creaky stairs, .hen they

stopped outside the bedchamber. The doorknob turned, and the Russian woman peered inside. "Are you all right, *cherie*?"

"Yes."

"You have not the headache?"

"No. I am tired."

"Everything is new to you, Ekaterina. When you are more accustomed to our ways, you will feel better. And soon the babe will settle, and everything will be all right."

The door closed again, and Alexei's sister moved into the hall. Katherine sat in a chair drawn up to the freshly laid fire and stared into the flames that licked and popped over still green logs.

Homesickness? No, it was more than that. It was disappointment that Alexei could not understand her, that he was so different from her. And no amount of learning different customs or language or anything else would ever change her opinion of that. As callous as her countrymen were, she did not think any of them—not even someone like Bellamy Townsend—would have refused to aid the thin, tattered serfs she'd seen that day.

Somewhere, possibly from Galena's room, angry voices rose, their words in heated Russian, and Katherine knew Alexei and his sister quarreled again over her. At least Galena tried to understand her, even when she did not agree.

She heard a door slam, followed by heavy steps in the hall, and she held her breath.

"You are not abed, Ekaterina?" As she looked up, Alexei came into the room, carrying a half-empty bottle of vodka in his hand. He walked closer to stand over her. He was obviously more than a little foxed. "You did not eat much," he muttered. "It is to be hoped you are not ill—we have too far to go in a closed carriage.

"I am not ill."

"Then get up and go to bed." He drank directly from the bottle, then wiped it with his sleeve. "Here—this will make you sleep better." When she did not take it, he pushed it at her. "Drink."

"You are disguised, my lord," she told him disgustedly.

"Disguised?"

"Drunk."

"If I am, it is none of your affair." He set the bottle down beside her and began to undress. "Come on—we leave at the first light."

Reluctantly, she rose and went to lie upon the bed. Turning her face toward the wall, she closed her eyes and pretended to fall asleep. She lay very still as she felt the feather mattress give beneath his weight. The room was quiet except for the crackling and popping of the fire.

He rolled against her back and reached his arm around her. His hand found her breast, and he massaged her nipple between his thumb and finger through the cloth. Still she did not move.

"Take off the gown," he said thickly against her ear.

She neither stirred nor answered.

"You like this, you tell me," he reminded her. "It is always 'Lexy, hold me.' Tonight I feel like holding you."

"I don't want to—not like this," she said finally, her voice low.

"I have come to you, Ekaterina—you see? I am here. Now—" His hand slid lower, over her abdomen, to her hip.

"Lexy, you are drunk," she whispered painfully. "I would that you did not ask it of me."

"Lena spoils you," he growled.

His mouth came down on hers, and his tongue forced its way between her teeth. She could taste the vodka, and it was as though every fiber of her being rebelled. She gagged and pushed him away.

"I'm going to be sick, Lexy!"

It took a moment for him to comprehend, then he pushed her away. "Boris!" he bawled for his manservant.

She lurched from the bed to the basin, where she was thoroughly, utterly ill. Bracing herself on her elbows, she heaved and heaved until there was nothing. Then she reached for the cloth on the turned wooden rung. Wiping her damp face, she faced Alexei.

He said something in Russian, then shouted again, "Boris!"

"It is all right—I am better."

"I do not sleep with the smell of *rvat*!" he snapped.

Someone knocked on the door, and Galena came in. "What is the matter?" She saw the basin, then turned to Kate. "Oh, Ekaterina, I am so sorry! But what good will Boris do for her, Lexy? Here, *ma petite*," she again addressed Katherine, "we must get you a clean gown."

"He can clean this up," he muttered. "And do not wait on her, Lena—there is Maria for that. You are beginning to act like an *Angleechahnka*!"

"You must not upset her in her condition!"

"Is that all you can think of, Lena?" he demanded angrily. "What of me?"

"You are drunk," she declared. "Go to sleep, and I will tend Ekaterina."

"Where in hell is Boris?" he repeated belligerently.

"I told him not to come."

"The *rvat*—"

His sister removed the basin from the stand and carried it to the chamber pot, where she emptied it. Putting on the lid, she said, "There. It is done, and I will set the bowl out in the hall."

"Lena, I have had enough of this!"

As Katherine watched, the Russian woman walked to stand over him. Leaning down, she brushed his hair back from his face, much in the manner of a mother tending her child. Then she pressed a kiss against his forehead. His arm came up to embrace her before she pulled away.

"Men! When they drink the vodka, they are as infants, Ekaterina. You must not worry over this. He will be fine in the morning." Coming back to Kate, she murmured, "And now we will get another night rail for you, and you will go back to bed, *n'est-ce pas*?"

As the older woman helped her out of the soiled gown, Kate whispered unhappily, "The fault was mine—I should not have denied him, but—"

Galena's head snapped back, and she glared at her brother. "Lexy, you will kill the child!"

"Lena, you remind me she is my wife," he retorted defensively. "Always you remind me."

"She is the little mother!" Galena found a clean gown from one of the traveling boxes and slipped it over Kate's head. "If he misuses you, you may come to my chamber, *cherie*," she told her.

"No."

As the door closed after the other woman, Katherine returned to bed. Lying down, she said nothing.

"You should not have told her," he said finally. "You worry Lena."

"I understand," she answered tiredly. But she didn't. "I just pray you will go to sleep until you are sober."

He turned onto his side, his back to her, and grunted his good night. Within a few minutes, he snored lightly as he slept off the effect of the bottle.

She lay awake, swallowing back still more disappointment. She knew that part of the problem between them must surely be her pregnancy. But as she lay there in silent misery, she could not help thinking of how different Bell Townsend had been when she was ill. The self-centered rake had been the one to act promptly, while her own husband had responded angrily.

Had Alexei not slept, she would almost have dared to ask him why he'd married her. But too much of her wished to cling to the notion that he'd loved her, that once she was at Domnya, everything would be all right.

Nothing could have prepared Katherine for Domnya. Not St. Petersburg. Not Moscow. Not Alexei's and Galena's prideful descriptions of it. As tired as she was after sixteen days of traveling rough and muddy roads, with only half a week spent in Moscow, she could only stare when she saw her new home.

It emerged suddenly out of thick-timbered hills, sitting on a bluff above the Moscow River, a huge, gray stone house with blackened chimneys that disappeared into the gray sky. As the carriage wended its way along the crooked road, the skeletons of winter timber gave way to an open parkland, then to a snow-dusted brown lawn.

Finally, for the last quarter mile or so, ruddy-faced women, perhaps as many as one hundred, raked piles of frosted leaves, then gathered them in dirty skirts. Behind the house, a tall column of smoke curled its way into heavy, hanging storm clouds.

"They are late, Lexy," Galena observed, her lips drawn thin. "It should have been done weeks ago. Now it will be too late to burn everything."

He stirred slightly, then sat up sleepily. "We are almost home?"

"We are home." She turned to Katherine, sighing. "The serfs are lazy when we are gone. I will discuss it with Popov tonight, and things will change. But," she added significantly, "you will see that none is hungry or in rags here. It is a matter of pride to us that Popov does not allow it."

"Popov?"

"He is the steward. Madame Popov oversees the kitchens and the housekeeping. Badin is responsible for the footmen and the wine cellars, and Raschev—"

"You give her too much to remember, Lena—let her meet them first," Alexei cut in, interrupting her.

"She is Countess Volsky," Galena countered. "They will expect her to know them. But perhaps you are right— if she greets Madame Popov, it is enough for today."

Popov. Madame Popov. Badin. Raschev. It did not seem so difficult to remember four people. "How many staff are there?" Katherine asked.

"Inside or outside?"

"Inside, as I should imagine those to be my responsibility."

"Well, you would have to ask Popov, of course, as I am not entirely certain. How many sweet cakes did we give in the house at Christmas and Easter, Lexy? Sixty, I think."

"Sixty-five, Popov said. But he was bringing two more into the house before winter."

Katherine nearly choked. "Sixty-seven servants?"

"Well, we are not so rich as the Sheremetievs, of course," Galena conceded. "*They* have two hundred serfs who merely put on plays for them. But we do very well with what we have. Besides what there is here, Lexy has nearly two thousand people at Dyeryivuhee, where we spend the summers on the Black Sea."

Katherine stole another sidewise glance out the window to the house, and her heart sank. She would not know where to begin learning how to be mistress of it. Her thoughts must have shown in her face, for Alexei's sister leaned across the seat to pat her hand.

"You must not worry over anything, Ekaterina. I shall be with you to guide you. Other than learning some of the names, you need only be concerned with yourself."

"I should wish to do what is expected."

Galena's fingers closed over hers, squeezing them. "What is expected, *cherie*, is a son for Domnya. It is all that is asked of you." Her expression changed, and she spoke rapidly in Russian to Alexei. There was no mistaking that she was displeased.

He leaned forward to look for himself, then smiled wryly. "Well, Ekaterina, you shall see Paul—and Olga Vladimovna."

"*Ta zhenshcheena! Ta zmyiya!*" Galena fairly spat the words out. "You must be careful, *ma petite*. She will poison you with lies."

"As if she could," Katherine protested.

"Good. She is the *zmyiya*," she repeated. "A snake—a viper." She looked at her brother. "How long do you mean to let them stay?"

"He was born at Domnya, Lena. I cannot—"

"Pah. He has a reason, and it cannot be good."

As the carriage finally reached the end of the drive, it rolled to a halt beside a long stone side porch. Before the coachman could reach for the door, a girl flew out of the house her dark hair swinging over her shoulders.

"Lexy! Lexy!"

Galena frowned. "Tati also?"

He threw up his hands as if he were defending himself. "I wrote that she could come home to meet Ekaterina Ivanova. She will return to school next week."

His sister's lips pressed tightly. "You did not tell me."

The carriage door swung open, and the girl stuck her head inside. "Is she here? Did you bring her?"

"Of course I brought her! Did you think I would leave her in Moscow?"' he countered, grinning. "Ekaterina Ivanova, this is Tatiana, our infant sister."

"I am sixteen!" the girl protested. Her gaze moved eagerly to Katherine, and her smile froze. "Ek-Ekaterina," she stammered. "I'd thought—"

"It does not matter what you thought," Galena interrupted her coldly. "You must welcome Countess Volsky."

"Yes—yes, of course. Your pardon, Ekaterina Ivanova—I did not mean to stare, but—"

"That is enough, Tati," her sister said firmly. "I see that Paul has come and brought that woman."

"She would not let him come without her. When I wrote, I only meant—"

"You wrote Paul? Tati, you know very well—"

"Well, it is not every day that Lexy takes a wife." The girl hung her head. "I did not think he would mind if I told Paul." Not daring to look at her sister, the girl added, "Viktor is come home also."

"What?"

Tatiana turned to Alexei. "Well, you did not say I could not tell them!"

He appeared uncomfortable beneath Galena's baleful stare. "No, no—it is all right. Ekaterina will wish to meet everyone, I am sure."

"I have looked forward to it all the way from England," Katherine assured her, smiling. "I have a younger sister also."

"The coachman is waiting, Tati," Galena reminded the girl.

"Oh—yes."

Alexei went first, then turned to lift his sister down. As she straightened her travel-wrinkled skirt, he reached for Katherine. His hands caught at her waist, then he swung her to the ground. As a tall woman emerged from the house, her arms crossed against the cold October day, he stepped in front of Katherine.

"Nyivyesta?" the woman demanded.

"The bride is here," Galena responded frostily. "Alexei, you will present Olga Vladimovna to Ekaterina."

"He will present her to me," Olga corrected stiffly. "It is my right."

"Yes, yes—we all know you are a prince's daughter," Galena retorted, her impatience evident. "But you are Olga Volskaya also—wife to Alexei's *younger* brother. Lexy?"

"Er—Ekaterina, as you have already heard, she is Olga, my brother Paul's wife."

"Prastoya!" Olga spat at him. "I do not kiss her!"

"Olga!" A tall, thin, almost austere man came up behind her. "There is to be no unpleasantness." He turned his attention to Katherine and forced a faint smile as he inclined his head slightly. "Ekaterina Ivanova."

Katherine was uncertain as to what she was supposed

to do; nonetheless, she extended her gloved hand.
''Paul?''

''My brother,'' Alexei muttered.

As the man bent to kiss her fingers, he murmured,
''You have surprised us greatly, Ekaterina. We had despaired that Alexei would take a wife. Indeed, it did not
seem possible.''

He looked older rather than younger than Lexy, and
aside from the height, there was little resemblance between them. He stepped back, and there was an awkward
silence. Finally, he turned to his wife and said something
in Russian. She glared at him for a moment, then stepped
forward to clasp Katherine's hands. Leaning forward
slightly, she brushed an utterly impersonal kiss on each
cheek.

''Welcome to Russia, *syistra*,'' she said, her voice flat.

''Thank you.''

Olga looked to Alexei. ''She does not speak Russian?''

''She will learn,'' Galena murmured. Then, unable to
completely hide her triumph, she added smugly, ''She
will have much time while we are waiting for Lexy's
heir.'' As the other woman reddened, she continued
smoothly, ''Yes, Olga—Ekaterina is *byiryemyinnaya*.''

Paul's wife stared hard. ''This is your doing, Lena—I
know it!'' she spat out. ''Everyone knows Lexy would
never—''

''That is enough, Olga.'' Paul moved between her and
Katherine. ''It is between Ekaterina and Lexy only.'' To
Katherine, he smiled. ''I wish you and the child well,
my dear.''

''Tati said that Viktor is here.''

''*Da*. And as is always the case,'' Olga said angrily,
''he is in need of money.''

''That is not your concern.''

''He asks Paul, saying you do not allow him enough!''

''Alexei, I am cold,'' Katherine said quickly, hoping
to escape the hostility.

''But of course, *daragaya*. There will be time for more

pleasantries later. Lena, perhaps you can see to arrangements for her.''

''We will find Madame Popov. Come, *ma petite*—you are not yet used to the climate.'' Without waiting for Katherine, she brushed past her sister-in-law, her skirt swishing.

As Katherine passed Olga, the woman repeated, *''Prastoya,''* under her breath.

Once inside, Katherine hurried after Galena. ''What is *prastoya*?''

''I told you she is a viper,'' Alexei's sister muttered. ''Popov! Popov!'' She pulled a heavy cord several times. ''Imbeciles! I am surrounded by imbeciles!''

A stern, stiff woman, as gray as the dress she wore, came down the stairs. *''Da, gaspazha?''*

''Ekaterina Volskaya.''

The woman curtsied low. *''Dabro pazhahluvat v Domnya, dahma.''*

Recognizing the words for a welcome, Katherine smiled. ''Thank you.''

Madame Popov appeared surprised. She looked to Galena. *''Ana gavareetye rooski yazik?''*

''Nyet. Angleechahnka.''

''She does not speak English?'' Katherine asked with foreboding.

''No. She just asked if you spoke Russian. I told her you were English. It will not matter, *cherie*, for I will speak for you.'' Galena ordered, *''Krahsnaya spalnya.''* As the woman nodded, she explained, ''There—I have told her to put you in the red bedroom. It adjoins Lexy's, and there is a sitting room and water closet on the other side.''

''Does anyone here speak English?'' Katherine persisted.

''We all do—the Volskys are educated, Ekaterina.''

''But the servants—''

''Unfortunately, no.''

It seemed overwhelming. Katherine exhaled fully, then nodded. ''I shall need a Russian tutor as quickly as possible.''

"Da," Galena agreed. "And until one is found, I will help you. But not today, I think. We are both too tired, and Olga has made me out of temper." She said something in Russian to the housekeeper, then turned back to Katherine. "She will show you up, and I shall come directly. But for now, I would see the men are careful with our trunks." When she saw the younger woman hesitate, she urged her, "Go on—one of the maids will draw a bath for you."

Daunted by being surrounded by people she could not understand and who could not understand her, Katherine followed the stern-looking woman up the stairs. At the top, the staircase spread out into a sort of foyer that tapered into a long, marble-tiled hallway ending in another, matching set of stairs that continued upward. Long Oriental runners muted her footsteps. Madame Popov stopped abruptly and threw open a door.

"Zdyiss."

"Thank you."

There was an awkward moment, then the woman nodded, obviously not understanding. Her expression utterly sober, she dropped another curtsy and was gone.

Katherine moved about the room in awe, touching the gilt trim on a chair, smelling the out-of-season roses in an exquisite Sevres vase. The awful thought that she, the plain Miss Winstead from Monk's End, did not belong here stuck in her mind. Finally, she sank into a chair and waited.

"Ekaterina?" Before Katherine could answer, Tatiana slipped into the room. "I told Galena I would speak with the maid for you."

"I am going to have to learn Russian," Katherine said grimly. "And sooner rather than later."

The girl plopped down in a chair across from her and reached into an open tin for a sugared date. "No doubt Lexy will get someone to teach you—if Lena will let him."

"I beg your pardon?"

"She is the Little Mother here." Tatiana made a face. "The Empress Ekaterina who married Peter the Great was called Little Mother also. She always had her way with him by being clever." She bit into the date, then chewed thoughtfully. "But Olga was right—none of us thought Lexy would wed. When he wrote me, I did not believe it. And Olga—well, Olga was furious!" She giggled. "She wishes to have Domnya, and Lena will see she does not. Even if it meant that Lexy had to marry, Lena would have him do it."

"I am told that there is difficulty between Lexy and Paul."

"By Lena, no doubt."

"Actually, it was Lexy."

The girl reached for another sugared date and popped it into her mouth. "Well, it is apparent enough that my sister chose you—you are a *meesch*." Her blue eyes met Katherine's. "A mouse," she explained. "But if you can tolerate Lena, who am I to complain?"

"Tati! *Von asyooada! Syaychass!*" Galena came into the room, shooing at her sister. *"Ookadee-tye!"*

Tatiana shrugged, then rose from the chair. "I am going, Lena." At the door, she turned back. "Welcome to Domnya, Ekaterina Ivanova."

"You must pay no heed to her—Olga has filled her head with nonsense."

"She said she came up to translate for the maid."

"Nyet. I said I would do it. She makes mischief because Lexy would not let her wed Genady Tcheramatov. Maria! Maria! That girl definitely goes to Boganin, for she is incompetent!"

"Dahma?"

"She would have a bath." When the girl stared blankly, Galena threw up her hands. *"Koopatsa! Doorak!"*

The girl blenched. *"Ya nye Angleechahnka."*

Galena turned to Katherine and sighed. "You will have to tell her if the water is too cold, I'm afraid. The word is *khalodnee*. If it is too hot, tell her it is *garyachee*."

Katherine repeated the words carefully, then nodded. "We shall manage, I am sure."

"Good. Anna will aid Maria with the bath." That settled, Alexei's sister started for the door, muttering under her breath something about Tatiana and *shkola*.

Footmen struggled in with huge kettles of steaming water and disappeared behind a large, carved wooden screen. The maid Maria could be heard, presumably directing them. More footmen came with kettles that did not steam. Katherine listened to them dispute, acutely aware that she had not the least notion as to what they said. Finally, the men left.

"*Dahma?*"

"Yes—that is, *da,*" she corrected herself quickly. Pointing to her own shoulder, she added, "Ya Ekaterina Volskaya."

The woman nodded. "*Dahma.*" She gestured for Katherine to stand, and immediately began tugging at the buttons of the traveling dress. When Katherine caught her hands, she looked up blankly.

"I can do it myself."

"*Nyet.*" Once again, the maid's fingers struggled with the tiny jet buttons.

"Please." Katherine sought the word in Russian, and tried "*Pazhahlsta.*"

The girl shook her head, then bent to lift the hem of the gown, pulling it upward. Undeterred, she appeared intent on undressing her. Unable to communicate, Katherine bent her head obediently. Then came the undershift, and finally the zona. Katherine stood naked and utterly embarrassed.

"*Nye troosee?*"

"I don't know," Katherine muttered.

The girl giggled and lifted up her plain wool skirt, revealing yellowed linen pantalettes. Pointing to Katherine's bare legs, she said, "*Khalodnee.*"

"We don't wear them much in England."

Another perplexed look.

"Look, I am *khalodnee,* Anna," Katherine said impatiently.

"*Da.*" The maid stood back, waiting for her new mistress to pass, then followed her behind the screen. She said something to Maria, and the other maid nodded, gesturing to the long copper tub.

Katherine surmised her bath was ready. Her face still red, she stepped into the water, and the shock was nearly unbearable. Struggling to get up, she gasped, *"Gary-achee—garyachee!"*

Maria hurriedly poured a steaming kettle from the fire into the water."

"Nyet! Nyet! Ya garyachee!" Katherine cried, rising from the water.

"Khalodnee, Anna—*khalodnee!"* Tears welled in Maria's eyes. *"Veenavat, dahma—veenavat,"* she whispered, her face a mirror of terror. *"Pazhahlsta . . ."*

"It is all right. Just put in the cold." When both women exchanged blank looks, Katherine reached for a large ewer and tested the water. It was cold. She poured it into the tub herself, then looked for another. "More cold—more *khalodnee."*

Finally, they managed to get the water right, and Katherine sank once again into the tub. Maria unstoppered a vial of scented oil and added it to the water. The fragrant scent of sandalwood permeated the air. Anna took a cloth and began soaping Katherine. After several attempts at explaining she'd rather do it herself, Katherine gave up and endured.

"Daragaya?"

Both girls cringed at the sound of Alexei's voice. He peered around the screen, then murmured apologetically, "I am sorry—I thought you would be done." He said something to Maria, and she went white, stammering some sort of explanation. As soon as he left, she burst into tears. The other maid dropped the cloth and tried to console her. Katherine finished washing herself.

When she was done and wrapped in a heavy woolen sheet, she came from behind the screen to find her husband sprawled across the bed. He gestured for Maria and Anna to leave, and they fled.

"You are feeling better, Ekaterina?" he murmured, watching her dry herself.

"I was not ill, Lexy—merely tired." She held out an

arm and sighed. "I will have to learn your language quickly or I will be burned in my bath."

"The water was too hot?"

"Definitely."

"You have but to tell Lena, and they will pay for the mistake. But you do not need to worry about Maria—I have decided to give her to my aide."

She swung around. "Is that why she was crying?"

He shrugged. "It does not matter. She is a miserable maid."

"But I like her," Katherine lied. "And if she does not want—"

"I told you—it does not matter," he interrupted curtly. "You can choose another. Lena will have Madame Popov find some girls for your approval."

Clearly, he considered the matter closed. But Katherine, who had been less than pleased with Maria herself, suddenly felt she could not let the girl be passed like a slave to a man she did not like.

"Alexei—please—I'd keep her."

He brushed her request aside. "Lena has decided she is unsuitable for you."

"But I want her! Lexy, am I your wife—or is it Lena?"

He gave a start, then recovered. "What do you mean? Only you are Countess Volsky, Ekaterina."

"Then Maria should be my choice, I think."

"Maria is a serf."

"I don't care. I would have some authority in this house."

"Ekaterina . . . Ekaterina . . . you do not yet understand." He rose from the bed and came to stand before her. Putting his hands on her shoulders, he smiled down at her. "If it means so much to you, I will ask Lena."

"I don't want you to ask her—I want you to tell her I intend to keep Maria. Otherwise, I shall do it myself."

"*Da.*" He brushed her cheek lightly with the back of his hand. "She would have you happy here."

"But would you? Lexy, I married *you,* not Galena. I love you, and—and it seems as though you do not really care for me—that Lena loves me more than you do. There, I have said it.''

"How could you say such a thing?"

"I don't know," she answered miserably.

"It is the babe," he decided. "But if you want, I will show you what I feel." His voice dropped nearly to a whisper. "Ekaterina—" His mouth sought hers, and as she felt the heat course through her, he pulled at the woolen sheet. "Let us not quarrel."

It would be quickly over—she did not doubt that—but she threw her arms around his neck eagerly. She wanted desperately to believe he loved her. And this was the only proof she had.

The Sherkovs' Moscow mansion was richly appointed, darkly ornate, in the old style. And as the winter set in, it became almost a prison to one used to the mildness of the English climate. Bellamy Townsend began to think he'd made a mistake, that perhaps he ought to have chosen the heat, the dust, and the insects of India.

He was going to remove to a hotel, and not a moment too soon, given the situation with Sofia. If she did not stop hanging on him, she was going to get him killed, and the irony would be that again he was innocent. Not because he was not attracted to the woman, but rather because he had a sense of survival in this backward place. Every time she tempted him, he remembered Galena Malenkova's warning.

He didn't like Russia, and he cared even less for the Sherkovs. Sofia was increasingly insistent, her husband nearly insufferable, the weather utterly intolerable. And the longer Bell stayed, the more he had to dissemble. As loath as he was to go somewhere he could not be understood, he did not think he could spend another week under the Sherkov roof.

The marshal was a blunt, boorish man, overgiven to boasting and drink, with the former increasing in direct proportion to the latter. After his second bottle of vodka, he was more than willing to take personal credit for the allies' defeat of Napoleon. And when he was not in his cups, his gout made him mean-spirited and cruel. Aside from vodka and vanity, his only other indulgence appeared to be Sofia.

And she detested Gregori, disparaging him behind his back. Spoiled, pampered, and petty, she relieved her boredom by flirting, heedless of the danger. Since Bell had been there, he'd observed her pressing against frightened equerries who suddenly disappeared—dispatched, it was rumored, to Siberia. And woe to the fellows foolish enough to appear to enjoy her attention. It was whispered they did not even get into exile. Whether Bell liked it or not, she was determined to be the noose around his neck. Whenever he mentioned leaving Moscow, she clung to him, begging him to stay the winter with them. He was now at the point where he was afraid to remain and afraid to run.

Lately he'd begun to feel that the marshal watched him, waiting like a bird of prey, ready for the moment Bell succumbed. It was as though they played a game, the three of them, and he was the only one who did not understand the rules. It was, he reflected wryly, his longest period of celibacy in nearly fifteen years.

On this night, sleet pelted the distorted windowpanes, and ice-covered branches rattled in the wind. As he locked his door, Bell loosened his cravat, and set down the half-empty bottle of vodka he'd carried up to his bedchamber. He was beginning to detest the stuff, he was beginning to long for a good port—or some Madeira even. But Gregori did not favor much of anything beyond his vodka, and Sofia's taste ran more to the sweet, heavy liqueurs of the East.

There was something wrong with a place where a man had to get drunk with a fermented potato. Nonetheless, he poured himself a glass and stood looking out the window. The yellow glow of lanterns below made the ice sparkle, and in another time and another place, he would have been struck by the beauty of it. But not tonight. Tonight he longed for England—and for Elinor Kingsley. And he wondered if she lay abed in Cornwall longing for Longford. Or if Longford had come home and she lay in his arms.

He drained his glass, then walked across the room to blow out the brace of candles beside his bed. He undressed quickly, for despite the noise of the fire that blazed in the hearth, the cold northern wind seemed to penetrate the walls of the house. Shivering, he pulled on a wool nightshirt more suited to a peasant than any English lord. Fingers already stiffening from the cold worked buttons from his chin to his chest. The damned thing was itchy, but he forgave that in his quest for warmth.

He moved again to the window. As he watched, an overladen branch broke and fell, shattering the thick layer of ice when it hit the ground. Man was not meant to live in a place like this—he was sure of that.

Even his ears were cold. He drew away from the window, chafing his hands. Walking to the fire, he leaned toward the flames, trying to draw the warmth before it fled up the chimney. Finally, he did the once unthinkable—he pulled on his borrowed nightcap. Despite his dislike of it, he could not help smiling at the irony of it all—he, Bellamy Townsend, buck of the *ton*, Aphrodite's Adonis, was getting into bed in a woolen nightshirt and a damned cap. If Brummell could see him now . . .

He turned around, found the bottle again, and took it to bed with him. The covers had been neatly turned back, and the sheets had been warmed, but he had no hopes of keeping them that way. He climbed between the feather beds, sinking deeply, shivering. Taking one last long pull from the vodka bottle, he put it down on the floor. He was becoming a sot—hell, he *was* a sot—no doubt at all about that.

He lay in the darkness, watching the flames cast eerie, licking shadows on silk-patterned walls, feeling empty and morose, probably from too much vodka. He was getting too damned moody, and he knew it, but he did not seem to be able to stop himself anymore. He'd trade each and every remarkable feature of his face for the chance to be Longford.

He let his mind drift, carrying him back to England, back to a time when Longford had been his best friend, back before Diana. Then he heard the click of a key in a lock, the unmistakable sound of a doorknob turning, and the hinges creaked as his door opened slowly. Pulling off the hateful cap, he sat upright. The door closed carefully, and the lock turned again.

"Don't be a fool, Sofia," he hissed at her.

She moved between him and the fire, and the outline of her body was visible beneath an all-too-thin nightshift. She knew he watched her now, and she lifted the gown over her head, letting it fall at her feet. She crossed the room slowly, deliberately, as the firelight bent her shadow over his bed.

"Sherkov—"

"Gregori could not waken if he wanted," she whispered, slipping between the covers beside him. Twining cold arms around his neck, she nibbled at his lips, murmuring, "I gave him laudanum for his gout."

"He had too much vodka. What if—"

She stopped his words with a searching kiss, and her naked body pressed into him. When she raised her head, her eyes were already darkened with passion. "I did not come to speak of him," she murmured as her hands roamed lower, feeling his manhood beneath his heavy nightshirt. Her mouth moved to his ear, and her breath sent a different shiver through him. He felt her fingers arouse him as she said softly, "I came for this."

His heart pounded as desire threatened to overwhelm him. "Not here—not now—"

"*Cher* Bellamy, you make me wait forever," she wheedled. "I tell you Gregori will not know."

He tried to stifle the feeling by drawing Kate Winstead to mind, recalling every barb she'd cast his way. Her words rang in his ears. *But you trespassed on my father's welcome.* He could hear the disapproval in her voice when she said it. And certainly he trespassed dangerously on Sherkov's. With an effort, he pushed Sofia Sherkova away.

"I cannot."

"But Gregori—"

"Not Gregori," he lied. Sitting up, he swung his legs over the side of the bed. "Sofia—"

She leaned against his back. "There is nothing you can tell me, Bellamy, that would make any difference."

"The time is not right!"

She sat back at that. "Why not?"

"I don't know. I just cannot do this—not now."

"Poor Bellamy," she murmured. "With Sofia it will be different."

"No. I cannot."

"You are impotent?" she asked incredulously. "Since when? And you did not tell me? You let Sofia Sherkova make a fool of herself, I think!"

Seizing on the excuse, he looked away. "It isn't the sort of thing a man tells a woman, but under the circumstances—"

"I don't believe you!" Nonetheless, she moved away from him. "You have the sickness, don't you?"

He knew he was going to regret it later, but he nodded.

"But you did not tell me! Why did you not say something to me before?" she demanded furiously. "I would not have wasted so much time on you!" She rolled off the bed and stared at him with loathing. "I want you out of my house! You are useless to me! No wonder you have come to Russia," she cried. "You do not want the English to know it!"

"Sofia—"

"Where did you get it?" she shouted.

"It comes from associating with whores, Sofia."

"You leave tomorrow!"

"I had planned to inquire of a hotel. Perhaps you know of one suitable?" he asked, his jaw tightening.

She calmed down at that. "No," she said finally. "Gregori will think it is a lover's quarrel. And he will think it strange you desert his hospitality for a hotel." She considered a moment, then decided. "You leave here to go—to Domnya. Yes, you have been invited for Christmas by Lena. She must have company for the English stick. I will write her in the morning."

"I'd rather you did not tell Madame Malenkov why," he said.

"I may—and I may not." She moved to the door for a moment to listen, then opened it. "Good night, *cher*

Bellamy," she said regretfully. "We could have enjoyed each other."

"I know."

He felt both relieved and chagrined. To get rid of Sofia Sherkova, he'd probably given himself the life of a monk.

The old man was already down for breakfast, and he looked sourly over his paper as Bell joined him, then nodded. For a moment, Bell wondered if Sherkov's head ached as much as his.

"My wife does not join us."

The hairs at the back of the younger man's neck stood. "Oh—is she ill?"

"Not at all. She said she did not sleep well last night—that my snoring kept her awake. I told her it was the laudanum, of course." He touched his wrapped leg and winced. "But with this, what is there to do?"

"I have heard gout is very painful," Bell murmured sympathetically.

"It is not the gout, sir," Sherkov retorted. "I was wounded—I took a ball in the thigh. It did not heal properly and has pained me for years. Gout," he pronounced definitely, "is for weak old men." Looking from beneath brushy brows, he met Bell's eyes. "I am still vigorous," he boasted, "if you know my meaning."

Bell unfolded his napkin and waited as a footman set a plate of smoked fish and poached eggs in front of him. When the fellow withdrew, he answered smoothly, "I did not doubt it. Madame Sherkov does not seem deprived."

"Deprived? Of course she is not! If there are no children, it is that she is barren! Is that what you are thinking?"

"Not at all. I had not even considered the matter."

"See that you do not." The old man leaned across the table. "What do you hear from the Malenkova? I understand from Sofia that she writes to you."

Not knowing what she might have said to her husband, Bell guessed. "She invites me to Domnya for Christmas."

"*Da*. She has asked us also, and Sofia does not wish

to go. She says with my leg, she does not think it wise.'' He peered closely at Bell. ''What do you think, Townsend?''

''I should think the decision yours,'' Bell said politely, wondering where the marshal intended to lead him. ''The winters here are quite harsh.''

''Harsh? Bah. You English do not know what harsh is, Townsend. Ask Napoleon, and he will tell you.'' He laughed loudly. ''Our winters swallow armies and starve them. In the winter, we crush fools who come here.'' For emphasis, he pounded the table. ''We crush them.''

Bell swallowed a bite of smoked fish, then washed it down with the dark, smoky tea. ''Napoleon was a fool to try invading in the fall.''

''Mother Russia guards her own, Townsend! It takes a Russian to live here.''

''Indeed.''

''You go to Domnya, eh? But I warn you—do not think you can seduce Galena Petrovna because she is a lonely widow.'' Again he leaned across the table, but this time he lowered his voice. ''Alexei Petrovich will not like it.''

''It surprises me she does not remarry.''

''If you would have my opinion of it, I think she poisoned Malenkov.'' As Bell's eyebrows went up, Sherkov nodded. ''She does not wed again, my friend. She would never leave Domnya. And why should she?''

''One would think a woman of her beauty—''

The old man interrupted him, indicating his question was rhetorical. ''She has everything there.'' He paused for emphasis, then repeated, ''Everything.''

''I heard that Malenkov died in the war.''

''Yes. Yes. Cyril was wounded, of course, but it was not until he went home that he died. So convenient.''

''Sir, what you are suggesting is repugnant.''

Sherkov shrugged. ''Well, she is back at her beloved Domnya—with Alexei Petrovich.'' He stabbed at a sausage on his plate and lifted it, gesturing. ''I would not advise an interest in the Malenkova, my friend. The Volskys are powerfully connected—their grandmother was a cousin of the Narrashykins, and their mother came to

Russia with the Czarina Maria Feodorovna. No, my friend—'' He stopped to savagely tear off a piece of the sausage with his teeth. ''—A seduction there, and you will not leave Russia alive. Nothing will come between Volsky and his sister.''

''They warned me about you.''

''Did they?'' The old man smiled broadly. ''Then you must heed them. We are all very dangerous, Bellamy Townsend.''

''What of the countess—what of Lady Volsky!''

''What of her?''

''Galena seems quite taken with her.''

''Galena Petrovna would be taken with anyone who could keep Paul from having Domnya.'' Sherkov leaned across the table yet again, but this time he lowered his voice. ''It is Olga Vladimovna who tells tales on her.''

''I was so famished I could not sleep.'' Sofia swept into the room, stopping only to brush a kiss on the old man's brow before turning to Bellamy. ''So, Lord Townsend—did you rest well?''

''Quite.''

''I am glad.'' Without waiting for a hovering footman to seat her, she drew up a chair.

''We were discussing the invitation to Domnya, my dear.''

''Ah, yes—dear Lena.''

''Townsend intends to go, he tells me.''

She looked at Bell and pouted. ''So you prefer the English stick? Should I tell Lena, do you think?'' Turning to her husband, she asked, ''Do we let him go, Gregori?''

''I have already warned him about Lena.''

''It will be such a house party this year,'' Sofia sighed. ''They invite everyone to celebrate that the stick gives Lena the child she has always wanted.''

''Katherine Volsky is not a stick, Madame Sherkov,'' Bell muttered. ''She is a lady of principle.''

''She is too skinny!'' she retorted. Then she smiled slyly, ''Well, perhaps not now. Now I expect she is fat.'' She reached to clasp her husband's hand. ''You know,

Gregori, I think we should go, after all. It might be most amusing.''

Bell polished off his eggs and rose apologetically. "If I may be excused, I should like to take a walk. I need to clear last night's vodka from my head.''

Both of them looked at him as though he'd lost his mind, "In this? Townsend, you will freeze.''

"I am trying to get used to the cold before it gets worse. Madame. Sherkov.''

"You had best take a footman," the marshal advised.

He escaped into the hall, where one of the maids mopped wet footprints from the marble floor. Seeing him, she smiled invitingly, and he obliged her with a quick pat on the rump.

Women. They were nearly always the instruments of his downfall. He exhaled fully, then went to get his own fur hat and coat. It was too much trouble trying to make himself understood, and even when they nodded, they often brought him something else. As he mounted the stairs, the maid giggled and went back to work.

Once suitably swathed in thick Siberian sable, he braved the Moscow street. The wind that hit his face nearly knocked him over—he had to lean into it to walk. But walk he did—all the way to the Moscow River, where he stood watching the great floating islands of ice move slowly past. It was December, and had he been in England, everything would be different. He could have breathed deeply without freezing his lungs. He could have smelled a roasting goose. He almost ached with homesickness.

But Harry Winstead had written him that Fanny's husband had threatened her with divorce, that it was on the betting books at both White's and Boodle's that he would call Bellamy out, so it had not mattered that there was no child. No, he could not go home—not yet. Maybe not for a long time.

He turned and started back down the street toward the Arbat. The cold was so bitter, so biting, that his face felt numb, and his breath crystallized in front of his eyes. As he passed a row of shops, he stopped to look in the steamed windows. One was a silk merchant, and the brightly colored scarves and shawls drew him. They at least reminded him of home.

It was nearly Christmas, and he was going to Domnya. He was going to hear another English voice. He thought of Kate Winstead and wondered if she were as homesick as he was. She would have everything now, everything that Alexei Volsky's money could buy her, everything except England. Harry had written that he thought her letters sounded as though she were a trifle out of sorts, saying it was probably her condition.

Bell hesitated, then ducked inside the shop to buy her the brightest shawl in the window. Then, afraid Volsky might take exception to Kate's gift, he bought another for Galena.

Domnya: *December 29, 1814*

The snow was deep, and huge drifts clung to the sides of the grand house, but two hundred serfs armed with naught but shovels and a draft plow managed to keep the road open for several miles. It was so cold that the river was covered with a thick layer of ice, and heavy, horse-drawn drays traversed it, carrying provisions from Moscow. Katherine watched from a window, feeling sorry for everyone outside in such miserable weather.

But her spirits were better than they had been in two months, and there was a festive air about Domnya that had nearly as much to do with her pregnancy as with the holidays. The sickness seemed to have passed, and she was feeling well enough to anticipate the coming company. Even Bell Townsend. She was going to hear English spoken again without a Russian accent.

She sat down at her gilded writing desk and wrote her brother, penning swiftly at first:

Dearest Harry,

In answer to your letter of 18 November, I am well, much fatter and healthier, I assure you, than when you wrote. Indeed, but the mails arrive indifferently here, so I was overjoyed when I received your news of home yesterday. I have read every page three times already, most particularly the part where you said Hargrove had invited all of you to a winter house party.

I do think he and Claire are quite suited, you know, and it sounds as though he may finally be brought up to scratch. Though I cannot imagine Claire and Lady

Hargrove could possibly be content to share him or the house. But as the Hargroves are so very rich, perhaps the dowager will move to another property.

I myself have been quite fortunate to have Galena with me, else I should not know how to go on. The Russian language is a difficult one to master, and full half the time I try to use it to get anything, I receive something else entirely! But Lena has promised me a tutor after I am delivered, saying I will have a great deal of time then to learn. As though I have none now.

Life here is more indolent than you could possibly imagine—there are servants for everything. In addition to Maria, I have three other personal maids! Whether I wish it or not, I am washed, dressed, and buttoned into my gowns—as though I am utterly helpless. If I would let it happen, I am sure someone would cut my meat for me at the table.

So I read a great deal, and Galena has been so very kind to order me English novels, which are unfortunately the same ones I read at home. Please, dearest Harry, when you write again, I pray you will send me something newer.

She stopped, thinking that it sounded as though she complained, but in truth she had nothing to do. And she blamed that on her inability to speak Russian. If she could communicate more, she could direct the servants better and take pride in running at least part of the house. As it was, she felt more the pampered guest than the mistress of Domnya.

Not that she faulted Galena, for Alexei's sister was exceedingly patient with her poor attempts at the language, always carefully correcting words and grammar. Still, it seemed as though she knew little more than when she'd arrived two and one-half months earlier. It would come with time, Galena insisted, but far too much escaped her, and anything said quickly was utterly unintelligible. Because of her difficulties with Russian, none of the servants sought her out willingly, preferring always to go to Galena. But it didn't matter—everything at Domnya always ran smoothly without her help.

But she carried Alexei's child, a child would tie him to her forever. She touched her swelling stomach, recalling how it had felt a scant four weeks before when she'd actually felt the babe move within her. When the birth was over, when she could hold this child they had made, she knew everything would be different. As it was now, whenever Galena was present, Lexy treated Katherine as though she were breakable. And even in the privacy of the bedchamber, he now behaved as though he believed it.

Galena and Lexy had already quarreled over baptismal names, one choosing Mikhail, the other Alexander in honor of the czar. In the end, Katherine had had to intervene, saying she much preferred to name her first son John for her father. They had acquiesced, but he would be Ivan in Russian, which somehow did not seem quite the same. Ivan Alexeievitch Volsky. If the babe should be a girl, everyone agreed she would be Alexandra. Alexandra Ekaterina Alexeievna Volskyaya.

Even Domnya's priest was pleased, going so far as to ask the prayers be said as far away as Moscow for this heir to Domnya. Katherine's pregnancy was, he insisted, a sign that God approved the marriage and would have her hasten her conversion to Orthodoxy. A mother, he had pronounced solemnly, must guide her child to right in matters of religion.

She sighed and dipped her pen again, continuing the letter.

Everything is so very different here, dearest brother. It is as though I have stepped back in time to another age, for people are owned here, and even the Orthodox Church condones it. Indeed, the church itself is quite medieval, choosing to follow the czar and the nobility rather than to lead it. And everyone clings to the old ways of doing things. For all that Catherine the Great encouraged Russia to modernize, I think she did not truly want it to do so. Here there are no machines for anything. Sometimes I marvel that I have a water closet.

How homesick I must sound to you. And in some ways I am, I suppose, for I find myself actually looking forward to seeing Townsend again, simply because he is English. But you must not worry for me, as I have Alexei and Galena.

She started to reach for another page of vellum, then heard the bells ring out a greeting. Hastily, she wrote in smaller script at the bottom and up one side:

I must leave you for now, best of all brothers, for the company arrives. But I do promise you I shall write what Townsend will not, telling you all the latest *crim-cons* I shall hear about him, and I expect they will be many. Why, oh why, are females so foolish?

I pray you will write again soon. Your best sister, Kate.

She sanded her letter, then folded and sealed it. Rising, she went to the window and lifted the dark, heavy damask curtains. As she watched, she could see Popov sending one of Domnya's huge sleighs to rescue someone. She watched eagerly now, knowing it would be some of the guests, hoping that it might be Bellamy Townsend.

"Dahma—dahma!" There was even excitement in Maria's voice as she rapped on the door. *"Anee edoot!"* The girl entered the room and stopped to catch her breath. *"Zhay* do come," she repeated.

For Katherine, Maria would do anything, including struggling to learn as many words in English as her mistress learned in Russian. The girl hovered her, eager to please the *"nyemnoguh dahma,"* saying nearly every day how grateful she was to have been saved from Boganin. She grinned at Katherine now.

"Ah, *dahma*—happy—*nyet*?"

"Yes—yes, I am."

"Kharasho."

Kharasho. Good. Yes, it was good.

"Ah, *cherie,* but you do not need to go down if you do not feel well," Galena murmured from the door. "I will make the excuses for you."

"No—no, not at all. As it is the first time we have had any guests of note, I am sure Alexei would wish me to greet them."

"Well, it is your decision, of course, but if it is only for Lexy—" Galena shrugged, then smiled. "Well, I can persuade him for you."

"Lena, I am fine—I have not been at all ill lately."

Alexei's sister turned to Maria. *"Yay nyi-zdarovitsa?"* The girl shook her head. "No sickness, *dahma.*"

"Vee gavaryoo parooskee!" Galena snapped.

"I am afraid the fault is mine," Katherine said hastily. "She learns English for me."

"Yes, yes, but she does not need to speak it to me." For a moment, the Russian woman's impatience showed, then she recovered. Smiling again, she reached to touch Katherine's arm. "Then it is settled. We go down together—yes? And everyone will say how your condition makes you beautiful."

Katherine looked down at the visible roundness beneath her gown. "Well, I don't expect everyone to think it. For me, it is enough if only Lexy is blind."

"Bah. He is besotted," Galena assured her. "Come—I can hear them already."

Below, in the marble-floored foyer, footmen took coats while Bell Townsend stamped the snow from his feet onto an already soaked grass mat. Beside him, Sofia Sherkova complained bitterly of the delays they had endured, and behind him, her husband grumbled about the effect of such cold on his war wounds.

"Ah, *mes cher amies!* Welcome to Domnya!" Galena Malenkova called down to them. "You are the first to arrive."

Bell looked up, saw Katherine Volskaya, and grinned. For all that he himself hated it, Russian life appeared to agree with her. Her face was fuller, making her nose seem shorter, her face somehow less plain, and even her obvious pregnancy was not unpleasing. And her welcoming smile made her actually attractive.

"You look well, Countess Volsky," he said.

The smile broadened at the sound of his voice. "As do you, my lord," she murmured, coming down.

"Truth to tell, I feel dashed cold—and they dare to tell me Siberia is worse."

"Much worse," Galena declared, holding out her hand to him. "Only wolves and criminals can live there. And sometimes not even the criminals," she added candidly. "But we are warm enough here, and there is a punch prepared, so perhaps you will like our Domnya."

"I am sure I will." He lifted her fingers to his cold lips, brushing them lightly. "Ah, Madame Malenkov, but you are more beautiful every time I see you."

Her laugh tinkled lightly. "Such address, *cher* Bellamy. If I thought you believed it, I could listen to you all the day." She turned to Sofia. "He is so charming, do you not think?"

"*Da*," the other woman agreed, her face suddenly grim. "But you must not think too much of what he says, for he flirts where he does not play."

"Galena! A word with you, please." Alexei stood in one of the doors that opened off the foyer. Nodding curtly, he acknowledged his guests. "Madame Sherkov. Gregori. Townsend."

Sofia Sherkova rolled her eyes, whispering loudly to Bell, "I hope he does not mean to be uncivil. When he wishes, he can be quite uncomfortable."

"No, no, of course he does not. Lexy, you must smile for Sofia," Galena coaxed him.

He obliged grudgingly, much as an unwilling child. "I am sure you will enjoy warming yourself before the fire with the milk punch."

Bell's nose wrinkled perceptibly, and Katherine hastened to assure him, "It is not at all what you would think—it is quite good."

"The milk—it is fermented," Sofia explained. "And there are spices. If you do not know what it is, you like it."

"Yes—just don't think about what you are drinking," Galena said.

"Good for the constitution," Marshal Sherkov spoke up loudly. "I say we find the fire and share a few cups between us."

"Galena—" There was no mistaking Alexei's impatience.

She sighed expressively. "Always he can do nothing without me. Ekaterina, will you see to everyone's comfort, *ma petite*?"

"Yes, of course."

As they disappeared into Alexei's study, a footman held the other door open. Waiting for Sherkov, who moved slowly, Bell leaned closer to Katherine. "We are not the only revelers, I hope?"

"No. Galena has invited Prince Pahlin and his wife and the Rostophievs. But whether Count Zelensky is coming is as yet uncertain, because of the storm and the distance. Alas, but Anya and Prince Golachev cannot travel so far in the weather." The light danced impishly in her eyes. "But you can hope Zelensky will not be here, for he is considered the most handsome man in all of Russia."

"I assure you I should welcome him. I tire of the role."

Sofia turned around. "And what of Paul and Olga? Surely they would wish—"

Her husband grunted. "If Olga Vladimovna comes, it will be unpleasant. The woman rules Paul, and I cannot stand that."

"Yet you tolerate Galena Petrovna."

"She has no husband to rule," he retorted. "Not that I did not pity Cyril Malenkov when he lived. It was a struggle between them."

"Aren't Viktor and Tati here?" Sofia asked.

"Yes, but I did not count them, for they belong here when they are not in school," Katherine answered.

The fire in the front reception room blazed invitingly, and the warm, enticing fragrance of sap floated in the air as the handful of green pine chips popped and crackled beneath the logs. A giant bearskin, its glass eyes fixed, stared incongruously from one of the lovely silk-covered walls.

Bell took the steaming punch from a footman and studied the massive bear head. "Dashed big fellow, wasn't he?"

"Yes. Alexei hunted in Siberia with Prince Pahlin, and that was his prize," Katherine murmured, looking away. "It seems such a waste that the poor beast must glare forever from a wall, doesn't it?"

Sofia looked at it, then shrugged. "Well, I suppose you could put it on the floor."

"Forgive me for sitting," her husband said from the depths of a tall wing chair. "Old wound, you know." His eyes took in the bear, and he nodded. "Magnificent animal—but dangerous. Poor Chelinsky was gutted in one swipe—got to be careful how you go about taking 'em. Alexei Petrovich is either a brave man or a fool—or both."

"Perhaps he had someone shoot it for him," Sofia suggested. "It is not uncommon." ·

"*Nyet.* The beast charged me, and I brought him down. If you will examine the skin closely, you can see where the ball entered its throat before severing its spine." Alexei walked into the room, his color heightened, and for a moment Katherine wondered if perhaps he'd been drinking. Taking a cup, he toasted the bear, mocking it. "May the best always win, eh?" He looked to her. "You do not have any, *daragaya*?"

"Not yet."

"Poor Ekaterina—she has lived on digestive biscuits Lena orders from Moscow for her, but now she is better." His mouth curved in a smile as he added significantly, "I told her she had to eat, that I did not wish a skinny son."

"Then you should have gotten a fatter wife in the first place," Sofia told him. "What if the sons, they are short like her—and the daughters, they are tall like Alexei Petrovich—then what will Galena Petrovna think?" she asked slyly. "It would be a pity if they did not get your looks, I think."

"Galena Petrovna would love them," Alexei's sister said coldly. She swept into the room, stopping next to Katherine. "Really, Sofia, but you ought to drink that— I am told milk is good for the complexion."

"Ah, Lexy," the other woman sighed, "but you must have the patience of a saint to live with her—no? And poor Ekaterina—what she must suffer here. Galena is so beautiful—so *very* beautiful—and—"

"Ekaterina is not your concern, Sofia," he responded curtly. "Galena will take care of her." He touched Katherine's shoulder lightly. "If you do not feel like eating tonight, you do not need to come down. I am certain everyone will understand."

"I am fine—truly." Out of the corner of her eye, she could see a footman trying to gain his attention. "Lexy, there is Boris," she murmured.

His irritation evident, Alexei went to the door, where the man spoke diffidently, his voice so low that Katherine could not hear. Her husband barked brief orders, then came back to set his cup down. "My apologies, but there is business that cannot wait." He beckoned to Galena. "See that Ekaterina does not tire herself." Leaning toward her, he whispered something quickly, his lips so close to his sister's ears that he appeared to kiss her.

"Go on—I will attend to everything. You will have enough time before supper," Galena answered him clearly in English. Turning to Katherine, she said only, "It is nothing to worry about."

He'd confided in his sister, not her, and Katherine felt as though Sofia Sherkova were staring pityingly at her. But Galena's hand touched hers, squeezing her fingers momentarily. "It is nothing," she repeated more loudly for them.

"Ah, Ekaterina Ivanova," Sofia murmured, "you let her manage everything for you? How very fortunate you are—but then she has always managed Lexy so very well."

"*Teeshe,*" her husband growled. "*Astaf-tye yeyo!*" To

Katherine, he said more kindly, "You must not mind her—it is that she is tired from the journey."

"Then perhaps Madame Sherkov would wish to retire to refresh her spirits," Galena offered stiffly. "Popov! Popov!" Without waiting for him to appear, she marched to the door, the heavy silk of her skirt swishing against her petticoat. "He will see you are directed to your bed-chamber, I am sure. Popov!"

Apparently, she found him just outside, for she could be heard speaking tersely to him. Almost immediately, a liveried footman appeared, bowing from the waist toward Sofia Sherkova. *"Slyedoo-i-tye zamnoy, Gaspazha."*

"Nyet," she snapped. *"Ya yishcho nye sabrahlsa!"*

Her husband rose unsteadily from his chair. "Well, *I* am ready, and if there is a fire in the chamber, I will go with you. My leg pains me, and I am tired. You can help me to bed and read to me."

She capitulated gracelessly. As the old man took her arm, Bell could not help smiling, thinking it was no more than she deserved. She passed him, her expression stony, and once she was in the hall, he heard her mutter, "One day everyone will know what she is. As for Ekaterina Ivanova, she is a fool that she does not see it."

"You chatter too much," Sherkov told her bluntly. "I do not wish to hear it."

"Men are blind," she complained. "Did you not see how she looked at Townsend? I wonder that Alexei Petrovich did not note it."

"It is not your concern." There was a pause, then the old man added, "And if Ekaterina Ivanova would bed the Englishman, that is not your affair also. If I discover differently, there will not be enough of you or him to feed three crows."

"Gregori . . . Gregori . . . how could you doubt me?" she crooned softly. "Do I not show you—and am I not at your side every night? Besides, he is unable, the maids tell me," she said. "Do you not trust me?"

Sherkov's answer was lost in the distance. Embarrassed that Katherine might have heard Sofia, Bell turned toward her. "The woman's a fool, Kate."

"That should suit you." But even as she spoke, she smiled. "You know, Bell Townsend, I never thought I should see the day when I actually wished for your company," she said softly.

"Blue-deviled?"

"No. Homesick for England and Harry."

"As am I, Kate—as am I." He went to the bowl and dipped another glass of punch for himself. Grimacing, he downed it. "I hate this place, you know."

"Here—or all of Russia?"

"All of it. For one thing, it's too damned cold by half, and for another, a man cannot get a decent drink. Vodka!" He fairly spat out the word. "It's made from a damned potato!"

"Poor Townsend," she murmured.

"You know what, Kate? I have even missed your barbs."

"Then it must surely be time for you to go home to England."

"Devil of it is, I cannot."

"Surely by now Hopewell must know Fanny lied."

"Everyone says I will have to wait for the spring thaws to travel much beyond Moscow. It took us two days to get here, when it should have been a matter of a few hours. Unlike England, where a coach can make ten miles to the hour, we are fortunate to have made ten hours to the mile."

"It isn't quite that bad," she corrected him, smiling.

"Dashed near it. All right—Sherkov boasted to me that we made three miles to the hour, Madame Honesty." Still carrying his glass, he moved to look out the window. "Look at it—and they say much of the country is worse."

"I take it there is much snow in Moscow?"

"Snow?" he said, choking. "Kate, you have no notion! I have not seen anything like this since the Frost Fair!"

"That wasn't very long ago," she reminded him.

"But that was an aberration! Here they expect this."

"Well, at least you have Sofia to comfort you," she observed wickedly.

"Like a plague of locusts," he muttered.

"You know what ails you, Bell? You have made a conquest you cannot escape."

"The devil I have," he retorted. "And she isn't a conquest, I assure you," he added, shuddering. "I can scarce abide her." Turning back, he sighed. "I'm removing to a hotel when I go back to Moscow."

"You could stay here, I suppose."

For a moment, he considered it, then he shook his head. "No. The next thing you'd hear is I am dangling after Galena Malenkova—or you."

"Nobody would believe it about me." Her hand rested on her stomach.

"How are you, really?"

"Once the sickness passed, everything was fine. I told you—sometimes I am homesick, but that's all. As you can see, I have filled out considerably."

His gaze rested briefly on her larger breasts, then returned to her face. "Most definitely," he said, teasing her. "And you are treated well?"

"I should have expected that from you," she admitted, blushing. "And, yes, I am pampered and cosseted until I cannot even do my own buttons." It was her turn to sigh. "If anything, he treats me too well, as though he fears I am too fragile for any use."

"And Galena?"

"She is worse. If she could, she'd put me in a glass case until the babe comes. I am to do nothing, Bell—nothing. One would think I am a queen awaiting the birth of the royal heir."

"And you do not like it—the hoyden in you rebels."

"Not the hoyden," she corrected him. "The woman."

"Tired of your golden cage already, Kate?"

"No, of course not!" she snapped crossly. "Everything is fine!" She caught herself. "I'm sorry—I don't know what it is about you that makes me want to rip up at you. If I just had Harry to talk to—" She looked up at him. "You are all I have of England over here, my friend, so I must learn to hold my tongue, mustn't I?"

"How you have sunk," he murmured, "to have to call

me a friend. Time was when you could not abide the sight of me.''

"That was then," she admitted candidly. "Now I have longed to hear you speak my native tongue the way God intended it.''

Before he could say anything further, Galena returned, obviously disgusted. "That Sofia—she has no breeding! Sometimes I think Gregori discovered her among the camp followers!'' She put her arms around Katherine, hugging her affectionately. "She is jealous of you, *ma petite,* for you have Lexy. For years she has made the eyes at him.''

"I should rather think her jealous of you," Kate responded.

"If she is, she has no reason." Galena's gaze moved to Bell. "You do not think I cast out the lures to you?''

"No.''

"Good. We are friends then, Townsend. Now, it is not enough that we must sit cooped up together in the house, I think. Tell me—do you skate? Perhaps later Lexy—''

"Not in years, I am afraid.''

"Then you must learn." Abruptly, her manner changed. "Poor Bellamy, you are tired of Sofia already—I can see it. Where could I send you to escape her, I wonder? Perhaps you could make mischief for my brother Paul. You almost make me wish Olga Vladimovna could see you . . . now she would be a challenge for you.''

"Dahma?" The man Boris stood uneasily in the open doorway.

Alexei's sister frowned her displeasure. *"Shto?"*

Katherine could not understand his answer, but seeing that Galena's frown deepened, she tried to intervene. "What is it?'' she asked quickly.

"That woman! She says the chimney of her fireplace smokes!'' Throwing up her hands in disgust, Galena added irritably, "I would she choked from it! But it is not your worry, Ekaterina—I shall tell him to carry her complaint to Madame Popov." She reached to pat Katherine's cheek. "You, little mother, must rest for your child's health.'' Before the younger woman could protest, she whirled to snap an order to Boris, then called out loudly, "Maria! Maria! *Syaychass!*"

"Really, but I don't—" It did no good, for Galena was not listening to her. Instead, she swished imperiously to the bellpull and yanked it almost violently.

"Da, dahma?"

"There you are, you lazy creature! You will put your mistress to bed—and see that she does not rise until it is time to dress her for dinner!"

"I am not tired, Lena," Katherine protested. "And there will be other guests. I don't—"

"Nonsense," Galena declared. "You must take care of yourself."

She made Katherine feel like a child herself, but the younger woman forced herself to admit Alexei's sister meant it as a kindness. Reluctantly, Katherine capitulated. "Well, I do not promise to go to bed, but perhaps I shall read. I am nearly finished with *Pride and Prejudice* again."

"Yes, yes, of course," Galena murmured dismissively. "You may read it in bed. And if you do not wish to skate, Townsend, perhaps you will wish a fire in your chamber. "Boris! Now, where is he? Boris! These serfs," she muttered, "they are like children. I have to watch them all the time."

The man returned, his hands held behind his back, his head lowered submissively. She said something in Russian that made him pale, then she turned back to Bell.

"You may follow him upstairs, and Popov will see that your trunks are delivered to your chamber."

She was too forceful, too imperious for a woman, and he did not like it. "Actually," he drawled, "I was thinking of calling for my cloak and walking outside to see the inimitable Domnya. I am afraid Sofia prattled about the place all the way here."

Katherine stared at him. "In this weather? Bell, you said you did not like the cold!"

"I need air. I'll see you at supper, Kate. Galena."

As he escaped, Galena shrugged, then turned to Katherine. "That poor man."

"Bell?"

"Ah, such a waste," the Russian woman murmured. "When Gregori was still trying to get up the stairs, Sofia told me he has lost his virility."

"He is old, Lena."

"Not Gregori, little one—Townsend."

Katherine stared, then she shook her head. No wonder he remained in Russia. But she supposed if it were true, that it was nothing less than his just desserts. For him, the pursuit of females had been his life. It had to be much as if Harry discovered his luck at the gaming tables deserted him. Yet, for all that she did not approve of his life, she could not help feeling sorry for him.

It was summer, and the fields were a rich, deep green. Her pony picked its way across the shallow ford as she leaned forward, eager to catch the first glimpse of him. Behind her, her sister complained. And then the black lacquered carriage came around the curve. She spurred the spotted pony, urging it forward, hoping to be the first to greet him. The carriage stopped in the road, and her father stepped down, his arms outstretched toward her.

"Aieeeeyeee! Aieeeeyeee! Aieeeeyeee!" Somewhere in the distance, a child screamed, intruding on her dreams. She lay there, her mind still grogged with sleep, thinking she'd only imagined the terror she'd heard. Then there was no mistaking the running footsteps on the stairs, the shouts of servants calling for help.

She swung her legs over the side of the bed and sat up. The awful stench hit her then, and she had to lean forward, her head between her knees, to keep from gagging. She swallowed hard and waited for it to pass. She felt clammy, nearly too sick to rise. And still there was the strange, sickly sweet smell—as though someone roasted a suckling pig in the house.

"Maria—" she called weakly. There was no answer— only muffled sounds coming from somewhere down the hall. "Maria—" she tried again.

Finally, she rose shakily. Picking up the wrapper on the bedside chair, she pulled it on and tied it, then found her slippers. The smoke burned her eyes. *Dear God, is the house on fire?* she wondered. Covering her nose, she moved to the bedchamber door, opening it.

A group of people were gathered near the end of the hall. As Katherine stared, more men ran up the back stairs. Then Galena saw her.

"You must go back, Ekaterina—this is not for your eyes."

"What—? What has happened?"

"It does not matter. You are not to concern yourself. Alexei, put your wife back to bed," the older woman ordered. "She must not mark the child."

"No." Resolutely, Katherine moved closer.

"It is nothing, I tell you!" Galena snapped. "Lexy!"

"Go back to bed, Ekaterina," he said. "I will explain everything later."

"I am not a child," she retorted, trying to see past him. "What has happened?" she asked again.

"I will not sleep in that room!" Sofia Sherkova shouted at someone Katherine could not see. "Gregori—tell them! My gowns—they are ruined by the smoke!"

"Be quiet, Sofia!" Galena shouted back. "Of course you will not stay there!"

Unmollified, the other woman protested loudly, "All I asked was a clean chimney! And now this! Everything is ruined!"

"What is ruined? For God's sake, will *someone* tell me what is going on?" Katherine demanded, pushing her way past two footmen. "What is this awful smell?"

"Ekaterina, it is not for you to see." Alexei moved to intercept her. "Come—"

But her gaze found her maid, and the girl stood, her face pale, her eyes a mirror of horror. "Maria—" Dodging beneath her husband's arm, Katherine faced her. "What is it?"

The girl stared. Before any could stop her, Katherine shook Maria. Wordlessly, the girl pointed through the open door. Katherine turned, seeing two men working with hooks, trying to dislodge something from the fireplace. Galena caught at her arm, pulling her back, but Katherine tore away from her. The smoke was thick, choking, and the men coughed continuously. The window was open, and the cold air drew the heat from the room, but smoke still billowed.

"Something is on fire!" she shouted, her eyes burning. "Lexy, something is still on fire!"

He nodded and turned away. This time, Galena grasped Katherine's arm tightly. "Ekaterina, you must not watch. For the sake of your child, you should not see this, I tell you!"

There were grunts, then a triumphant cry as the hooks pulled the obstruction down into the grate. Galena tried to cover Katherine's eyes, but she was too late. Despite the soot, despite the blackened flesh, it was unmistakably a small child. A man with a bucket of water doused it. Galena pushed Katherine at Alexei, muttering, "Take her away."

"No!" She turned wildly to Sofia Sherkova. "Madame—what—?"

The woman shrugged. "There was a bird's nest—they sent him up."

A man tried to explain plaintively, but she could not make sense of the Russian words. "Get it out of here," Alexei growled, looking away.

"*It?*" Katherine's voice rose almost hysterically. "Lexy, that is a child—isn't it?" She turned to her maid, and tried to regain control. "Maria?"

"Oh, *dahma*," the girl whispered, her eyes enormous. "He not go up—they make him—" Her throat constricted visibly, and she could not go on.

Katherine searched the impassive faces of the men, then she looked to Madame Popov. "You let them burn up a child?" she asked angrily.

"Ekaterina!" Galena said sharply.

"For a bird's nest, you let them kill a child?" Katherine demanded again. "What kind of woman *are* you?" She dropped to her knees before the grate and reached to gingerly touch the curled figure. The smoldering flesh disintegrated beneath her touch. Tears burned her eyes. Drawing back in horror, she could only whisper, "What kind of *people* are you?"

"It was a serf," Sofia Sherkova muttered. "Tell her it was a serf."

"He was someone's son!"

"Serfs are like rabbits," Marshal Sherkov observed contemptuously. "They will not miss one mouth when there are so many."

She rose to face her husband, her hand on her rounded abdomen. "Lexy, tell me you would not miss this one!" When he did not answer her, she moved between him and Galena. "Whoever is responsible for this must be punished—do you hear me, Lexy? A child is dead!"

He raised his hands, then dropped them. "It is unfortunate," he murmured, not meeting her eyes.

"Unfortunate?" she shouted at him. "It is criminal! Is no one going to do anything? Does no one care?"

As Galena glared at him, he caught Katherine's arm again, trying to drag her from the room. "Ekaterina, you do not understand—the boy was a serf. I cannot punish Madame Popov for this. Come—you must not think on what you cannot help," he murmured soothingly. "It is not good for you."

"No!" Wrenching free, she ran from the room.

"Ekaterina! Ekaterina!"

She had to get away from all of them. She could scarce breathe for the tightness in her chest. Brushing past a returning Bellamy Townsend, she ran down the back stairs, nearly colliding with one of the maids coming up, then out into the cold winter air.

Bell started to go after her, but a footman was already in pursuit. Galena called to the fellow, shouting something. The footman turned back. Both Alexei and his sister were in the hall, and when they saw him, Alexei held out his hands helplessly. Galena sighed, then shook her head. "I told her not to look. Now perhaps she will wish to be alone."

"What the devil—?" Bell moved closer. "Will someone explain all the noise—and what the hell is that smell?"

It was Sofia Sherkova who answered him. Coming into the hall also, she bore a look of supreme disgust. "Ekaterina Volskaya is possessed of too much silly English sensibility! A serf is dead, and she would hang us all for it! She does not even care that my clothes, they are all ruined!''

He pushed past all of them, then stopped when he saw men lifting the small burned body into a blanket. ''Good God! It is a child!'' Turning to Marshal Sherkov, he demanded, ''What happened?''

The old man glared for a moment, then looked away. ''It is unfortunate, of course—but the chimney smoked. When Sofia complained of it, they sent a sweep and the boy.''

''There was a bird's nest in it,'' Sofia explained defensively.

''It had to come out before the house burned,'' Alexei insisted. ''There was nothing else to do.''

''Of course it did,'' Galena murmured soothingly. Looking at Bell, she added, ''I'm afraid the boy was sent up to get it down.''

Maria's chin quivered, then she burst out, saying, ''He—'' She groped helplessly for a word and could not find it. ''He cry!'' she wailed finally. She went to the grate and picked up a blackened stick. Gesturing with the stick, she poked up the chimney from below, jabbing as though she were forcing something. ''He cry,'' she whispered, dropping the charred wood back into the grate. ''Then nothing.''

Bell nodded grimly. ''He suffocated.'' Turning back to the others, he could not hide the contempt he felt. ''What kind of people are you?'' When no one answered him, he shouted it. ''What kind of people are you?''

''It was a serf—a serf!'' Sofia insisted. ''And you have no right—''

''Be still, Sofia!'' Galena snapped.

His jaw worked visibly as he sought to control his temper, but they were all looking at him as though he were the one who was mad. Finally, Sherkov cleared his throat. ''It is different in your country, but here we do not—''

''And your czar claims to be enlightened,'' Bell mut-

tered, pushing past them. "You make me sick—all of
you!"

In the hall, he found a maid still polishing the dark
wood panels. "*Dahma* Volskaya—where?" he demanded
curtly.

"*Dahma narroozhoo.*" As she spoke, she pointed to
the door.

"She'll freeze," he muttered. "Why didn't anyone
stop her?"

It was a useless question. The girl's expression did not
change. He opened the door, and a blast of icy wind hit
his face. He pulled his fur-lined cloak closer and plunged
outside again. She couldn't have come out in this, she
couldn't have, he told himself, but then he saw the small
footprints of a woman in the snow, footprints of slippers
rather than boots, and he knew better.

The cold cut through Katherine's silk wrapper, and the
snow filled her slippers. Her feet sank deeply, making
her stagger awkwardly as she sought shelter in the stable.
Tears clung in crystals to her lashes, and the bright snow
blinded her. She pounded on a door.

"*Dahma! Shto?*" someone asked.

"Leave me alone!" she cried. "Get out!" He backed
away obediently, then stood there at a distance, staring
at her. "*Astaf-tye menya! Oohadeetye!*" she repeated.
"Just go!"

"*Da, dahma.*" He turned to a gathering group of men
and boys and barked something at them. They looked at
her, then moved away, muttering to themselves.

She ran the length of the stables, past the occupied
stalls, then stumbled blindly into an empty one, where
she dropped to her knees, sobbing against a bale of hay.
Even in the musty cold of the stable, she could still smell
the burned flesh. She closed her eyes, seeing again the
small, blackened form of a child. She had to gag back
the bile that rose in her throat.

A child was dead, and no one seemed to care. Not
Alexei. Not even Galena. Dear God, but was she the only
one not mad in this awful place? No matter how long she
lived, she would never forget what she'd seen. Fingerless

fists where hands had been, features burned beyond recognition.

She sobbed until she choked, then she lay her head against the hay, letting the tears roll down her cheeks. She hated Russia. She hated Domnya.

"Kate?"

She heard Bellamy Townsend's tentative voice, but she could not answer. Shivering uncontrollably, she curled up against the hay, hoping he would not find her. She didn't want to speak to anyone.

The stall door creaked behind her, and he stood over her for a moment, then he dropped to his knees beside her. "For whatever comfort it gives you, Kate, I do not understand them either. When I saw it, I was as sick as you are."

"You c-could not b-be." She lay, her face away from him, her cheek still against the hay. She felt his hand smooth the wrapper over her shoulder.

She was freezing cold, and she did not seem to know it. Sharing her horror, he sought to comfort her by drawing her into his lap. She resisted at first, then turned her wet face into his shoulder and sobbed. Holding her close, he pulled his cloak around both of them.

"How c-could L-Lexy allow it? How c-could Galena?" she cried. "Bell, they l-let a little b-boy die, and they are not even a-ashamed of it!"

He shifted her in his arms, trying to give her warmth. She was so cold, it frightened him. He held her silently for a time, letting her weep against him, as he silently cursed all of them—Sofia, Gregori, Galena, Alexei. Finally, he could stand it no longer.

"Don't, Kate," he whispered into the crown of her hair. "It isn't your fault—it isn't your fault. These Russians are not like us. They don't understand us."

"I d-don't understand them!"

"Shhhh. I know—neither do I."

"It was a little b-boy—he could not have b-been above five," she said brokenly. "What d-did he ever do to d-deserve—? Bell, he b-burned to death!"

"The smoke probably got him first." As soon as he

said it, Bell wished the words back. "I don't think he
felt it," he added lamely.

"I heard him scream—I h-heard him!" She clutched
his shoulders as though she had to make him believe her.
"I did not know what it was, but his cries woke me up!"

"There was nothing you could have done."

"M-maybe I could have stopped them—if I'd known—"

"Shhhh." Without thinking, he tilted her back and
brushed his lips against hers. "Don't, Kate," he whispered. "Please don't cry."

Her arms closed around his neck, clinging to him, and
he could taste the salt of her tears. His hands twined in
her dark hair, and for a moment, he lost himself in her
response to him. His mouth moved on hers, seeking more
as her lips parted with an eagerness he'd not suspected.
Suddenly, she struggled to sit, her face white, her dark
eyes filled with self-loathing. She was shaking.

"You must think me no better than—than—" she
choked out.

"The fault was mine, Kate." He let her stand and turn
away from him. "Look, I'm sorry—truly. I guess I forgot
who you were for a moment."

"I have n-not the excuse. I was merely lonely." Wrapping her arms about her like a shield, she started for the
open half door. "I'd b-best go back."

"It's an old habit—one that does not end easily." He
held out his hands, then dropped them. "I guess I am as
lonely as you are."

"You?" she asked incredulously.

"Surprising, isn't it?" He fell in beside her, and when
she sank nearly knee-deep in the heavy snow, he caught
her elbow. "Here—you are going to catch your death."
Reluctantly, he shed the warmth of his cloak and threw
it over her.

The cold wind cut like a knife through his clothing,
slicing to the bone, and crystallized snow whipped around
him, stinging his face. When Katherine stumbled against
him, he wrapped his arms around her and struggled with
her to the house.

Galena was waiting when they reached the house, her

displeasure obvious. "Ekaterina, you risk everything with your foolishness!" she snapped.

"Leave her alone," Bell gasped, trying to exhale the cold air from his lungs. "She's got to get warm."

Galena went to the foot of the stairs to call for Katherine's maid. "Maria! Maria!" Turning back, she said, "Maria has prepared some tea for Ekaterina, and Madame Popov will bring up the laudanum. Come," she ordered the younger woman, "we must get you into your warmed bed, and hope you have not harmed yourself or your babe."

"I d-don't want any l-laudanum, Lena," Katherine protested. "I won't d-drink it."

"You are behaving as a spoiled child," Alexei's sister countered.

"She is found?" Tatiana Volskaya asked.

"Yes." Nearly ignoring the girl, Galena marched toward Katherine's bedchamber. Once inside, she spun around to face her. "Ekaterina," she said stiffly, "you have shamed Alexei Petrovich in his own house."

For a moment, Katherine gaped, then she found her voice. "*I* have s-shamed him! Lena, he did not c-care that a little b-boy burned to death in this house!"

"You will not shout."

"I will shout if I wish, Lena! I am m-mistress of Domnya!"

"There was nothing he could do, I tell you! Go to bed, Ekaterina."

"No. I am n-not a child, Lena—I am *with* child! And there is a d-difference!" Pulling off her wrapper, Katherine went to one of the ornate wardrobes and drew out a dress. Still shaking almost uncontrollably from the cold, she announced, "I am going to d-discover the m-mother of that boy and tell her how s-sorry I am this has happened." Moving away from Alexei's sister, she dragged the gown down over her head and tried to button it with cold-stiffened fingers. When Maria attempted to assist her, she shook her head. "I am n-not a helpless ninny! There—you see, I have d-dressed myself!" She strode to

her writing desk and found her allowance box. Emptying
it, she stuffed the money in one of her reticules.

"What are you doing, Ekaterina?" Galena demanded.

"Money c-cannot replace the boy, but perhaps she will
be able to use it."

"You cannot give that to a serf! Boris!" Galena
shouted. "Boris!" As Katherine went back into the hall,
the older woman caught her. "Boris! Ekaterina, look at
yourself—you are sick!"

"Leave me alone, Lena!"

Galena barked orders to the burly manservant, and he
took Katherine's hand apologetically. *"Ee dyomtye sam-
noy, dahma."*

"I don't want to c-come with anyone!"

"You have frozen yourself, Ekaterina! If you do not
care for your own health, think of your son!"

"When I h-hold my son, I shall think of that boy's
m-mother," Katherine countered.

"Dahma, please," Maria pleaded.

"Speak Russian, you idiot!" Galena snapped, round-
ing on the maid furiously. "You have nothing to say in
the matter! Madame Popov, the laudanum!"

It was obvious that Boris did not want to hurt Katherine, but as Galena's temper heightened, he literally
picked up her and carried her to her bed. The main
housekeeper came, bottle and spoon in hand, and while
Galena held Katherine down and Boris forced her mouth
open, she poured two full spoons into the younger woman's mouth.

Katherine gagged and nearly brought it up. "You are
supposed to put it in water!" she cried. *"Vada*, Maria!
Vada!"

But it was Galena herself who carried the water back
to the bed. Standing over Katherine, she said sternly,
"You will drink, then you will sleep. And in the morning, everything will be better, Ekaterina. Tonight I will
tell everyone you are ill."

Defeated, Kate turned on her side and rolled into a
ball. "I do not believe Lexy knows you do this to me,

Lena,'' she muttered as Maria threw a heavy blanket over her. "Lexy would n-not t-treat me thus!"

Ignoring her now, Alexei's sister gestured to the warming pan, indicating she wanted it. Dutifully, Maria filled it with coals and brought it back. Moving Katherine's feet over, she slid the hot pan between the covers. Satisfied, Galena left.

Katherine felt sick all the way to her soul. How could they not care? Even a man like Bellamy Townsend cared. They were so wrong, so very wrong.

Maria removed the pan, she slid her feet to the hot place on her bed, seeking the warmth. Already she could feel the effect of the laudanum, and she was so dizzy she could scarce think. She closed her eyes against it and tried not to fall into the black pit of sleep.

On the morrow, she was going to reason with Alexei. On the morrow, she was going to make him understand how wrong things were at Domnya. On the morrow, she was going to make things different.

But as she ceased struggling, as the cold subsided, she no longer tried to think. Instead, she clung to the kindness in Bell Townsend's voice, the warmth of his fur-lined cloak, and finally to the remembered comfort of his kiss. The drug made her detached, giddy even. And as she finally succumbed, she wanted to tell Claire that Bell Townsend had kissed her.

Downstairs, Alexei Volsky faced Bell over a large glass of brandy. For a long time, he sat, saying nothing, then he rose and walked to the fire. Finally, he cleared his throat. "It was a mistake for Lena to invite you."

"There is nothing between myself and Kate."

"I am not speaking of Ekaterina." His face fixed on the red-orange flames, he exhaled heavily. "I am asking you to leave."

Bell gave a start. "Today? It's dashed nasty out there, Alexei," he protested.

"The morning will be soon enough. I will send you in my own coach, so you will not be excessively inconvenienced."

"Because of Kate? Look, I know—"

"I don't want you in the same house with Galena Petrovna."

"And if I tell you there is nothing there?"

Alexei shrugged. "It would not matter. There is Sofia, and that is enough. Sherkov is not a fool forever, I think, and we do not need him for an enemy."

"I despise the woman. As for Galena—"

"I do not wish to discuss my sister with you," Alexei said coldly, effectively cutting him off. "And you do not serve Ekaterina by reminding her of England. She is not this Kate you call her—she is Ekaterina Ivanova Volskaya."

"She is overset because of the boy's death, Alexei."

"Precisely." The Russian's lip curled disdainfully. "You think I have not seen your climbing boys, eh? But there you make them think everyone is free, and here we do not make the pretense. She will have to learn to live here."

"I promised her brother I would see she is well treated."

"And you have seen it. Ekaterina Ivanova has everything—everything Lena can buy for her. And when you are back in Moscow, you may write him that."

"I see. And will Kate know I am leaving?" Bell managed to ask evenly.

"When she wakes up tomorrow, I will tell her."

But later, sometime in the night, long after everyone else was abed, Bell sat, his feet warmed at the fire, his glass of vodka in his hand, thinking of Katherine Volsky. If he did not say anything to her, she would hate herself for encouraging him, and he couldn't leave her like that. He had to tell her that it meant nothing to him, that it ought to mean nothing to her.

She'd been too ill to come to supper, Galena had said, but Bell suspected it was more than that. For some odd reason, Alexei Volsky was jealous, and Bell suspected he did not let her come down.

His gaze traveled to the still-unwrapped silk scarf, and he felt his resentment grow. They weren't even going to let him give it to her, they weren't going to let him see if she liked it at all. Well, damn them all—damn them all to hell! He stood unsteadily and reached for the scarf. He'd be hanged if he let Volsky give it to her. Even if he roused the house, he would do it himself.

Scarf in hand, he made his way up the long, nearly dark hall. At the end, a sputtering candle burned in a chimneyed sconce, and he stood there uncertainly, wondering which door was Volsky's. Finally, he rapped on one, ready to demand to see Kate.

A still-dressed maid answered, her finger over her lips. "*Dahma?*" he tried. "Ekaterina Volsky?"

"Da." She eyed him strangely for a moment, then laid her head on her hands as though she slept.

He understood. "Volsky? Alexei Volsky?"

She shook her head.

Alexei wasn't with his wife. Bell held out the scarf, then pointed into the room. "For Ekaterina—*pour madame.*"

She stepped back, indicating the bed where Katherine lay, then she went to pick up the bottle and held it out to him. He unstoppered it and sniffed. They'd given her laudanum to make her sleep.

"All right." While the maid watched him, he refolded the scarf, then he gave it to her. "For Ekaterina," he repeated. "From me."

She nodded.

It was the best he could hope for, he supposed. At least he wouldn't be relying on Volsky to deliver his gift.

January 15, 1815

It had been perhaps the worst Christmas of Katherine's
life. Despite the exquisite and expensive presents given
her, she had felt incredibly lonely and left out much
of the time. When Bell Townsend had gone, it was as
though he'd taken whatever holiday there was left with
him. Not that she had felt much like celebrating anything
after the death of the little climbing boy. But that had not
mattered to the others—they'd merely been festive without her.

She'd been glad enough to see them go—Sofia with her
flirting manners, Sherkov with his irascible temper,
Prince Pahlin with his cold reserve, and Vera Pahlina,
his wife, who had spent much of the time regaling her
with the horrors of each of five childbeds. Now only Tatiana and Viktor remained, and in five more days, barring
more snow, they were supposed to return to school.

She sat in the huge book room, her chair drawn up to
the fire, wondering if this new storm would ever end.
Whenever her gaze strayed to the multi-paned windows,
she could see that the snow rose above the sills. Three
English feet, Galena had told her. At that rate, the
younger Volskys would be with them until spring.

Tati reminded her somewhat of Claire—lovely and
spiteful, while Viktor was shy, reserved—more like the
absent Paul. But at least he never cast barbs her way,
unlike Tati, who pried far too much, then muttered in-
sults when denied. Katherine could almost like Viktor.

Resolutely, she turned her attention to the book Harry
had sent her, Jane Austen's *Mansfield Park*. Under other
circumstances, she would have been delighted with it,

but just now she was rather blue-deviled. It was her pregnancy, she supposed wearily. That and the fact that Alexei now seemed to have completely deserted her bed, saying she needed her rest.

She stopped and tried to remember what she'd already read. It was no use. Her mind simply would not stay the course. She marked her place and set the book aside.

"Oh, there you are, Ekaterina!"

She looked up to see Tati, her face flushed with cold, her body bundled in cherry velvet trimmed with sable, and she felt a stab of envy. "So you have been romping in the snow?" she asked, forcing a smile.

"Yes." The girl came in, stomped the snow from her feet before the fire and pulled off heavy woolen mittens with her teeth. "You should have been there—we made a fort and defended it." Tati swung around to face her. "But I forget—Lena will not let you."

Ignoring that, Katherine asked mildly, "Who won?"

"Lena and Viktor—but then Lena always wins, doesn't she?"

"But you had Lexy."

"You must be besotted," Tati decided. "He lets her win, you know. Next time, I shall insist on Viktor." Moving to the bellpull, she rang for assistance. "I shall have a hot punch, I think—do you join me, Ekaterina Ivanova?"

"No."

"I suppose she does not let you do that either. It must be very tiresome for you here—I do not know how you stand it."

Katherine started to deny it, then held her tongue.

"Well," the girl sighed, "I should not like it. When I am wed, I shall make sure there is no other woman there to rule in my place."

"Tati—"

"But then I do not mean to be anyone else's oven. In fact, I am not at all certain I would wish to bear a child at all." She moved closer to Katherine. "You do not appear very comfortable, you know, but then Sofia said you might have twins."

"Leave her alone, Tati." Chafing his cold hands, Alexei's youngest brother entered the book room. "Did you order the punch?"

"If I have not, it is that the fool does not come."

"Which fool?"

"Any of them." At that moment, a hapless servant dared to show his head, and Tatiana rounded on him, berating him loudly, reminding Katherine of Galena. *"Ideeot!"* she shouted at him as he quaked before her. Then she made a shooing motion before turning back to her brother. "See, Viktor, you must be firm. Now we have the punch promptly," she added to Katherine. "Ekaterina, you are too kind, and it gets you nothing."

"I told you to leave her alone, Tati."

She regarded him haughtily. "You like the English mouse, Viktor? She was a stick, but now she looks like a pear, I tell you."

"Go to your room, Tati." Even as she spoke, Katherine could not believe she'd done it. When the girl did not move, she repeated, "I said you are to go to your room, Tati."

"You order *me*?" the girl demanded incredulously. "I do not think so, Ekaterina."

"And when the snow stops, you will return to school early," Katherine added evenly. "Until you are civil, I do not want you in my house."

"*Your* house? I do not think you dare tell Lena it is your house," Tatiana scoffed.

"I am Countess Volsky, and I have my marriage lines to prove it."

"Really?" The girls' eyebrow raised disdainfully. "And who has the ordering of the servants? And who approves everything? No, Ekaterina, Domnya is Galena Petrovna's."

"It is Alexei Petrovich's." Moving swiftly into the book room, Galena stopped before her youngest sister. Before the girl could raise her arm in defense, the woman struck her hard, leaving a hand print on her face. "And you will do as Ekaterina Ivanova tells you—do you hear me, Tati? Go to your room and have your maid pack your clothes for school. You also, Viktor.''

"Lena, I did nothing," he protested.

"You did not protect Ekaterina from her words."

"He tried," Katherine spoke up. "And it is not his place. Please—I do not mind if he stays until the next term starts."

"How long, Lena? How long do you think you—" Tatiana got no further.

Galena slapped her again, this time sending the girl reeling. "You will hold your tongue, Tati, or Lexy will not pay your allowance," she said coldly. "Apologize to Countess Volsky."

"Your pardon," the girl mumbled, her posture giving the lie to her words. As she passed Katherine, she muttered under her breath, *"Gloopee meesch!"*

"What did she say to you, Ekaterina?" Galena demanded.

"Nothing of import," Katherine lied.

"She called her a foolish mouse," Viktor said.

"That girl! She will not bother you again—I swear it. If she has to go to school in Siberia, she will not insult you again." Galena moved to put her arm about Katherine's shoulder. "I am so sorry—so truly sorry, Ekaterina. You must not let her behavior upset you."

Katherine pulled away. "The truth, Lena, however it is said, is still the truth."

The older woman appeared hurt. "Ekaterina, I only do for you what you cannot yet do for yourself." She peered more closely into Katherine's face. "You are beset by blue devils again, little one?"

"Yes. Perhaps it is the weather."

Viktor regarded her sympathetically. "It is different here, isn't it?"

"Yes."

"When you have grown old here, you will think of yourself as Russian," Galena assured her. "You will wish for nothing of England."

"Would you like to play chess, Ekaterina?" Viktor asked suddenly.

"Well, I am not very good at it," she conceded.

"At least you will have company."

"Yes. Yes, I think I would."

"Very well." Galena spoke rapidly to the boy in Russian, and he replied shortly in kind. Satisfied, she turned to leave. "I am going up to see that Tati packs everything, *mes enfants*.

"Yes, Little Mother," he murmured.

She spun around suspiciously. "What did you say?"

"I only meant that you are more like the Great Peter's Ekaterina than our Ekaterina is."

"See that you remember it always," she snapped.

As soon as she was gone, two serving boys returned with a steaming bowl of punch and cups. As they were arranging the silver tray, Viktor began setting up the chess board on one of the reading tables.

"I warn you, Ekaterina—I am the best in my school," he told her.

"Well, I must surely be the worst of your opponents," she murmured, taking the chair across from him. "In fact, I am not at all certain I can remember how to play it at all."

"Then I will be kind." He turned his head to say something to one of the servants, then returned his attention to her. "I told him that you would like a shawl as it is chilly in here."

She smiled. "Now that reminds me of Lexy—he is forever saying I must take care of myself."

He looked up, regarding her soberly. "I hope I am different from Alexei Petrovich. I should prefer to remind everyone of Paul before he married Olga Vladimovna. It seems to be the fate of the Volskys to be ruled by strong women," he added, sighing. "My mother was such a one before Lena."

"This is not a very happy family, is it?"

"Was yours?" he countered.

She thought of her brother and her father, then of her mother and her sister. "No, I suppose not. We were divided, Papa, Harry, and myself on the one side, Claire and Mama on the other."

"So are we. I think perhaps every family has its secrets, Ekaterina Ivanova." He stared at the board for a moment, then made his first move. "Your turn."

"I don't suppose you would wish to call me Kate?" she ventured wistfully.

"Kate?" He appeared to consider the name for a moment, then shook his head much as Alexei had done. "I don't like the sound of it."

"Surely there must be an informal name for Ekaterina here."

"Rina—or Kati."

"Oh. Well, I cannot say I like the sound of those, either."

"You are homesick, aren't you?"

"Terribly," she admitted.

"Your friend Townsend did not stay long."

"He is not precisely my friend—and no, he did not."

"Lexy was jealous," he said matter-of-factly.

"I cannot think why."

"You have known him a very long time, Ekaterina?— this Townsend, I mean?"

"Yes. But only through his friendship with my brother. He and I never used to deal well together." She made a tentative move, then sighed. "I used to despise him, you know. I'm afraid he was never a very admirable person, particularly where females were concerned."

"Neither is Lexy." He shook his head. "Now that, Ekaterina, was a very bad move. Look—you will lose your pawn already."

"I told you I do not know the game very well," she reminded him.

"Very well. We will clear the board, and I will try to teach it to you."

"All right."

She watched him turn the chess board at an angle so that she could better see what he did. He was as much an enigma as the rest of his family, this solemn boy who sat across from her. There were so many questions she wanted to ask him, and yet she could not, for she was afraid of the answers.

Viktor Volsky was very patient, pointing out each mistake gently, showing her how to anticipate his strategy. But he still won quickly.

"Oh—your pardon, Ekaterina—have you seen Lena or Madame Popov?"

It was Alexei. She half rose to stop him before he disappeared. "Wait—"

He stopped. "Something is the matter?"

"No, of course not," she said hastily. "It is just that—well, I have scarce seen you today." Not wanting to beg for his company, she indicated the chess board. "Viktor teaches me, and I thought perhaps you might wish to play."

"No. I am sorry, Ekaterina, but there is a matter I must attend. Perhaps later."

He was gone. She sat back, her disappointment evident, then she managed to square her shoulders. "Well, where am I?" she asked, looking again to the chess board.

"About to lose your queen."

"I am not a very good pupil, am I?"

Viktor's hand covered hers, squeezing it briefly, then he released it. As she looked up in surprise, he said quietly, "You have a friend in this house, Ekaterina."

"You?"

"Yes. I know how empty everything is here."

For a moment, she was taken aback, but there was nothing in his expression to distrust. And he certainly did not appear to be a boy in the throes of calf love.

"Thank you, Viktor—I shall always remember that."

"Please do."

"Yes—well, if I am about to lose again, I think I shall withdraw from the field. I am rather tired, you see, and my back pains me." This time, she rose with effort, grimacing. "It feels as though the little fellow is sitting on my spine."

"Shall I ring for assistance?"

"No. I have but to walk up the stairs to my chamber." She stopped at the door, then turned back to him. "Thank you for entertaining me this afternoon, Viktor."

"I had nothing else to do, Ekaterina."

She climbed the stairs slowly, thinking how much breath the babe took from her. She felt incredibly weary at the top, so much so that she held onto the baluster for a moment before going on. She did not know how she could wait another three months before delivering her child.

Once inside her chamber, she found herself alone, and instead of ringing for Maria, she sank into a chair. Using one foot to remove the slipper from the other, she looked down and saw that her ankles swelled. It was all of a piece, she supposed. She'd been plain before, but now she was simply ugly.

Acute loneliness washed over her, and with it came the most intense yearning for Harry and England she'd felt since her arrival in Russia. Her gaze swept the room as her mind attempted to bolster her spirits. She had everything, she told herself—everything. Even the gown she now wore was of the best silk Alexei's money could buy. She was as pampered as a princess, if clothes, jewelry, and luxurious surroundings meant anything. But she was alone amid all the opulence.

Out of the corner of her eye, she saw the bright silk scarf Bellamy Townsend had brought her; the scarf he'd not even stayed to give her. On impulse, she rose and went to pick it up, shaking it out, wrapping herself in it. It belonged to a peacock, not a sparrow, Tati had said. Odd, but he'd once called her that also—"a sparrow with lion's teeth," he'd said. Only she didn't feel like a lion at all. Just now she felt more the wounded sparrow.

She walked back to her desk and opened a drawer to find the note he'd left also. "Dearest Kate," he'd written, "I'm afraid I've been given the heave-ho, possibly because of your husband's fear of Sherkov. At any rate, I hope you will wear the scarf in health, knowing I chose the brightest thing I could find in this dreary place. Think of the other as a kiss between friends. Your servant, Townsend."

Icy branches rattled against her windows, making her shiver more from the sound than the cold. Reluctantly, she laid the scarf aside and lay down upon her bed. Pulling her covers up, she turned over to hug her pillow.

Something crackled beneath it, and when she slid her hand there, she felt a folded paper. Mystified, she pulled it out and sat up, opening it to the snow-bright light, and as she read it, her blood went cold inside.

In Tati's feathery hand, it said: "If you would know why he does not share your bed, you will have to go to his after midnight."

It was the girl's final attempt at spite. Balling up the paper, Katherine threw it across the room before lying down again. What was she supposed to find—that he had taken one of the maids to his bed? Yet even as she thought it, every fiber of her being denied it. He loved her. He'd married her and brought her to Russia as his countess. If he neglected her, it was because he believed she needed to rest. He wanted to take care of her. Yes, that was it— he did not come to her because he feared for her health. Because she was being sent back to school early, Tati had acted out of revenge.

S he could not sleep. Somewhere in the distance, the faint sound of church bells vied with the cries of the wolves. She rolled over and tried to see the clock, but it was in shadows. Clutching her heavy nightgown close, she rose from the bed. Despite the glowing coals in the fireplace, the room was cold. For a moment, she warmed her body over them, then she lit a candle and sought the clock. She needn't have bothered—somewhere within the cavernous house, a bigger one struck thrice. It was three o'clock in the morning.

She listened, but there was no sound after the chimes, indicating everyone else slept. Moving to the desk, she saw where Maria had picked up the crumpled paper and laid it there. Part of her denied the implication, and part of her wished to know the truth of it. She'd had to force herself to lie through the twelve bells of midnight, then one bell, then two . . . and now three.

Unable to stand it any longer, she got her wrapper and pulled it on, tying the sash around it, and then she found her fur-lined slippers. She would say she was cold, and he would not turn her away. She would say she could not sleep without him.

It was dark in the hallway, so dark that she could not even see the pattern of the carpet beneath her feet. She was dizzy, light-headed, and shivering as she kept close to the wall, moving noiselessly. She stopped outside his door, thinking perhaps she ought to turn back, that she ought not let Tati poison her mind. But something deep within her demanded to know. She turned his doorknob, almost hoping it was locked, then held her breath as the door opened inward.

She waited, taking stock of nearly everything before she dared to move. Stubby candles still burned in their holders, and long wax icicles hung downward from the iron stand, indicating that Alexei had retired quite late. The room was unfamiliar, the furniture heavy, baroque. Near the bed, a fire still crackled and spit, and the heavy, carved bed cast strange, distorted shadows that bent at the ceiling.

It was a big bed, medieval almost, swathed in red hangings so dark they appeared black. The curtains were pulled closed to shut out drafts from the tall, multi-paned windows. Resolutely, Katherine crossed the floor to it, her footsteps hidden in the depths of the thick carpet. Once there, she put her candle in a guttered sconce, then shed her slippers and wrapper and parted the bed hangings to slip inside.

In the darkness, her hand caught in silky hair, and a woman turned over, murmuring sleepily, "Lexy?"

It was as though Katherine's heart stopped and her stomach knotted. *Tati had known Alexei would not be alone.* She shook, this time not from the cold, as she backed out of the bed. As though she were in a trance, she moved to pick up a brace of dying candles, then reached to pull the heavy curtains with unsteady hands.

The flickering orange and yellow light fell on Galena's red hair as it spilled in a tangled mass across a satin-covered pillow. Alexei's sister sat up, and the heavy coverlet fell from her bare shoulders. She blinked, then stared, her expression stunned.

"Ekaterina!"

Alexei rolled over and reached for Galena, mumbling, "*Shto?*"

"*Ana zdyiss*! She is here!" Clasping the covers to her bosom with one hand, she held up the other helplessly. "Oh, Ekaterina—"

Katherine felt sick all the way to her soul. She turned and stumbled blindly from the room, ignoring Galena's shouts of "Ekaterina! Ekaterina!"

Katherine leaned against the wall, unable to breathe,

unable to think, as the knot in her stomach tightened. Wave after wave of nausea hit her until she could swallow it back no longer. Bracing herself with one arm, she leaned forward to retch again and again, heaving despite her empty stomach.

"*Dahma!*"

Having heard Galena, Maria hurried into the hall in her nightdress. Catching Katherine from behind, she held her. "Bed—bed, *dahma.*"

"No—I—" Katherine strangled, unable to answer.

"Bory! Bory!" the girl shouted. "Boreeees!" As Katherine sank to the floor, her head between her knees, Maria knelt beside her. Looking to Alexei Volsky's open bedchamber door, she understood. "Oh, *dahma,*" she whispered. "I try for you not to know—I try," she repeated over and over again.

But Katherine leaned forward, her body hunched in a ball, her arms hugging her knees, rocking. As footsteps could be heard scrambling in the servants' quarters overhead, Maria put her arms around her. "Dahma, no—your babe."

"I wish I were dead" was the muffled answer.

"No, no—the babe—"

"I don't want it." Katherine's eyes were oddly dry when she lifted her head. "They lied to me, Maria—*they lied to me!*"

Alarmed, Maria called loudly for Boris again.

"Be still, you fool!" Galena hissed, coming out into the hall. Then, realizing she spoke to Maria, she snapped, "*Zamalchee! Zamalchee!*" She pulled the girl away roughly, then slapped her. "*Zabood-tye!* You will forget!" As the first footman raced down the stairs, she shouted him away, making a shooing motion with her hands.

Still dressing, Alexei came up behind his sister. She nodded to Katherine and spoke in English for the younger woman's benefit. "She will be all right, I promise you. Come, Ekaterina—we will get you to bed."

"Don't touch me!"

"*Daragaya—*"

"And don't call me that!"

He looked helplessly to Galena. "What do you want me to do?"

"Carry her to her bed."

Despite the awkwardness of her body, Katherine struggled to her feet without his help. "If you touch me, Lexy, I swear I will bring the house down about your ears," she said evenly.

He dropped his hand. "She does not want—"

"Fool! *Doorak!*" Galena rounded on him. "It does not matter what she wants! We must think of the child!"

"But she does not want—"

As though nothing was different, the Russian woman coaxed, "Alexei will help you, Ekaterina. Come— everything will be all right, I promise you."

Katherine stared at her in horror. "What kind of people are you? Lena, I saw you—I saw you—"

"When you are in bed and Maria has brought you a soothing *tisane*, we will speak."

"I don't want anything." Turning away, Katherine started back to her bedchamber.

"Ekaterina—"

Before either of them stopped her, she got inside and closed her door, locking it. She felt empty, hollow, as though there was a great void beneath her breastbone. Sinking into a chair before her nearly dead fire, she stared, unable to think beyond what she'd seen. She would not cry—she dared not, for fear that once she started, she could not stop. She closed her eyes and swallowed, thinking that she must surely have gone mad.

The cold did not matter anymore. Nothing mattered. She did not even hear them pounding on her door, nor did she hear Maria begging her to open it. She was utterly, completely numb, and still she wished she were dead.

How could she have been such a fool? How could she have believed he loved her? And Galena—there were no words for Galena. Galena had betrayed her.

The doorjam splintered, and Boris came sprawling inside. Embarrassed, he righted himself and pointed to the few coals left. He was going to make her a fire.

"*Daragaya*—Ekaterina—" Alexei came to stand over her.

She did not answer.

He tried again. "Ekaterina. Please."

"Tell Galena I do not wish to hear it," she said finally.

"She said you would not know. I did not want to hurt you, little one." She was too cold, too controlled. Mistaking that for reason, he plunged ahead with the speech Galena had given him. "Nothing has to change, Ekaterina. You are still my countess, and—"

"Please don't."

"But you must listen to me," he pleaded. "I am telling you that it will be all right."

"All right?" Her voice rose in disbelief as something seemed to shatter within her. "*All right?* Alexei, everything is very wrong! I loved you, Lexy—I *loved* you! And you—you—" Words failed her for a moment.

"I said I did not want to hurt you."

"You lied to me! You came to London, and you courted me, and you made me believe I was loved with the flowers, with the sweet notes—with this ring even! It was cruel—the cruelest hoax I have ever believed!" When he did not respond, she forced herself to look at him. "Everything you said was nothing but a lure! You made me love you so she could have a child!"

"I will honor you, Ekaterina, I swear it. As the mother of my children, I will honor you."

"Did she tell you to say that also?" she demanded. "Were any of the words spoken between us yours? Or were you merely Galena's puppet on strings?"

"I will still be your husband. We do not have to change anything," he said evasively. "The other has nothing to do with you."

"Nothing to do with me?" Her voice rose hysterically. "Lexy, are you mad? You—you come to me telling me that everything is the same! Well, it isn't! There is a word for what is between you and Galena, Alexei—it is *incest*!"

"I cannot help it, Ekaterina."

Angry, bitter tears burned her eyes. "Was I ever anything to you, Lexy? Did you ever feel anything for me?" Once again, her voice was shrill. "Answer me—for God's sake, *answer* me! Did you ever love me?"

He looked away. "You are my wife."

"Your wife! No, I only thought I was your wife! You married me for this, didn't you, Lexy?" She rested her hand on her rounded stomach. "Galena could not give you an heir, so she chose a plain girl to do it for her!"

"Ekaterina, I am sorry. What can I say to you? I have loved Lena all of my life."

"Not like that surely!"

"At first it just happened—I was sick, and there was no one to care for me. My father did nothing, for he had other sons—and my mother was too busy to come home from Moscow for me. I was fourteen, Ekaterina, and I still remember the feel of Galena's breasts as she held me."

"And that is supposed to make it right? It is a sin!"

"I told you—I cannot help it. When my father forced Lena to marry—the night she went to Cyril—I nearly lost my mind. I wanted to kill Papa and Cyril both."

"Were you going to wish me dead also?" she cried. "After this child was born, were you going to get rid of me? Was Galena going to brew something for me?"

"No, no, of course not. You read too many of those English gothic romances." He ran his hand across his face. "I would have returned to your bed and got another. I wanted us to be a family, Ekaterina—you, me, and Lena. I wanted there to be children at Domnya."

It was too much for her to comprehend. She buried her head in her hands and began to sob uncontrollably. He started to touch her, then drew away. "You do not understand, Ekaterina."

"You fool! You were supposed to console her!" Galena told him furiously from the door.

"Lena, I cannot—she will not be consoled," he retorted defensively.

"Then leave us." As he brushed past her, she muttered, "I must do everything for you." Crossing the room to where Katherine sat, she dropped to her knees and smoothed the younger woman's hair. "Ekaterina, I am so sorry you had to discover Alexei's secret. Poor Ekaterina," she murmured. "My poor little Ekaterina."

Katherine's shoulders shook beneath her touch. "It will be all right."

"Never!"

"But you still have everything he gives you. You are Countess Volsky. You live at Domnya. You will rear your children here." Galena put her arms around Katherine. "Ekaterina, I have seen that you have everything you could wish for—a handsome husband, a title, wealth, children. You would have had none of that in England." Her hand stroked the younger woman's tangled hair. "Lexy needs me, but only you can give him an heir, so he needs you also. No one else has to know. You will fill Domnya's nursery, and you will be honored for that. You can give Lexy something I cannot, so between us, we make a family."

A great shudder passed through Katherine as she sought calm. "I-I would you did not touch me, Galena. I cannot bear it."

Alexei's sister reluctantly drew away. "What an innocent you are, Ekaterina Ivanova. You think husbands are faithful to their wives? Look at your own country, where ladies have children by different lovers and the husband does not complain. And the women—" She paused scornfully. "The women, they pretend they do not know about the other women their husbands keep."

"In my country, a man does not sleep with his sister."

"No? I am a stranger there, and I hear about your poet Byron."

"I don't want to live like that. I don't want to live at Domnya." Twisting the folds of her wrapper, Katherine declared, "I won't live like that."

"I can give you another house, or jewels, or fine furs, Ekaterina. I have made you Countess Volsky, and I am willing to share Alexei with you." Galena looked meaningfully at Katherine's swollen belly. "You carry that child for me as well as for Domnya. Now, as we are understood, you will drink whatever I make for you, and you will know that it will not harm you. There is nothing I would do to injure you or the child." She struggled to rise. "Alexei is a weak man, Ekaterina, and I am sorry for it. But together we hold him, and together we watch his children grow. And no one has to know anything about how it is between us."

Feeling utterly beaten, Katherine said nothing. If Alexei was mad, so was Galena. And there were no words to make anything different. She had been cheated of her dreams, and they seemed to think she should be grateful.

"Ekaterina, we love you," Galena coaxed. "Come, let us not quarrel over this. I make everything right for you. When the snow is gone, we go to Moscow and buy you dresses for after the babe comes, eh? And Czar Alexander will be godfather to him. You will be the envy of all Russia, I tell you." Leaning to kiss Katherine's cheek, she murmured, "You will feel better after you sleep."

"I cannot sleep forever, Lena."

"It will not come to that, *ma petite*."

After Galena left, Katherine walked to the window and stared out into the darkness. For a moment, she considered hurling herself down into the dead garden below. But the child within her stirred, changing positions, hitting her ribs with an arm or foot, and she knew she could not. Neither could she stay at Domnya.

She hurt—as surely as if someone had driven a knife between her breasts, she hurt. And no matter how far she went away from Alexei and his sister, she knew she would always feel the pain. She had been such a fool, she thought bitterly, and despite what Galena said, nearly everyone knew. Sofia. Olga. Tati. And Viktor. How they must have laughed at her naïveté.

"Dahma?" Maria asked tentatively. "Better? You better?"

"You knew, didn't you?"

"Da."

"And you did not tell me."

"Nyet."

"I suppose it was fear."

"Shto?"

"I do not blame you, Maria, but I will never forgive them." Perceiving that the girl sympathized but did not understand all her words, Katherine sighed. "Nothing," she said finally. *"Neechevo."* Seeing the cup the girl carried, she shook her head. *"Nyet—ye nye pyoo*—I don't want to drink anything.*"* There was no mistaking the apprehension in the maid's eyes. *"Here—"* Taking the cup, Katherine carried it into the water closet and poured the contents out. *"Go back to bed."*

Long after Maria left, Katherine stood at the window, her arms crossed like a shield before her. Forcing her thoughts away from Alexei's betrayal, she let her mind return to England. Just now she missed her papa terribly, perhaps more than any time since his death. When he was alive, she was held, comforted, shielded against unhappiness. But John Winstead was dead, leaving only Harry who loved her. And somehow she could not write Harry about what was happening to her. It was simply too humiliating to put into words.

There was a faint, stealthy knock at her door, and for a moment, she suspected her mind tricked her. But as she listened, she heard it again. And again. She held her breath, hoping whoever it was would think her asleep, but the sound became more insistent. It would not be Alexei or Galena, she was certain, for they believed she'd drunk the laudanum-laced *tisane.* But she did not want to face anyone—the pain was too deep, too raw for any to see.

The door opened a crack, just enough for a tentative, whispered, "Ekaterina?" It was Viktor.

"If you have come to console me, I am beyond reason, I think," she said.

The boy slipped inside and closed the door quietly. "I have come to help you escape them."

"Viktor—"

"No—no, it is not impossible."

She clasped her arms more tightly, scarce daring to believe him. "How?"

"They will not come down when I go back to school. I can take you to Paul and Olga, and they will not know until it is too late," he answered simply.

"And what of the driver? Or the coachmen? Or the ostlers? I thank you for the thought, but I'm afraid we should be discovered.'' She forced a small smile. ''I do thank you for the thought,'' she said again.

''Ekaterina, I will say you are my manservant.''

She looked down at her bulging belly. ''Like this?'' she asked incredulously. ''Viktor, it is obvious I am increasing.''

''We leave at first light, and you will be bundled warmly against the cold. If you carry a heavy fur rug in front, none will notice,'' he argued eagerly. ''You have but to pull the cloak hood over your face, Ekaterina.'' When he could see she was still uncertain, he added, ''You can take some of your clothes in my trunks. Maria will pack them when everyone is asleep.''

Maria. She shook her head. ''I cannot leave Maria to Lena's certain wrath.''

''Bring her then. Ekaterina, it is your only chance to escape! Do you want Lena stealing your child from you? She will make him as weak as Lexy!''

''And how do we get Maria out of the house?''

''I told you—no one ever comes to see me away. I will say that you have sent her to procure some herbs for you in the village, and I will order a carriage to come for her there.''

''Why would the same carriage not take her and bring her back?'' she countered.

''Ekaterina, they are serfs. Whatever I say, they must accept whether it makes sense or not. They do not dare to question me.''

''But when Galena discovers I am gone, she will send after me. If not for me, for my child.''

''We do not go to Moscow, Ekaterina. I will take you to Omborosloe, and I do not think Lena will wish to push Olga too far. Olga,'' he declared somberly, ''will not hesitate to spread the scandal to discredit her.''

''If she has known all these years—''

''Suspected—not known,'' he corrected her. ''It has been whispered, but not proven. Only I knew for certain, for I was with Papa when he caught them together at the summer house.''

"Why do you do this for me?" she asked suddenly. "Why would you risk Lexy's anger?"

"Because of what Lena has done to him. She has made him into nothing."

The truth was so painful that she did not know if she could face Olga Vladimovna.

It was as though he guessed her thoughts. "Paul will welcome you, Ekaterina—and Olga will also, for her own reasons."

"I see."

"It is your only chance."

"And the whole world will know what a fool I have been," Katherine observed bitterly. "They will say I should have known he could not love a plain female."

"They will blame Galena Petrovna. And you are not entirely plain, Ekaterina—when you smile, you are not plain at all," he reassured her awkwardly. "It makes your eyes shine."

She didn't want to go to Omborosloe—she wanted to go to England. But England was so far away that it could not even be contemplated, given the weather. And if she stayed at Domnya, now that there would be no need for pretense, she would be reduced to nothing more than the oven Tati had said. She would be but a pitiful creature, and everyone would know it.

"How long have you known?" she asked finally.

"Since I was a small boy. I heard the quarrel, and I will always remember my father's fury. If he had not died before he could do it, I think he would have given Domnya to Paul because of Lena."

She did not know what Lexy would do about the child, whether he would demand her own return or not, but she knew she could not stay there. She could not let Lena rear her son. She exhaled heavily, then raised her eyes to meet Viktor Volsky's.

"All right. I will go."

It had been an arduous three-day journey because of drifting snow and low temperatures, with Viktor, Katherine, and Maria huddled together beneath the fur rug in the carriage, taking turns being in the middle for the greatest warmth. No fewer than five times the driver and coachman had wanted to turn back, but Viktor managed to shout them down. It was a wonder, Katherine reflected wearily, that the poor fellows had not frozen to the box. They were used to it, Viktor said, but she knew better. They could not be.

The roads had been nearly empty of travelers, but every time she heard a horse or carriage, her heart paused. She did not believe she'd actually escaped Galena and Alexei until the coach came to a halt before Omborosloe.

She was so tired, so very tired, and her feet were numb from the cold, so much so that she did not know if she could walk. While Viktor jumped down to explain everything to his brother and Olga, she and Maria remained pressed together beneath the fur, both shivering uncontrollably. If they were turned away, the maid predicted tearfully that they would die.

"N-nonsense," Katherine muttered, utterly unconvinced herself.

It seemed as though they waited an eternity, but finally it was Paul rather than Viktor who opened the carriage door. "You must be careful of her," he cautioned a man with him. To Katherine, he said, "Do not try to do anything—Ivan will carry you, Ekaterina."

She half rose to lean out the door, then quite literally fell into the manservant's arms. He lifted her easily and started up the stone stairs, while Paul himself guided an unsteady Maria behind them.

"Welcome to Omborosloe, Ekaterina Ivanova," Olga murmured, leaning to kiss Katherine's cold cheek. "What a terrible ordeal you have suffered, but you are safe now. Come, we must get you into something warm, and then we shall speak over some spiced tea—unless you prefer the coffee, of course."

"T-tea w-would be f-fine."

"Poor Ekaterina. Yelena will see you to your chamber and soak your feet in cold water," Olga said soothingly. "Then I shall come up to you with the tea."

"C-cold water?"

"Unless you wish to lose your toes. Already Viktor soaks his. That boy—what was he thinking to bring you out in such weather? But of course he had not the choice, little Ekaterina, for you could not stay at Domnya. How Lena must be vexed just now."

"Let the girl thaw out," Paul spoke up. "You may pry later."

The man Ivan carried Katherine up the wide staircase and down a long hall to a bedchamber. Following him were Yelena and a stumbling Maria, who complained she could not feel anything either. Already, another two maids had prepared a pan of water and were in the process of filling a tub.

There was a voluble exchange between Maria and the others before the little maid explained, "You cold, they heat you."

"I h-hope s-so. G-go warm yourself." When the girl did not move, Katherine pointed at Maria, saying, "*Tee—zhara.*"

Too tired to protest, Katherine allowed the maids to undress and wrap her in a blanket, then she sat shivering with her feet in the cold water. They stung and burned as the feeling came back. Satisfied, the maids gestured for her to lay upon the bed, where they pounded and pummeled the warmth back into her body. Finally they bathed her, letting her soak in the warm water until the chill receded from her bones.

It was not until she was swathed in a heavy gown and another blanket and seated before a roaring fire that Olga came up to her. As Katherine watched, the other woman poured two cups of the steaming liquid, then added chunks of brown sugar and a finger of brandy to each.

"This will make you feel better," she declared, handing one over. She waited until the drink was sampled, then nodded her approval. "Yes, yes—much better."

"Thank you."

"There is no need to thank me, Ekaterina. I would do anything to deny Galena Petrovna Domnya—anything." She drank deeply, then sighed her satisfaction. "Yes, you must stay at Omborosloe until the child is born. Galena will be in a rage, but what can she do, I ask you?"

Katherine felt uneasy. "What about Alexei? Can he demand my return if he discovers I am here?" she asked nervously. "I don't know anything of your laws."

"The laws are what Alexander chooses to make them." Olga reached to pat Katherine's hand. "My father is powerfully connected, so you must not worry. When we are done, Galena Petrovna will not dare show her face in Moscow or St. Petersburg," she declared with conviction. "It will cost Alexei Petrovich Domnya to stop me from exposing him for what he is."

"Olga, all I want is a divorce," Katherine protested. "And to go home to England."

"No," the other woman contradicted, "you shall have revenge."

"I have to protect my child—I left Domnya to protect my child."

"Yes, yes—of course. But you are in no condition to travel now, anyway—and there is the weather." Olga finished her cup, then set it aside. Rising, she towered over Katherine. "You must leave everything to me, Ekaterina, and Galena Petrovna will wish she had never been born. I suggest you let Yelena warm your bed that you may rest. You have suffered a terrible shock, and it cannot be very good for you or the child."

After she left, Katherine sipped the rest of her brandied tea slowly, thinking that Olga Vladimovna was as managing as Galena. But there was no warmth or kindness in her, not even in pretense.

Rested, bathed, and dressed in a burgundy velvet gown, Katherine went down early to sup. She hoped to find Viktor, but discovered Paul instead. He came out of his study, and when he saw her, his expression was somber. For a moment, she thought he meant to tell her that Alexei had sent someone to take her back to Domnya.

"Ah, Ekaterina, you are looking better." But as he spoke, he did not look at her. "Would you care for some wine or tea before dinner?" He held the door as though he did not expect her to refuse.

"Yes, of course."

"Tea—or wine?"

"Wine will be fine."

"Good. We have some of the French variety, I think." Gesturing to a chair with one hand, he pulled the bell cord with the other. "Some of the champagne, Ilya," he ordered the servant who came. Turning back to Katherine, he studied her for a moment, then sighed. "First, Ekaterina, I must tell you I am sorry for what you suffer at the hands of my family. Given the circumstances, it was wrong of Alexei to marry anyone."

"I was a fool," she admitted simply. "I should have known he did not care for me."

"No, no—he can be quite persuasive, I am sure."

'She did not spare herself. "He only wanted a child for Galena."

He nodded. "Lena grieves for the babe she lost." He moved away to stare into the flames that licked the neatly stacked logs on the grate, then he cleared his throat. "I do not fault Viktor for bringing you here, but I fear you have not improved your situation."

Her heart thudded painfully and her stomach knotted. "I see. You think I should go back."

"Not at all." Returning, he poured two glasses of champagne and handed her one. Sipping his, he looked over the rim. "I think, Ekaterina, that you must do what is right for yourself and your child."

"But Viktor said I should be welcomed here. And Olga—"

"My Olga and Galena are very much alike, I am afraid, although each would deny it."

"She said I could stay—that I could stay until my child is born." She felt a sense of hopelessness. If he turned her out, she had nowhere to go. "Please—at least that long."

"Ekaterina, where the babe would have been Galena's treasure, it will be Olga's pawn."

"I'm afraid I do not understand, sir."

"Paul. We are family, Ekaterina Ivanova, and I want to help you." Again he peered at her above his glass. "My wife, I am afraid, is so taken up with envy and perceived slights that she will do anything to bring my sister down. I, on the other hand, do not want to see my family ruined." He finished his champagne and set the glass on the table. "I think, Ekaterina, you must decide whether you would have revenge or the child."

She stared into her champagne, thinking perhaps she'd had too much, that perhaps her brain was too fogged to follow what he said. "You think Lexy will attempt to take my babe?" she asked him.

"I think that if you tell this tale of incest, they will make every attempt to put you in an asylum, my dear," he answered soberly. "And if they do not, Olga will trade the infant for Domnya."

"Not while I breathe," Katherine declared. "I should rather die than raise my child at Domnya."

"Alas, but that too can be arranged. My wife, Ekaterina, is a Narransky—and the Narranskys have intrigued for centuries. What they dare not do openly, they will achieve anyway—by exploiting weakness, by threats—and sometimes by poison."

"Are you saying Olga would have me killed?" she asked incredulously.

"I am saying she is not beyond it—unless you are willing to let her use the child to bring my brother down."

She sat very still, her mind trying to understand that she faced the possibility of an insane asylum or death, that she'd allowed herself to be caught between two scheming women. Putting aside her glass, she clasped her hands in her lap and tried to think rationally.

"There is nowhere else to go, I am afraid," she said finally. "Unless—no, it would not serve," she decided. "He came here to escape scandal rather than cause one."

"An Englishman?"

"Yes. And I do not even know where he is." She looked at her hands. "Before Christmas, he was with Marshal Sherkov and his wife. Now he has removed to a hotel somewhere in Moscow."

"Could you trust him, do you think?" he probed gently.

The image of Bellamy Townsend came to mind. She shook her head. "I don't know. I have no claim on him, other than he is my brother's friend."

"Could he perhaps be persuaded by money?"

The irony of everything bore down on her, and she smiled wryly. "Unless he has lost it, he is possessed of a considerable fortune. Besides, I cannot think he would help me, for he has such a shocking reputation that we both should be ruined. I do not think he would risk being ostracized forever for anyone." She studied her hands again for a moment. "Indeed, I know he would not. He has run from every scandal of his making, so why should he wish to embroil himself in mine?"

"I see." He put his fingertips together and contemplated the fire again. "Well, then I shall have to think of something else, *n'est-ce pas*? In the meantime, you must not worry. You have—what?—three months perhaps?" he guessed.

"Yes."

"It is enough time to discover a way out, I think."

"Ekaterina Ivanova, you are down early," Olga observed, coming into the room. "Ah, Paul, you have entertained her, I see."

"Yes."

"I have told her we will protect her."

"But of course."

"You see, Ekaterina? You will stay here with us, and

Alexei will not dare demand your return." She looked around briefly, then asked her husband, "But where is Viktor?"

"He is more afraid of Galena than you are, my darling. He has already left for school."

"The Volskys!" she spat out. "They are all weak men."

Surprisingly, Paul did not dispute it. "What are we having for supper tonight?" he asked as though he'd not heard the other.

"Lamb, dumplings, sour cabbage soup—too much to remember, I am sure. "We did not expect a guest, but no doubt the cook will manage. If you are finished, Ekaterina, you may come with me, and I will show you Omborosloe. It is not," she declared with a withering look at her husband, "nearly so big as Domnya."

Katherine covered her empty glass with hand. "Er, I find myself rather tired from the journey, and if you do not mind it, I should prefer to finish my champagne."

"Champagne?" The other woman's eyebrow lifted. "You gave her champagne, Paul?"

"To celebrate her escape, Olga," he told her.

"Ah, yes—a celebration is in order. Little Ekaterina, we have but begun. Before this year is out, we will live at Domnya," she predicted smugly. "You will go home in triumph."

"I don't—" Katherine caught his warning look. "That is, I hope that Lexy will not be there."

"Humph! He will be most fortunate to be *here,* if I have anything to say," Olga assured her. "Very well, you may drink your champagne without me." She looked down to where Katherine's feet were visible beneath the hem of her gown. "How long have you had that?" she asked suddenly.

"What?"

"Those ankles."

"You mean the swelling? For the last several weeks, I'm afraid," Katherine admitted ruefully. "Increasing tends to make one rather ugly, doesn't it?"

"Well, I do not like that. Paul, do you see? We must

have the doctor to examine her." She smiled thinly at Katherine. "Nothing must happen to the child, Ekaterina."

"He won't come in this weather, Olga," her husband reminded her. "As he gets old, he prefers to stay by the fire, mumbling over his vodka. Would you have a drunkard tend her—or do you not think perhaps she ought to see Karasov?"

"In Moscow?" Again, her eyebrow rose perceptibly. "Why would you say that?"

"Because you are concerned. Kanin is worthless if anything goes wrong."

"It is something to consider," she conceded. "Yes, for once, you are right. I do not like those ankles at all. When my sister Natalya swelled like that, she lost the child. And I am sure it would ease Ekaterina's mind to know that everything is all right."

"Perhaps you should go with her," he suggested.

"Why would you say that? You know very well that I despise Moscow in the winter. Unless the czar is there, it is a worthless place."

"Ekaterina knows no one there."

"She will know you," Olga declared with a finality that brooked no argument. "You will take her."

"You know I am not very good at such things," he countered. "She should have a woman with her."

"You are not very good at anything," she snapped. "And she will take her maid."

For a time after his wife left, Paul stared absently, making Katherine acutely uncomfortable. Finally, she broke into his thoughts. "Actually, I do not mind seeing this Kanin, for one doctor is very much like another, I expect." When he said nothing, she added, "And I have traveled more than I cared to these two days past."

"No, Ekaterina," he said, "if Olga Vladimovna says you must go to Moscow, you will go. She would be more unforgiving than Lena if you lost your child."

Moscow: *January 26, 1815*

T
he hotel corridor was empty as they searched for
the number given them by the clerk. Then Katherine found it—#16, and for a moment, she stood
there, composing what she would say. Behind her, Paul
Volsky waited. Finally, she squared her shoulders and
tapped lightly on the door. She heard movement within
the room, and her heart pounded in her ears. She knew
he was going to turn her away.

Bell opened the door in his shirtsleeves, apologizing
for the lapse, then he stared at her.

"Kate! What the devil—?"

"Please—I'd come inside. And Paul."

As he stood back, she hurried past him, and the man
with her urged him to close the door. He swung around
to face them, his eyebrows raised.

"Never say this is an elopement?" he murmured.

"Of course not!" She caught herself, knowing she had
to put her case to the touch quickly or lose her nerve.
"Bell, I have nowhere else to turn!" she blurted out.
"You are my last hope!"

"I suspect," he decided wryly, "that you have come
to enact me some sort of Cheltenham tragedy." But
something in her face told him she was utterly serious.
"All right, Kate—out with it." As he spoke, he shoved
a chair at her. "But first you'd best sit—you look fagged
half to death." Before she could speak, he retrieved his
chased silver flask, opened it, and handed it to her.
"Have a sip—it will revive you."

Her hands were shaking as she took it, and when she

drank, liquid fire shot to her stomach. Coughing, she pushed it away.

"Ugh!"

"You are supposed to sip it."

It was several seconds before she caught her breath. In half-strangled words, she asked, "What was that?"

"Your national drink. Vodka." Screwing the lid back on, he set the flask aside. "Now—to what do I owe the honor?"

She didn't know whether to look at him or not. Finally, she met his eyes. "I have left Alexei, you see."

"What?" He gave a start, and his eyes narrowed. "No. It won't fadge, Kate—nobody would believe it. Besides, I have given up my penchant for wives."

"Monsieur—"

"Who the devil is he?" Bell demanded.

"Alexei's brother, Paul Volsky. He brought me here." She sucked in her breath, then let it out before trying again. "I would not have turned to you, Bell Townsend, if I had anywhere else to go, but I do not." When he said nothing, she looked to her hands in her lap. "It is a very lowering tale to tell, you see," she began, "and I don't even know how to tell it." Raising her eyes, she could see he was regarding her skeptically. "I have been such a fool—such an utter fool! I should have known he could not love someone like me!"

She looked like the veriest waif—her face was red from the cold, her nose ran, and her dark eyes seemed too large for her pale face. He reached for his flask again, and this time, it was he who drank, gulping, gaining time.

"It would be more affecting if you'd blow you nose, Kate," he told her brutally. Pulling his handkerchief from among his effects on a table, he tossed the folded cloth at her. "Keep it."

She blew loudly, then wadded it in her lap. "It is so humiliating that I do not even know where to start."

"The beginning."

He was giving her no encouragement, none at all. "Lexy does not love me, Bell."

He supposed she'd discovered Alexei Volsky was no more faithful than any other man. "It was to be expected, Kate. Most husbands keep a bit of fluff here and there," he said finally. "And most wives learn to live with it."

"Bell," her voice rose incredulously, "Alexei's bit of fluff, as you call it, is Galena!" As his face mirrored his disbelief, she nodded. "I know. I caught them, Bell—I caught them!" She stopped to blow her nose again, then spoke more calmly. "I caught them in Alexei's bed—and—and Galena said I should stay, anyway—that no one else need know. She said I could be Countess Volsky and bear his children—but I cannot! I cannot!" She touched her rounded belly, and her voice dropped. "All they wanted of me was this, Bell."

He felt acutely sorry for her, but he knew he could not help her. "I don't know what you think I can do about it, Kate. Perhaps you ought to go to the authorities here. Surely the Church—"

"The Church will do what it has always done, monsieur," Paul spoke up. "What is impolitic, it will ignore."

"Bell, I want to go home," Katherine pleaded. "I don't want to have my babe here. I want to keep him safe—surely you can understand that."

"Look, I'm sorry about Volsky, Kate—truly sorry. But if you have come to ask me to take you to England, I cannot."

"You do not like it here any more than I do."

"No, I don't," he admitted readily. "But I cannot very well run across Russia with a count's wife in tow, can I? Besides, it is winter—not even the Russians go very far in winter," he reminded her. "And it wouldn't look right."

"Right now, I am beyond caring how it looks."

"You haven't thought. Look at me, Kate—it is Bell Townsend! Do you know what everyone will say? That you have run away with me! Maybe even that the bun in your oven is mine! Do you want that?" He shook his head. "No, I don't think so, Kate. We should both be ruined forever." Unable to look at her, he addressed Paul angrily, "What were you going to do—dump her on my doorstep and flee?"

"No, of course not," the Russian answered.

"Then you can dashed well take her back with you."

"Listen to me, Bell—*listen to me!*" Kate cried. Biting her lip to still its trembling, she fought back tears. "If I go back to Domnya—or if Lexy finds me—I shall be committed to an asylum for the insane. They will take my babe, and Galena will have him, Bell. For this child's sake, I pray you will get me out of Russia."

"We would not have a chance," he told her more gently. "Think on it—even if the weather were better, we should not know the roads. We should be caught like ducks on a pond, and you must surely know it."

"For Harry, then—I'd ask you for whatever Harry's friendship means to you, Bell," she said, her voice husky from suppressed tears.

"You do not listen, do you?" he countered. "What about this Paul? Let him hide you—or go to the English embassy even. I'm sorry, Kate, but I am not your man."

"Vicomte Townsend, if I take her back to Omboros-loe," Paul said quietly, "Olga will use the child to bring my brother down."

"Who the hell is Olga?"

"My wife. She is Prince Narransky's daughter, and there is more of him in her than in his sons, I think. The Narranskys," he went on, "are a powerful family, and they will stop at nothing to gain their ends."

"It still has nothing to do with me," Bell countered.

"Please, Bell—I don't want my child used as a pawn between Galena and Olga," Katherine pleaded.

"Kate, even if I would, I could not. It would all come down on my head, and I cannot stand the consequences of another scandal. I can give you money, but more than that, I cannot do."

She swallowed hard, then gathered the shreds of her dignity. She'd begged, and he'd refused her. Standing, she managed to speak with a calm she did not feel.

"I told Paul you were the last person I should ask.

Nevertheless, I thank you for listening to the tale.'' She pulled her cloak closer over her distended abdomen. ''Good day, sir.''

''I'm sorry, Kate.'' She held out her hand to him, and as he took it, he felt the small, almost frail bones. ''Kate—''

''It is all right.''

His eyes met Paul Volsky's. ''You are taking her back with you?''

''No,'' she answered for him. Surprising herself, she decided, ''I shall stay in Moscow until the snow thaws, and then I shall hire someone to take me out of Russia.''

''Ekaterina, it is not possible,'' Paul insisted. ''They will search for you here.''

''It is a large place. I shall discover another hotel and register under another name. You did bring papers, did you not say?''

''Yes, but—'' Seeing that she was indeed serious, the Russian sighed and reached into his coat. Drawing out a thin leather folder, he produced two official-appearing documents. ''You may perhaps need both of them if you engage anyone to take you across the border. The names are Albert and Elise Chardonnay.'' As Bell's eyebrow rose again, he explained, ''In the late war, they were of some use for spying, but now they are not needed. I have paid a small bribe for them.'' He smiled faintly. ''With the Narranskys for relations, one never knows when one must flee.''

''Thank you, Paul,'' Katherine said sincerely.

''Is there a warrant out for the Chardonnays' arrest?'' Bell wanted to know.

''I was assured there is not. But she will have to remember to always speak French at the borders. In Russia, unless she is stopped, it will not make any difference. The serfs cannot speak the language or read at all.''

Katherine carefully folded the papers and inserted them into her reticule. Some unfathomable impulse prompted Bell to ask, ''Where do you intend to stay?''

She looked to Paul Volsky, and he appeared to consider the matter. ''There is a respectable hotel—not so patronized by the nobility as this one," he murmured. "It is in the next block—on the corner."

"Very well, then," Katherine decided, nodding. "I shall inquire there of a seamstress, for I have left nearly everything at either Domnya or Omborosloe."

"I did not think it wise to alert Olga by letting you pack more," Paul said soberly.

"Have you got any money, Kate?" Bell asked her.

"Yes. When Viktor—Alexei's youngest brother—offered to help me, I brought my quarter's allowance." Her mouth twisted ironically. "In that, at least, Alexei was quite generous."

"Come, Ekaterina. I will take you to the hotel," Paul insisted, taking her arm. "Good day, Vicomte Townsend."

As he closed the door after them, Bell knew it would be but a matter of time before she went back to Alexei Volsky, one way or another. She'd been a fool to run, he told himself, and she was an even greater fool to attempt living alone in her condition in Moscow. And Paul Volsky was as much a fool for letting her stay.

But it wasn't his affair. It was one thing for Harry to ask him to look in on her, quite another for anyone to expect him to risk his life for her. He picked up his flask and drained it, then went in search of another bottle. Finding one, he sank into a chair, and staring moodily into the fire, he drank. For all his wealth, for all his looks, he felt utterly empty inside. He had no honor, he had no purpose, and he simply could not care about anyone or anything. He was an utterly worthless fellow, and he knew it.

"Vicomte Townsend?"

Even the way it was asked made Bell reluctant to answer. He swung around and saw a uniformed officer approaching him.

"Yes?"

"Perhaps we could be private?" The fellow coughed into his gloves. "It is a matter of some delicacy."

The hairs on Bell's neck rose, but he managed to maintain an utterly bored mien. His eyebrow rose perceptibly. "Captain, I assure you—"

"It is Colonel—Colonel Bashykin, monsieur," the officer snapped.

A faint smile played at the corner of Bell Townsend's mouth. "Colonel, then. You must forgive me—not a military man, I'm afraid."

"You are English."

"Yes." Bell looked around the sparsely occupied lobby. "Perhaps you would care to sit?"

"Not here—in your room." The officer regarded him closely. "There is perhaps some reason we should not go to your room?"

"Not at all." Shrugging, Bell led the way up the narrow stairs. Opening his door, he stood back. "Maid hasn't been in yet, I'm afraid, and I am not much of a housekeeper," he murmured apologetically.

The man walked in and surveyed the room. Is this all there is, Monsieur?"

"There is a suite—the bedroom is over there, and I sit out here where I can see the street."

Rather than sitting, Bashykin opened the other door,

then went in to examine the wardrobe and the chest, pulling out drawers, looking into them. His gloved hands poked beneath Bell's laundered inexpressibles. Finally, he returned to the sitting room.

"You travel alone, Vicomte Townsend?"

"Alas, but my valet did not like the weather, and I cannot say I entirely blame him." Bell dropped into a chair and lay back, stretching his feet out before him. Looking up, he indicated another seat. "Be my guest, by all means."

The officer sat on the edge of the chair. "You are acquainted with Countess Volsky, are you not?"

"Yes."

"When is the last time you have seen her?"

"I was at Domnya before your Christmas," Bell responded easily.

"You are quite certain?"

"Is anything wrong? Has something happened to her?"

"I will ask the questions, monsieur." Bashykin put his fingertips together and flexed his fingers. "Are you familiar with the Narranskys?"

"No, I am afraid I've not had the pleasure."

"It is not a pleasure, monsieur!" the officer snapped. "They have ways of discovering the truth."

"How very gothic."

"What?"

"An attempt at levity merely. Er-what precisely is the connection between Countess Volsky and the Narranskys?"

"The Narranskys." Bashykin studied him, then appeared to relent. "Countess Volsky is a relation of Prince Narransky by marriage, and he is very concerned for her health, monsieur. We fear she has been abducted."

"Abducted," Bell repeated blankly. "From Domnya?"

"Where does not matter. It is most important that she is found before any harm comes to her."

"And you think I may have abducted her?" Bell demanded incredulously. "My dear Captain Bashokin, Kate

Winstead and I have never dealt very well together, but
I can assure you—''

"Colonel Bashykin—Ba-shee-kin," the officer interrupted him coldly. "And naturally, I do not accuse you.
However, if you should be contacted by the countess, it
is expected that you will give me her direction, that I
may return her to her family safely."

"Does her husband know this?"

"There is madness in that side of the family, monsieur. It is Prince Narransky who would help her."

"You think she may have bolted then?"

"Bolted?"

"Run away from Domnya?"

"Perhaps. And now we are afraid something terrible has
happened to her. But whether she has fled or whether she
has been abducted, she is vanished, monsieur—vanished,"
Bashykin repeated for emphasis."

Bell appeared to consider it for a moment, then shook
his head. "I shouldn't think she has fled. The last I have
heard, she is increasing, and I cannot think she would
wish to run anywhere under the circumstances."

"Increasing?"

"She is with child."

"Yes, I believe that is correct. And that makes the
matter even more imperative, monsieur."

"She wouldn't wish to contact me," Bell was positive.

"No, not at all. But if I should see her, I shall be certain
to inform Count Volsky."

"Not Count Volsky, monsieur. Me." He produced a
card and handed it to Bell. "Vicomte Townsend, you
must send her to me." The colonel stood, his body stiff,
and inclined his head slightly. "Otherwise, monsieur, I
cannot guarantee her safety—or yours." He slapped one
glove against another. "Good day, Townsend."

As the officer left, Bell could hear him muttering under
his breath that the English were imbeciles. Not that he
cared what the good colonel thought of him. His thoughts
turned to Kate, and he considered warning her. But he
supposed that for a little while at least, Bashykin would
expect it, and there was the possibility of being followed.

Instead, he sat there, thinking Kate Winstead had gotten herself into a devil of a coil. He would wait perhaps an hour, then ask at the desk for the direction of a barber, in case any listened.

Having made up his mind, he reached for last night's bottle and took a long pull of it. If he lived ten years in Russia, the Almighty forbid, he would never truly like the taste of vodka. Nonetheless, he prepared to pass his hour with it.

Before much more than half that had elapsed, there was a quick, sharp rap at his door. When he did not immediately answer it, his caller pounded. Bottle still in hand, Bell opened it, then stood back, trying not to betray anything.

It was Alexei Volsky.

"Where is Ekaterina?" The Russian demanded.

"I suppose I should be surprised," Bell managed to murmur, "but you are the second to inquire of her today."

Volsky's head seemed to snap back. "The second?"

"Yes." Moving to the table, Bell produced the card and read, "Vasily Bashykin. And he does not like to be mistaken for a mere captain, I am afraid. But I expect you know him."

The count seemed to have paled. "No, of course not."

"I collect it has something to do with a Prince Narransky's concern for Kate." Enjoying himself now, Bell added, "He told me she has bolted—run from Domnya."

"It was a family quarrel merely, and I have come to take her back."

"I thought the Volskys merely sent someone, according to Madame Malenkov."

"These are not ordinary circumstances, Townsend. Her condition has made Ekaterina volatile, and she does not know what she does. We believe she is ill."

"And I'd always thought her a sensible girl," Bell murmured.

"Not any more. She has become more and more irrational as her time nears, and we are afraid she may hurt herself. For her safety and the safety of my child, I must find her."

"Odd—that's what Bashykin said Prince Narransky wished—her safety, I mean."

"He will have no use for her after the child is born," Alexei snapped. "I must find her first." He caught himself. "You have not seen her—you swear it?"

"I have not seen Kate since Domnya," Bell lied.

"She has not been the same since that unfortunate incident. And now Galena is beside herself with worry. Poor Lena—she loves Ekaterina so very much."

"I'm terribly sorry."

"Viktor took her to Olga after the quarrel, but as soon as Olga wrote Galena of it, Ekaterina disappeared."

"Perhaps Olga lied—whoever Olga is."

"No, of course you do not know of them." Alexei met Bell's gaze for a moment, then he looked away. "If you hear of Ekaterina—if she comes to you—"

"I am to contact this Bashykin," Bell finished for him.

"Not at all—no, you must not!"

"All right. Then I will send to you. But I am returning to England after the spring thaw, you know. Have you considered that she may already be attempting to go home?"

"We have considered everything! Everything! And she cannot travel very far in this. I cannot think she could even get to Moscow, but Lena—"

"I own it would surprise me." Bell went to the window, where he observed the colonel in a carriage, conferring with a soldier. "But perhaps you would wish to inquire of Bashykin yourself. Kind of him to wipe his coach windows, don't you think?"

Alexei looked for himself, and his complexion darkened. Without so much as a word of farewell, he stormed from the room, and Bell could hear him running down the stairs. In those moments, he made up his mind.

He waited only long enough to see the confrontation begin, then he threw a change of clothes and the stuff of his toilette into his bag. While they were going at it, he was going for Kate. He only hoped she'd kept both papers that Paul Volsky had given her.

It did not take him long to get down the back of the

hotel, where a dilapidated town carriage waited around the corner for custom. Out of sight from the street, he negotiated rapidly, digging into his purse, waving a lifetime of money before the driver. Gesturing that he should go around the block the other way, turn at the next corner, and wait in the alley, Bell held his breath as they made their way down the snow-packed street.

Before the elderly coach rolled to a full halt, he was already out of it, half running, half walking as he crossed the marble-floored lobby. At the stairs, he gave up all pretense of leisure and ran outright.

She heard him rap on her door, and she held her breath. "Kate," Bell Townsend said as softly as he could, "for God's sake, let me in."

Still in her nightshift, she hurried to the door. As soon as she threw the bolt back, he pushed inside. "Come on—there's no time. We've got to leave now."

"What—?"

"Not what, Kate—who! Not half an hour ago, a Colonel Bashykin called on me, saying the Prince Narransky looked for you. And now Alexei is here."

Her eyes widened. "In Moscow? But how—?"

"I don't know." His gray eyes met hers soberly. "All I know is that we don't have any time." He drew her to the window and pointed down the street. "Alexei and Bashykin are having a devil of an argument down there just now."

"But—"

"Come on," he urged her impatiently. "We can speak in the coach. Just bring the papers."

"But how could Alexei find me?"

"Does it matter? I'm telling you to come on!" Even as he spoke, he went to the wardrobe and took out her small traveling bag and stuffed her clothes into it. Carrying it to the dressing table, he scooped the contents into it. When she did not move, he flung her cloak at her. "Put this on—we've got to go now, Kate! I don't mean to take a ball in my chest for you."

"I cannot go in my nightgown, Bell!"

"The devil you can't!" Dropping the bag at her feet,

he picked up the cloak and pulled it around her. "Get your slippers. Hopefully, when they are done, we will be already on the road."

"I cannot wear my slippers."

He looked down at her feet in disbelief. "God, Kate—you should have seen the doctor."

"I was afraid he might give me away—and I could manage to get them on until yesterday."

He dropped to his knees and tried to force the slippers on. Finally, he'd gotten her toes into them. "You'll have to walk on the back half, but there's no help for it. Once we are down the road, we'll find something for you." Rising, he picked up the bag again and caught her hand. "We'll take the back way out. I have bribed a fellow to bring the coach 'round to the alley."

"But you don't have a coach."

"I do now," he answered tersely.

He half dragged, half carried her down the service stairs, past the barrels of garbage set out for the poor, and into the run-down alley. Beggars looked up from their scavenging, then went back to digging in the foul-smelling mess. A dilapidated coach, its black paint peeling, its iron wheels reddened with rust, awaited at the end. Pulling her after him, Bell Townsend ran toward it. Opening the door, he tossed her bag inside, then heaved her in also.

It wasn't until she was leaning back against the worn leather seats that she dared to ask where he'd gotten it. He wiped the steam from a cracked window before answering.

"It was waiting for street custom, so I offered the driver fifty rubles, which is more than he makes in half a lifetime. I expect he knows it is a matter of life and death for all of us, else I'd not pay so much."

"You are stealing it?" she asked with disbelief.

"I didn't take the time to discover if he owned it, Kate."

"No, of course not."

"I thought we should abandon it at Kharkov and hire someone else to take us to Kiev," he explained. "At

Kiev, perhaps we can purchase something to get us the rest of the way.'' He met her gaze soberly. ''The devil of it is that once they realize I am gone, I expect they will have a fair notion of my direction. All we have on our side is haste.''

As the carriage traversed the back streets, he watched nervously, seeing the possibility of being stopped at every corner. When he looked up, Katherine Winstead was regarding him oddly.

''You changed your mind,'' she said softly.

''And I expect I am a damned fool for it.''

''Why?''

''I don't know.'' He turned to look out the cracked window, then he sighed. ''I guess I am tired of what I am—maybe I find myself in need of redemption just now.''

''For whatever reason, I shall forever be in your debt,'' she told him quietly. ''To me, today you are as Galahad.''

''No, I am everything you have ever thought me.'' As a chunk of ice flew up beneath him, he frowned. ''We may wish we'd stayed in Moscow, you know. Although the roads are bad now, I expect them to get worse. And the farther one gets from the city, the less anyone maintains them. Besides, the clerk at the hotel said more snow fell south this time.''

''It could not have,'' she declared positively. ''All I saw all the way from Omborosloe were deep drifts. The peasants were only able to clear a small path through them.''

''Never in all of my thirty years have I seen anything like Russian weather,'' he muttered.

She shifted uncomfortably on the cold seat. ''I hope you brought my dress.''

''Both of them, but they are going to be sadly creased, I'm afraid. I just stuffed them in the bag.''

She was already cold, and they'd not even left the city. With an effort, she drew up her feet and covered them with the bottom of her cloak. It didn't matter, she told herself. She was going home to England.

As silence descended between them, she watched the snow-topped buildings, their blackened chimneys spitting soot onto the snow, loom ahead and then disappear behind them. As miserable as she felt, there was a certain exultation. She was going home.

Suddenly, the coach stopped, nearly throwing her to the floor. She caught the rope and righted herself. "What—?"

"I told him that as soon as it was safe, we'd like some food and hot bricks for the journey. And," he added, "I told him he could buy a pint of vodka for himself."

"Wonderful," she muttered. "We shall have a drunken driver in bad weather."

"I knew your gratitude couldn't last. At least we are on the road, aren't we?"

"Yes." She sighed heavily. "But I should still prefer a sober driver." She peered across to his window. "*Bylee Beek,*" she read aloud. "White Bull. They even name their establishments like we do at home."

"Clever of you to note it," he murmured sardonically.

"Well, when I was with Alexei, we did not stay in such places, except when we traveled between St. Petersburg and Moscow, and then I did not note any names. But I expect they had them."

"Perhaps you were too besotted to see what was around you."

"Or perhaps they were a different sort of establishment. What do you suppose is keeping the fellow?" she asked anxiously. "Is he waiting for them to warm the bricks?"

"I expect it is the food. I ordered some bread and cheese for you, because I wasn't certain as to how queasy you might be, and something with meat for me. I didn't expect you'd eaten, and I know I haven't."

"I cannot. The thought of food sickens me."

"I'd heard that that eventually passes."

"It did, but it seems to have returned." She forced a smile for him. "But do not worry over it. I don't cast up my accounts any more—I just feel as though I could."

"You cannot live on nothing, you know. You'll be skin and bones."

"Thank you," she retorted acidly. "My feet do not seem to know it. Or my middle."

"Well, you had best take care of yourself," he advised, "for I am no hand at all at playing nursemaid."

"I don't expect you to be."

The door opened and a filthy fellow stuck his head inside. Grinning, he handed Bell a greasy, rolled paper, followed by the silver flask. As he withdrew, Katherine decided, "He is more than half-gone already."

Ignoring her, Bell unwrapped the paper and sniffed at the contents. "Not an English pasty," he murmured, "but it will suffice." He bit into it, then grimaced. "Tough mutton."

There was a tapping on her side, then the fellow pushed a large loaf of bread, followed by a hunk of moldy cheese at her. Her stomach revolted.

Seeing that she put her food on the seat, Bell reached for his small penknife and began paring off the mold for her. "It's not half-bad, if you don't think about it."

For the last time, the bribed ostler returned and set a row of heated bricks in the floor. Then she heard him climb onto the box above.

"Watch out—you'll burn your feet."

"There should be a cloth over them, but I daresay he forgot that," she said.

"If he ever knew it." Bell unscrewed the lid of his flask and peered inside. "More vodka," he decided, disgusted. "I told him I should rather have wine."

"Perhaps he didn't understand you."

"I know a few words of Russian."

"If you learned them from Sofia, I wouldn't repeat them in company."

"Unworthy of you, Kate," he chided. "Actually, I employed a tutor as soon as I got here. Unfortunately, I was not a particularly apt pupil. As soon as I got the merest basics, I discharged him. Everyone in the Sherkov's circle preferred French, you see."

"They distance themselves from their serfs that way.

I think Lena and Lexy only spoke Russian when they were afraid I might understand them—or when they conversed with the servants.''

He began eating in earnest, stopping only to wipe his fingers on the paper or to drink from his flask. She watched, but made no move to taste her cheese and bread.

"Go on—try it," he urged between mouthfuls.

"All right."

In truth, she still felt awful. But to satisfy him, she broke off a small piece of bread and chewed at it. As soon as she swallowed, her stomach knotted. She slipped the rest of the piece beneath her cloak, hoping he would think she'd eaten it.

He didn't. "You know," he told her, "much depends on your staying well."

"I am well enough," she lied. "I'm just not hungry."

"All right, but you'd best save it. I mean to get as far as I can before we stop for the night." His own meal finished, he rolled up the remnants in the paper, opened the door, and tossed it. Pulling his hat forward to cover his eyes, he leaned back, his flask between his legs. "Maybe you can sleep until you feel more the thing," he suggested.

"Do you think we can make it?" she dared to ask him.

"To England? I don't know—but we can dashed well try."

"I know you could have left me at the hotel—or let them discover me. I am extremely grateful that you did not." When he said nothing, she went on, "I could not go back to Domnya, Bell—I could not. I should rather die than face Alexei again." Her gaze dropped to where her hands rested on her stomach. "I feel so terribly, utterly foolish, Bell."

"You could not have known."

"I was too plain for someone like that."

"You shouldn't say that."

"Well, I am."

"You were merely green, my dear. If any is at fault, it is Harry. He should have realized something was wrong with the offer."

"I daresay we were all overwhelmed at my good fortune," she recalled ruefully. "From disgraced baron's daughter to Russian countess—it was quite a climb for me." A small, harsh laugh escaped her. "In truth, I was a caged sparrow set among peacocks. Now I know that Galena chose me because I had no hope of outshining her."

"You cannot look back, Kate."

"And I cannot look forward, either," she retorted bitterly. "I left England in triumph, and I shall return in disgrace."

"You are being incredibly unforgiving of yourself, don't you think?"

"How can I be anything else? It is all my fault—I could have told Harry I didn't want Alexei." It was as though all the hurt of the past three months spilled over. "Everyone knew it but me, Bell—from the moment I arrived at Domnya, everyone *knew*. I was a *meesch*, Bell! A mouse—an English stick—and finally a stick with a beehive in the middle! But I didn't care as long as I believed Lexy loved me. How they must have laughed behind my back—Madame Popov and the others. They knew he only loved Galena."

When she looked over at him, it appeared Bell Townsend slept. His eyes were closed beneath the shade of his hat, and his flask remained between his knees. In repose, he looked like the Adonis Brummell called him.

She felt even more foolish for speaking the pain in her heart to him. A man like Bellamy Townsend could not possibly understand the betrayal she felt. She swallowed hard, trying to stifle her self-pity, then closed her eyes and tried to think of something else, of England, of Monk's End, and of Harry.

"We'll make it to England, Kate—I promise you I'll get you there somehow," he said quietly.

He hadn't been asleep at all. He'd merely been silent, letting her rattle on, because he had no glib words of comfort, no patently easy way to ease the grief and bitterness she felt. All of his charm, all of his vaunted wit were useless just now. As he'd listened to her, he felt an intense pity for her, a sadness that whispered words, a few caresses, and stolen kisses could not heal what Alexei Volsky and his sister had done to her. If they could, he might have tried.

It was so cold they had to stop. The driver had come down from the box to tell them he could no longer feel his hands or his feet. And while it did not snow, the wind swirled and drifted what was already on the ground across the road, making progress slow and tedious. Wiping his cracked window with his sleeve, Bell peered out into the dusk and saw a cluster of lights perhaps a quarter of a mile ahead.

Telling the frozen driver to get inside with Kate, he climbed out and sank to the top of his boots in the snow. Muttering curses, he took the lead horse's bridle and started walking toward the lights. The wind flapped his cloak about him and bit into his face. Afraid of damaging his lungs, he took quick, shallow breaths, and as he exhaled, it seemed that the steam froze on his lips.

He plodded blindly, making slow work of the short distance, until he thought he could go no farther. But when he raised his head, he was less than one hundred feet from an old rock house. It was perhaps the most welcome sight in his life. He picked up his pace, striking for it. When he reached it, he pounded loudly on a crude door, shouting in Russian for help.

A sturdy woman opened it, then motioned to her husband, who helped Bell inside. When a youth pulled at Kate's carriage door, she leaned gratefully into his arms. The driver had to be lifted out and carried.

It was a crude place—a single room with a large fireplace at one end, a table and benches in the middle, and one bed, surrounded by pallets at the end farthest from the fire. Battered tin dishes were laid out on the table, and some sort of stew simmered in a hook-hung kettle. The odor of onions lay heavy on the steamy air.

Children, ranging from a babe in cradle to the youth who'd aided Kate, watched silently as the woman brought out a bucket of water for frostbitten feet. The thought crossed Katherine's mind that they were all serfs; that if any knew they'd helped her, they'd be severely punished.

They didn't understand French, and Bell's Russian was inadequate, but somehow the driver managed to convey that they were traveling to Kharkov. The word elicited a look of disbelief from the husband, but apparently the driver finally convinced him they were not entirely insane. Katherine heard him say something sympathetic to her, then realized that he thought someone had died. She nodded. The woman patted her stomach and smiled, revealing a mouth without teeth. She nodded to that also.

Three more elderly tin bowls joined the others on the table, and the man gestured to Kate to remove her cloak. She was still in her nightgown, so she demurred. But Bell moved to put his hands on her shoulders.

"I doubt they will know the difference, and you are covered," he whispered. "Besides, I collect they have offered us shelter for the night."

"Here?"

"There isn't an inn—it's just a sort of peasant village, I think, and most houses are like this or worse. I collect they belong to a Prince Bolskoi or something. Go ahead—take off your wrap," he urged. "I'm going back for what the driver didn't drink of the vodka. It's the least we can offer, and I don't think they have much use for money."

"No, of course not."

"Madame." The man gestured to a bench, shooing his children down to the other end of the table.

His wife reached for Katherine's cloak, and everyone stared at her high-necked, finely woven rail. The woman's rough hands smoothed the delicate satin and lace trim, then touched the tiny satin-covered buttons one by one. It was as though she did not know it was a nightgown.

"Za-myichah-tyilnee," she murmured, making Katherine almost ashamed to be wearing it.

"Yes, it is lovely—*spaseebuh."*

Then the woman looked down to where Katherine's slippers did not entirely cover her feet, and she shook her head. *"Plakhoy."*

It was bad. Katherine nodded.

Their driver ate with his feet still in the cold water, while Bell sampled the boiled beets, onions, and potatoes, all of which were dark red from being cooked together. "Go on—it isn't half-bad," he urged Katherine. "I think there's some kind of fat in it."

"I cannot." When the woman filled a bowl and pushed it her way, she pushed it back apologetically, then touched her stomach. *"Minya tasheet,"* Kate explained.

"Da." Rising, she came to stand in front of Katherine. Without warning, she pinched her guest's cheeks, then stood back, shaking her head. *"Plakhoy,"* she repeated. Moving away, she went to a small cupboard and took out a cracked cup, then she reached into a straw-covered cold hole and dragged out a crock of milk. Pouring a little into the cup, she brought it back to Katherine.

With so many children, the milk was precious, but it was a gift that Katherine could not refuse. She managed to drink it down as the woman nodded her approval. After that, a loaf of hard, dark bread was produced, and a chunk given to Katherine first. There was no butter or cheese to go with the heavy, grainy bread, but somehow she ate it.

Once everyone had eaten, a girl removed the dishes into a wash pan while one of her brothers brought in snow to be melted over the fire. The man offered Bell the only real chair in the place, then sat cross-legged on the floor before the fire. With great ceremony, the three men in the room shared the small amount of vodka, making toasts over little more than thimbles of it.

One by one, the children disappeared into a dark corner of the room, where they shed their clothes and rolled into straw-filled sack pallets. Some sort of argument developed, and the man barked out a ruling. One of the pallets emptied as four children scrambled to huddle together.

The woman busied herself shaking out the covers on the bed, then beckoned Katherine over to inspect it. Bell rose and walked to stand behind her. "I think she's telling you there is no vermin."

"I cannot sleep in their bed," she protested.

"I collect they don't have many guests," he responded. "Let them enjoy it."

"Bell, I cannot."

But the woman had already gestured for Katherine to sit on the side of it, and Katherine understood it when she asked, "You like?" in Russian.

"It's very nice—*Kharooshee*," she murmured appreciatively.

Touching Katherine's stomach, the woman insisted, using the words for "for you" over and over again. She looked at Bell, smiling broadly, and he nodded. Satisfied, she turned her attention to the pallets.

"I'm afraid we've got the bed, Kate."

"I cannot sleep with you."

"I told you—I don't snore. Besides, we'll be warmer." His fingers touched the rounded collar of her nightgown. "And you cannot say you are not sufficiently covered. It must have been dashed cold at Domnya."

She pulled away. "It was."

"Go on to bed," he advised. "I'm going to drink with Yuri and Vanya until it's gone. You won't even know when I come to bed," he promised. "And I won't touch you." When she just stood there, he sighed. "Look—pretend I am Claire, and I will pretend you are Harry."

She could feel the blood rise in her face, but there was no help for it. As he turned back to the others, she hastily climbed into the bed. The sheets were like ice, making her shiver, but she doubted they had such a thing as a warming pan. The wind outside whipped at the oiled paper over the windows, making a racket, reminding her that she was at least sheltered for the night. But she felt guilty over the thin featherbed. She ought to have insisted on one of the pallets.

As she snuggled deeper, seeking to make a warm place, the woman came to stand over her, smiling down at her. Very carefully, almost tenderly, she placed Kate's fur-lined cloak over the covers before saying good night.

Ever so slowly, the cold receded in the small place Katherine made in the featherbed. Drawing her knees up against her distended belly, she cradled her pillow and tried to sleep. She was so tired that every bone ached, but it didn't matter. She was going home.

When she awoke during the night, the room was in darkness, save for the fire at the other end. It was so cold that her nose hurt above the covers, but the rest of her body was warm. She tried to move, to adjust her cramped position, but found she could not. Bell Townsend's arm was wrapped around her, and his leg lay over hers. She lay there, listening to his even breathing, wondering when he'd come to bed.

She ought to be scandalized, and she knew it. But his body warmed her, and he was asleep, so he did not even know what he did. Lying there, she felt an intense gratitude to him. For all his protests, he'd come to her aid, and now he was risking a great deal, possibly even his life for her. For if Alexei caught them—or Olga—she dared not think of the consequences.

Finally, unable to stand the cramp in her leg any longer, she shook him. "I've got to turn over," she whispered. "Please."

"Unnnnhhhhhh."

He didn't move. This time, she pinched his arm. "Please—I've got to turn over. My leg pains me."

"Sorry," he mumbled, turning away. "Forgot."

He didn't make any sense, but she didn't care. Almost as soon as he moved, she could feel the cold. Sitting up gingerly, she massaged her leg, trying to work the cramp from the calf. Wriggling her toes, she finally managed it, and she lay back down, pulling up the covers, staring at the blackened ceiling.

Beside her, Bell breathed softly. Her thoughts turned to all the women he'd been with, and she wondered if any of them had meant anything to him. He'd said he'd

offered himself and his name to someone, who'd taken
another. Somehow it did not seem possible. For as much
as she herself had avoided him, she knew that he was
considered the premier catch by nearly every female of
her acquaintance. She was beginning to wonder if her
reasons for disliking him had had as much to do with
guarding her own heart as with his reputation.

And yet as she lay there listening to him, he no longer
seemed forbidding; he no longer seemed dangerous even.
It was perhaps that she was no longer green, that she no
longer had a girl's romantic illusions about any man. All
of that had died at Domnya.

She let her mind wander to Alexei, remembering how
much she'd loved him, how wonderful she'd thought him,
how fortunate she'd believed herself when he'd offered
for her. And it had all been a sham. A very real ache
tightened her chest, and she wanted to cry. She felt utterly, completely alone, utterly, completely betrayed. Hot
tears burned her eyes. He hadn't wanted her, he hadn't
loved her—and neither had Galena.

She was so cold, so cold she felt empty inside. She
didn't want to think of Lexy anymore, she didn't want to
think of Galena. She just wanted to go home. But first
she had to survive. And it was numbing cold in the room.

Unable to stand it, she finally rolled over against the
warmth of Bell Townsend's back and pulled the covers
over her head. If he said anything about it, she would
pretend she'd been asleep.

He awoke sometime before dawn, but no one was about
yet. The floor around the bed was a tangle of pallets, and
somewhere either Yuri or Vanya snored. When he lifted
the covers, he could see his breath. Laying down again,
he felt an odd movement against his back, but Katherine
hadn't stirred. Then he felt it again. Something like a
bubble or a small ripple. She was lying against him, her
stomach pressed into his back, and he realized suddenly
that what he felt was her babe.

An odd longing washed over him. He was nearly thirty,
and he'd sown far more than his share of wild oats, yet
he did not know if any of them had resulted in a child or

not. And until now he hadn't cared. Very gingerly, he turned onto his back and reached to touch her abdomen. For a moment, there was nothing, then he felt it move again. Alexei Volsky's child, gotten by a cruel hoax. Once it came into the world, she would be forever reminded of how deceived she'd been.

He removed his hand guiltily, thinking how very hypocritical he was. In his own way, he'd been no better than Volsky. No, that was not quite true—he'd never promised to love anyone. Except Elinor Kingsley.

Ahead of them, the horses plodded on the snow-packed road. Inside the coach, Katherine rested her feet on a rock heated from Vanya's fireplace. She wore loose, black wool shoes, having traded her kid slippers to his wife for them. And beside her, on the seat, a dingy cloth held the rest of the loaf of dark bread.

"You know," she said finally, "over here the *boyars* do not even believe Vanya or his family are people. They are merely property." She looked at Townsend. "They shared the best they had with us."

"I know. I gave the woman a few small coins to buy food. More than that would have raised suspicion."

"Do you think she believed we were French?"

"I don't know. I didn't show the papers, because I didn't think they could read."

"No, of course not."

"She seemed rather disturbed by your feet. I think she wanted you to do something about them."

"No. I am all right." But even as she said it, she looked at her hands. Her wedding ring was nearly cutting her finger. Covering it, she tried to work it off, but couldn't. "I am all right," she repeated.

"I don't know." He studied her face for a moment and frowned. "You look as though you have put on weight overnight."

"It is the child. None of us look very well when we are increasing, I expect."

"Well, when we reach Kharkov, I think we ought to find a doctor before we go on."

A wave of dizziness hit her, followed by nausea. She

gripped the rope that hung over the door and held on until it passed. She felt cold, damp, and utterly sick. "All right," she managed, swallowing. "At Kharkov."

"Kate, you look like death. Here—" He caught her as she leaned forward. "You'd better lie down."

She didn't protest when he pushed her back against the seat and lifted her legs. Instead, she drew them up against her and lay with her eyes closed. He leaned to pull her cloak more closely about her.

"I don't think I was meant to do this," she whispered.

"What are you feeling?" he asked anxiously. "Does anything hurt?"

"No. Dizzy—that's all."

"God, Kate—you gave me a fright."

"I'll be all right."

She looked little, fragile under the cloak, and the fur was dark against her pale face. He reached to clasp her hand where it held the cloak above her breast. "It's not all that far to Kharkov," he tried to reassure her. But he knew differently—it would be days before they got there. "Maybe there's something on the way. Surely we'll pass something."

"Tula."

"What?"

"We can stop at Tula."

"All right." He released her hand and sat back, but as his head passed the window, he didn't like what he saw. "Damn."

"What?"

"It's started snowing again. And Yuri's already turning to ice. He won't want to go on in this."

"He's got to—we've got to escape," she said miserably. "We've got to."

"We will." He looked out the window again and muttered, "I expect the weather is better at the poles, don't you?"

"Yes."

"Feeling more the thing yet?"

"No—but I daresay I will."

He didn't have much hope of it. She didn't look well

at all. He stared bleakly at the falling snow, seeing not the beauty of it, but rather the hardship it brought. And he wondered how far it was to Tula.

The carriage wheels would not turn, despite the fact that the horses strained in their harnesses. The man Yuri plodded back to the coach itself and opened the door. The biting wind had burned his face raw, and his blue eyes had nearly disappeared behind the ice that hung from his eyebrows.

"No go—we die," he said.

Bell got out and tried to help him, but nothing moved. Finally, he came back. "We're going to take the horses and try to ride for help, Kate. Keep inside, and for God's sake, keep bundled up."

"Bell—"

"There's no help for it, Kate. And there's no time to argue. It's freezing out here."

"Please be careful."

He forced a smile. "I do what I can."

She pulled her cloak tight over her arms and watched them until they disappeared in the snow. Everyone was wrong, she decided wearily—hell wasn't hot—it was Russia. And Bell Townsend was going to freeze to death because of her. Then she would die there. No one would even know what happened to them.

As forsaken as she felt, she tried to pray. *Please, God, deliver us. Please let them find help . . . please.* Poor Bell—he'd not asked for this, and she was sadly regretting that she'd begged him to do it. *Please, God, watch over him, for he has done this for me.* It was as though she spoke to no one.

She drew her legs up onto the seat and lay on her side, trying to shelter the life within her. She did not mind dying so much, she reflected unhappily, but she did not want to take her child or Bell Townsend with her. No, that wasn't even true—she didn't want to die either. She wanted to live to hold her son or daughter in her arms. She wanted to live to see her child grow. She'd left Domnya for him, and she'd fled Omborosloe for him, and now possibly it had all been for naught.

She didn't know how long she lay there, only that she was cold. And so very, very tired. She closed her eyes and tried to think of other things—of summers long ago at Monk's End, of Papa swinging her in the air, of Harry slipping on the rocks and falling into the stream, of the profusion of roses and honeysuckle in the garden, of playing Find Me in the maze . . .

"Madame! Madame!"

At first, she thought she had dreamed it, but then someone was pounding on the door. She sat up and straightened cramped legs. The window was frosted over, but she could see the distorted image of a bearded man. And she heard the crack of ice breaking as he pried open the door.

"Madame Chardonnay?"

Help had come. Her throat was too tight for speech. All she could do was nod.

He turned to say something to others behind him, then thrust himself through the door. His arms slid under her, and he lifted her as he backed out. Other arms caught her, passing her down a line, until she was laid among the furs on a heavy, horse-drawn sled.

The driver spoke to her, telling her she was going to be all right, adding that Monsieur Chardonnay was also. But the other fellow was not so fortunate—or at least that's what she thought he said. Something about his feet.

The snow fell so hard that she could see almost nothing, and the man's black coat disappeared in a thick layer of white. But ahead of them, the bells on the horses jingled, keeping time to the plodding steps. Behind them, riders disappeared, obscured by a vertical blanket of snow.

She felt an intense gratitude to God, to Bell, to everyone. She was going to live and so was her child. She was still going to have someone to love, someone to hold, after all.

Seemingly out of nowhere, tall spires of a chapel rose, and stretching behind them was a charter house. Bells pealed, cutting through the air, and the smell of bread was everywhere. The sled moved the length of the long building, then stopped at the end, where bearded, black-robed men waited. They were perhaps the most welcome sight of her life.

"You are all right, Kate?" Bell Townsend whispered as he reached for her.

She nodded.

"Ah, Elise, we are saved by monks!" he said more loudly in French. "So fortunate, do you not think?" He put his arm around her, steadying her. "Can you walk?" he asked low.

"Yes."

"There are some younger sons of the nobility here who speak French," he cautioned her.

They were shown to the guest house: a small, square room, adequately furnished, but austere. The monk who led the way announced proudly that it had once been occupied by Peter the Great during a crisis of faith. Walking to the bed, he gestured with his hands to show how far the tall monarch's feet had extended from the end of it.

Already a goodly fire blazed in the hearth, and heavy tapestries covered the windows to shut out the cold. Beside the fireplace, there was a small shrine made of a simple table, a clean linen cloth, an icon of Christ, and two candles. As Katherine's gaze moved around the room, she saw the single bedstead, a table, several wooden chairs, and a handwoven rug between the bed and the fire.

The black-robed monk took a piece of kindling to light the candles. Making the Orthodox sign of the Cross over the shrine, he said a prayer, then turned to Bell and Kate and blessed them also.

As soon as he was gone, Bell pulled one of the chairs closer to the fire. "Yuri may lose his toes," he told her, "so I think we'd best look at yours."

"I am all right—if I ever get warm." Nonetheless, she sat and let him remove the black wool shoes.

Her feet were swollen more than before, and the skin

was mottled, worrying him. He caught her hands and looked at them, seeing the same thing there. He hoped it was just from the cold. Trying to keep his voice light, he said, "They are bringing hot cider, so I expect you'll warm up soon enough."

"I hope so. Bell—"

"What?"

"I was so frightened. I thought I should die out there—and—"

"Don't—it's over."

"I prayed for you—I prayed for all of us—Yuri even."

"Then your prayers must have been answered. We couldn't see anything, you know, and yet we stumbled straight into here." He held the woolen booties toward the fire, warming them. "I think that as soon as you drink your cider, you ought to go to bed."

"What are you going to do?"

"I'm going to see what they can do for Yuri." His gray eyes met hers briefly. The man risked his life for fifty rubles."

"It is a fortune to him."

"Not if he cannot spend it."

He was still on the floor beside her, and as his head bent over her feet while he retied the wool shoes on her feet, his pale hair shone with reflected fire. She had to resist the temptation to smooth the disordered waves.

"I was terribly wrong, Bell—you aren't a shallow person at all."

He didn't say anything until he stood up. Then he stared into the fire for a few moments. "No," he said finally, "you were right."

"Bell—"

"And I cannot say I am very proud of what I am." He swung around to face her. "I could say the difference between us is that I was born with a pretty face, but it's more than that."

"You wrong yourself."

"Kate, don't let gratitude change your judgment. I am every inch the frippery fellow you have always thought me. I have smiled and charmed and used every ruse at my disposal to gain what I have wanted, I assure you.''

"Not with me.''

"No, but do not delude yourself. If I haven't, it is only because you are not in my style.''

"And I am Harry Winstead's sister,'' she reminded him.

"And you are Harry's sister,'' he agreed. "But if I had any real compunction about anything, I wouldn't have cuckolded Longford. Always remember that, Kate—always remember that.''

"She was very beautiful.''

"And I was drunk. But that doesn't excuse anything. He was supposed to be my friend.''

"No, I suppose it doesn't, but everyone says he has forgiven you.''

"He wanted to be rid of her.'' He laughed harshly. "Rich, isn't it? The pendulum swings, Kate—the pendulum swings. I took his wife, and now the woman I wanted to wed chose Longford.'' His manner changed abruptly. "How maudlin we are today—nothing like a taste of mortality to do it, I suppose.''

"I suppose.'' She sighed. "But if I ever told anyone how kind you have been, none would believe it.''

"Don't, I pray you. You'd ruin my rep.'' He bent to heft another log onto the fire, then poked it until it settled into place. Rising, he dusted his hands on his pantaloons. "Go to bed, Kate, before those feet get any bigger. Pretty soon you'll be wearing my boots.''

He was grateful there was no mirror. As she sat across from him at the table, he could see that the swelling had moved to her hands and face, making her appear considerably fatter than she was. And her skin was a mottled pink and gray. When he touched her hand, his print remained for some time.

She pushed at her food, not eating any of it, despite the fact that it was quite good. He'd tried urging the dumplings on her. And the meat-stuffed cabbage. And the cheese-filled crepes. All to no avail. Despite the fact that she'd eaten little, she felt bloated, full.

They ate alone in the guest house. He supposed it was due to some reluctance to have a woman at the monks' table. He didn't care—he would as soon forgo the religion, anyway. He had no more acquaintance with the Almighty than any other buck of the *ton,* and probably considerably less.

"You aren't feeling very well, are you?" he said finally.

She was dizzy, nearly too sick to sit up, but she shook her head. "I'll get better."

"You're lying to me."

"All right—I am ill."

"What seems to be the matter? Other than the fact I can see you are all swelled up, I mean."

"How very kind you are to note it," she muttered. "As though I cannot see for myself." She let her head drop into her hands. "I don't know, Bell—I don't know. I cannot seem to think. My head pounds, and I am so dizzy I feel as though my mind is separated from my body. There—I have said it."

"I'll get you a doctor, Kate."

"And what can he do?" she asked miserably. "He will merely say I am increasing."

But she didn't tell him the worst of it. She was afraid for her babe. In the hours since they'd arrived, she'd only felt the child stir once. It was because he'd gotten cold, she told herself. It was because everything had gone wrong since Moscow. Tomorrow, she would feel it move again, and everything would be all right.

"If you aren't going to eat, you'd best get back to bed." He pushed his own half-eaten food away and stood up. "I'll find out the direction of the nearest physician."

"You cannot go out again in this snow!"

"I'll have to."

"No! Please, Bell—don't leave me alone again. If anything should happen to you, I—" She started to say she'd perish, but then realized how that must sound. "—I'll never see England again," she finished lamely.

"Maybe they'll be kind enough to send someone."

"And maybe I don't need a physician!"

"And maybe you do!" He ran his fingers through his disordered hair. "I'm sorry, Kate—I shouldn't rip up at you—not after all you've been through. But I have no experience with any of this. Look—I'll feel better if it is determined you are all right."

"And what if Alexei finds me?" she cried out hysterically.

"Kate, if we cannot get out, he cannot get in," he answered reasonably. "Besides, I told you—he'll not want to get out himself in this weather. And I can dashed well guarantee that no one is going to risk his life for another man's wife."

"He came to Moscow!"

"Which is far different from here. Leave off, Kate—right now I'd say Volsky is the least of our worries."

"Bell, I am afraid!"

"Of what?"

"I don't know!"

"Damn!" He walked around in front of her and pulled her from her chair. "If you don't take care of yourself, we are both in the basket! I'm putting you to bed!"

"You are shouting!"

"So are you!" He caught her arm and propelled her toward the bedstead. Still holding her, he reached to yank back the covers, then he pushed her onto the mattress. "If you get up before I get back, I'm abandoning you!" He twitched the heavy blankets up over her, then stood back. "You know, Kate Winstead, if you weren't Harry's sister, I wouldn't be doing this, anyway."

She swallowed hard, trying not to be sick before him. "I know," she whispered.

The anger left him. Moving to the foot of the bed, he lifted the covers and removed the ugly wool shoes. "I'm sorry, Kate. For once in my life, I don't know what to do."

"Neither do I. Bell, I am so sick—so very sick."

"I know."

"I'm going to need the washbasin."

He brought it to her and waited, but she merely lay there, her eyes closed. Despite the cold, he could see the perspiration on her brow. He had to get help.

"Don't do anything foolish—please. Just lie there until you are better."

She swallowed visibly. "All right."

Throwing on his cloak, he went out into the bitter, biting wind, crossing the long, narrow courtyard to the chapter house. The monks were still eating—much plainer fare than he and Kate had been given. He walked to the head of the table to speak to the bearded man with the rings on his fingers.

Speaking in French, he said, "My wife is very ill, and it is not near her time. Is there a physician who will come?"

Someone down the table spoke up in Russian, then they all shook their heads. "I am afraid it is impossible," the monk said. "The roads, they are impassable." He regarded Bell sympathetically. "And we are unskilled in the problems of women."

"She is bloated to twice her size," Bell argued desperately. "Her hands and feet—"

The monk lifted his ringed hands, then dropped them. "We can pray, monsieur—it is all we can do."

But another monk rose and came to whisper in his ear. As he nodded, the man turned to Bell. "There are herbs for too much water in the body, monsieur. But if it is anything else, there is nothing we can do."

"We can pray," his superior reminded him. "For Madame Chardonnay, we can pray."

"Pray!" Bell fairly spat the word back at him. "She doesn't need prayers! She needs a doctor!" Turning on his heel, he strode from the chapter house angrily. Did no one understand? Unless he did something, he was going to take Harry Winstead his sister's corpse—he knew it in his bones.

When he went back to her, Kate was sitting on the edge of the bed, her head hung over the basin. The very little she'd eaten had come up. Cursing silently, he found a cloth and wiped her face.

"You are all right, Kate—you are going to be all right." But his voice rang hollow in his own ears. "Just lie down a bit."

"The doctor?"

He didn't know why he did it, but he lied. "He's coming."

"Good. The pain—"

"What pain?" he asked sharply. "What pain, Kate?"

"I don't know—in my back—it hurts."

"In your back," he repeated, relieved. "That's good, isn't it? I mean—"

"I think so. It is probably from riding in the carriage so much."

"You are unused to traveling."

"Yes." She lay back. "I'm just tired, Bell—so very tired."

"You are going to be all right." He walked to the window and looked out into the dusk. "We shouldn't have tried this, you know. We should have tried to hide in Moscow."

At least he hadn't said he should have left her. But she did not see how she could go on—even if the snow ended, she didn't see how she could go on.

"Bell?"

"What?" He swung around almost angrily.

"You won't leave me, will you?"

"No. For what it's worth coming from a scoundrel, I won't leave you." He walked back to the bed and sat on the edge. Taking her hand, he leaned over her. "If I knew how to help you, I would." He felt her hand tighten in his. "It's all right, Kate."

"No." She sucked in her breath, then let it out slowly. "The pain is getting worse."

"Where?"

"In my back."

He squeezed her fingers reassuringly, then released them. Finding a towel on the washstand rack, he carried it to the fireplace and held it close to the heat, the way his old nurse had done for his growing pains in what seemed an age ago. As it warmed, he folded it, keeping one side to the fire. Satisfied that it held the heat, he carried it back to her.

"Here. Let me put this under your back." He waited a few moments, then dared to ask, "Is it any better?"

"Yes," she lied. "When does the doctor come?"

"It'll be awhile."

He went back to a chair and pulled it to the warmth. Sitting, he stared morosely into the fire. He was discovering what he'd suspected for a long time—he was an utterly useless man. None of the things he'd pursued—the women, the games, the admiration of his fellows—none of that really mattered. He had no truly useful knowledge, only Latin and Greek, history and grammar, literature, and a smattering of politics. Very futile things when one was pitted against imponderables like weather—and mortality.

Damn her! Why hadn't she told him she was sick before they left Moscow? Why hadn't he insisted she see the damned doctor there? The answer, he had to admit, was there had been no time. They'd set off pell-mell, at a time not determined by them but by some overdecorated colonel named Bashykin.

He glanced around the darkening room, wishing he had something to drink. But here, as everywhere else, there was the ubiquitous vodka. Didn't these fools know potatoes were to be eaten? Nonetheless, he heaved himself up and went to get the bottle that had been left with supper. Uncorking it, he carried it back to the fire and began to drink. By the time he was a quarter of the way through it, he wouldn't mind it.

Someone rapped on the door, and he rose reluctantly to answer it. One of the monks held a small flask in one hand, a lantern in the other. *"Pour madame,"* he murmured, holding it out.

"What is it?"

The monk gestured to his hands and feet, then puffed out his cheeks. It was for the swelling. He spoke again, this time in rapid Russian, indicating it was to be mixed with something. When Bell couldn't understand him, he left the flask and went back outside. Returning with his hands full of snow, he put it into one of the cups, then carried it to the fire. Before it melted, he poured some of the contents of the ornately painted flask into it. Then he pointed to where Katherine lay on the bed.

"I'll give it to her. *Merci*."

After the monk left, Bell stirred the slushy snow and medicine together, then tried to rouse Katherine.

"Kate, you are to drink this."

She raised a hand to push the cup away. "Can't."

"Come on." He lifted her shoulders and held it to her mouth. "For God's sake, drink it. It's for the damned swelling."

She swallowed some, then pushed the rest back. "Ugh—what is it?"

"I don't know. One of the monks brought it." He let her lie down. "Maybe you'll feel better."

"I hope so," she whispered. "I hope so."

It was dark and cold away from the fire. He set the cup down on the floor and reached to touch her forehead. It was cool and damp. Sighing, he removed his boots and lay down beside her. Pulling the covers up over them both, he turned to her.

"I expect everything will look better tomorrow, Kate. At least you have not gotten an inflammation of the lungs from the weather," he consoled her. "For that alone, we ought to be thankful."

"Bell, something's wrong—something's very wrong!"

He came awake with a start, aware only that she clutched his shoulder convulsively. He tried to roll over and draw her into his arms, but she was frantic.

"Bell, I cannot stand this!"

"You are all right," he mumbled, stumbling from the bed. "You must be dreaming." As he tried to soothe her, he fumbled for the flint and managed to spark a candlewick. "Do you need something?"

"The pains—" She sucked in her breath and held it, then exhaled with a moan.

"What the devil—?" Still holding the candle, he threw back the covers with his other hand, and then he saw the dark, wet stain. "Oh, God," he groaned.

Her eyes were dilated, and she was panting. "Got to get up—going to ruin the bed—"

"No—don't move, Kate." He looked wildly around the room, then saw the tablecloth on the small table. He grabbed it, sending the evening's dishes clattering to the floor. Wadding it, he thrust it under her. "Where does it hurt?" he asked foolishly.

"My back—everywhere. My babe—"

"It's too early for the babe, Kate. It must be something you ate." But she hadn't eaten anything, and they both knew it.

"The doctor—"

"I'll go now."

The pain must've been intense even before she awakened him. She'd bitten her lower lip until it bled. He felt utterly, totally helpless, and he knew something was very wrong. He flung himself across the room, pulled on his cloak, and raced to the door.

"Please don't leave me, Bell!"

"I'll be back in a trice," he promised.

The chapter house was dark, but he pounded on the door loudly, shouting until he was hoarse. Finally, he could hear the muffled shuffling of feet, then the ancient door swung inward. It was the brother who'd brought the medicine.

"She's got to have a doctor!" he shouted at the monk, as though the very volume could make him understand. "Her time has come!"

"Le medicine—"

"It didn't help! I tell you she's bleeding!"

"Monsieur." An older, austere brother appeared behind the other one.

"Tell him to get a doctor for my wife! A physician!" He groped for the Russian word, then shouted, *"Vrach! She needs a vrach!"*

"Oui, monsieur, mais—"

"I'm telling you there is something wrong! *Vrach! Vrach!* Can you not understand? She needs a *vrach*!"

The older monk indicated the younger one. "Yvgeny—"

"He damn well poisoned her!"

He didn't have the time to argue with them. Spying the table behind them, he pushed past them and took the cloth from it. "She's bleeding," he muttered as he left.

When he returned, she was lying on her side, her knees pulled up, and her head hung over the edge of the bed. On the floor, he could see where she'd vomited again. "It's the babe!" she gasped. "It wants to come!"

"It cannot be very big, Kate. You've got to let it."

"No!" she cried. "It is too early—it cannot survive!"

He sat down on the other side and tried to force her onto her back. "Kate, listen to me! I don't know what to do either, but God knows, I'll try to help you."

She clutched at his arms. "If I lose my babe, I want to die, Bell—I want to die!"

"Stop it!" Realizing she was terribly frightened, he

tried to speak more calmly. Smoothing her damp hair against her temple, he told her, "I don't want to take a corpse home to Harry—he'd never forgive me. Just try to breathe—just try to get air."

"Bell, this babe is all I have!"

"Shhhh. Just try to stay calm, Kate—just try to stay calm."

She wanted to turn away again, but he wouldn't let her. Instead, he rolled the cloth and pushed it between her legs. They were wet and sticky, and her gown was soaked. It was so dark he couldn't even see what he did.

Someone pounded on the door, and he felt a surge of hope. But when the door opened, it was the same monk who'd brought the useless medicine earlier. The fellow carried a lantern, and as he moved closer, the yellow light showed the woman on the bed. He spoke calmly, soothingly, then raised his hand over Katherine, blessing her.

He turned to Bell and held up one finger, then said the word, "*Vrach.*"

"He said the doctor's coming, Kate," Bell told her.

She looked up at him, then shook her head. "He said it will take a day for him to get here."

"A day and she'll—" He caught himself before he voiced his worst fear. "Never mind," he muttered.

As the man withdrew, Bell dragged a chair closer to the bed. "You've got no one but me, Kate, but I'll do anything you ask." Tears rolled down her face. "For God's sake, don't quit," he whispered, taking her hand. "You are going to survive this."

"No."

There was so much blood in the bed that he was afraid she hemorrhaged. "Let's get you out of the gown."

Humiliated, she turned her head away from him. "I cannot," she croaked. "Please."

"I told you a long time ago—you haven't got anything I haven't seen somewhere else." Before she could fight him, he raised her up and pulled the gown above her hips. Leaning her forward, he managed to get it over her head. "You are a mess, Kate."

"I know," she managed miserably.

"All right, we know it's got to come out, don't we?"

"No." She clutched at her abdomen and tried to raise her knees. It was obvious that she was in intense pain. *"Nooooo!"*

"And we know there are heathens all over the world who do this without any help at all," he went on, as much for his benefit as for hers. He put his hand on her distended belly and felt the intensity of the contraction. "All we've got to do is wait, Kate—all we've got to do is wait."

But it was a long wait. For hours, it was the same thing over and over. The pain would come and she would gasp, then hold her breath and draw up her knees until it passed. Both tablecloths had long since been soaked. She was tired, so very tired, and he could see it. Unable to do anything for her, he got up and paced, then returned with a damp cloth to wipe her face.

"If you are waiting for the doctor, you are doing a deuced good job of it," he complained.

"I know," she gasped.

Her hands were red from gripping the bedstead, and her mouth bled from half a dozen punctures. Never in his life had he felt half so sorry for anyone or anything. Finally, he could stand it no longer.

"You cannot go on like this, Kate—you cannot. I am told there are places where the women just go out into the field and squat, you know. Maybe if you tried to sit up—maybe—"

But her eyes were glassy, distant, and her hands closed convulsively on the bedpost. It was as though her whole body rose up, stiffened, then fell back, as if the wind had left her. Between her legs lay a small, bloody thing.

"It's all right, Kate—it's over! You did it!"

"No," she moaned. "Not yet."

He reached down to pick up the tiny creature just before the afterbirth arrived. Wiping the babe with a corner of the sheet, he could see it was a deep bluish purple beneath the blood, and he knew it did not breathe, that it could not live. For a moment, he could only stare at it, seeing the tiny face, the miniature hands and feet, It was a boy.

Sensing her despair, he forgot his horror, and he began to rub the little body vigorously, trying to stimulate life. Finally, he bent over it and tried blowing into the tiny mouth. When it neither breathed nor moved, he felt nearly overwhelmed by the hopelessness of everything he'd done. Not knowing what else to do, he laid the still, blue infant across Katherine.

She held it close and crooned to it, her voice breaking, and he felt tears sting his eyes. "I'm sorry," he whispered, his throat aching. "I'm terribly sorry, Kate."

She began to cry then, sobbing as though her heart had broken. "Now I have nothing, Bell—nothing! I am truly accursed, Bell—accursed!"

"Kate . . . Kate . . ." Very gently, he lifted the babe away and wrapped it in one of the blankets from the bed. Using his penknife, he cut the cord, then dumped the afterbirth into the washbasin.

At dawn, the monk came back to stare at the tiny babe. Kneeling, he said prayers over it, then he summoned his superior.

When they returned, they dragged a clean feather mattress and fresh bedding. The older monk made the Orthodox sign of the Cross over the dead infant before approaching Bell. He had to know, he said, whether they would name it before it was buried.

Bell repeated the question to Katherine, but she would not speak. Telling them he would answer later, he managed to persuade them to leave. Her nightgown was ruined, leaving only the two dresses and an undershift. She did not resist when he put her into the latter and helped her to a chair before the fire.

Salvaging half a sheet from the ruined bed, he tore it into strips, then rolled them and set them aside. Then he dragged the soiled mattress to a corner and replaced it with the clean one. Somehow he managed to get the sheets on, then the blankets. Rummaging through the other bedclothes, he took a top cover and folded it, then laid it between the sheets.

"Come on—let's get you back to bed."

She walked as though she were in a trance, and at his bidding, she crawled under the covers. He moved the folded blanket beneath her, then found one of the rolled rags and thrust it between her legs.

"You are still bleeding as though you have been slaughtered," he muttered more to himself than to her. "Can you drink something?"

She didn't answer.

He pulled the covers up over her and went to build up the fire. Then he sat before it, the bottle of vodka in his hand. He ought to have been thoroughly, utterly disgusted by what he'd seen, but he wasn't. Just now, he was more inclined to weep for Kate Winstead. She hadn't had much of a life, not with that harridan mother, not with Alexei Volsky—and now this. Life wasn't fair—it wasn't fair at all.

Instead of drinking, he stood up and kicked the chair out of his way. Moving to the bed, he looked down at her. Her hair was still wet, but her eyes were closed, and her skin was as waxy as a candle. She looked almost bloodless, making him again afraid. He had to put his hand over her nose to know that she still breathed.

"Kate, you've got to live," he whispered. "I promised you I'd see you to England."

She was utterly exhausted, and she'd lost far too much blood. He lay down again beside her and covered his shoulders. Turning against her back, he held her close, his hand touching her oddly flacid stomach, and he felt a sense of loss. It did not seem right that the babe who'd moved beneath his hand wasn't there anymore. It wasn't anywhere.

Sometime during the morning, someone crept in and removed the mattress and the dead infant, leaving instead a small icon on the table in the corner. The candles were lit.

When Bell awoke finally, it was afternoon, and someone was shouting through the door. He rose groggily to open it. A man in a heavy greatcoat introduced himself as the *vrach*, saying he'd ridden by sled half the night and day to reach Madame Chardonnay.

"Yes, of course." Bell ran his fingers through his hair, trying to clear his thoughts. "The birthing is over."

"And the babe is dead."

"Yes."

"I'm sorry. Your first?"

"Yes." Bell stood aside and gestured toward the bed. "She hasn't been well, I'm afraid. Her feet and hands and face have been swollen, and now this."

The doctor nodded gravely.

"She has taken this very hard," Bell added. "And she's lost a terrible amount of blood—or at least it seems that way."

"May I see her?"

"Oh. Yes—of course."

"Monsieur Chardonnay?"

It was another monk. Leaving the doctor to attend Katherine, Bell went to speak with him.

"Monsieur, would you have the child buried here?"

He hadn't thought about it at all, but he could think of nothing else to do with it. He nodded.

"And the name? Do you wish a name to be given?"

"I haven't asked K—I haven't asked Elise yet."

"The choice is yours, monsieur."

The less said to Kate, perhaps the better. "All right. John, for her father."

"Jean?"

John or Jean—it was the same thing. He knew she would not want it to be Ivan. "Yes."

"And prayers?"

"Yes."

"We are all saddened by your loss, Monsieur Chardonnay. Please convey our condolences to your wife."

"I will."

The monk hesitated, then told him, "Basil drove much of the night to find the physician for you."

"Thank you. Thank you very much."

"It was not I—it was Basil."

Bell walked to where his coat lay over a chair, and he

reached for the slender leather folder that held his money. Drawing out some of it, he held it out. "For Basil—'tis twenty rubles."

"He is sworn to poverty here, monsieur. But if you would wish to give it for prayers for your son, I will take it."

He didn't want to pay for prayers for anything of Alexei Volsky's. But the babe had been Kate's also.

"Yes—of course."

Behind him, the doctor cleared his throat. "Monsieur, a word with you, please."

"Is she all right?"

"She has a small fever, so I will have to examine the afterbirth to be certain she has passed all of it."

"But is she all right?"

"As to that, I am uncertain. She is very weak and very sad, I think. But the birth could not be helped, I am afraid."

"I don't understand."

"Usually, we know something is wrong when everything begins to swell. Many times we not only lose the child but also the mother. It is as though the child poisons the mother."

"Then she should get better now that it is over?"

"Monsieur, I am a doctor, not a soothsayer," the physician protested. "Much depends on her. She must want to get well. Now, under ordinary circumstances, I should suggest bleeding, but—"

"No!"

"Monsieur, you do not let me finish my words. As she has lost much blood, I do not think it would be wise to take any more."

"Your pardon."

"You have it. Now, I think she must drink. Not the wine, for it causes phlegm—nor the vodka, for it heightens the temperature."

"I see. Milk, then."

"Water. Pure water. Not from the river, but from the cleanest snow."

"All right."

"And plenty of meat. Let them kill a pig for her. Or a sheep, if she prefers it." He eyed Bell for a moment. "I do not suppose she would drink calf's blood?"

"She has a queasy stomach."

"A pity. Blood will replace blood, after all."

"It wouldn't stay down." Bell was certain.

"And she must not travel while the bleeding is so heavy. Later, perhaps when it is normal, she may ride in a sled or carriage."

"All right."

"But the greatest thing to fear is her mind. It will take her some time to accept what she has lost. Women are different than we are—they have not the fatal notion, eh?"

"No, I suppose not."

"I have come a very long way under very trying conditions, monsieur. Very trying conditions. At night."

"I collect we are negotiating your fee," Bell murmured.

"Not at all. It is five rubles to a Russian, ten rubles to a Frenchman."

"I see."

"I lost my uncle and two brothers to the French."

"I'm sorry."

"But you do not speak as a Frenchman, monsieur."

"Actually, I have lived for some time in England. My family fled there in the Terror," Bell lied.

"An émigré, then?"

"Yes."

"Then for you it is five rubles, my friend. You go home and fix what that devil Napoleon has done, eh?" He poked Bell in the ribs. "But first your wife must put on meat over her bones."

"I will see that she does."

"I do not doubt it."

Bell waited until he was nearly out the door. "Wait!"

"Yes?"

"Er—how long does this heavy bleeding last?"

The doctor chuckled. "So young—so eager. The worst will be over in a week or a little more. But you must not touch her until she is well—two months perhaps."

He only wanted to know when she could travel, but at least the rest of it indicated that unless something else went wrong, she'd recover. The worst she faced was her grief, and he did not know how to deal with that.

When he turned back, he noticed the bucket of melting snow by the fire. Someone must have left it while he slept. Taking a cup from the table, he dipped the cold water from it.

"Kate," he said, sitting on the bed, "you are going to drink this and get well."

"I don't want anything" was the muffled reply.

"Oh, yes, you do—if not for yourself, for me. I'm too damned homesick for England." He leaned closer to her ear. "The sawbones told me to give you calf's blood, so you'd dashed well be grateful 'tis only water."

Her back was to him and her shoulders shook, making him think she cried again. "Don't—please don't."

But it was a harsh, bitter laugh. "Don't you see, Bell— now they will not want me! Now that I have lost my babe, nobody will want me! I am of no use to anybody!"

"Stop it, Kate! Stop it!" He grasped her shoulder hard. "Don't be a peagoose! You are going back to England, I tell you!"

"But no one wanted me there, either! Without my child, I am nothing!"

"Don't do this to me!" he shouted angrily. "We've been through hell, Kate—hell! Give us the day to let it pass, for God's sake!" But as he shook her thin shoulders, the anger left him. "Come on, Kate," he coaxed, "just drink the water."

"All right. "I'm not very grateful, am I?"

"No, you are not."

She gulped it down noisily, and he carried the empty cup back to the table. This time, when he sat down with the vodka, he intended to drink all of it. He hadn't been this weary in his entire memory. He uncorked the bottle and took a swig, then sat back, his legs stretched toward the fire. She didn't know what nothing was, he reflected tiredly. At least she was possessed of character.

On the bed, Katherine turned her face into her pillow.

She'd never had many illusions nor many dreams—until Alexei Volsky came into her life. And then she'd dared to think she could be like other females, that she could have a husband to love her, children to be loved by her. Now she would never have either. And she had wanted her son so terribly, terribly much that she could not bear knowing he would never sit on her lap, never grow up.

In the chair, Bell heard her soft sobbing, and he wanted to cry with her. Resolutely, he drank his vodka, thinking what he needed wasn't the responsibility of Katherine Volsky, but rather a soft voice and a warm body to lose himself in. And yet as the drink hit his stomach, he could feel the hot, wet tears sting his eyes.

On 9 February, 1815, Jean Chardonnay, as the monks had erroneously christened him, was laid to rest in the small walled cemetery beside the monastery. Katherine was still abed, making Bell feel it incumbent to attend the ancient ceremony, then to watch as the monks cleared two feet of snow before hacking at the frozen ground with picks. It was difficult to make a hole big enough. At grave side, he had been given a clod of frozen dirt to throw in after they'd lowered the small, hastily contrived casket.

Afterward, the monk called Basil came up to him, saying, "You must not bury your grief inside you, monsieur. You must not let your wife weep alone."

He had no grief. Only sorrow for Kate. Still, he nodded.

"It is well that you found us," the monk went on. "Here you will have the peace to recover."

"How long before the road is passable?" Then, realizing it sounded as though he rejected their hospitality, he hastily tried to make amends. "That is, you must know we shall always be grateful to all of you."

"And to St. Basil." The man smiled. "And I am the most fortunate, for I carry his name."

"To the monks of St. Basil. We shall never forget the service you have done us."

"Our prayers have been with you in your loss, monsieur."

"Our thanks."

"As for the roads, it is difficult to tell. Sometimes we are snowed in for a month and more, and sometimes not.

We have hopes the road will be open before the 26th of February, because the metropolitan of Moscow comes then.''

"It is a rather arduous journey for him."

"Yes, but it is a pilgrimage. Everyone will try to clear the way for him, and the landholders will send their serfs to help. But if it snows more, he will not come."

"And then he goes back to Moscow?"

"Not then. If the weather permits it, he continues to Tula, where he will say Mass."

Returning to the guest house, Bell found Katherine curled up in bed, her face turned away. "Buck up, Kate," he told her, "the snow has stopped, and they will be clearing the road to Tula."

"I don't want to go anywhere" was her muffled reply.

"You've got to—or see me hanged."

"They won't care anymore."

"A man like Alexei Volsky has his pride, I expect." He leaned over her, touching her shoulder. "You've got to get well, Kate. In another week, we'll have to travel."

"I cannot."

"The place will be overrun. They've got the metropolitan of Moscow coming. He's seen you before, hasn't he?"

"Yes," she answered dully. "He registered me as Ekaterina Ivanova. Lexy was going to have him christen the babe."

"I know." Once again, he felt helpless. "It's over, you know." He dropped down to sit beside her and began rubbing her shoulders through the lawn undershift. "I named him John for your father, thinking perhaps you'd prefer that. But they wrote it as Jean, since we are supposed to be French."

"I don't care."

"Yes, you do—you care very much. And I know that. But it's over, and you've got to get well and go on."

"It'll never be over—never," she whispered fiercely. "He was all I had left in this world—all I had left in this world!"

"You still have Harry. We've got to get you back to

England, Kate.'' His hand moved to smooth her wild, tangled hair. "He'll let you cry all over him.''

"I know. B-but I cannot wait to cry!'' she sobbed.

He lifted her, holding her close, letting her give vent to her grief. "It's all right, Kate—it's all right,'' he repeated over and over. "Shhhh—you are going to make me cry with you.''

Finally, he could stand it no longer, and he set her back from him. She rubbed at her eyes with the back of her hand. "I'm sorry. I know you m-must think m-me naught but a silly female, but—''

"I think we are going to have to clean you up again.''

She looked down at the blood on her undershift and nodded. It was as though she'd lost all dignity, all privacy for the most intimate of functions. "I'll try—I can try.''

"No. If you stand up unaided, you are like to faint. Besides, when we are out of here, I intend to forget all of this. I won't even remember I saw you like this,'' he promised.

Backing off the bed, he went to find his own bag. Rummaging through it, he discovered the hated nightshirt. Carrying it back, he held it up for her to see. "I'm not a big man, Kate, so you won't be completely lost in it.''

"You are a lot bigger than I am.''

"At five feet nine? How can you say it when you have seen Harry?'' he quizzed her.

"You have eight inches on me,'' she reminded him. "And I've never heard it noted that you are small.''

"Not small—just not big.''

"And what will you do if I am in your nightshirt?''

"I'll sleep in my clothes.'' He forced a grin. "Despite what you have always thought me, I am not entirely lost to propriety.''

"Yes, you are—but it doesn't matter,'' she said wearily.

He rinsed out the washbasin and tossed the water out the door, then refilled it from the kettle by the fire. Dropping a cloth and a chunk of homemade soap in it, he carried it back to her.

"We'll need to wash you first.''

"I cannot let you do this for me."

The intimacy born of desperation had already passed, and he knew it. "All right. Let me help you to a chair before the fire, and you can take whatever time you need to wash yourself. While you are doing it, I can find something to put beneath you in the bed."

She smiled wanly. "In another life, you must surely have been a nurse."

"No, if I had another life, I must've been a rodent," he countered wryly. "And now I am being punished for it."

"You have been terribly kind to me."

"I'm not kind, Kate. I just want to survive. I want to get back to England, that's all."

"You could have left me."

"And gone where? In case you have not noted it, there is snow and ice everywhere." He set the washbasin down and caught her beneath her arms as she slid off the bed. "God, but you are thin now that the water is gone," he muttered. "I could almost carry you."

"Don't."

"Don't worry. I don't intend to." He pulled her undershift down to cover her legs. "By tomorrow, I expect you to do this yourself."

"Bell, I don't want to do anything."

"I know—you want to die, but it won't fadge just now. If you do, I shall be blamed for it. Come on." He walked her to the chair, then brought the basin to her. "Do whatever you have to, and I won't look."

"Everyone in England will know me for a fool."

"Does it matter?"

"No," she lied.

"You'll have Harry," he reminded her. "And you can live quietly at Monk's End."

"With Mama."

"It was you who wished to go home, Kate."

"But I thought—I thought I should have my child with me."

He swung around at that. "Please, Kate—don't. I'm not a very kind fellow anyway, and I've done everything

I can. What's done is done, and it cannot be changed—no more than I can change what I am. I cannot take any more of this, I'm afraid.''

"You could leave me here."

"God. Is that what you want? Or are you like every other female of my acquaintance?'' he demanded angrily. "None of you tells the truth!''

He went back to the bed and yanked the bloody, folded cloth from where she'd lain. Then he flung his nightshirt across the room at her. Carrying the soiled cloth, he headed for the door.

"Where are you going?''

"To get something for a pad! Take care of yourself while I am gone!''

She felt utterly, totally miserable, thinking he felt her an ingrate. She wasn't an ingrate at all, she wanted to cry after him. He just didn't understand—she'd lost her child! Hurt turned to despair. She'd lost her husband, and now she'd lost her child. Couldn't he see? She had no one.

Outside, his temper cooled in the frigid air. He had no right to rip up at a sick woman, he told himself. And he had no right to resent what she could not help. She was weak, she was frail, and she needed him. Shivering, he went across to the chapter house to beg another cloth for her.

When he returned, she was still sitting in the chair. But she had his wooly nightshirt buttoned up to her chin. And on the floor beside her, the water in the basin was pink. He walked to the table and picked up a rolled piece of the torn sheet.

"I have already gotten one,'' she said, reddening.

"It looks decidedly better on you than me,'' he declared, his eyes on the hated shirt. "But it will itch you to death.''

"Actually, it is quite warm.''

There was an awkwardness between them. "Are you feeling better?'' he asked finally.

"Yes.'' She looked up at him, her dark eyes nearly

overwhelming her pale face. "But you cannot ask me not to mourn."

"I'm not asking it. I'm asking you to get well."

"How—how did he look?" she managed to ask.

He'd not seen the babe after the monks put him in the box, but he lied to her, "He looked fine, Kate."

"Did they wrap him warmly?"

"Yes."

"And will they mark his grave?" Her chin quivered, but she did not cry. "Somehow that is terribly important to me."

"Are you quite sure you want that?"

She did not want Alexei or Galena to have her son, not even in death, but neither did she want her babe to lie there, a nameless child in a distant place.

"Yes."

"I told you—he is listed in the register as Jean Chardonnay. I had to sign it."

"I know."

"Then we will have it marked that way."

"Thank you."

"I gave twenty rubles for prayers."

She nodded.

"Come on, Kate—you are shivering. Let's get you back into bed."

Because she was so weak, she managed to sleep for a time, leaving him to wander about the small room. The place was like a prison, he reflected gloomily, and it did not matter that Peter the Great had retreated there in some crisis of faith. He was stuck there, utterly, inexorably stuck there. And when he got out, when he got her back to England, there was going to be hell to pay—any way he cut the cards, there was going to be hell to pay. And no matter how much she thought otherwise, she was utterly unprepared for what was going to happen to her. He wasn't even sure he could come about himself.

The first two days after the loss of the child had been the worst. She ached, body and soul, and her breasts had to be bound to ease their pain. After that, she began to improve, eating and drinking everything Bell gave her. But after four days, he was restless and irritable.

While it had stopped snowing, nothing showed any signs of thawing, and Yuri was speaking of seeking asylum there. To make matters worse, the monk named Basil did not think the roads could be cleared before the metropolitan came on the 26th. Barring some further complication, given the state of the roads, even the best driver could not get them the thousand or so miles to Warsaw in less than seven weeks. That would make it mid-April. They'd be damned fortunate to be in England before May.

And Bell did not know if he could stand it unless Kate recovered completely. His newly discovered kindness was being tried by his less-admirable self. Finally, for want of anything else to do, he managed to acquire some pasteboard and scissors from the monks. He was amusing himself, he decided ruefully, like a grubby schoolboy.

He sat at the table, utterly absorbed, his head bent low over his work. When she could stand it no longer, she rose from the bed to watch. He was carefully cutting squares.

"What are you doing?"

"Making cards."

"Cards?" she asked incredulously. "Game cards?"

"Yes." He looked up at her. "I'm trying to get them all the same size, so they can be shuffled." He could see she was unimpressed. "While you may have been too ill to note it, a monastery is a dashed dull place for me, I can tell you."

"But they are all plain."

"Ah, Kate, you have no imagination. I expect to put the marks on them."

"Can you even draw?"

"Indifferently. But does it matter?"

She picked up one of the pieces, eyeing it critically. "Well, I expect I could do that for you."

"Do you know the suits, the sequences?"

"I was born a Winstead," she reminded him. "And, while you may not recall it, Harry and I beat you at Monk's End once. But," she added judiciously, "I think your mind was elsewhere."

"You never forgive, do you?"

"Yes. I have come to realize she was a foolish woman." She sat down opposite him, asking, "Do you have a pen and ink?"

"In my box. I'll get them for you."

When he came back, he set the inkpot before her, then drew out his penknife and sharpened the quill. "Try not to make extra blots," he advised her. "We don't want to be confused."

"No, of course not." Taking the pen, she began making neat, rounded numbers on the corners of the cards. "You know, it would go much faster if we only put the suits next to the numbers. Otherwise, we shall be forever drawing hearts and spades."

"And clubs and diamonds—there are four suits," he reminded her.

"You know very well what I meant."

"I think you are on the mend, Kate," he decided. "I begin to recognize your tongue."

"You have never brought out the best in it, you know," she murmured, bending her head over a card.

"At least I have heard it. If you had spoken half so

much to an eligible *parti,* I daresay you might have taken. But everyone thought you tongue-tied, as I recall.''

"No. The only ones who gave me twice-over were elderly or stupid. The rest all wanted to make sheep's eyes at Claire.'' She drew a heart beneath a bold Q. ''It doesn't look quite right, does it?''

"What it needs is the queen.''

"That I cannot do very well.'' Nonetheless, she outlined a head with a crown on it, then added a wimple. ''Now, if we can only tell her from the king,'' she murmured wryly. ''She looks quite medieval, I think.''

"At this pace, you'll not be done ere the snow thaws.''

"But at least I shall be occupied.''

"I'll do half of them. Which do you want—diamonds, spades, or clubs? You've already started the hearts.''

"It doesn't matter.''

"Spades then. Balance the good with the evil. I'll take the clubs and diamonds myself.''

It took nearly half an afternoon of cutting and drawing before the deck was done and neatly stacked by suit. He went to pour her some more of the melted snow, then carried it back to the table. ''I think I am going to see if perhaps somewhere in this place there is a wine cellar. And if there is, I mean to offer money for something besides the damned vodka.''

While he was gone, she attempted to shuffle the pasteboard cards, but the edges were not smooth enough. Finally, she turned them face away and sifted them back and forth. Satisfied, she stacked them again, and reached for the water he'd left her.

Although she'd known him for more than half her life, she'd never imagined any kindness in him. He was Bellamy Townsend, Viscount Townsend, to be exact, and he was the object of a great deal of admiration and even more gossip. She sipped pensively, thinking how wrong everyone was about him, and most especially how wrong she herself had been. But who could have thought him capable of anything beyond himself? And yet she knew she owed him her life.

"You aren't blue-deviled again, are you?'' he asked, shutting the door.

"Actually, I was thinking about you," she admitted.

"Well, don't. None of this does anything to my credit, you know. Besides, if you tell, no one will believe it."

"I know. But you *are* a surprise. I'd always thought you too self-centered to help anyone."

He sat down and pulled the cork from a bottle of wine with his teeth. It popped loudly. "I am," he acknowledged, pouring some of the dark red liquid into a cup. "But I owed Harry."

"Still—"

"And if you are going to start hanging on me like every other female of my acquaintance, I'm going to wish I'd left you in Moscow."

"I have not turned around quite that much," she answered dryly. "I have merely discovered a modicum of decency in you."

"And that's about all there is, I'm afraid." He started to shuffle the cards.

"I have already mixed them."

"Oh?" He eyed her for a moment, then cut them. "The first rule for a gamester is to trust no one, my dear."

"What are we playing?"

"Well, as there are only two of us, it cannot be whist, so I expect it will have to be loo."

"I haven't played it in ages."

"And I daresay I haven't played it for longer than you, so we should be fairly even." He pushed the ink pot and the quill closer to her. "Just keep count of the tricks," he advised her.

They played throughout the waning hours of the afternoon, until one of the monks brought bread and stew. Pushing the cards aside, Bell handed Kate a bowl and spoon. She did not protest, but began eating it.

He sat back, his drink in his hand, watching her. She was too slender by half, too pale by more than that, and her hair was a fright, but there was something about her that drew him. Despite that certain waif-like quality, there was also a quietness he found he liked. She was utterly lacking in artifice, and she was, in all likelihood, the only truly honest female he knew. Rather than puffing herself up, she was far too hard on herself.

He caught himself and stared reproachfully into his wine. He'd either had too much or he'd been too long without the solace of a woman, he supposed.

"I know my hair needs combing," she murmured.

She'd known he watched her. "Actually, I was thinking you were almost as good company as your brother," he lied.

"Really? But he rarely loses," she reminded him.

He looked at the score of tricks and grinned. He'd won nearly two-thirds of them. "All right, then you are better."

"It's a whisker, and I know it."

"No, when we are not running and you are not ill, you are a very pleasant female."

"I lose at cards, you mean."

His manner changed abruptly. "I don't know if you ought to go back to England, Kate."

Stunned for a moment, she stared. "But why?" she asked finally. "And where else would I go?"

"I don't know."

"I will not go back to Alexei and Galena, Bell—and there is no one else here. I hardly think Paul and Olga would want me, now that there is no child to dangle before Galena."

"No—no, of course not."

"And I cannot sue for divorce in Russia," she argued. "Katherine Winstead against Alexei Volsky? Paul said they would put me in an asylum for the insane!"

"You won't be welcome in England. I've thought and thought—while you slept these last days, I thought of little else."

"I shall apply for a divorce from Alexei. Beyond that, I do not care."

"Yes, you do. Ask Diana—ask Longford's former wife what it is like. She's had to go abroad nearly for life."

"And Lady Holland is a Whig hostess, though she is divorced!"

"But you aren't Lady Holland, Kate. And she's not

received anywhere, either. Yes, the politicians flock to her table, but what about their wives?''

"I don't know."

"I do. Deuced few of 'em are to be found, I can tell you."

She stared at her food for a moment. "I don't care. If I have to live at Monk's End for the rest of my life, I don't care."

"What if Lady Winstead won't have you?"

"Then I shall live with Harry. And don't say that Harry won't have me, because he will—I know it."

"All right. But you will not be received anywhere. And there's worse to think about."

"Nothing could be worse than living with a man who does not love me. Nothing could be worse than living with a man who shares his bed with his sister."

He regarded her soberly, then sighed. "Even if you are charged with adultery?''

"Alexei would not dare face me in court."

"He won't have to—he can engage a solicitor. And how's it to look that you will have spent months traveling in my company?''

"You are afraid, aren't you, Bell?"

"Not for me," he lied. "I can come about, Kate—but you cannot."

"I have nowhere else to go—nowhere. So I am prepared to pay for my foolishness. As for being cut, I never liked most of those people who will cut me, anyway." She sipped her water, then met his gray eyes. "And if you are afraid you will be expected to marry me, I can assure you it will not happen."

She was too green, and she didn't understand how terrible it would be. But any alternative he could envision wasn't much better than taking her back to face the censure of the entire *ton*. And given that the case would involve the Russian count, he did not see how Harry could keep it out of the newspapers. She would be fortunate if she could show her face anywhere.

Impulsively, he stretched his hand across the table to

clasp hers. Her fingers tightened momentarily. "We cried friends, Kate," he said huskily.

"I pray you will not regret it." She withdrew her hand and stood. "I think I liked it better when I was losing at cards." Moving away, she regarded the fire for a time. "It must be quite different for a man," she said slowly. "You have your bits of fluff, and when the passion has passed, you find another. We aren't like that at all—or at least I hope we are not. We want it to last forever, you see."

The fire reflected off the angles of her face, softening them, haloing her hair. And the sadness in her eyes was haunting. He could not stand it.

"Don't you think that is what we want, Kate? Only we are about in the world enough to know that it doesn't happen."

"But *why*?"

He came up behind her and laid his hands on her shoulders. "It just doesn't. So instead we look for a female to do us credit—show to advantage, display social graces—that sort of thing."

"Then you might as well have a pretty puppet."

"Alas, but that's precisely what most of us get. And when we get tired of playing with it, we return to our bits of fluff."

"How very lowering for us."

"You console yourselves with our money."

"Not Galena. She consoled herself with my husband."

"Poor Kate," he murmured sympathetically.

"I don't want your pity!" She shook him off angrily. "I have a surfeit of that for myself."

"What do you want? I haven't much else to give."

She closed her eyes and swallowed hard. "I want," she whispered, her voice anguished, "to go to sleep and never wake up. But I cannot. And so I will go on."

"Kate—"

"I will be all right."

"It might be better for both of us if I married you."

It was as though her stomach sought her feet, and for

a moment, she thought her heart had stopped. "What did you say?" she asked hollowly.

"Don't rip up at me," he said hastily. "I just think it might solve things better. And we would not have to expect anything of each other."

"You cannot even pretend to have any deep affection for me, and I cannot pretend the right sort for you. I doubt I shall ever care for anyone after Alexei."

"No, of course not. But I could take you to Paris—or Italy. Let Alexei sue, Kate," he reasoned, "and when it is done, we marry abroad. Then, although you are not received, you will not be utterly invisible either. In time, we'll go home and come about—like the Hollands, if you will."

"An arrangement, then?"

"Yes. I probably won't be much of a husband, but at least we will not be at daggers drawn. I've seen you closer than any female of my acquaintance, and I've discovered a liking for you, Kate. I don't want to see you hurt further."

"No." She turned to face him. "Just now, you are perhaps the dearest friend I have on earth, maybe even the only one, and I thank you for it, but we should make each other utterly miserable."

"Think on it."

"Adonis and the Antidote? I think not. Besides, I do not mean to admit to that which I have not done."

"It happens all the time, Kate."

"Not to me. Unlike you, I've not had the experience of having Parliament declare me guilty of adultery. Your pardon—I shouldn't have said it precisely that way," she said quickly. "But I should very much rather have them decide Alexei guilty of incest, thank you."

"All right. But you'd best think on it, before you are so certain." He sighed heavily. "I only hope you know what you are about."

She moved away. "If you do not mind, I have been up far too long. I think I shall wash up a bit and go to bed." She waited until she had nearly the whole room between them. "I do thank you, you know," she said softly.

"Some Adonis, Kate," he murmured wryly. "You are the second female to turn me down."

He went back to the table and picked up the nearly empty bottle of wine. Returning to the fire, he sat down, his back to her, and drank. He ought to feel relieved, he told himself, but he didn't. He just felt damned lonely. And the devil of it was, he didn't even know if he'd offered to save her or himself.

Brest, Byelorussia: *April 10, 1815*

He sat before the fire in the small inn room, feeling a sense of accomplishment. He was nearing the end of keeping his promise to Kate Volsky, and he told himself he was glad, but there was also a sense of imminent loss. On the morrow, they would attempt crossing the border into Poland.

They had spent three weeks at St. Basil's while she recovered, followed by nearly seven more on hellish roads, fighting first the snow and cold, then the rain and mud, averaging less than twenty-five miles a day much of the way to Brest.

He waited while she undressed behind a makeshift screen. The incredible intimacy between them had passed with St. Basil's, and now there was a certain constraint to forget. As her body healed, it somehow seemed improper to continue sharing a bed. So now he slept on a pallet like a peasant, but he didn't entirely mind it.

Still there was that bond born of survival that he found he could not and did not entirely want to break. He'd watched her endure more suffering and hardship in two months than any woman ought to have to bear, and while she'd grieved, she'd gone on. He felt an intense admiration for her, but at the same time it angered him that Alexei Volsky had closed her heart. She was too young to go on alone, too young to wither. She deserved to have someone to love her.

The irony was not lost on him. Two months ago, he'd believed love was naught but romantic nonsense foisted on men by women. Or the means of seduction. Now he was seeing the price Kate had paid for believing herself in love with Volsky. There was so much hurt, so much bitterness, that he doubted she would ever entirely recover.

She emerged from behind the screen in her nightgown and wrapper, with her hairbrush in her hand. The firelight silhouetted her body, showing that she'd gained much of the weight she'd lost during her pregnancy, that if anything, her breasts were fuller, her face softer, and her dark hair longer. She no longer looked plain to him at all. Even the nose she claimed to hate did not appear as long as she thought. There was a definite appeal to it, in fact.

He uncrossed his legs and rose to face her. "Are you tired?" he asked.

"No." She smiled. "Surely by now you must know no female would admit to fatigue after shopping."

"I'd almost forgotten." His fingertips brushed her cheek lightly. "It's good to see you smile again, Kate," he said softly.

She had no answer to that, so she merely murmured, "I thank you for the shawl, by the by."

"You practice too many economies, when it comes to yourself."

She spied the small, linen-covered table pulled close to the fire. "What's that?"

"I thought perhaps we should celebrate our last day in Russia," he said, turning back to it. "After a great deal of haggling, I have cajoled our innkeeper out of two bottles of authentic Madeira, some bread and cheese, and a small bit of excellent caviar."

"I am really not very hungry." As she saw his smile fade, she relented quickly. "But I daresay I will taste the Madeira with you."

"We could play cards also."

"You have already forgotten I won the last time?" she teased him.

"No. In fact, I like to watch your face when you win. You are like a cat over cream."

"And you are not, I suppose?"

"I play them considerably closer than you do."

She got the cards from his bag, then brought them to the fire. "The table's too small," she decided, dropping to the floor. Besides, this reminds me of when I was a child at Monk's End with Harry. We were used to sit on the rug before the hearth."

He joined her, taking one bottle and the tray with him. Filling both glasses, he handed her one. "You'd best watch it," he warned her. "It's rather strong."

She studied the amber-colored liquid for a moment, then shook her head. "Actually, it looks rather innocent to me."

"Too much, and you will have a devil of a head in the morning." He sipped his, savoring the taste of it. "Go on—try it."

It was perhaps a bit strong for her taste, but she forced herself to drink of it. Setting it aside, she began sifting the pasteboard cards. It had been a sort of private jest between them that they were too economizing to buy a real deck. Satisfied, she passed them to him for his cut.

"No—I trust you."

Her eyebrow lifted. "Since when?"

"I don't know—I just do."

"No wonder I am winning."

Her head was bent low as she distributed the cards, the crown of her hair so close he could have reached out and touched it. And this night, he was acutely aware of everything she did. He closed his eyes momentarily to still the racing of his pulse.

"Is something the matter?"

"No." He drained his glass and refilled it, before passing her the bread and cheese."

"I cannot. I will become positively fat."

"You are not fat at all, Kate."

There was a softness in his voice that gave her pause. For a moment, she looked at him, seeing the open-necked shirt, the tousled hair, the almost boyish smile. He was in truth Adonis. Taken back by what she felt, she turned her attention to the cards in her hand.

"More, Kate?"

"I have not drunk this yet." But as she spoke, she

sipped the wine. "You know, Bell, I think I am going to lose."

"I certainly hope so. Do you want another deal?"

"No—it wouldn't be fair, would it?" she said, sighing. "I shall just have to play it out."

He filled her glass, anyway. Then he took the first trick. And the second. And third. "You were serious, weren't you?"

"Yes. It is all of a piece, I think. I am not very lucky at anything."

"You are too young to say that."

"Am I? I am now three and twenty, and I am about to be divorced from a man who did not love me." Her dark eyes met his. "I am not at all likely to ever get another offer, you know." Her mouth twisted crookedly. "And now I shall never have children, either."

"You don't know that."

This time, she tossed off her whole glass. "No, not even old Mr. Thurgood would have me now, I'm afraid. You are beholding a scarlet woman, Bell."

"I don't think so, Kate. I think you are magnificent."

Her eyes widened, then she blinked. "I thought," she told him severely, "that you were not going to offer me any Spanish coin."

"I'm not."

"But you cannot—"

She got no further. Still kneeling, he reached out to her, taking her face in his hands. As time seemed to stop, he slowly, deliberately bent his head to hers. And her breath caught in her chest when his lips teased, then his mouth possessed hers hungrily. Her arms came up to twine about his neck, and she leaned eagerly into his kiss.

He could feel her whole body tremble, and he forgot she was untouchable, that she was Harry's sister. He lay back, taking her with him, then rolled onto his side to face her. Her eyes were large and luminous in the firelight, then they closed as he kissed her again.

Some small voice within her told her it was wrong, yet she was suddenly alive again, and she did not want to give up the moment of being held by him. And even when she felt his hands at the ties of her wrapper, she did not want to turn him away. Instead, she returned kiss for kiss, savoring the closeness, the feel of him.

"Open up!" someone shouted at the door. "It is the authorities!"

"What the hell—?" Bell rolled away, then struggled to stand.

There was a determined pounding. Frightened, Katherine sat there on the floor for a moment. Forcing herself to rise, she looked to him.

"It cannot be, Bell—it cannot!"

"I don't know," he muttered. "You'd best get the papers."

He opened the door, then stood back. Two uniformed men walked inside. "Monsieur Chardonnay, you are French?"

Bell nodded.

"And your wife?"

He nodded again.

One of the men looked to Katherine. "Turn around, madame—please."

As she turned to face him, she tied her wrapper at her waist. His eyes lingered there for a moment, then he shook his head.

"Is something the matter?" she managed to ask.

"*Non.* There are Imperial warrants for a woman and her paramour."

"I see. And you think that—"

"*Mais non.*" There was a flash of white teeth beneath his dark mustache as he smiled regretfully. "I am told she is *enceinte*, and that her time nears." He bowed stiffly. "*Pardon*, madame. We are sorry for the intrusion.

"*De rien*," she responded.

"*Bon soir, monsieur.*"

"*Bon soir*," Bell murmured.

The two men clicked their heels together, then withdrew. Bell looked to where Katherine stood, and he knew the moment between them had passed. Reason told him it was for the best, that she would have too much remorse, anyway.

"It's all right, Kate."

Disappointment warred with relief. "I know," she said finally.

"I must be reforming," he decided. "I've not had a woman since I left England."

"Not even Sofia?"

"Certainly not Sofia."

"I forgot—she said you could not."

"Not could not, Kate—would not." He walked to her and lifted her chin to look into her eyes. "You were my conscience, you know. In the end, I would not trespass on Sherkov's hospitality, no matter how much I disliked him."

For a moment, she thought he meant to kiss her again, but he dropped his hand. Exhaling, he nodded toward the bed. "I expect we ought to just go to bed and get up deuced early, don't you think?"

"Yes."

"We don't know what awaits at the border itself."

But long after the candles were doused, long after she'd gone to bed, she lay awake, listening, and she knew he did not sleep either. Across the room, a log popped as it burned in the hearth. Never in her life had she been as aware of anyone as she was of him now. Her hands crept to her lips as she relived each kiss, and she knew that had the soldiers not come, she would have given herself to him.

She came out from behind the screen, wearing one of the two new gowns she'd had made in Brest, a dark green traveling dress trimmed in black. The seamstress had fitted it well—it curved over her breasts without a wrinkle. As he watched, he could not help thinking she no longer looked like the starving waif he'd brought out of Moscow.

"What do you think?"

He rose to pick up her curled-brim bonnet and set it on her head. After tying the black grosgrain ribbon under her chin, he stepped back to view her critically. Dissatisfied, he undid the ties and moved them to one side. This time, he made larger loops with the bow.

"I think, Madame Chardonnay," he murmured, "you are quite fetching."

"Fiddle. You've merely forgotten what your barques of frailty looked like."

"You know, Kate, you need to learn to take a compliment."

She moved away to pull on her black silk gloves. "What if they do not let us cross? What if we are arrested?"

"It won't happen," he assured her. But for all his bracing words, he was not entirely convinced himself. It would be the first time they actually had to put the papers Paul Volsky had given them to the touch.

She made a face at herself in the mirror, then straightened her shoulders. "I am ready, I suppose."

"I hate it when you do that."

"What?"

"You look like a monkey who does not like what he sees."

"I suppose so." She looked up at him. "We cannot all be Bellamy Townsend, you know."

"For which you ought to be grateful." He draped a fringed black silk shawl over her shoulders. "Do you know how lowering it can be to know everyone admires you merely for your face?"

"No. But I should be willing to discover it," she admitted truthfully. "Do you know how very lowering it is to discover no one looks at you because you have a beautiful sister?"

"I was an only child."

"Ah—I'd forgotten. You were your mama's angel, weren't you?"

"That, Kate, was utterly unworthy of you. And you have a deuced long memory."

"Yes, well—I am ready, I think. I just wish it were all over, that somehow I was already in England."

"You won't think so after you are there." Nonetheless, he held the door open for her. "Well, Elise—it is now or never, is it not?"

Despite her gloves, her hands felt as cold as ice. Still, she nodded. "Yes, Albert, it is."

He offered her his arm, and together they went downstairs to eat before they drove to the crossing. On the stairs, he looked down to where her hand rested on his coat. "You'd best take off your ring, lest it is recognized," he said low.

"Yes, of course."

In the small public room, the same two officers ate. As Kate passed them, she nodded politely. "Ah, madame," one said, "do you and monsieur join us?"

Not wishing to draw suspicion, Bell nodded. It was, he decided, much like the mice eating with the cats. But it couldn't be helped.

Finally, they escaped gracefully and headed by carriage for Siedice, a small Polish town. As expected, they were stopped on both sides, but ironically, it proved the Poles who were suspicious. After the Chardonnays' papers were examined carefully, one of the guards asked them to come inside, where he explained that a necessary stamp was missing. He called for his superior, who was temporarily engaged.

Bell stood there, his face impassive, his mind in turmoil. Surely after all he and Kate had endured, it could not come to this. Behind him, he heard her gag, then retch, bringing up her breakfast at the crossing guard's feet. She held her head with one hand, the wall with the other. Recoiling, the guard turned to her.

"Please—I am unwell," she gasped.

The fellow hastily scrawled his approval on the papers, then shoved them at Bell, advising him to get his wife some air. What had begun with deliberation ended speedily. As Bell took Kate's arm, he murmured apologetically that she was *"enceinte."*

But once outside, he was concerned. "Are you quite certain you are well enough to ride?" he asked anxiously. "It must have been the excess of grease with breakfast."

"It was my finger." Leaving him to contemplate that, she climbed into the carriage. "When he was not looking, I felt the need to act rather promptly."

"Your finger, my dear?" he said as he heaved himself onto the seat opposite her.

"Yes," she admitted, smiling smugly. "When we were children, Claire had quite a facility for escaping her lessons. She was ill a lot, you see."

"You know," he said, grinning, "you are a remarkable woman, Kate—you never cease to surprise me."

"Well, I much preferred being sick to going back to Russia, so I cannot see anything very remarkable about that."

"No, Kate, you are—you are."

Even as he said it, she felt a tremor of awareness course through her. "I expect you say that to every female, don't you?" she said, trying to keep her voice light.

"Only to you, my dear—only to you," he insisted low.

Since there had been no great need for haste now, they drove rather leisurely to Warsaw, where he would deliver her into the hands of the British ambassador. Both of them faced that with trepidation—and with a sense of impending loss.

But every word spoken, every gesture appeared fraught with nuance now, making Katherine wonder what he truly thought, if the shared kisses of the night before were on his mind as much as hers. And she knew she had to stop thinking about something that probably had no meaning at all for him. She knew also that anything beyond those kisses was literally a road to ruin.

He leaned back, his hat pulled forward to hide his thoughts, telling himself he had no right to touch her—not now, not ever. For all her pluck and renewed spirit, he knew there was a fragility beneath, that she was not the sort of female to take disappointment twice. And no matter how much he thought otherwise just now, he knew in his heart he'd disappoint her. It was not in his nature to love with constancy. The fact that he no longer thought of Elinor Kingsley ought to prove it.

It began to rain, a mixture of mist and drizzle, turning into a heavy, pelting downpour. Bell hit the roof of the passenger compartment, signaling his driver to slow down, then he yelled for him to find a place for the night.

As he leaned forward, he was but inches from her, and his very presence was as heady as the Madeira of the night before. She forced herself to look out the window into the storm. Lightning flashed overhead, making the horses skittish, so she hoped they would stop soon. She needed space between herself and Bell Townsend, before she acted the fool.

The small town was an old one, medieval in character, and the narrow houses clung to each other on each side of the cobbled street. The carriage rolled to a halt before the painted sign of a hanging ham.

Bell jumped down to go inside, affording her a respite from the tautness she felt. Even then, she had to close her eyes and force herself to remember the pain of Lexy's perfidy. The last thing she needed, she knew, was to throw herself at Bell Townsend's head. For when it was done, she would not even have him for the friend he'd become.

He returned to tell her that there were rooms to be had with the meals, and it appeared the sheets were clean. She nodded. He reached for her, lifting her, letting her slide the length of him before he set her down. But then she wondered if she'd only imagined it, that it was her own mind that deceived her.

Inside, one of the tavern maids eyed him saucily, reminding her again of what he was. And as he wrote in the yellowed register, the girl all but fell into him. He was so accustomed to the reaction that he did not even appear to notice.

While Katherine went up to wash and change, he remained downstairs with a glass of dark beer. She was to join him for supper when she was ready, he said. But when she looked back, the maid was hovering him, and she suspected there was more to it than that.

In the bedchamber, Katherine took her time, savoring the most thorough washing she could get out of a basin and lavender soap. The smell of that latter made her homesick all over again. She unpacked the other dress from its tissue and held it up, letting the dark blue twill unfold. As plain as it was, it was a pretty gown, and when she'd been fitted for it, Bell had said it became her.

Once dressed, she passed the small dressing table mirror and stopped to make her usual face. But this time, she was drawn to get her case and sit down before it. Taking out her brush, she dragged the tangles from her hair, then she twisted and pinned it. It was too severe, and she knew it. Pulling a few strands, as Galena had taught her to do, she framed her face with delicate wisps. And then she did the unthinkable. She took out the rouge pot and tried to put on just enough to give her the blush of youth without the paint of age. Then she made her face.

He was waiting, telling her apologetically that he'd already ordered for her, that he'd not expected her to take so long.

"They have lavender soap," she explained. "I have not felt so clean in an age."

"You look quite lovely, you know," he said softly.

"Fustian."

"Kate . . . Kate . . . whatever am I to do with you? When a man says you are in looks, you are supposed to accept it," he chided.

"Even when the man is Bellamy Townsend?" she countered.

"Yes."

"All right." She looked at her plate curiously. "What is it?"

"I don't know. I don't speak Polish, I'm afraid, but as nearly as I could tell, the girl recommended it."

"I expect if you could understand her, she recommends something else as well."

"Now that is a universal language, my dear."

"I wouldn't know."

"Never say the Russian did not speak soft words in your ear?" As soon as he'd said it, he saw her wince, and he wished he'd held his tongue. "I'm sorry—I didn't mean to pry."

She was silent for a moment, then she sighed. "No, I don't think so—or if he did, Galena fed them to him. He only said or did what she wanted, you know."

He covered her hand. "It must have been hell for you."

Her eyes were hot, her throat too tight for speech. She had to swallow hard to answer. "Not at first. At first, I was so very grateful that I thought he loved me. Now I do not know what I felt. It was as though I had a dream of what he was like, I suppose," she said haltingly. "And the dream died in small pieces, bit by tiny bit, and still I clung to the shreds until I found out why he could not love me." She pushed her plate away and rose. "I'm sorry—I shall be back in a moment."

He caught her hand again and held it. "It was not my intent to make you cry."

"No, I am all right." Mastering herself, she sat down again and reached for her fork. "Well, whatever it is, I expect I shall like it." But as she took the first bite, she looked up to discover that he still watched her. And it was as though something inside her caught, holding her breath in abeyance. She had to force herself to chew, but she scarce tasted the food in her mouth. "Aren't you going to eat?" she asked, once she'd swallowed. "I think it is made of pork."

"Kate, you are pluck to the bone," he murmured softly. "Volsky was a fool."

"I suppose if one has to be something, pluck is a worthy attribute, isn't it?"

"Yes. It goes far deeper and is far more lasting than mere beauty."

She regarded him, trying to fathom the turn of his thoughts, telling herself he simply made conversation. Ruefully, she smiled. "For the shocking flirt and altogether shallow fellow you claim to be, you are quite brave yourself."

"Only when I have to be."

"No. What you did for me at St. Basil's was truly heroic. I shall be forever in your debt—forever."

He appeared to be toying with his wineglass, tracing the edge idly with a fingertip. When he looked up, the expression in his gray eyes was utterly sober. "I don't want gratitude, Kate."

"I cannot help giving it, Bell." The tension she felt was too great. She looked down at her nearly full plate, then shook her head. "I'm not very hungry, I'm afraid. Perhaps it is but that everything is nearly over and that we are safe, but I find myself worn to the nub, so to speak."

"If you want to retire, I can bring you something up when I come," he offered quietly.

"No. I think I shall go to bed."

But once upstairs, she merely put on her nightgown and wrapper and sat in the darkness. She was weepy, blue-deviled, and so taut inside that she knew if she let herself cry, she'd never stop. So she stared unseeing into nothing, not even aware that the rain had stopped, or that the stars shone.

She heard the key in the lock, but she did not move.

He let himself in, removed his boots, then said tentatively, "Kate?"

"I am over here."

"Why aren't you in bed? You'll take your death sitting here like that."

"I just hadn't gotten up yet."

"I came up to see how you fared—if you needed anything."

"No."

He walked to stand behind her. "Are you quite certain?"

"I just wish to be left alone."

"No, I don't think so."

She drew in her breath and let it out slowly. "Bell, if you wish, I will not notice if you go back downstairs."

His hand touched the back of her neck lightly, sending a shiver down her spine. "But I don't want anything downstairs."

She ducked away and stood. "Please, Bell—I—"

He closed the gap between them and reached to hold her face, massaging her temples with his thumbs. Very deliberately, he moved closer and brushed her lips lightly, letting his breath caress her cheek.

"I want you, Kate—please," he whispered. "Let me give you what Lexy did not—let me show you what you have missed."

"No—" But even as she said it, she could feel herself shatter into pieces at his lightest touch. Her arms slid around his back, clinging to him. "Can you love me, Bell?" she asked, anguish in every whispered word.

"I can try."

He kissed her deeply then, tasting, probing, taking, until her knees were weak. And his hands moved from her face to her shoulders and down over her back and hips, holding her close to him. The odd thought crossed her mind that although he was not so tall as Alexei Volsky, he was strong and solid. And she did not think she'd ever wanted anything in her life as much as she wanted him to hold her like this.

Finally, he released her to catch her hand, to take her to the bed. His hands found the ties of her wrapper, loosening them, then he slid it off her shoulders, down over her arms, until it fell in a swoosh at her feet. It wasn't until she felt him raise her gown that she was afraid—she didn't want him to see her.

"No," she said, catching at his hands.

"All right."

As she stood there, shivering as much from desire as from cold, he shrugged out of his clothes, leaving everything in a tangled heap beside her wrapper. His gray eyes caught the moonlight from the window as he reached for her. He studied her face for a moment.

"Kate, you need this as much as I do," he said softly.

She nodded mutely.

This time when he kissed her, there was nothing but her nightgown between them, and she could feel the heat of his body as it rose against her. He backed against the bed and took her down with him. Rolling her over onto her back, he began exploring her eagerly, touching, tasting, feeling—her forehead, her eyes, her temples, her lips, her neck. And as he found the sensitive hollow of her throat, she felt him work her gown upward. She moaned and parted her legs to receive him.

But he was in no hurry. "No," he murmured against her ear, "we've just begun." He raised up enough to draw her gown all the way to her neck. Then he lifted her shoulders and pulled it off. "I like the feel of your skin, Kate. You are so smooth, so warm."

His mouth traced fire from her throat to her shoulder to her breast, and his tongue licked, teasing her nipple until it hardened. He sucked it, and she felt the wetness between her legs. Her hands caught his soft, waving hair, and her fingers opened and closed restlessly, urging him on, and still he did not take her.

She moved beneath his touch, tantalizing him with her body, striving almost mindlessly for ease of the terrible yearning within her. At that moment, there was nothing beyond what he did to her. His hand moved lower, touching the soft thatch before his fingers slipped inside. Her head went back, and her body arched to receive him. Her legs opened and closed around his hand, until she could not stand it any longer.

She heard the labored gasps, the distant cries, not realizing they were her own, and then he took away his hand and guided himself into her. Her nails raked his bared back as she bucked beneath him, and her legs, which had urged him on so desperately, locked around him, holding him tightly. And still he rode, rocking, thrusting, sending wave after wave of ecstasy through her. Her hands clawed at his hips as his own animal cries vied with hers, then she felt the flood, and as the waves subsided, she knew peace.

Unlike Alexei, he lay there for a time, his weight on his elbows, gasping for breath, looking at her. Then the reality of what she'd done came home to her, and she wanted to hide in shame. His hand touched her jaw lightly.

"Don't, Kate," he gasped. "I need to be held as much as you."

"But what you must think—" she croaked miserably.

The moonlight caught his smile. "I think I want to do this again and again." Sobering, he withdrew from her and eased his body off hers. Turning away, he spoke, his voice oddly strained. "I don't want to take you to Warsaw, Kate. I don't want to send you back to England."

"Bell—"

"I've thought of little else for days. Let's go to Italy and live where it is warm. Let's live where no one cares about Bellamy Townsend's rep—or about Alexei Volsky."

Her throat ached as she shook her head. "Bell, I cannot."

"We don't need revenge—let him get the divorce."

"You don't understand." Grateful that he could not see her face, she tried to explain. "As ridiculous as it may seem after this, it is still a matter of my honor to me."

"I cannot go to England with you," he said, his voice low. "They would crucify you for it."

"I know."

He was silent for a time, seeking the means to persuade her, finding none beyond what they'd done. But he was still a gambler inside.

"All right. But give me a week before I take you to the embassy."

"I cannot bear a child out of wedlock, Bell," she said desperately. "As much as I would stay, I cannot."

"I'll be careful—as much as I know how, I'll be careful," he promised. "Just let me love you for a week."

It had been a bittersweet compromise. He'd asked for a week, and she'd promised three days. More than that frightened her, but he would not understand. As for her, she felt torn, guilty, in more ways than one.

Bell Townsend had taken her out of Russia, he'd saved her life, and she was acutely aware that she owed him dearly for it. But she also suffered guilt for giving him her body, for risking a bastard child. And whether she was now an adulteress or not, she had to see her divorce laid at the right door. For her own honor, she had to see the grounds were incest, because she knew she'd done all she could to be a wife to Alexei, and he had nearly destroyed her pride.

On this, the last of the three days, Bell still slept, his face a deceptive mirror of innocence, his tousled hair giving him the appearance of a little boy. As she propped herself up on an elbow to study him, she wondered how she could have ever thought she loved her Russian count. Looking back, she still felt the fool every time she thought of Alexei—if any had courted her, it had been Galena.

Not so with Bell. He made her feel as though she'd come to him a virgin, that the quick, furtive gropings Alexei had given her were nothing. Her face softened as she watched the rhythmic rise and fall of his chest beneath the covers. Bell Townsend was one hundred times and more the lover—patient and passionate. And although she had no illusions about his constancy—even though she knew the bliss she felt just now could not last—she also knew she loved him.

He sighed, then opened his eyes, and the innocence fled in that instant. There was a sensuous light to the gray eyes, a sensuous curve to the mouth that sent a thrill through her. He rolled over and wrapped his arms around her, holding her as Lexy never wanted to. She lay there quietly, savoring the closeness she felt.

Finally, he sat up and yawned. "Don't move," he murmured. "Got to find the chamber pot."

She turned her face toward the wall, not caring if she heard him or not, only knowing he would not wish to be watched. It was as though there was nothing about him that she did not know, and nothing about her that he had not seen, And given that, it was to her a marvel that he still wanted her.

When he was done, she heard him pour water from the pitcher into the basin and splash his face. When he came back, he was wide-awake. He eased himself the length of her back and reached around her to explore her breasts. She closed her eyes, feeling the intense excitement of what he did to her.

His lips brushed the nape of her neck as his hands worked their magic, eliciting such a need that it always seemed nothing could fulfill it. She bit her lip to stifle a sob that rose in her throat as he tugged her onto her back.

She settled beneath him, her dark eyes made darker with desire, and he felt a certain reverence for her. Unlike the wantons who'd come before her, she was still his pupil, she was still eager to discover what his body could do for her. And she gave of herself wholeheartedly. He could not look in her eyes and not think Alexei Volsky had been the greatest fool on earth.

"Why don't you ride?" he asked her softly.

"What?"

She could still blush after everything they'd done. He nodded. "You can do the work this time, Kate."

"Oh, but—"

He rolled over, pulling her on top of him, and he tasted one of her breasts, nibbling at the nipple, watching it harden.

She lay above him, her legs straddling his, feeling the

growth of his manhood beneath her, and she knew a sense of power. It would be as though she took him.

His hands moved over her, playing with her breasts, sending shivers coursing through her as they skimmed her bare hips. And the now familiar, aching wetness was there, ready for him.

"Lift up," he whispered.

As she did, she felt him ease inside, and the exquisite anticipation took possession of her whole body. It was as though every fiber of her being wanted what they did. She moved tentatively, discovering what she liked.

"Move, Kate," he urged her. "Do whatever you want."

She moved with abandon, rocking, sliding, rolling her body around his, seeking the ecstasy she wanted. And then she felt it, the undulating waves of satisfaction, and she drew up her knees to prolong it.

"You'd better get off," he warned her, gasping.

But instead, she closed around him and moved until he could not stop bucking beneath her, until he moaned as he came.

"Now, that, Kate, was not my fault," he gasped, catching his breath. "I told you to get off. You could have used your hand."

But she hadn't wanted to. She'd wanted to feel him. Still, now that it was over, she realized the risk she'd taken. One week with Alexei, and he'd gotten her with child.

"Would it matter to you?" she asked suddenly.

"No."

He could see her hurt in her face, and he sighed. "You have to learn how to ask your questions, you know. I collect you are asking me if I would mind having a child. In that case, the answer is no, I would not. If you are asking if it matters if the child were out of wedlock, then the answer is yes."

He still hadn't said how he would feel if she had the child, but she knew she did not want to know. She moved off him and lay down, her head on his shoulder.

After a time, he eased her off and sat on the side of

the bed. He was almost afraid to ask, but he forced himself. "I don't suppose you have changed your mind one whit, have you?"

"No."

"Kate—"

"I have to go back, Bell—I have to. For myself—for Harry, I have to defend what is left of my honor. Even after this, I have to think I have some worth left in me."

For all that had passed between them, he knew that she was ashamed of giving him her body, ashamed of being what she'd perceived she'd become. And no words of love, no pledge could change that she was still Alexei Volsky's wife. But he didn't want to go, not yet. He wanted to lie back down beside her, to smooth the dark, tangled hair, to kiss her parting lips, to feel the heat of her body around his.

"What difference can four days make?" he asked, his voice harsh.

"What if I were to bear you a child?" she countered.

"I'd find a way to marry you."

"You cannot." She sat up behind him and laid her hand on his bare shoulder. "Bell—"

He felt a surge of unreasoning anger as he drew away. "Then there is not much more to say, is there?" He rose, his back to her. "I expect we ought to press on to Warsaw."

"Please, Bell," she whispered, "I pray you will not make me cry."

He was empty, devoid of the address that had always gotten him everything he wanted. His shoulders settled in defeat.

"All right."

The last leg of the journey was a quiet one, and the silence intensified with every mile. At first there had been some attempt at desultory conversation, but finally even it had lagged. He stared out his side of the carriage, his fine profile held as steady as a bust of Alexander the Great. For her part, she did the same most of the time, but every once in a while, she could not help stealing a glance at him.

He was like stone. And her heart was like a rock within her breast. But every time she wavered, she reminded herself of the scandal she would bring down on Harry. At least if the grounds were incest, perhaps the Winsteads could not be blamed for it. And certainly if she went off to Italy with Bell, neither one of them could ever go back to England, no matter what he said.

Then, out of the graying sky, Warsaw loomed on the horizon, and it was as though Kate's whole being turned to ice. As the horses plodded ever closer, she could see the bridge in the distance. And finally, they crossed the river. The city sat on either side, and it was as cramped and medieval as Siedice, only it was of a much grander size.

"Well, it will not be long," he said finally.

"No. Are we going to a hotel first?" she dared to ask.

"No."

"Bell, why does it have to be Italy? Why can it not be England?"

He didn't look at her, but he answered, "Because I have always run, I expect. I am not a man for unpleasantness." As the spires of a large church hovered over them, he added, "I never could. It was always easier for me to part friends—even with Longford."

Finally, the carriage stopped, and Bell and the driver got down to seek directions. Coming back, he slumped into the seat across from her again.

"It isn't far."

"How far?"

"A matter of blocks."

"What if the ambassador will not receive me? I mean, Poland is supposed to be independent, but everyone knows that Czar Alexander is above it all. And now that Napoleon has escaped—"

"Then I suppose you will go to Italy." He regarded her for a moment, then looked outside once more. "I am not taking you to England, Kate. You'll have to ask the ambassador for a letter of transit to Berlin, I expect, and then from there to Rotterdam, if you've no wish to be at sea very long.''

"I expect it will be another month ere I am home.''

"I don't know. The roads ought to be better.''

It was as though they had suddenly become strangers. But he was punishing her for not going to Italy. Again, the carriage stopped, and this time, she could see the British flag flying over the building.

He jumped down and shouted to the driver on the box. The fellow came down and opened the boot. Leaving the horses standing, he preceded them, carrying Katherine's case and the box of things that they'd bought in Brest. Already it seemed as though that had been a lifetime ago.

They were ushered into a small antechamber while a clerk, having been informed of the presence of a Russian countess, went to get the ambassador. She sat on the edge of her chair, certain that the interview was not going to be pleasant. But it would be nothing in comparison to what she would face in England.

A gentleman came in and was directed to her by the clerk. "The ambassador cannot be reached, I am afraid, but perhaps as his personal aide, I may be of assistance?''

"It is to be hoped.'' She extended her hand and managed a smile for him. "I am Katherine Volsky, sir.''

"Countess, it is an honor,'' he murmured, bowing. "Arthur Pritchard at your service, of course. You have but to tell me what you require.''

She sucked in her breath for courage, then let it out. "I am seeking to return to my home in England, sir.''

"I see.'' He regarded her curiously now. "But cannot your husband do that for you?''

"I have left him,'' she announced baldly. "And I cannot think he would wish to aid me. It is not a pleasant parting, you see.''

"Madame—''

"I am going home to seek a divorce, sir.''

He looked at her as though she announced she wished to commit a murder. "Countess, are you aware that divorce is unattainable for females?'' he asked awfully.

"I am aware that the only ground open to me is that of incest," she replied evenly. "And in this case, it applies, I can assure you."

"I see," he murmured, obviously disbelieving her. "And you are wishing us to facilitate your journey?"

"As an English citizen in a foreign land," she reminded him.

"Madame, although Poland is by treaty independent, you must surely be aware of its rather integrated policies with Russia. Your request could be construed as an impediment to the conduct of His Majesty's business here."

"It is my right to ask your assistance, sir."

"It will have to be taken under advisement, I'm afraid, and direction must be obtained from His Majesty's government."

"I assure you Prinny won't care." Bell stood up, making his presence known.

"Townsend! What the devil are you doing here?"

"Hallo, Arthur. You find me returning from a repairing lease in Russia, and I have escorted Lady Volsky from Moscow at her brother's request," he lied smoothly. "Er—to put it delicately, I collect Count Volsky has an unholy attachment to his elder sister."

"Really?" For an instant, the man was diverted, then he returned to the matter at hand. "It is still a nasty business, I'm afraid. And given the situation with the French monster—"

"Hang Napoleon!" Bell snapped. "Lady Volsky is English!"

"But she is married to a Russian, and that puts a rather different significance to the matter."

"Look at her, for God's sake! The man's depraved, I tell you, and you would prate about waiting for direction?"

"Townsend, I assure you—"

"She is an innocent in the hands of a husband who shares his bed with his sister," Bell argued more reasonably. "It is your duty to offer her sustenance and assistance."

"Sustenance most assuredly. But I must say it is highly

irregular to see that you have brought her to me," Pritchard declared stiffly.

"Does she look to be in my style?" Bell countered. "I am telling you I undertook the business on the direct commission of her brother, Baron Winstead."

"That is all very commendable, my lord, but—" The man appeared to waver slightly. "If it were not for the divorce, and—"

"And if it were not for my presence?" Bell finished for him.

"Precisely."

"But I am not going to England at this time, so there is no one to know—with the exception of yourself, of course. And if you provide the papers, I cannot think you will want to mention me at all."

"How did you get here?"

Bell reached into his coat and drew out the well-creased documents Paul Volsky had given him. "We came as Albert and Elise Chardonnay."

"As man and wife?"

"As brother and sister," Bell lied again.

Pritchard perused them slowly, then looked up. "These declare that the Chardonnays are wed."

"But most of the innkeepers do not ask."

"No, I suppose not." He turned to Katherine. "When did you leave Moscow, Countess?"

"In early February."

"Given the weather, it is a miracle that she is here at all. Much of the time, we couldn't make three miles per hour."

"And we were snowed in for sometime near Tula," she added.

"Tula? I should think so." The ambassador's aide still eyed Bell suspiciously. "Terrible time of year—even the French menace could not travel in Russia in winter. Most of them froze, poor devils," he murmured.

Bell's patience was at end. "Look, I must go—I just promised to get her this far, that's all."

That was perhaps more persuasive than anything else

he had done. "It is your intention to leave her here now?"

"In your capable hands, old fellow—provided she is given assistance home. I told you I have no intention of proceeding on to England just yet."

"Not financial assistance," Kate hastened to explain. "I have quite enough money of my own."

"Devilish glad to hear of it. I suppose for humanitarian reasons, I could send you with our next dispatches out," the man decided. "You would, of course, be accompanied. Terrible times, though. The French devil marches north, you know. But I expect Old Douro will contain him—always does, doesn't he? Just wish they'd hanged him rather than exile—saved us a good deal of trouble."

"Yes. Thank you," she murmured.

Relieved, Bell exhaled, then turned to Kate. "Yes, well, if it is settled, I shall push on. This part, at least, of your ordeal is over, my dear."

"Where are you going?" Pritchard asked curiously. "And will you not need papers also?"

"No. I went to Russia as Bellamy Townsend."

"Ah, yes, of course. Very well, Countess Volsky, Baxter will discover someone for your bags."

"Thank you."

To her dismay, Bell was already walking toward the door. "Your pardon, sir," she said hastily, excusing herself. "I had intended to give a small token of my appreciation to the driver. He has endured so much."

"It's very kind of you," the man murmured.

She caught him in the street. "Bell, were you not even going to tell me good-bye?"

"I expect I will see you in England someday, Kate."

"But—"

"And I always try to leave my friends happy." His mouth twisted for a moment, then he managed to smile. "If you had wanted, you could have come to Italy," he reminded her.

That was it. She stared incredulously. "Then none of it meant anything at all to you, did it? You did not care

a button for me?'' Her voice rose, prompting him to draw
her into a corner. "Bell, I—"

"Look, Kate, we have been through hell together."
He caught her arms and held them for a moment. "I will
always feel bound to you for that alone, even if we did
not count the other. But since you are determined in this,
I cannot aid you now."

"I see. I do not expect you will write, will you?"

"Not until everything is over."

"You asked me for a week," she reminded him desperately.

"And you did not give it."

"I gave everything else."

For a moment, she thought she'd gotten to him, but
then he said soberly. "In the event there is a child, I
want to know, Kate. I'll send Harry my direction."

"And what good will that do?"

"I won't saddle you with a bastard." He set her back
and started to leave again.

"You offered to marry me—at St. Basil's, you offered
to marry me! Surely—"

"The offer is still on the table, Kate. Look, you cannot
stand out here like this—not if you are going to England."

She waited until he was nearly to the curb. "I am not
twice the fool, Bell Townsend! Hell will freeze before I
pick it up!"

He winced, but did not turn back to her. It was hard
enough to leave her, as it was. He'd long thought he was
an empty fellow, but now the tightness in his throat, the
very real pain beneath his breastbone gave the lie to that.
He almost wished that he hadn't been so damned noble,
that he'd not given her the choice at all. He should have
just carried her off to Italy with him, and they both could
have taken the consequences later.

He swung up into the carriage, then allowed himself
one last look through the window. She stood there, looking not like the waif he was used to think her, but like
the woman who'd chosen what was left of her honor over

him. He raised his hand to her, then tapped the roof, telling the driver to go.

Turning, she walked back to the embassy, where a guard regarded her curiously. "Is aught amiss, miss?"

"No." But as she mounted the steps, she wanted to cry. Everything was amiss. Twice she had been fooled. And this time, the pain was far greater.

May 16, 1815

The Winstead town house looked much as it ever had. For a moment, Katherine stood there, drinking it in. She was in England. She was home. Still, she had to take a deep breath before going up the steps. She'd written from Hamburg that she was coming, and there had been no way to get a response.

Her heart pounding, she climbed the portico steps and lifted the knocker. It seemed as though it took forever for anyone to answer. Finally, the door opened inward, and Dawes stood there, regarding her. Turning around, he directed a footman to inform her ladyship that Countess Volsky is returned.''

"Can I not come in?" she dared to ask.

He didn't answer.

It was Claire who came out first. "You!" she cried with loathing. "I shall despise you forever! And Mama will not let you in this house either! You miserable, wretched creature, you have quite cut up all my hopes!"

Behind her Lady Winstead appeared. "Mama—?" Kate said tentatively.

"You are a viper in my bosom!" her mother declared. "A viper, Katherine."

"Mama, may I please come inside?"

"I don't think so. As it is, you have cost Clarissa the match of the Season," the woman said coldly. "I know not how we are to hold our heads up, I am sure."

"Mama, you have not even heard what happened!"

"We have heard enough," Claire sniffed spitefully. "The notice is all over the papers—Count Volsky has charged you with adultery. There is to be a hearing at the bishop's on the matter.''

"*What?* Alexei is here?'' Kate asked incredulously. "He cannot be! I have traveled more than three months to get here! And the port at St. Petersburg was frozen!''

"Under the circumstances, Katherine, I cannot welcome you into this house.''

"Did he name—that is, who does he accuse with me?'' Kate managed to ask.

"Nearly everyone, I collect.''

"But it is not true!''

"The damage is done, Katherine. I'm afraid it cannot be repaired.''

"I see.'' Gathering up what little dignity was left to her, Kate's chin came up. "Then I shall just have to go to Harry.''

"If he will have you.''

The door closed on her. Deep, bitter anger welled like bile inside her, but like everything else, she was impotent to stop it. She turned back to the hackney that had brought her, and remounting the step into it, she ordered the driver to her brother's address.

He was not at home, and his man refused to admit any unattended female, even one who styled herself as a countess, he said. So she sat on the narrow stoop of his lodgings and waited, with her bag and box on the ground at her feet.

"Kate!''

"Oh, Harry—I pray you will not turn me away! I have been forever getting home!''

"No, of course not.'' But he made no move to put his arm around her. Instead, he looked up and down the street. "Your things, Kate?'' he asked, indicating the bags.

"Yes.''

He shouldered the box and carried the case up the steep stairs. As the door opened to his voice, he unloaded everything on his man. "My sister is coming to stay,'' he said merely.

"Mama would not let me into the house.''

"I know. It's a devil of a mess, I can tell you. Not that she ought to have done it—my house, after all. But she's mad as fire."

"So I have noted."

"Cannot blame her entirely. Hargrove finally came up to scratch just before the scandal broke. It was hell after that—he and his mother called on Claire and told her they had no wish to ally themselves with such a family."

"I'm sorry. But when did this come out?"

"About two weeks ago."

"And Alexei is here?"

He shook his head. "Apparently Volsky has engaged an English solicitor, and he only means to send depositions himself."

"Harry, for whatever it means to you, I did not commit adultery at Domnya."

"I didn't think you had. At least not with your groom, nor with a footman. It wouldn't be like you."

"Mama said Alexei is claiming I have fornicated with nearly everybody."

"Yes. He's got affidavits from four or five of them."

"Harry, none of the grooms or footmen can read or write! They are serfs, and he owns all of them!"

"And he also accused Bell."

She knew he wanted her to deny that also, and she could not. "He brought me out of Russia."

"The devil of it is that they are demanding Volsky's child by you. Given the circumstances, you will have to give it up, I expect."

"God defeated him in that, at least." She sat down, not knowing where to begin, nor what to tell him. "It was February, Harry, and the roads were so bad that we had to stop. I could not have gone on, anyway, for I was too sick." The telling was so painful still that she had to keep her eyes on her folded hands in her lap. "There was no doctor, and something went so very, very wrong." Hot tears stung her eyes, and she had to stop to swallow the lump that rose in her throat. "He was born dead, Harry," she whispered. "He is buried at St. Basil's monastery, somewhere between Moscow and Tula." She felt his hand on her shoulder, and she turned against his body to cry. "Please, Harry—I do not want Lexy or Lena to ever have him! I don't want them to have my son's body!"

"Shhhh. It's over, Kate, and you are home." He smoothed her hair over her ears, then his arm held her. "I wish I'd known—I'd have tried to help."

"All I had was Bell, Harry," she sobbed. "All I had was Bell! And there was no doctor until long after it was over!"

"Shhhhh. Don't—Kate, don't."

"He helped me—I think he saved my life! They—they buried my babe without me—but he was there—and—" She stopped to sniff her running nose, and she wiped her streaming eyes with the back of her hand. "Harry, I am the most miserable of females!"

"God, Kate, you have been through hell, haven't you?" he murmured softly. "We had no notion."

She sat back finally and withdrew her handkerchief from her reticule. After blowing her nose, she composed herself. "Do you want me to tell you what happened at Domnya?" she asked quietly.

"Not if you want to wait."

"They made a fool of me, Harry—both of them. It was Lena's notion that he should marry me, you see, and he did not want to."

"He did not appear reluctant to me."

"Well, he was. I think I even disgusted him, if you want the truth of it. But she wanted a child desperately, and she could not have one. As Tati so crudely put it, I was but the oven for her bun."

He pulled up another chair beside her, then sat forward to take her hands. "It doesn't make any sense, Kate. Why the devil would they come to England for a wife for him?"

"They wanted a green one, I guess—and one who could not make sense of the rumors about them." She looked up, shaking her head. "And I was green, wasn't I?" she recalled bitterly. "He has been sleeping with her since he was a boy. I gathered she seduced him."

"The bastard. The miserable bastard," he muttered.

"I should have known almost as soon as I got to Russia. Lena managed everything—she even sent him to my bed when he balked. Harry, she made him sleep with me! And she kept him away when she thought it might harm the babe! I thought she was my friend! Harry, I loved her for her kindness to me! But to her I was like a child she could deceive. She even treated me like one, sending me off to bed whenever I was inconvenient."

Still holding her hands, he looked to his manservant. "I think you'd best get her a bit of brandy."

"I'd rather have water, I think."

"Make it brandy," he insisted. As the man went to fetch it, he turned his attention again to her. "Can you prove any of this, Kate?"

"I don't know. I suppose all I can do is try to convince the bishop, then hope if he believes me, the courts and Parliament will also."

"It'll be fodder for the gossips for years."

She settled her shoulders. "You sound like Bell. He told me not to come back. He said Lexy would claim I committed adultery to cover the incest he has committed with Lena. But—" She appeared to study her slippers for a moment, then looked up again. "But it is a matter of honor to me."

"You know you will not be able to show your face in London, don't you?"

"Harry, they were going to take my child."

"But now that is not relevant, is it? Kate, we've got to try to protect you. Do you want to tell this to everyone?"

"If I must."

"They are all men," he reminded her. "And adultery is far easier for them to believe than incest."

"I don't care anymore," she said tiredly. "They may believe what they want, but they have to listen to me. Harry, Lexy and Galena expected me to condone what they were doing—can you not see how very wrong they were? She told me I could continue to be Countess Volsky—that I could have more of his children! As though it was not wrong!"

"You are overset, Kate. Here—here's your brandy. After you drink it, you can lie down, then later we can think what is to be done."

"I don't want to lie down! I'm sorry," she apologized, "but I don't. That's all Lena ever wanted me to do. And I have sat most of the way from Moscow." Recovering her composure again, she told him, "Harry, I have to tell you about it—there is no one else to listen just now." Going on, she explained, "When I first ran away from Domnya, I went to Alexei's brother at Omborosloe. But I had to flee there because Olga—Paul's wife—wished to take my babe also. She was going to sell it back to Lena for Domnya."

"I cannot follow you," he admitted.

"All right." She took the brandy and sipped it, then drew in her breath. Letting it out, she tried again. "Alexei and his sister sleep together, Harry."

"That much I got."

"And when I discovered it, they tried to persuade me that it didn't matter to me—that I would still have everything. But they only wanted an heir for Domnya. I don't know what they would have done if I'd stayed."

"I understand that also. After that, I cannot make sense of the rest."

"But I ran to Olga and Paul Volsky—only she was nearly as evil as Galena. She wanted to trade my babe to Galena for Domnya."

"But she was giving them what they wanted," he pointed out.

"Galena wanted a child even more than she wanted Domnya. She would have forced Alexei to exchange Domnya for Omborosloe if she could have a child."

"Ah. All right—now I understand that also. So you had to run away from this Olga?"

"Paul asked if I had anywhere else to turn, and there was no one—so I told him I would ask Bellamy Townsend, who was in Moscow then. He very eagerly took me there, hoping Bell would help me escape from Russia."

"That must have been amusing. Bell's not over-given to helping anyone, not even his friends."

"He didn't want to—in fact, he turned me away. He said I should be ruined to come home in his company. But I would not go back—I took a hotel room and hoped the weather would improve enough that I could engage someone to take me out of the country."

"At least he was truthful."

"I know. But then he discovered that both Alexei and the Narranskys—Olga is Prince Narransky's daughter—looked for me. And Alexei wished to have me committed to an asylum, while the Narranskys wished to have me arrested—or some such thing. Only then did Bell help me." She sipped the brandy and tried to decide what he thought. "You believe in me, don't you, Harry?"

"Yes. But as much as I love you, I cannot quite think the tale ought to be repeated. It will be said you have read too many gothic romances, you know."

"Well, I haven't. And I cannot think this can go to criminal court as there is no one to charge here. Somehow it does not seem possible that Alexei will send servants over to testify."

"There is Bell. It would not be the first time he was named as correspondent, you know. There is a precedent in the Longford affair," he reminded her.

A harsh little laugh escaped her. "Bell has gone to Italy, I'm afraid. He's gone—bolted."

"You sound bitter over it."

"No. I owe him too much to be bitter. He saved my life, you know. I think I could have bled to death when my son was born."

He stood and walked about the room, pacing as she watched him. "I don't think I'd say much about Bell, Kate. I'm not even sure I would mention him. You could just say you hired someone to bring you out."

"If I lie in that and am discovered, then no one would believe the other," she pointed out calmly. "I shall have to tell everything." But even as she said it, she knew she did not wish to admit what she'd done with Townsend.

"I think," she said finally, "that I will lie down, after all."

"Yes." He seemed to seize on the notion. "We can talk about this more later. Though I don't know what the devil to do—other than hire you a solicitor, of course."

"I know. But if you will but speak with me, if you will but stand with me, nothing else matters."

"You know I will." He handed her her glass of brandy. "Here—you'd better take this with you. While you are resting, I mean to call on Mama."

"She won't listen."

"Then she can go to Monk's End—or lease herself another place. The properties are mine, Kate, and we are going to live in the town house. I'll be damned if I expect you to stay in bachelor's lodgings."

His guest bedchamber was small, owing possibly to the fact that it was part of a bachelor's establishment. She sank tiredly onto the bed, wondering if she'd been wrong to come home after all, wondering if she should have reached for at least some happiness with Bellamy Townsend.

But reason told her that there would have been too much guilt—and God knew she had enough of that now—that she would have only gotten herself hurt further. In the carriage with the diplomatic courier, she'd had a great deal of time to think, and she'd come to realize that she could not change Bell. He might profess to love her, and he might even persuade himself to believe it, but he lacked stability—he lacked commitment to any ideal, to anyone.

Still, she missed him so intensely that there were times she thought her heart was breaking. He'd been there for her too long, she'd clung to him too much, for her to ever forget what he'd done for her. And once they'd parted, she'd almost tried to write him, to say anything to make him come back for her. But less than a week after she moved into the embassy, her monthly course had come. So she had not the excuse.

S he had ceased to exist. She still ate, breathed, and tried to survive, but she had ceased to exist. Bell and Harry had tried to warn her how it would be, but nothing could have prepared her for the price of leaving Alexei. Even if somehow she were exonerated, she would still be utterly invisible to nearly everyone. She could have done almost anything else. She could have even openly flaunted a dozen lovers. And it would have been forgiven her. But she could not divorce Alexei, nor could he divorce her. And the scandal of either thing alone had put her quite beyond the pale.

When she went to Hookham's to borrow a book, the clerks stared at her, and if she went into the reading room, it suddenly emptied. If she shopped, those she knew pretended she was not there. If she went to the theater with Harry, her former acquaintances would speak to him, all the while looking straight through her as though she were not present. On the street, even when accompanied by a maid, she rarely encountered anyone she knew directly. Most would cross the street to avoid her.

Since her return to London, she had been given the cut direct, the cut indirect, and nearly every other slight imaginable. Invitations to Harry often carried small, handwritten notes in them, advising him to come alone. And the number of those invitations themselves had declined drastically.

Her mother and Claire had gone home to Monk's End, where the same vicar who had known Kate most of her life—had married her to Alexei even—now denounced her from the pulpit. Mama's letters to Harry did not refer to her by name, only as "that miserable creature who has wreaked such misfortune on all of us."

But Mama and Claire's removal from London had meant she was at least at home in her room. But even that had caused a considerable row, for Dawes and Mrs. Simpkins, the housekeeper, had at first gone about with their noses far too high, until Harry confronted them with being turned off. Now they were icily civil to her. But she again had Peg. Upon hearing that Harry might be returning home, the maid had simply allowed herself to be discharged so that she could stay.

The solicitor Harry had hired for her had managed to get the ecclesiastical hearing postponed, saying that his client was exhausted from her journey and from the terrible loss of her child. The meeting with the bishop was now set for the following week.

She was in the book room, reading everything she had missed while in Russia, when a footman entered, then stood there, clearing his throat apologetically.

"Someone to see you, my lady."

My lady. Despite the ignominy of everything else, she was still Countess Volsky. She looked up from her book. "You must be mistaken. I am not at home."

"Yes, ma'am."

He'd already turned to leave, but she could not help her curiosity, for who would be foolish enough to risk seeing her? "Who is it?" she dared to ask.

"He says he is Lord Leighton."

George Maxwell. Here? "There must be some mistake, Jem. I daresay he has come to see Harry."

"Yes, my lady."

He withdrew, leaving the door half-open. She could hear him tell Leighton that she had gone out. Settling back in her chair, she turned the page of her book.

"I usually know a whisker when I am told one, my dear." The Scottish viscount stood in the doorway, smiling at her.

"Are you not afraid you will be named as my paramour?" she asked bitterly. "I should not be seen speaking with me, were I you."

"No." The grin turned into a smile. "Rich men are generally forgiven almost anything. And so far my perceived character has remained unblemished." Without waiting to be invited in, he crossed the room to her and chose a chair close by. Dropping into it, he reached into his coat for a moment, then brought out what looked to be an envelope. "Had business in London, actually." He leaned forward to hand her the envelope. "Bell Townsend asked me to deliver this to you."

"Oh?"

"Said he did not want to send it through the post under the circumstances—said he didn't want it to fall into the wrong hands."

"I don't know why," she muttered. "He has no rep to save, does he? And neither do I."

His hazel eyes rested on her for a moment. "As much as I have been known to wish him at Jericho myself, Lady Volsky, I daresay he's not as bad as most think him."

"No, he could not be."

"He warned me you might be angry with him," Leighton murmured.

"Why should I be? Though I do not suppose you have heard the whole tale, I expect it will come out that he rescued me from Russia. Indeed, I owe him a great deal."

"He has asked me to support you in this unfortunate situation."

"I do not think there is anything anyone can do, my lord, but I thank you for the offer. You are quite kind, sir."

"Yes." He smiled again, this time ruefully. "I have it on the best authority that I am the sort of man a female should marry."

"Whoever said that?"

"It doesn't matter. But it is a lowering assessment, don't you think?"

"Well, I don't know you very well, of course," she admitted. "But I have always heard you have no enemies."

"A man with no enemies must be a rather dull fellow—or at least I think so. Take Bell, for instance—or Harry. Now they lead far more dangerous lives."

"But not always admirable ones."

"I don't know about that. But," he added, sighing, "if I have not lived rakishly, I expect it can be attributed to my rather Scottish upbringing. The Presbyterians, I have found, are a rather dour lot."

"Is that why you live in Cornwall?"

"I live in Cornwall for the weather, my dear. My ancestral estate sits on rather dreary rocks above the North Sea. A deuced cold place, actually."

"I should expect."

"In Cornwall, I still have the sea, but I am not expected to freeze my knees in winter." He put his fingers together and contemplated her for a moment. "If you will tell me what I can do to support you, Lady Volsky, I will do it."

"There is nothing anyone can do, I'm afraid."

"Bell wishes me to hire Patrick Hamilton for you."

"What?" Her voice rose incredulously. "It is my understanding he represents murderers and criminals!"

"Lady Volsky, he is the best to be had, and I think I can obtain his services. We were at Eton together."

"I am not a criminal, sir—but I thank you for the offer."

"Bell said I was to beg you to take Hamilton," he told her. "He will pay him for you."

"No, I shall just have to tell the truth and hope I am believed."

Leighton hesitated, then shook his head. "I am sure your brother would agree that you should have Hamilton. Sometimes, my dear, truth is not enough—and the man is a genius."

"But he comes rather dear, doesn't he? I have heard his fee is quite literally everything a man has got."

He started to admit it, then caught himself. "For murder perhaps, but for something like this, I should doubt it."

"How much?"

"Townsend—"

"I could not accept Bell's money, sir. If I should engage Mr. Hamilton, I would have to pay him myself."

"I can but speculate, of course, but I should expect no more than a hundred pounds," he answered, hoping he'd given her a figure she could afford, knowing it was going to cost Bell at least ten times that.

She really didn't wish to hire a solicitor at all, but if she could perhaps get the best for one hundred pounds, then she might have to reconsider. "Are you quite certain of that?" she asked.

"I can ask him."

"Then I expect I ought to speak to him," she decided, sighing. "It would possibly relieve Harry's mind a great deal." She met Leighton's gaze for a moment. "He does not seem to think I can win this, you know."

"You are rather calm about it."

"Hysterics would serve nothing, sir."

"You know you rather remind me of Lady Kingsley— Lady Longford now."

"Lady Kingsley? I shouldn't think so in the least. You flatter me, for she is perhaps the loveliest woman in England."

"You both have incredible pluck."

"Only you and Townsend have seemed to think so," she admitted ruefully. "And even he thought I should run."

"Well, I expect I should go." He drew out his watch and flicked open the cover. "I am due to meet Hamilton within the hour. No—no need to see me out, I assure you."

She sat there for a time after he left, wondering why Bell had written to her through Leighton. Looking down at the unopened envelope, she wanted to consign it to the fire, but there wasn't one. She did not need any more pain, not now—not ever. And yet as she studied the bold, dark script, she wavered. Finally, she broke the wax seal and unfolded the single sheet of paper.

Dearest Kate,
By now you may well be wishing yourself in Italy, I expect, but you must not lose your spirit. You are

the most remarkable woman of my acquaintance, you know. I think of you often, whether you choose to believe that or not, and my conscience pains me that I did not go back with you. I find myself salving it continually by reassuring myself that I could only have made things worse for you.

I trust this finds you well, and that everything is as it ought to be. If not, I pray you will tell me, and I shall come home on the instant. I meant what I said about that—and about the other also.

In my absence, I am commending George to you. Unlike the rest of us, he is possessed of solid rock beneath that handsome face. In all my years of his acquaintance, I have never known him to fail anyone. And he is not without influence where it can be counted most, so I have asked that he engage Hamilton to represent you. I know you will dislike the notion, but one ought to always get the best in hopes of some advantage. God keep you, Kate.

As ever,
Bell

At the bottom, he'd carefully printed an address in Florence.

It was, in her opinion, a decidedly unloverly letter. She read it, telling herself she ought not to have expected anything more of him, then she carried it upstairs to her room. Sitting at her cramped desk, she unstoppered her ink bottle, found a piece of paper, and chose a pen. She wrote quickly.

Dear Lord Townsend,

Thank you for your inquiry as to my health. It is quite good and need not concern you. As for Leighton, he has kindly called on me, offering to engage Mr. Hamilton, as you have asked him. I think the act of doing so must surely make me appear to be guilty, but I expect Harry will require it. However, I intend to pay every penny of his fee myself.

At the end of it, she added, Katherine, Countess Volsky, as much as she hated the name. Folding it, she scrawled the address on it and sealed it with a blob of wax. In the morning, she would ask Harry to send it for her.

Then she flung herself onto her bed and indulged herself with a good bout of tears. She no longer wished to be beautiful, nor did she wish for wealth and fancy gowns. All she wanted in this world was for Bell Townsend to come home to her, she told herself tearfully. But she knew it wasn't true—what she wanted most was for him to love her.

The post came, but she paid no attention to it. She was in the kitchen, tasting a sauce for Harry's favorite fish, when she heard him come home. Then she heard him run up the stairs, apparently taking them two or more at a time. Almost immediately, he came back down the servant's stairs, only this time he was shouting.

"Kate, where the devil are you?"

"In the kitchen!" she called out. "Seeing to your dinner!"

"What the deuce are you doing in here?" He stopped, then sniffed. "Is that what I think it is?"

"Only if you are smiling. Otherwise, I shall throw it out."

"What a saucy baggage you are become, Kate," he complained, lifting pot lids.

"You are the only one who seems to think so, and I pray you will not repeat it. I do not wish to be mistaken for someone like Lena."

"No, of course not. Didn't mean anything like that, and you know it. Why the fancy dish? Are we having company?"

"You jest, of course. I was trying to show the cook how it is made at Monk's End."

"Mmmmm. Excellent. Peas to go with it?"

"Yes. And an apricot tart also, but I had to pay dearly for it at Gunther's."

"You went out?"

"I sent Jem." She untied her apron. "By the by, Lord

Leighton called, saying that Bell wishes me to get Hamilton for my defense.''

He whistled low. ''Hamilton? Deuced good notion, if you can get him. But—''

''Leighton says for this, he could obtain his services for a hundred pounds, Harry.''

''I don't—'' He knew that much for a hum, but Bell was right. There was none better. ''Yes, well, I think we ought to do it—don't you?''

''I suppose. If you don't think I shall appear even more guilty by doing so.''

''No. I think you need every advantage. It's going to be decided by a bunch of old men, Kate—and men tend to believe men.'' He looked down at the mail in his hand. ''Almost forgot why I was looking for you—you've got something from Moscow—or at least something from Russia. That is Russian, isn't it?'' he asked, holding it out to her.

''Moskva—Moscow. Yes.''

''Want me to open it for you? I mean, in the case that it might prove unpleasant?''

''No.'' She wiped her hands on a cloth and addressed the cook. ''You must not boil it, or it will curdle. And when it has thickened, skim it as it cools.''

''Yes, my lady.''

As she turned back to him, she made a face. ''At least if nothing else can be said for this mess, I shall most likely not be a titled lady much longer. Do you think they will let me be Katherine Winstead when it is done?''

''I expect you will be Katherine Volsky.''

She sighed. ''I fear you are right.''

''Your letter, Kate,'' he reminded her.

''All right. But I think I shall take it into your book room to read it.''

''Are you quite certain you do not wish me to look at it first?''

''Well, it cannot contain much gunpowder,'' she retorted. ''It is too flat.''

''I didn't expect it to explode, Kate. You know, you

are in a queer mood, aren't you? It is as though you are determined to be cheerful.''

"And you are complaining? Dearest Harry, if you wish, I could weep buckets over you.''

He followed her in and watched as she sat down to open the stiff paper. Another, smaller piece fell to the floor. He was afraid for her, afraid that some newer threat had come, but her face was oddly still as she read.

"Is it from Volsky?'' he asked finally.

"No.'' She handed it to him. "You may read it for yourself.'' She bent down to pick up the other one.

The script was tight and narrow, the sort that was difficult to follow, but he repeated the words aloud, scarce understanding the import of them as he read aloud.

> Dear Ekaterina,
>
> I am sorry it has taken me so very long to write you, but long have I worried of your health. Galena is still furious with me for helping you escape, and she says that before she is done, you will be ruined, if she has to make every serf at Domnya swear he has lain with you.
>
> As for Alexei, he has cut off my allowance, but Paul provides me with what I need. Paul is not like the rest of them, as I am sure you must know by now. And he agrees with me that what they did to you was inexcusable. If we have any regrets, it is that you had to discover Alexei and Galena together for yourself. It was not something those of us who knew could tell you, for you seemed to love my brother so very much, and then there was the child.
>
> Enclosed is Tati's letter of apology to you. I wish you and the child the best.
>
> Your brother for life, Viktor Petrovich Volsky.

He looked up. "Do you know what this means, Kate?''

"Yes. I shall be free of him,'' she said simply.

"What does the other one say?'' he wanted to know.

She held it up, and the paper shook as she read from it.

Ekaterina,
Paul says I must apologize for my terrible surprise, but I felt you were so much the English fool. I wanted you to surprise them, to see Lexy and Lena together in the bed. It sickened me to see that you believed they loved you.
Tatiana Volsky

"Who is that?" Harry asked.

"Alexei's youngest sister."

"What a pleasant, charming family they must be," he murmured. But as he said it, he couldn't quite suppress an ever-widening grin. "Damn, Kate—I knew I had the luck!" Dragging her from her chair, he swung her in his arms. "I knew you could not be what they called you!"

She held onto him, smiling through tears. "You were the only one, Harry—the only one."

He stopped and set her down. "Hedged my bet though."

"I beg your pardon?"

"I went to St. Margaret's and prayed."

"You?"

"Don't look at me like that—I didn't even put it into the books, I swear it."

"Oh, Harry!"

He sobered suddenly. "But it's not over yet, you know. No matter how the bishop rules, there will have to be a trial to adjudge Volsky the guilty party—and it will have to go to Parliament. It's still a deuced nasty business. You'll still need Hamilton, if we can get him."

"And I still shall not be received, but I don't care about that. I'm free of Alexei, and that is all that matters."

"You'll get damages, you know."

"I don't want any money from him."

"Hamilton could cost more than any hundred pounds," he warned her.

"All right. I'll ask that Lexy pay him."

His mind was already racing ahead. "I'll try to get Shackleford to introduce the bill. It ought to come up in the autumn, I expect. Then we can set you up in a tidy place of your own."

She knew she'd forced a drastic change in his life-style, that in the ordinary way of things, he'd be spending most of his time in gaming hells and in cyprians' beds. She felt an overwhelming gratitude for him. Standing on tiptoe, she pulled his head down to where she could kiss his cheek.

"I love you, Harry." Then as she let him go, she added, "But I don't want Shackleford to do it. I want Leighton. He's so terribly kind, I think."

"George?"

"Yes."

"Tell you what, Kate—you put on your best gown right now, he said impulsively."

"What?"

"And I'll send 'round to the Pulteney for a table. Katherine Winstead, we are going to celebrate!"

"Harry, you are insane! The fish—"

"Let Dawes eat it. I'm buying you champagne—and we are going to eat beneath everyone's noses, I tell you. We shall show 'em you've got spine, Kate."

But as she sat before her mirror, seeing the same face she'd seen for twenty-three years, she felt an intense sadness. Her gaze fell on Bell Townsend's letter, then on hers back to him. She patted her hair into place, then went to tear hers up.

Once everything was over, once Parliament had ruled her a divorced woman, there was nothing left in England for her. Harry certainly didn't need to be saddled with a scandalous sister. She was going to Italy, Florence to be precise, and take Bell's offer off the table. And then she was going to make him love her.

Florence, Italy: *June 10, 1815*

He sat looking out his villa window onto the hills below, seeing the beauty of the city, the Cathedral Square, the six bridges across the Arno River, wishing that Kate were there. She was never far from his thoughts, despite the fact that she'd never answered his letter. When he'd written it, he'd hoped she'd not conceived, but now he almost wished she had.

At least that way, she'd be with him now. Instead, she was all but alone in London. Oh, she had Harry, and he knew that, but Leighton had written that the censure of the *ton* was total and utterly unmerciful.

At least she'd taken Patrick Hamilton. That had cost him nearly a thousand pounds already, but there was no help for it. To salvage his own conscience, he had to give her every advantage he could. And even that had not worked for him. Regret haunted him every day, and longing shared his bed every night.

"Signor?"

The dark-haired maid peered inside the door, but he shook his head. Time was when he'd have taken her to bed with scarce a thought. But no more. It was rich, it was—with the passing of his thirtieth birthday, he had a sense he was finally growing up, that he was finally paying the price for all his earlier follies.

He wanted Kate Volsky more than anything now. She was no longer Harry Winstead's plain little sister, but rather the woman he'd shared not only hell but a grand adventure with. He could close his eyes and see her, her dark hair tangled against his shoulder, her dark eyes lit with desire. God, if Volsky had only known what he had.

In his memory, there was no plainness in her face, but rather a loveliness born of inner dignity. Volsky had betrayed her, she had lost her child, and he'd run to the relative safety of Italy rather than stand with her. Or so it seemed. He knew he couldn't have gone back, that he could only have made everything worse for her. But that no longer eased his conscience. Nor did the fact that he'd written Harry, promising he'd stay away until everything was over. He hadn't acted out of any nobility, but rather to save what was left of his miserable reputation.

If only he knew she was all right. Harry had answered, saying she was bearing up, and Leighton had praised her resolve, but she'd said nothing. She probably hated him now. She probably thought she had been nothing more than another brief affair in his life.

There was a knock at his door, and he rose reluctantly to answer it.

"Oh, 'tis you," he murmured.

"One would almost think you wished me at Jericho," Jack Bangston observed.

"No," he lied.

Bangston, another exile, was younger than Bell, still caught up in the heady throes of his salad days, and to him Bell was the epitome of all he wished to be. His fawning admiration was fast becoming onerous. Nonetheless, Bell stepped back to let him inside.

"Missed the Borodino affair," Jack said, dropping into a chair. "Dashed nice little piece there, I can tell you. Actually, I'm glad you wasn't in attendance. Got pretty feet and hands—and the face of an angel."

"A paragon, I am sure," Bell muttered.

"God, I hope not. Perfect though—her husband must be fifty, if he's a day. I can tell by her eyes she's bored beyond belief."

"You'd better watch yourself. I expect her family wouldn't approve."

"Got to be discreet—learned that from you, you know."

"Discretion, my dear Jack, was not invented by me."

"You know what I mean."

"No."

"Dash it, you've got to. Bell Townsend, ain't you?"

It was obvious that Bangston had been drinking, and Bell was in no mood for maudlin admiration. "Take my advice, and leave the girl alone," he said coldly.

"Odd—coming from you. Always wanted to be just like you, you know."

"Then you are a bloody fool."

The younger man blinked. "Coming it too strong," he protested weakly. "Every man wants to be what you are."

"Then they are all fools also." Bell turned away and walked to the window. "You want to know what I am, Jack?" he asked rhetorically. "I am a man corrupted by his face. I have been given so much in this life that I am utterly empty."

"But you are Bellamy Townsend. Dash it, but—"

Bell swung around at that. "Maybe I am tired of being Townsend," he said almost angrily. "Maybe I am sick of what I did—did you never think of that? What do you see, Jack? Look at me—I am thirty years old, and I am a sot—an utter sot!" He ran his fingers through his disordered hair, then fixed the young man with sober gray eyes. "And I am a coward."

"Huh? But—"

"A coward, Jack—a complete coward. You behold a man who has run from everything."

"I say, but you are being deuced hard on yourself, ain't you?"

"No. I am not nearly hard enough. If I had any spine, any nerve at all, I should be in England right now." And as he said it, he knew it for the truth. "Even the worst of rakes must reform sometime, or they die with nothing. And you know what, Jack? I don't want any of it anymore. I don't want any more faithless beauties. I don't want to take anything that's not mine anymore."

"You in some sort of queer mood?" Bangston asked, bewildered.

"Maybe. But I am going home."

"What?"

"Home. England."

"But you cannot!" Bangston caught himself. "That is, well, I always knew you wasn't hanging out after the likes of Lady Volsky, but—"

Bell walked to where a decanter of wine sat on a sideboard. Unstoppering it, he poured a glass, then handed it to Jack Bangston.

"Ain't you joining me?" the younger man asked curiously.

"No. My salad days are over, Jack."

"Now I know you are in some sort of queer start—I know it." He gulped from the glass. "Damme, but what are you going to do in England?"

"Pay the piper." Bell's gray eyes rested on Bangston for a long moment before he added evenly, "And then I shall hope to wed Katherine Volsky, if she will have me."

S he took her seat at the table and wiped her damp hands on the skirt of her demure dark blue dress. Hamilton had insisted on examining her wardrobe himself, and he'd chosen it, not knowing it was a reminder of Bell Townsend and her flight into Poland. He only knew that it made her look like an incredibly improbable siren. He'd even insisted she wear no rouge, that her hair be pulled back severely, making her look even older than she was. Finally, she'd had enough and retorted that if she looked too awful, they would not blame Alexei for anything.

Three churchmen, all in robes, filed in to sit across from her. It was to be a preliminary, informal meeting to determine how the charges would be presented to the bishop—or in this case, to the Archbishop of Canterbury, given that Alexei Volsky was a Russian count. The clergyman across from her, a cathedral dean, studied her critically for a moment, and she wondered if he thought it a miracle that Volsky had noted her at all.

Papers were shuffled, and throats were cleared. On one side of her, her brother reached to squeeze her hand. On the other, the Honorable Patrick Hamilton, a renowned younger son, sat, his face utterly inscrutable. If a man ever played his cards close, as her father used to advise, it was Mr. Hamilton.

The dean read for a moment, then coughed. "I collect this is Katherine, Countess Volsky?"

"Yes."

"Are you represented here?" he inquired, knowing

she was. Patrick Hamilton did not show up for anything as a spectator, that she had ever heard.

"Yes. Mr. Hamilton is with me," she answered. "And my brother, Baron Winstead also."

"An irregular business—very irregular," he murmured, turning his attention down the table. "Is Count Volsky in attendance?"

"Reverend, he remains in Russia—at the czar's court, but he is represented by myself," a gentleman in a dark green coat said.

"And you are? For my records, you understand."

"William Berry, Reverend."

"Yes, I see." He looked again to Katherine. "And you do not believe there is the possibility of a reconciliation to be effected?"

"No, Reverend," she murmured, keeping her eyes down. "I am seeking a divorce from my husband."

"Most irregular," another of the clergy mumbled.

"Reverend sir, it should be noted that Count Volsky is desirous of a divorce also," Berry spoke up. "On the grounds of adultery. And," he added, "he sees no possibility of reconciliation."

He said it as though he had dropped a cannonball on the table. Hamilton sat silently, his expression benign, making no objection on her behalf.

"Yes, I see that," the dean, a Peter Hervey, said. "Very well, gentlemen, as it is to be determined which grounds will be presented for the archbishop's consideration, I should like to ask that you state your cases as effectively as possible. Er—is there a determination as to who shall speak first?"

Patrick Hamilton looked down the table, then addressed the panel, "Reverend Hervey and members of the panel, I have not the least objection to listening to Mr. Berry."

Berry appeared almost gleeful to hear it. "I am prepared," he declared importantly. "I shall show that Countess Volsky has committed adultery on numerous occasions, both at the count's ancestral home of Domnya and other places."

Hamilton set out his ink pot and a freshly sharpened pen. "Would you care to enumerate the other places, that I may write them down?"

"In due time," Berry snapped. "But first we shall deal with Domnya." He looked across to the dean. "You will note several sworn affidavits from Countess Volsky's co-participants in this delicate matter."

"May I see them?" Hamilton asked.

"Reverend Hervey, I cannot speak if I am to be continually interrupted."

"But it is counsel's right to see specific documents pertaining to Katherine Volsky's guilt or innocence, is it not?" Hamilton said mildly.

"He can look at them later," Berry protested.

"Very well, but I shall stipulate that each be noted singly and brought to the attention of all present."

"Yes. Certainly," Hervey agreed. "Mr. Berry?"

The man appeared peeved, but he nodded. "Very well. It is determined that on October 30, the countess engaged in a furtive liaison of improper nature with one Boris Petrovsky, footman to Count Alexei Volsky."

"It is *alleged*," Hamilton murmured. "I pray you will note that stipulation, sirs." He turned to Katherine. "Madame, do you know a Boris Petrovsky?"

"I didn't know that was his name, sir. He was always called Boris, although I assume the Petrovsky must come from Alexei's father, Count Peter Volsky."

"Why that assumption?"

"Because it comes from a patronymic—I daresay he was born at Domnya when Alexei's father was count," she answered. "And as he is a serf, and therefore owned, I expect he was so named."

"Really," Berry complained, "this is most irregular."

"For the court's edification only," Hamilton inserted smoothly.

"This is not a court!"

"But surely protocols must remain the same?" Hamilton addressed the dean.

"It would perhaps be practical, particularly since we

do not entirely understand the significance of Russian names. Er—Countess, you say this Boris is a serf?''

''Yes. And a serf is a slave.''

''A formidable slave to cuckold his master,'' Hamilton murmured.

''Reverend Hervey, I object most strenuously!''

''Very well. Point taken,'' Patrick Hamilton told him. ''Proceed. I collect you have other supporting documents?''

''There is the matter of one Bran Petrovsky, a groom, I believe.'' Looking again to the dean, Berry added, ''The translation of his statement indicates that this was a continuing relationship until the countess chose to desert the bed and board of her husband.''

''Did he sign the translation—or the original?''

''Both. Really—''

''May I see it?''

Hervey nodded, and one of the other men passed it to Katherine, who gave it to her solicitor. He handed it back to her without looking at it at all. ''Is that Bran Petrovsky's signature, so far as you can determine it?''

''He cannot write.''

''He cannot write?''

''No. He is a serf also, and Alexei does not allow them to be taught.''

''If he cannot write, he cannot read, I would suppose.''

Nearly apoplectic, Berry stood up. ''I cannot proceed with this farce, sirs! Either I present my evidence or I leave!''

''You are presenting it,'' Hamilton reminded him. ''We are merely ascertaining its authenticity. ''Surely this panel must agree that if a serf cannot read, he cannot know what he has signed, and if he cannot write, he cannot sign it at all.''

''Most irregular,'' Dean Hervey agreed. ''But that is not to say he is lying, is it? Perhaps Lady Volsky is merely saying that none of them read to serve her own interest.''

At that, Hamilton drew out a lengthy document. ''You

will please note this report, which was prepared for Catherine the Great, stating the deplorable conditions of the serfs. I believe you will find on page 22, approximately two inches from the bottom, where it is stated that illiteracy among the serfs is nearly universal.''

"This is preposterous! The woman's been dead for years!''

"And, gentlemen," Hamilton continued, unperturbed, "here is a similar report commissioned by Czar Alexander I, autocrat of all the Russias. As you will read, the conditions of the serfs are said to have worsened.''

"It does not matter what the conditions are!" Berry retorted angrily.

"It matters very much if every deposition concerning the alleged adulterous activities is taken from serfs, whose very lives depend on the whim of their master, in this case, Count Volsky himself.'' Hamilton passed the second report across the table. "In a court of law, this evidence would be considered tainted by the manner of its inception.''

"Dean Hervey, I must protest!''

"Very well. Are there other, less—er—tainted documents?'' Hervey inquired mildly.

"There is a statement concerning Viscount Townsend. I have a letter obtained from our embassy in Warsaw, stating that Townsend brought Lady Volsky there—nearly two and one-half months after she left her husband, sirs!'' Berry declared thunderously. "Now, if that is not adultery, I am sure I do not know what is! Everyone is aware of Bellamy Townsend's reputation, I assure you!''

There was a brief pause as Hervey read the letter, then shared it with the other two clergymen. Clearing his throat, he looked at Katherine.

"Countess, you arrived in Warsaw with Viscount Townsend?''

"Yes.''

"A considerable length of time after you left your husband?''

"Yes.''

"Were you with him all the time?''

"No. I left Domnya to flee to Alexei's brother and sister-in-law at Omborosloe." She had to be careful, for Hamilton had said she must not confuse the issue by discussing the Narranskys. "I was ill—I was increasing, you see—and Paul Volsky took me to Moscow to see a doctor. There was considerable swelling in my face, hands, and feet." Looking directly at the panel across from her, she said softly, "I elected to stay in Moscow, and Paul did not object."

"You were increasing?"

"Reverend Hervey, it is in our documents also," Berry insisted. "If you will but look—"

"What happened to your child?" the dean asked gently.

"It was stillborn." Tears welled in her dark eyes, making them bright. "That—and the deep snow and bad roads—is why I did not get to Warsaw until April," she said, her voice breaking. "I'm sorry."

"And you were with Bellamy Townsend the entire time," Berry pointed out.

"Yes. And I should have died without him. Twice I nearly froze to death—and once I nearly bled to death."

"Lady Volsky, my condolences," Dean Hervey said quietly.

Hamilton was ready to make his move. "If that is all he has to present, I am prepared to speak for Countess Volsky," he said.

"She has not explained Townsend! She cannot explain Townsend away!"

"Nor does she make the attempt. We concede that Lady Volsky fled from her husband to his brother to Moscow, and that once in Moscow, she applied to Viscount Townsend for his assistance."

Hamilton rose to walk behind Katherine. "And because of a long-standing friendship with her brother, one which dates back to his childhood, Bellamy Townsend could not turn her away. I submit to you that, yes, Townsend's reputation is not unspotted, sirs, but I would ask that you look at Countess Volsky, that you use your powers of imagination, if you will, and see this woman, her face swollen until her eyes nearly disappeared, her hands swollen until her wedding ring disappeared in the folds of the flesh, her feet so bloated that she could wear no shoes—'' He paused dramatically. "And I would have you tell me that this woman could possibly be the object of his affection—or that she would be seeking an adulterous liaison in that condition!''

It was clearly a daunting picture.

"Gentlemen, you have only the word of a vengeful husband and his illiterate slaves to support the accusation of adultery,'' he said, his voice dropping.

Berry rose at his end of the table. "We have considerably more to support our contention than Lady Volsky can present to support hers. Dean Hervey, distinguished clergy, I submit to you that the only person here or anywhere to give any evidence against Count Volsky is his wife. It is a case of her word, which Alexei Volsky emphatically denies.''

"Mr. Berry, while we have not yet deliberated, I must tell you that I do not personally see substantiation of your assertions of adultery. I would expect the archbishop to refuse to take these charges to ecclesiastical court,'' the dean declared.''

They were not going to give Alexei Volsky a divorce. She was not publicly an adultress. But Hervey's next words sent a new chill through her.

"I do not believe there are sufficient grounds for a divorce. Under the circumstances, perhaps a separation may be negotiated.''

"Count Volsky is prepared to accept a separation—on condition that Lady Volsky produce the child.''

"If it was stillborn—''

"Then he wishes her to prove that.''

"I suppose that is not without merit. Lady Volsky?''

"I do not want my son's body returned to Domnya.''

The three men looked at each other, and she could sense she was losing again. She turned to appeal to Patrick Hamilton. "Please—if you could go on. Tell them I do not wish a separation. I want a divorce from Alexei Volsky.''

"As there is no evidence of the heinous charges she has made against a member of one of Russia's finest families, I must object deeply to any presentation of lies," Berry said. "Before I listen to anything further, I must demand to know where Alexei Volsky's legal heir is."

"And I cannot tell. I do not want my son buried at Domnya."

Hamilton opened a leather folder and extricated the two pieces of paper. "In England," he said, "the only avenue of divorce open to a woman of any class is that of incest committed by the husband. It would be very easy to believe that Lady Volsky, in a desperate attempt to leave Alexei Volsky, would use this charge to gain her freedom. However, if it please you, I would like to submit these two letters, which were sent to her, for your consideration."

"Dean Hervey—"

But the dean had already read Viktor Volsky's letter, and the priest beside him had Tatiana's. Hervey looked up, his sympathy now evident in his expression.

"You will see that these are authentic—sent from Moscow to the Winstead town house in London," Hamilton pointed out.

"Lady Volsky, who is Viktor Volsky?" Hervey asked.

"My husband's youngest brother."

"And Tatiana?"

"His youngest sister."

"And who are Lexy and Lena?"

"My husband and his oldest sister."

"Lady Volsky, I know this must be repugnant to you in the extreme, but I must ask you—Did you in truth see your husband in an indelicate situation with his own sister?"

"Yes." She knew he wanted more than that. Sucking in her breath, she let it out slowly, before she spoke, her voice low, husky almost. "I thought I loved Alexei, and I thought he loved me. But we were wed on short acquaintance, and when I followed him to Russia, I soon discovered that it was Galena—his sister—who determined everything. She even determined whether or not he came to my bed. Everyone knew it but me. Then Tatiana told me to go to his bed. When I did, they—Alexei and Galena—were together, and they were unclothed.''

It was as though he wanted to reach his hand across to her. But instead, he turned to the others at his side. ''Gentlemen, I suggest we take Lady Volsky's petition under advisement.''

It wasn't enough for Patrick Hamilton. ''Dean Hervey, it would seem to me that Countess Volsky has suffered immeasurably at the hands of a cold husband, whose sister used her in the quest for a child. I would ask that before we adjourn, a determination be made as to this panel's recommendation to the court.''

He didn't even mention the archbishop, making it clear he expected it to go to the ecclesiastical court. Hervey looked down at the papers before him.

''If you and Baron Winstead would care to wait in the outer room with Lady Volsky, we will discuss the matter. I do not expect the considerations to be weighty. Someone will inform you within the hour.''

Harry rose. ''I thank you all for the justice you give my sister.''

Outside, he hugged her. ''Kate, I have not the least doubt as to how they will rule. Not the least doubt.''

When he released her, she turned to Patrick Hamilton. ''Thank you, sir—from the bottom of my heart, thank you. I know why you are so very highly recommended.''

He smiled. ''I always wished to be an actor, you know, but such is not to be for respectable younger sons. The practice of law allows me to follow my heart. But,'' he reminded her, ''it is not over yet. There is still the criminal court, and then Parliament.''

''I know.''

Berry did not wait. When Katherine looked around her, he was gone.

''Mr. Hamilton,'' a clerk said finally from the half-opened door. ''You may speak with Dean Hervey now, if you wish.''

''Wait here.''

She closed her eyes and held her breath. Then she felt Harry's hand clasp hers. "Buck up, Kate," he whispered.

Hamilton could not have been gone above a minute. He returned, grinning.

"Countess Volsky, your husband has been charged with the commission of incest."

London: *September 11, 1815*

It was the last step, and Patrick Hamilton had said she did not need to be there to hear it, that perhaps it would be less painful if she did not. But she could not wait idly at home while the bill of divorcement was debated and passed. It was a formality, Lord Leighton had assured her, but she had to see for herself.

She had spent much of the past week packing, ostensibly for a retreat to the sea, but she'd not yet told Harry she intended to cross it, that she intended to go to Florence. He'd try to dissuade her, she knew that. He'd tell her Bell Townsend would not make any woman a decent husband, she knew that also.

And she could not even say that Bell would marry her, or that he had not found another woman after her. But he'd haunted her dreams, he'd made her ache herself to sleep far too many nights for her to just forget him. She had to at least see him, to see if he still had his offer on the table. In many ways, she was not the same weak creature he'd taken across Russia. She'd finally gotten the spine and the pluck he'd given her credit for. And she was going to put it to the touch.

But she was not without a sense of reality. She knew he might not want her. But if he did not, he'd have to say it to her face. If he did not, he would have to tell her that those nights in Poland had meant nothing to him. And if he said that, she'd come home utterly defeated.

The court has already found Alexei guilty, and they had assessed him enough money to make her wealthy for a lifetime. The Russian ambassador had already delivered half of the settlement to Harry, and between them, he and she put it away where neither could touch it without the advice of Patrick Hamilton.

She adjusted her hat in the mirror while Peg fidgeted with her hair, pulling the tendrils about her ears as Galena had once done. She was about to make the same face at herself, but she could see Harry's reflection behind her.

"Lud, Kate, but you look as though you are moving," he observed. "Is there anything you have not packed?"

"Yes."

"And you have ordered everything to be picked up tomorrow?"

"No. Some of it goes today."

"Good of you to tell me," he said. "Were you just going to let me come home to an empty house?"

"Of course not, stoopid!" She turned around. "Well, how do I look? Harry, I know it is nearly over, but I think I am more frightened today than I have ever been."

"You look fetching. Truly. It would not surprise me in the least if Patrick Hamilton came up to scratch."

"What fustian."

"Fellow's halfway to head over heels," he murmured, testing her. "You couldn't do much better, you know."

"Oh?"

"And, his career doesn't depend on his wife."

"You are making every bit of this up."

"No."

"Harry, I am the next thing to an Antidote!"

"Kate, I won't lie and say you are a beauty, but you are not hard on the eyes, either. Thing is, a man's got to know you to appreciate you."

"Thank you."

"That's why you did not show to advantage on the marriage mart, you know."

"You are my brother."

"I know of two others who think so also."

"Who? Hamilton and who? Leighton?"

"Possibly. Maybe even Bell," he suggested slyly.

Her breath caught in her chest. "He—he never said so, did he?"

"You should know that better than I, I'd think."

"Have—have you heard from him lately?"

"Not lately."

"Oh. Well, I daresay he must be enjoying Italy."

"I daresay."

"I owe him everything, you know," she said, her voice dropping low. "Sometimes I have wished I hadn't come home, but then—"

"It was truly a matter of honor, wasn't it, Kate?"

"Yes."

"Leighton said you reminded him of Lady Longford—she used to be Lady Kingsley."

"For my spine, Harry—for my spine."

"Are you ready?" he asked suddenly.

"Yes. Do I need the rouge pot, do you think?"

"No."

He waited until they were down in the foyer, then he recalled that he'd left something. Running up the stairs, he went to her bedchamber rather than his. A cursory search of her packed boxes yielded nothing.

"Peg, they are coming for some of her boxes today, aren't they?" he asked her maid.

"Yes, but—"

"Here—" He dug out a piece of paper with an address on it and handed it to her. "She copied down the address wrong. Give them this."

As he hurried back down the stairs, the maid looked at the paper, wondering how Katherine Volsky could have mistaken Florence, Italy, for some place in Cornwall. She exchanged the cards nonetheless. Her ladyship might be mad as fire, but Peg herself was an English girl, and the thought of jaunting off to Italy had not been very appealing anyway.

The gallery was packed with the curious, some of whom had merely come to see the notorious Countess Volsky, the woman who had traveled thousands of miles to escape a dastardly husband. Not that many actually sympathized with her. To them, the civilized thing to do would have been to ignore it, to amuse herself with another Russian nobleman while Count Volsky enjoyed his sister's company improperly.

"Er—" The elegantly attired gentleman drew out a wad of bank notes and held them up. "Ten pounds to anyone willing to give up a place."

That section nearly emptied. For ten pounds most could push and shove their way in somewhere else. The gentleman moved to the front and sat down before removing his dove gray hat. Leaning back, he combed his blond Brutus with his fingers. And then he waited for a glimpse of her. He'd not been half so eager to see any female since his salad days.

He'd written Harry he was coming home, but Harry had asked him not to try to see Kate until everything was over. Truth to tell, he hadn't pushed the matter—he didn't even know of his welcome. He only knew that he loved her desperately, that the months in Italy had been hell. For weeks after he'd left her in Warsaw, he'd turned over and reached for her in the night, then awakened with the knowledge that she wasn't there.

Harry said that Patrick Hamilton, the solicitor he'd hired with Bell's money, a man Bell knew only by repute, was completely taken with her. And he could tell by Leighton's letters that George had not exactly been least in sight either.

Bell knew he didn't deserve her, and he never would. He knew that. But he also knew that out of the dozens of women he'd held, out of the dozens who'd played the game with him, she was the only one he wanted to keep forever.

He saw her come in with her brother, Leighton, and a man he took to be Hamilton. It was enough to give his heart pause. Leighton he'd known was tall and handsome. But so was Hamilton. Both of them had to be several inches taller than he was.

He strained to see her as she was surrounded, and then watched her as she sat down. It had been a nasty, bitter business, but she carried herself with dignity. God, how many times she must have had to listen to how foolish she'd been, how gullible. How many times she must have had to repeat her heartbreak publicly, telling how it felt to discover that her handsome husband had preferred his older sister to her.

Hamilton, Leighton, and several others met together for a moment in a corner, then Hamilton came back. Bell did not miss the language of his look, nor the way he bent his head close to Kate's. And he saw the way that she looked up, the way she smiled. He'd been away too damned long.

Then he saw why they had conferred. The bill was presented, read in its most sanitary language, saying nothing more than that Katherine, once Winstead, now Volsky, should be divorced from her husband on the grounds that he had deserted her bed and committed incest with his sister. There was a rumbling of "hear—hear," then a passing vote. It had been so easy, he marveled at it.

Katherine was a free woman. There was a near mob scene below as people gathered to congratulate Patrick Hamilton. In a way, he was one of their own, and he'd won the woman's freedom for her. Bell started down the back stairs, deciding he'd call on her later. Right now, the moment belonged to those who'd fought for her. Even to a man he'd paid a thousand pounds to save her.

As he came out into the front, he saw her again. Somehow Harry had managed to get her out. For the first time since he'd been seduced at fifteen, Bell felt like the callowest of youths.

"Kate!" he called out on impulse.

At first she didn't hear where the word came from, and then he shouted more loudly. She turned around, and her heart rose in her throat.

He was as she remembered. His tousled blond hair still made him look almost like a little boy, and his gray eyes were as arresting as ever. She stood there, waiting, hoping.

He'd been in a hurry. Now he walked slowly, stopping before he reached her. He had to know—he could not wait half a day to put it to the touch. He grinned crookedly.

"Hallo, Kate."

"Bell."

"I didn't want to run any longer. And I don't give a damn about my rep anymore. And I don't care if I am never invited to another party anywhere." He knew he was bungling it badly. "The offer is still on the table, Kate," he said. She stared at him, and for an awful moment, he was certain he was too late.

Then she smiled. "I was going to Florence to pick it up, Bell. My bags and boxes are all packed."

"Oh, God, Kate."

She could feel his arms around her, she could feel the soft superfine of his coat, and she could smell the Hungary water he'd worn for her. He was there. He'd come home to her. She clung to him as though he were her life, savoring the feeling of his cheek against her hair, of his breath against her cheek before she gave herself up to his kiss.

"Bell, for God's sake—not here!" Harry hissed at him.

"I love you, Kate. *I love you, Kate.* And I don't want to go to Italy—I've traveled too damned many miles for you already, he murmmured against her lips."

"Oh, lud!" She stepped back self-consciously.

"What is it?"

"My bags—they are on their way to Florence! And I bought all new clothes in hopes you would like them!'

"You can go naked for all I care," he said, smiling foolishly.

"No—I sent her clothes to Cornwall," Harry admitted. "I thought she meant to take you."

"Cornwall!" she wailed. "Why on earth Cornwall?"

Bell's smile turned to a full grin. "I've bought a house there—a big, grand house with room for children. And you can see and smell the sea from the windows. We don't ever have to go through any of this again. It won't make any difference if we are received."

Patrick Hamilton had been watching with an intense

war of emotions in his breast. He stepped forward manfully, however, to offer his services.

"I can arrange to facilitate a special license, for a fee, of course."

"What do you say, Kate? Do you really want a worthless rake for a husband?" Bell asked her.

"No. I want a *reformed* one," she told him happily.

Duchy of Cornwall:
September 15, 1815

"You know, I do not think I can ever get enough of you," he murmured into the crown of her hair.

She ducked beneath him and stood away from her desk. "I was writing to Harry to tell him how we are." But even as she said it, she felt the same intense desire for him. "You know," she whispered softly, "we are spending all our time in bed."

"I know." He looked over her shoulder to the unfinished letter, reading where she'd written to her brother. "Well, Adonis has wed the Antidote, making her supremely happy." Leaning past her, he dipped her pen in the ink pot and carefully struck out the words "Antidote" and "her," replacing them with "Original" and "him."

"Now, where were we?" he asked, opening his arms for her.

He drew her against him, heating her body through the lawn nightgown with his own. He'd explored nearly every inch of her, and she was still the most seductive creature of his memory. His thumbs massaged her temples, drawing her head closer, and then he tasted her lips, savoring the soft, pliant feel of them as they parted. And then he was drowning in his own desire.

"Come to bed, Kate. There must be a hundred ways to show you how I feel."

"And I want to know every one, she admitted shamelessly."

His hands loosened the ties at her neck, then pulled
her gown down over her shoulders. His head bent lower
as he sampled each breast. He could feel her body quiver
as her nipples hardened. It was going to be good again.
The gown caught between them, then slid to the floor at
his feet. She stepped back, hesitated, then her smile
beckoned him as she backed to the bed.

As he followed her down into the depths of the feather
mattress, he wondered yet again how he could have ever
thought her plain. "You know what, Kate?" he whispered huskily against the hollow of her throat. "You are
beautiful—absolutely beautiful in every way."

For her answer, her arms closed around his shoulders,
and her body moved beneath him, enticing him. He raised
his head to hers, letting her tongue tease him, and as she
brought her legs up, he possessed her body and her mouth
at the same time.

She welcomed him eagerly, her hands urging him on,
touching him, tracing the muscles of his back and his
hips, taking what he gave her, carrying him with her,
until he could wait no longer. He could not tell whether
he heard her cries or his, and it didn't matter. He lay
there, sated, not wanting to move, feeling the warmth of
her body around his.

When he looked down, her dark eyes were even darker
with remembered passion. And her smile was as warm
as any he'd ever seen. He kissed her before he left her,
then rolled onto his side and pulled her close.

She buried her head into the gold, curling hairs on his
chest, knowing she was going to love him forever. He
looked down at her, feeling a tenderness as intense as
his earlier desire.

"What do you think of when we are like this?" he
asked her.

"Falling stars," she answered huskily. "When I close
my eyes, they are everywhere."